CHARLIE BROWN
BROWN
HERE WE GO AGAIN

Other *Peanuts* AMP! Comics for Kids Books

Snoopy: Cowabunga

Charlie Brown and Friends

Charlie Brown: Pow!

Woodstock: Master of Disguise

Snoopy: Contact!

Snoopy: Party Animal

CHARLIE BROWN

HERE WE GO AGAIN

A **PEANUTS**™ Collection

CHARLES M. SCHULZ

Andrews McMeel
Publishing®
a division of Andrews McMeel Universal

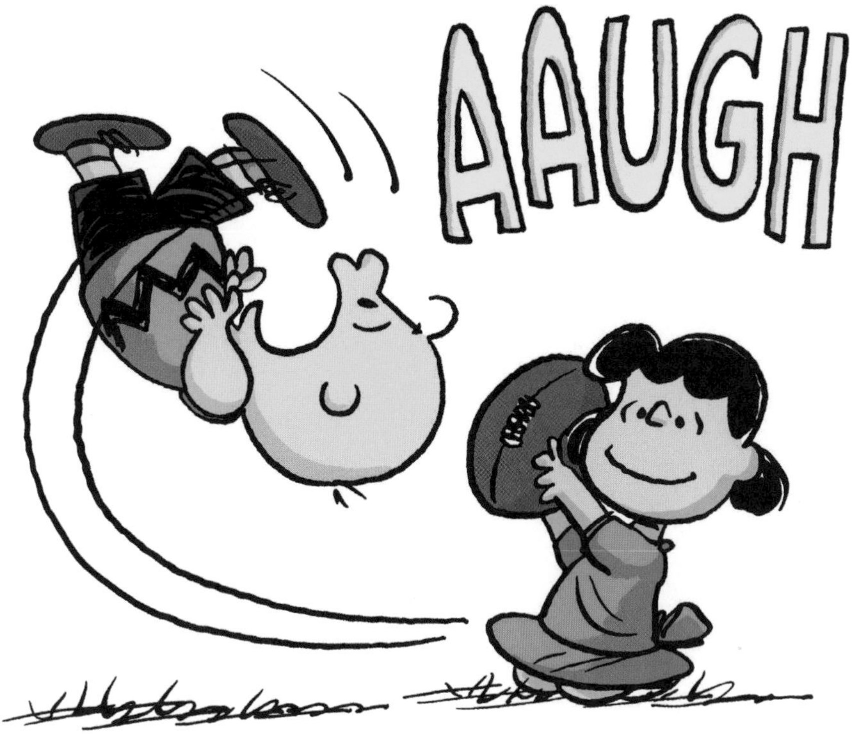
AAUGH

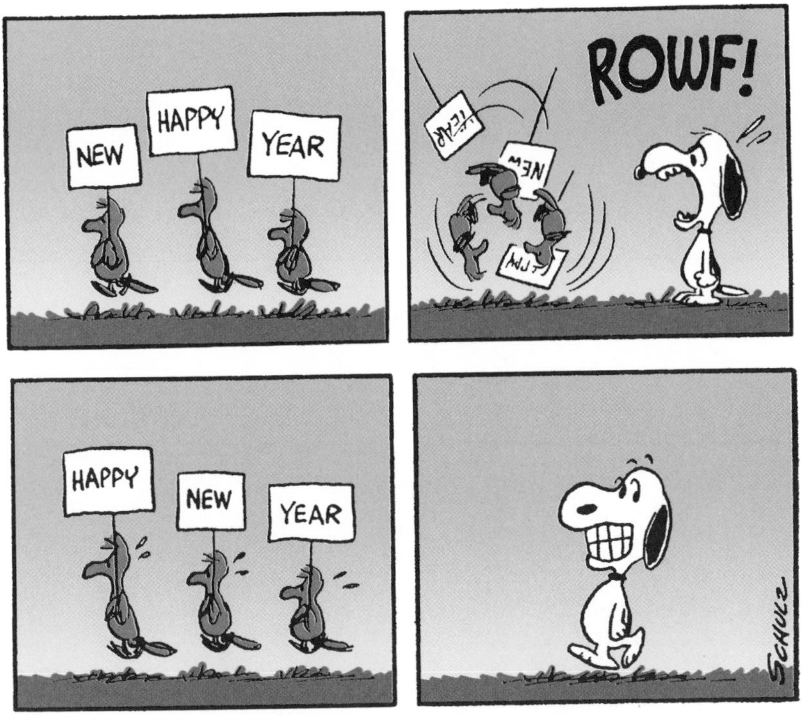
NEW
HAPPY
YEAR
ROWF!
HAPPY
NEW
YEAR
SCHULZ

AAUGH! AAUGH!

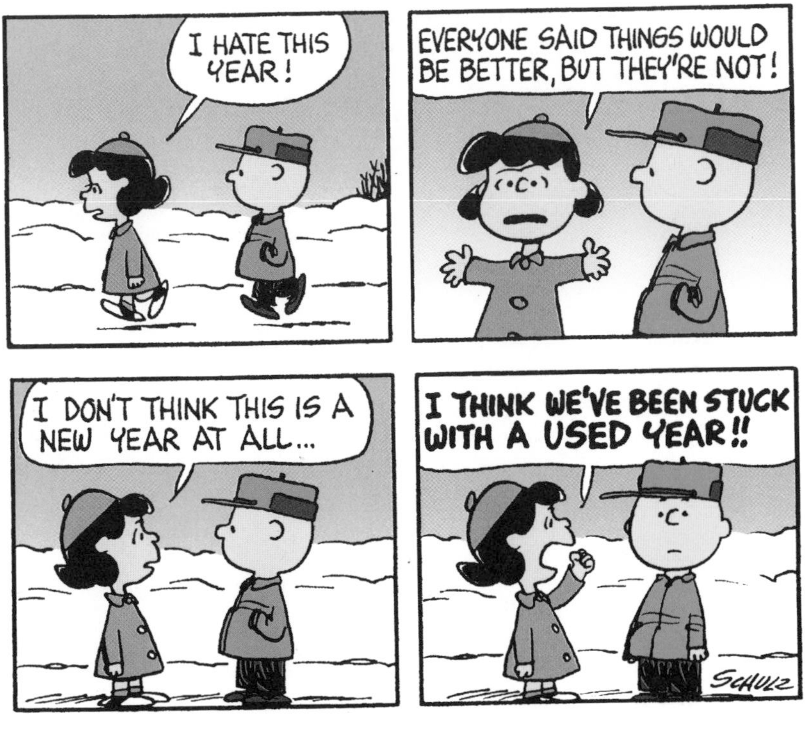
I HATE THIS YEAR!
EVERYONE SAID THINGS WOULD BE BETTER, BUT THEY'RE NOT!
I DON'T THINK THIS IS A NEW YEAR AT ALL...
I THINK WE'VE BEEN STUCK WITH A USED YEAR!!
SCHULZ

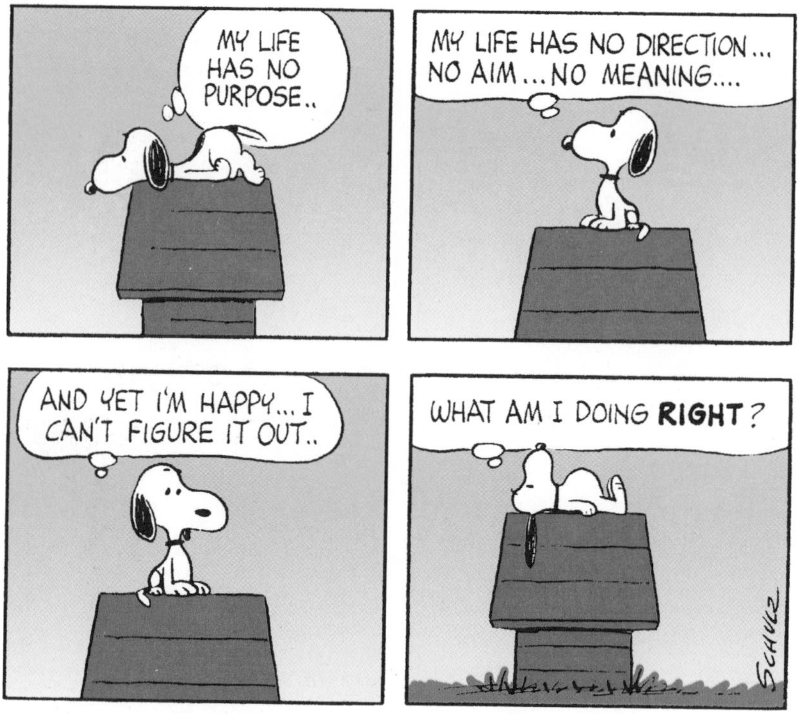
MY LIFE HAS NO PURPOSE..
MY LIFE HAS NO DIRECTION... NO AIM...NO MEANING....
AND YET I'M HAPPY... I CAN'T FIGURE IT OUT..
WHAT AM I DOING **RIGHT**?
SCHULZ

AAUGH! AAUGH!

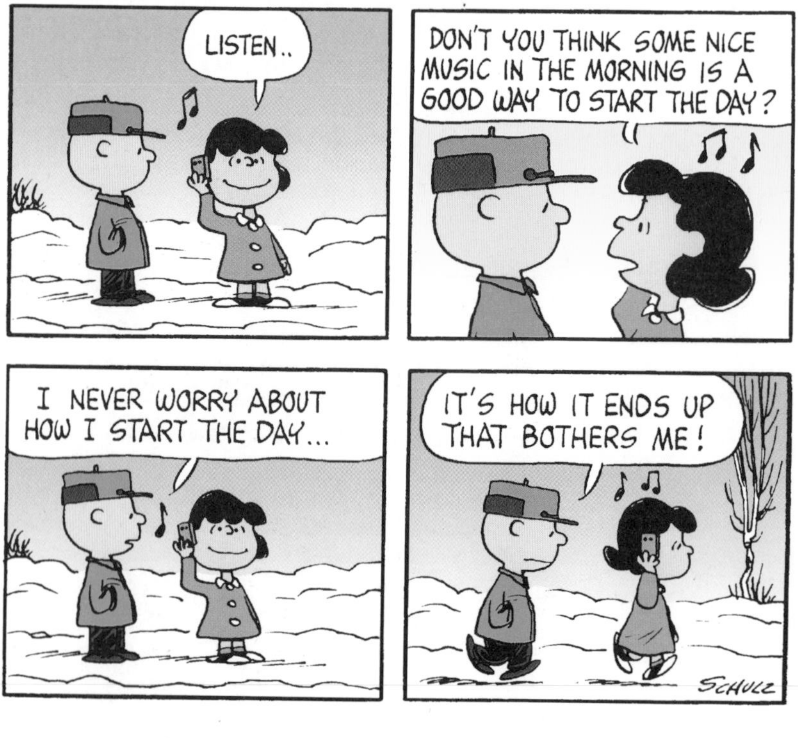
LISTEN..
DON'T YOU THINK SOME NICE MUSIC IN THE MORNING IS A GOOD WAY TO START THE DAY?
I NEVER WORRY ABOUT HOW I START THE DAY...
IT'S HOW IT ENDS UP THAT BOTHERS ME!
SCHULZ

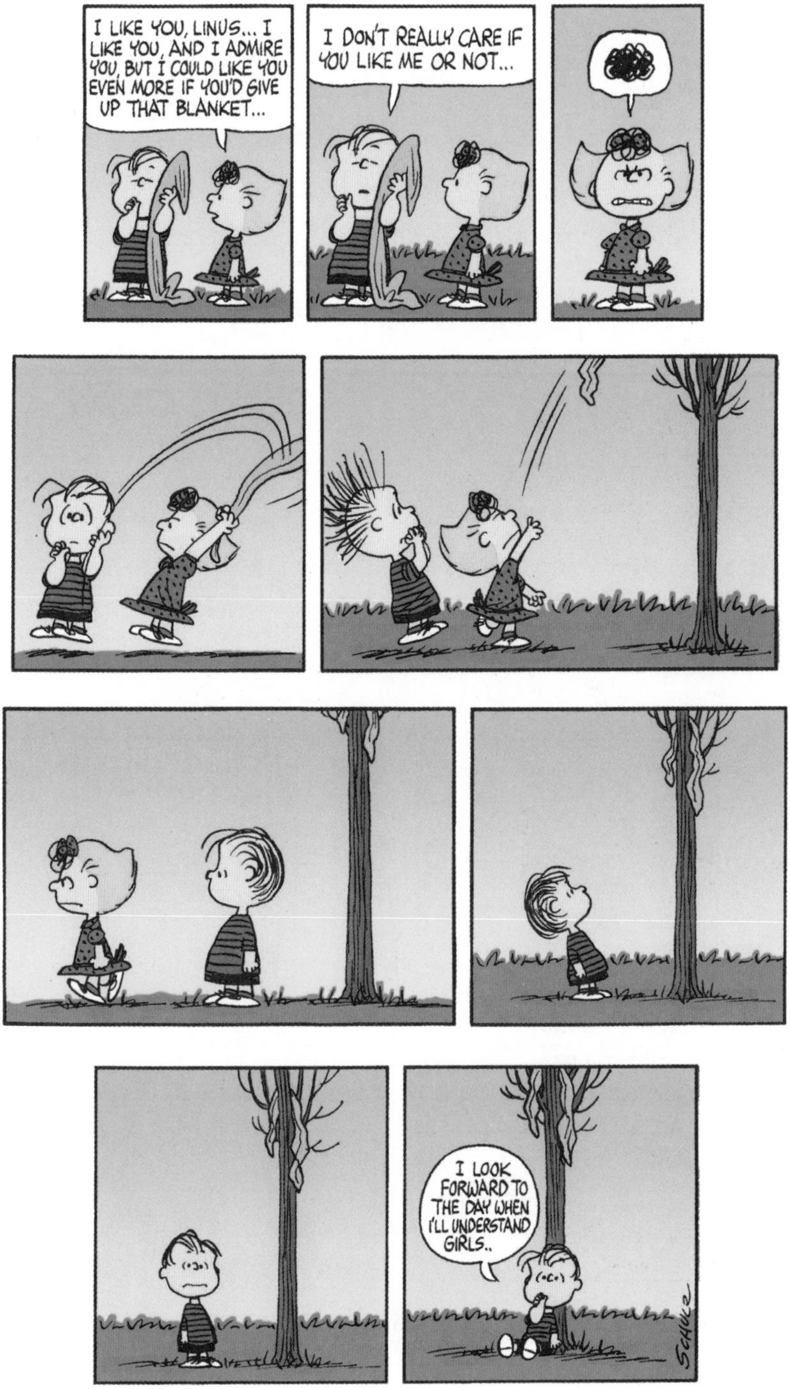
I LIKE YOU, LINUS... I LIKE YOU, AND I ADMIRE YOU, BUT I COULD LIKE YOU EVEN MORE IF YOU'D GIVE UP THAT BLANKET...
I DON'T REALLY CARE IF YOU LIKE ME OR NOT...
I LOOK FORWARD TO THE DAY WHEN I'LL UNDERSTAND GIRLS..
SCHULZ

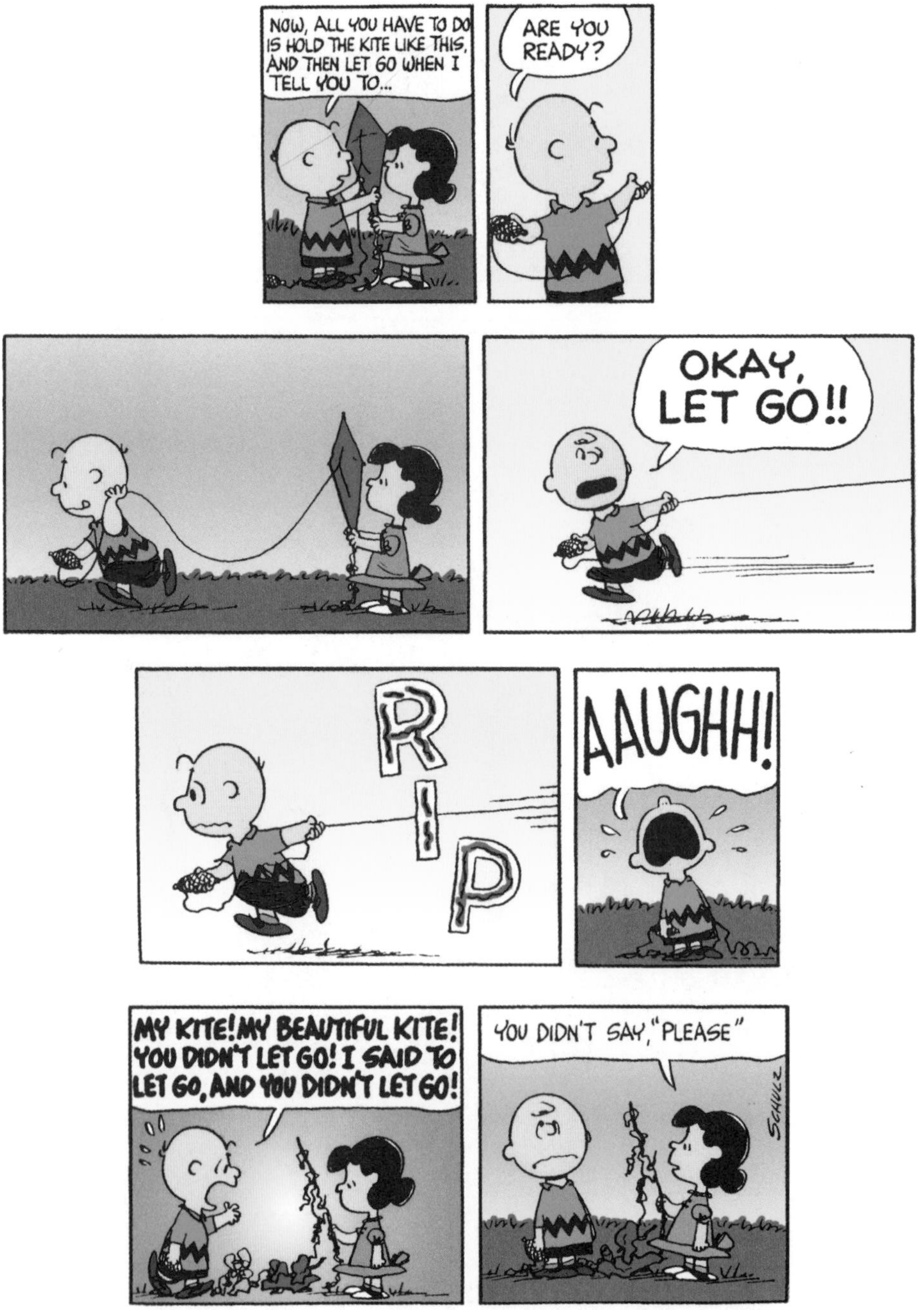
NOW, ALL YOU HAVE TO DO IS HOLD THE KITE LIKE THIS, AND THEN LET GO WHEN I TELL YOU TO...
ARE YOU READY?
OKAY, LET GO!!
R I P
AAUGHH!
MY KITE! MY BEAUTIFUL KITE! YOU DIDN'T LET GO! I SAID TO LET GO, AND YOU DIDN'T LET GO!
YOU DIDN'T SAY, "PLEASE"
SCHULZ

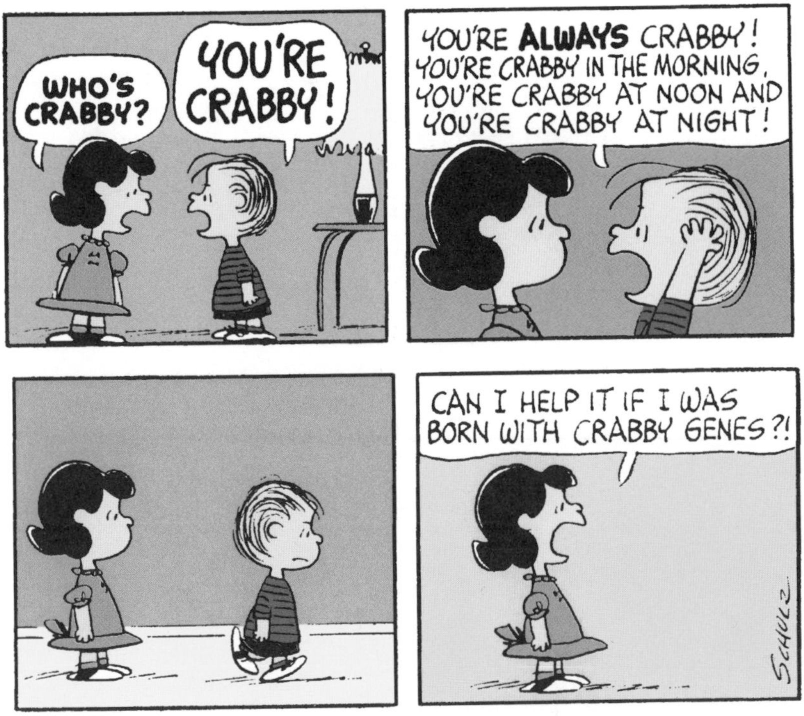
WHO'S CRABBY?
YOU'RE CRABBY!
YOU'RE **ALWAYS** CRABBY! YOU'RE CRABBY IN THE MORNING, YOU'RE CRABBY AT NOON AND YOU'RE CRABBY AT NIGHT!
CAN I HELP IT IF I WAS BORN WITH CRABBY GENES?!
SCHULZ

AAUGH! AAUGH!

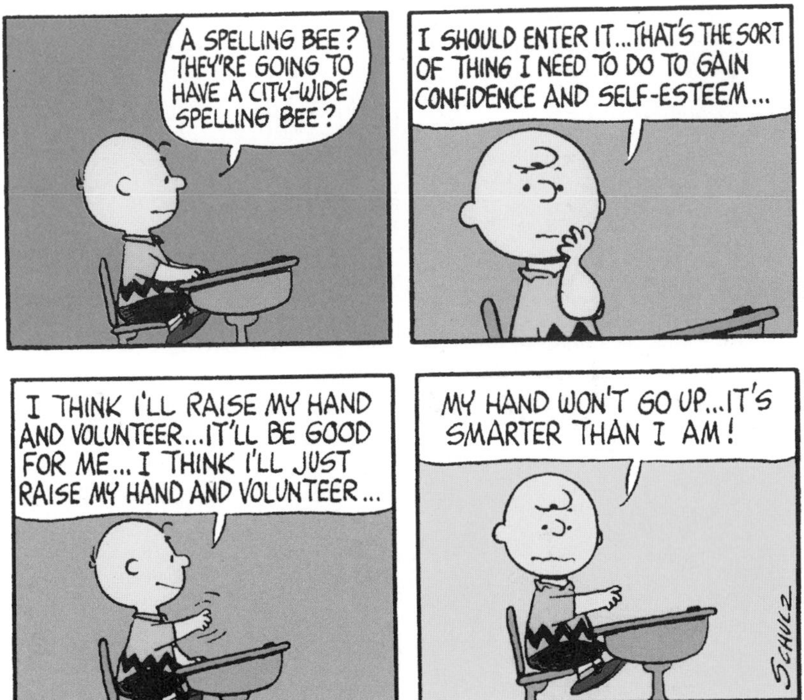
A SPELLING BEE? THEY'RE GOING TO HAVE A CITY-WIDE SPELLING BEE?
I SHOULD ENTER IT...THAT'S THE SORT OF THING I NEED TO DO TO GAIN CONFIDENCE AND SELF-ESTEEM...
I THINK I'LL RAISE MY HAND AND VOLUNTEER...IT'LL BE GOOD FOR ME... I THINK I'LL JUST RAISE MY HAND AND VOLUNTEER...
MY HAND WON'T GO UP...IT'S SMARTER THAN I AM!
SCHULZ

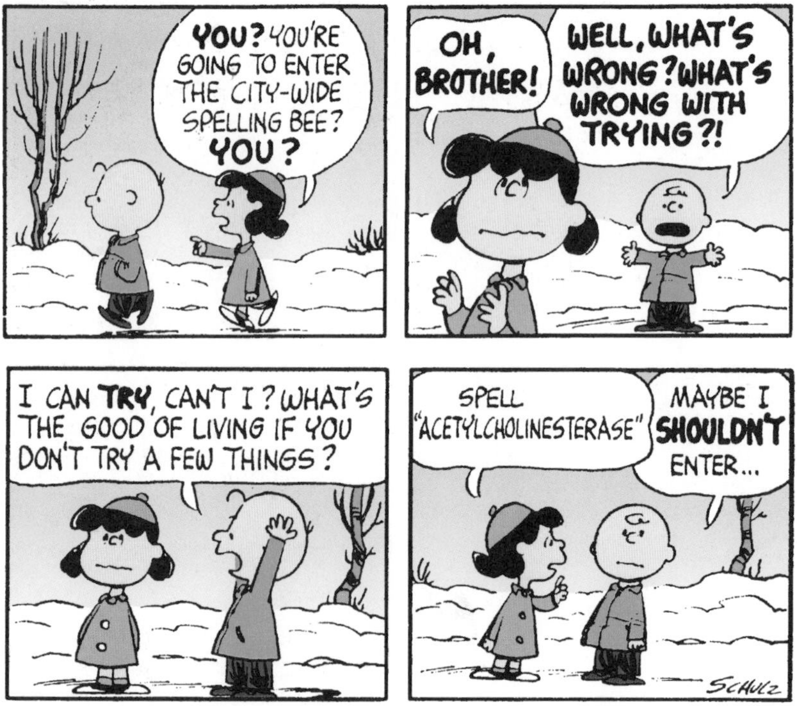
YOU? YOU'RE GOING TO ENTER THE CITY-WIDE SPELLING BEE? YOU?
OH, BROTHER!
WELL, WHAT'S WRONG? WHAT'S WRONG WITH TRYING?!
I CAN TRY, CAN'T I? WHAT'S THE GOOD OF LIVING IF YOU DON'T TRY A FEW THINGS?
SPELL "ACETYLCHOLINESTERASE"
MAYBE I SHOULDN'T ENTER...
SCHULZ

AAUGH! AAUGH!

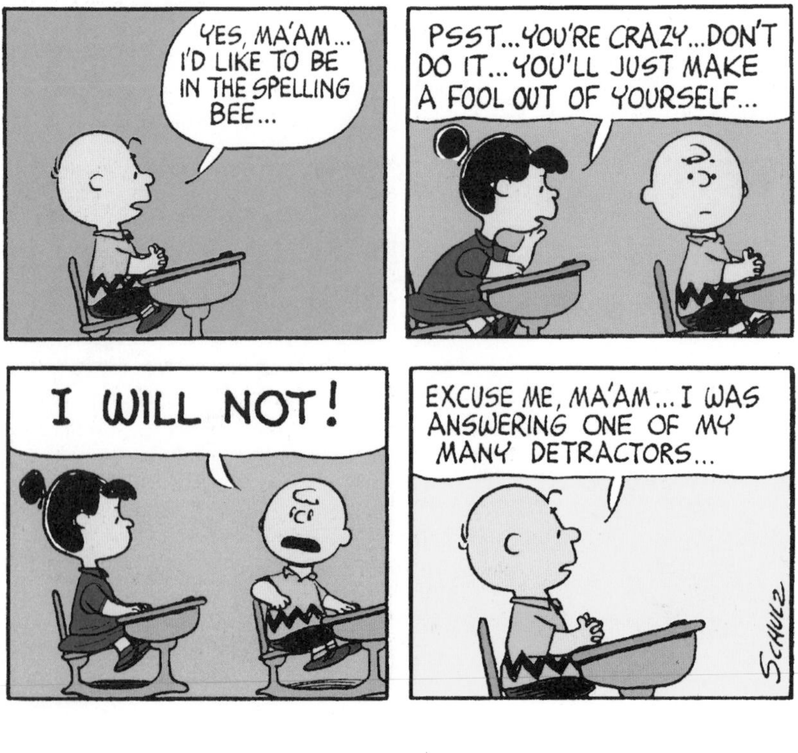
YES, MA'AM... I'D LIKE TO BE IN THE SPELLING BEE...
PSST...YOU'RE CRAZY...DON'T DO IT...YOU'LL JUST MAKE A FOOL OUT OF YOURSELF...
I WILL NOT!
EXCUSE ME, MA'AM... I WAS ANSWERING ONE OF MY MANY DETRACTORS...
SCHULZ

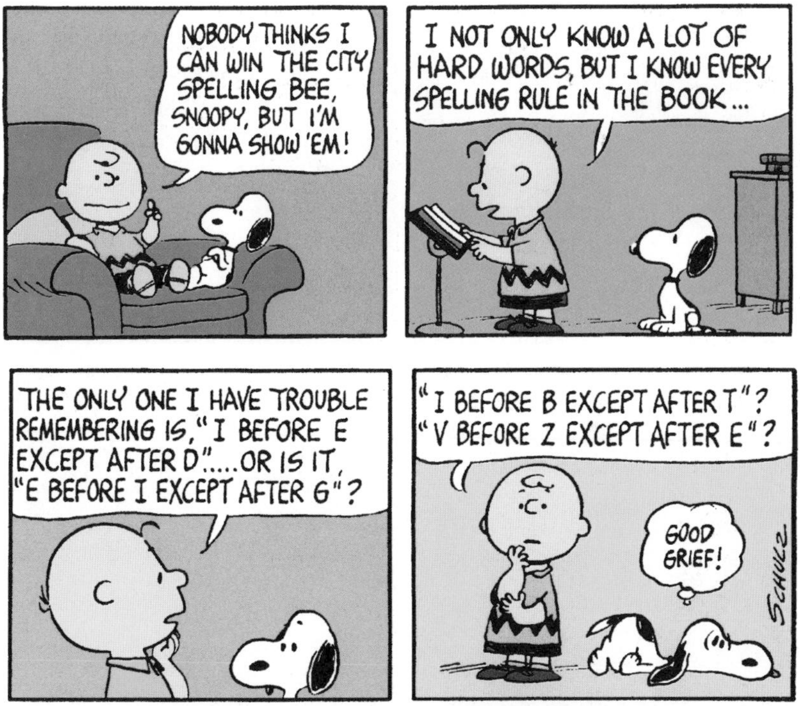
NOBODY THINKS I CAN WIN THE CITY SPELLING BEE, SNOOPY, BUT I'M GONNA SHOW 'EM!
I NOT ONLY KNOW A LOT OF HARD WORDS, BUT I KNOW EVERY SPELLING RULE IN THE BOOK...
THE ONLY ONE I HAVE TROUBLE REMEMBERING IS, "I BEFORE E EXCEPT AFTER D".....OR IS IT "E BEFORE I EXCEPT AFTER G"?
"I BEFORE B EXCEPT AFTER T"? "V BEFORE Z EXCEPT AFTER E"?
GOOD GRIEF!
SCHULZ

AAUGH! AAUGH!

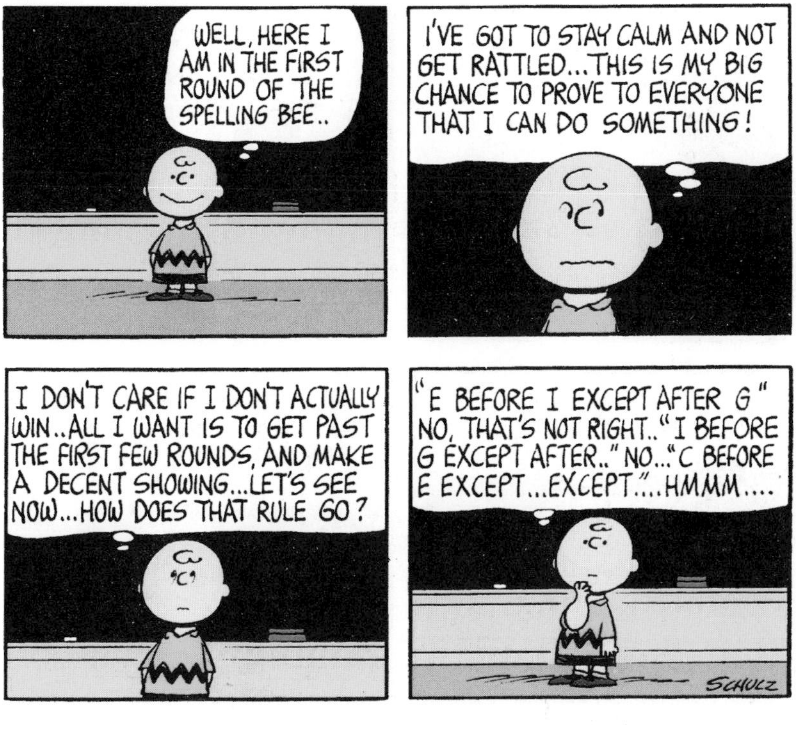
WELL, HERE I AM IN THE FIRST ROUND OF THE SPELLING BEE..
I'VE GOT TO STAY CALM AND NOT GET RATTLED...THIS IS MY BIG CHANCE TO PROVE TO EVERYONE THAT I CAN DO SOMETHING!
I DON'T CARE IF I DON'T ACTUALLY WIN..ALL I WANT IS TO GET PAST THE FIRST FEW ROUNDS, AND MAKE A DECENT SHOWING...LET'S SEE NOW...HOW DOES THAT RULE GO?
"E BEFORE I EXCEPT AFTER G" NO, THAT'S NOT RIGHT.."I BEFORE G EXCEPT AFTER.." NO..."C BEFORE E EXCEPT...EXCEPT."...HMMM....
SCHULZ

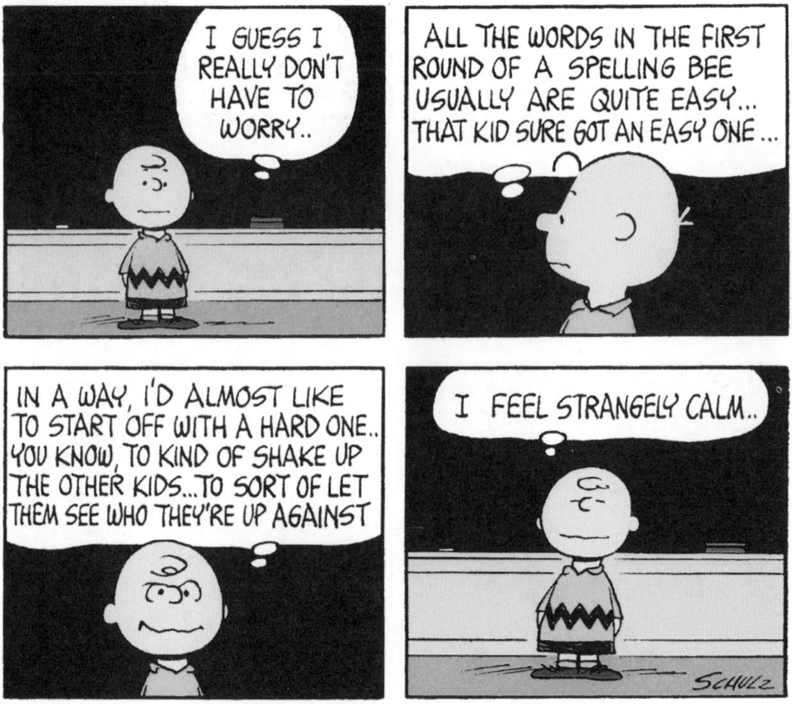
I GUESS I REALLY DON'T HAVE TO WORRY..
ALL THE WORDS IN THE FIRST ROUND OF A SPELLING BEE USUALLY ARE QUITE EASY... THAT KID SURE GOT AN EASY ONE...
IN A WAY, I'D ALMOST LIKE TO START OFF WITH A HARD ONE.. YOU KNOW, TO KIND OF SHAKE UP THE OTHER KIDS...TO SORT OF LET THEM SEE WHO THEY'RE UP AGAINST
I FEEL STRANGELY CALM..
SCHULZ

AAUGH! AAUGH!

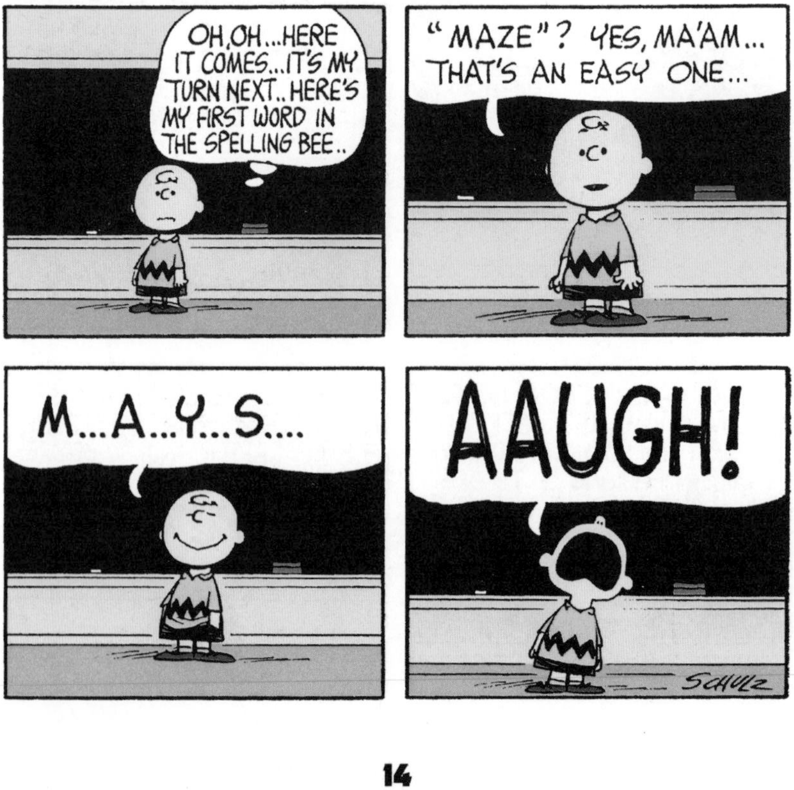
OH,OH...HERE IT COMES...IT'S MY TURN NEXT..HERE'S MY FIRST WORD IN THE SPELLING BEE..
"MAZE"? YES, MA'AM... THAT'S AN EASY ONE...
M...A...Y...S....
AAUGH!
SCHULZ

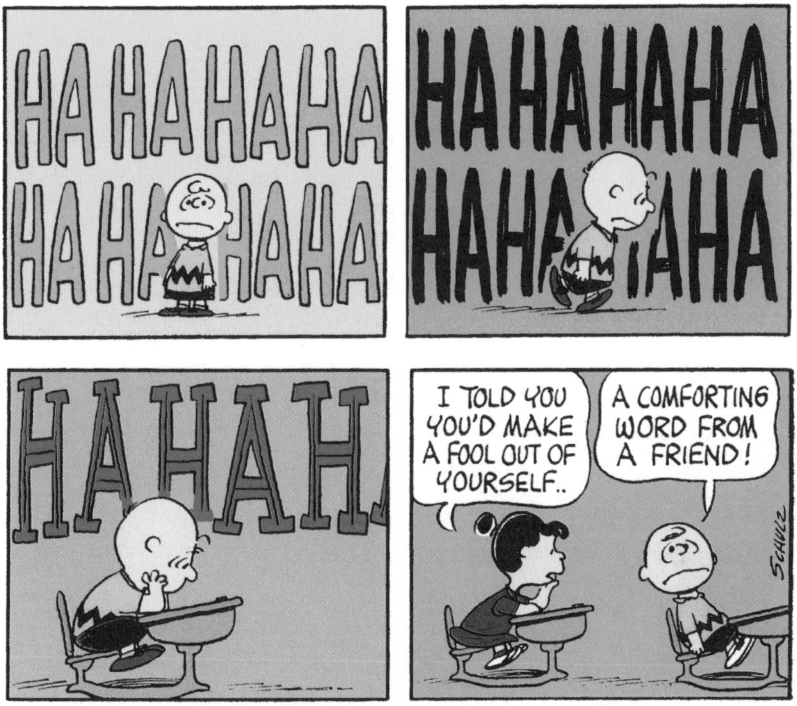
HA HA HA HA
HA HA HA HA
HAHAHAHA
HAHA AHA
HAHAH
I TOLD YOU YOU'D MAKE A FOOL OUT OF YOURSELF..
A COMFORTING WORD FROM A FRIEND!
SCHULZ

AAUGH! AAUGH!

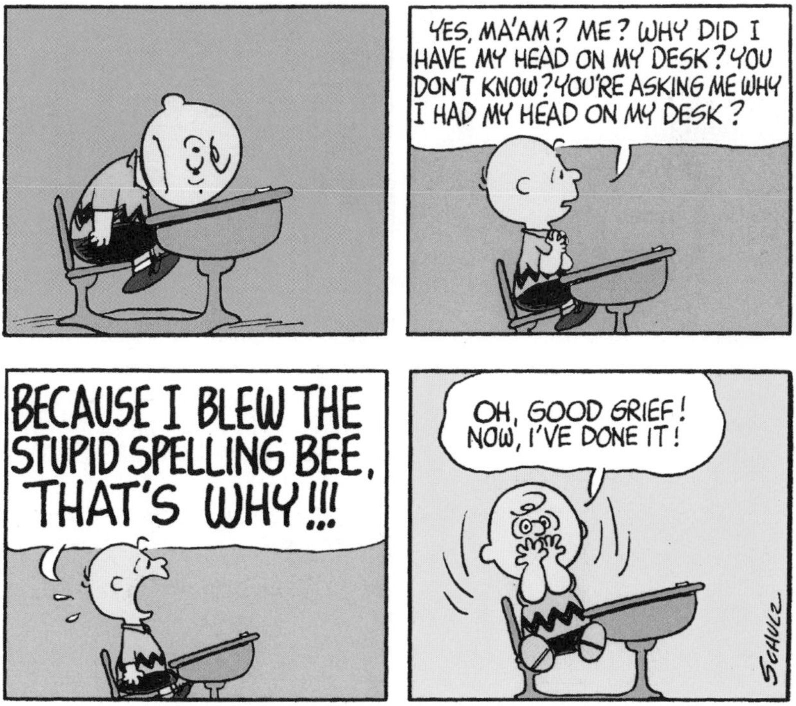
YES, MA'AM? ME? WHY DID I HAVE MY HEAD ON MY DESK? YOU DON'T KNOW? YOU'RE ASKING ME WHY I HAD MY HEAD ON MY DESK?
BECAUSE I BLEW THE STUPID SPELLING BEE, THAT'S WHY!!!
OH, GOOD GRIEF! NOW, I'VE DONE IT!
SCHULZ

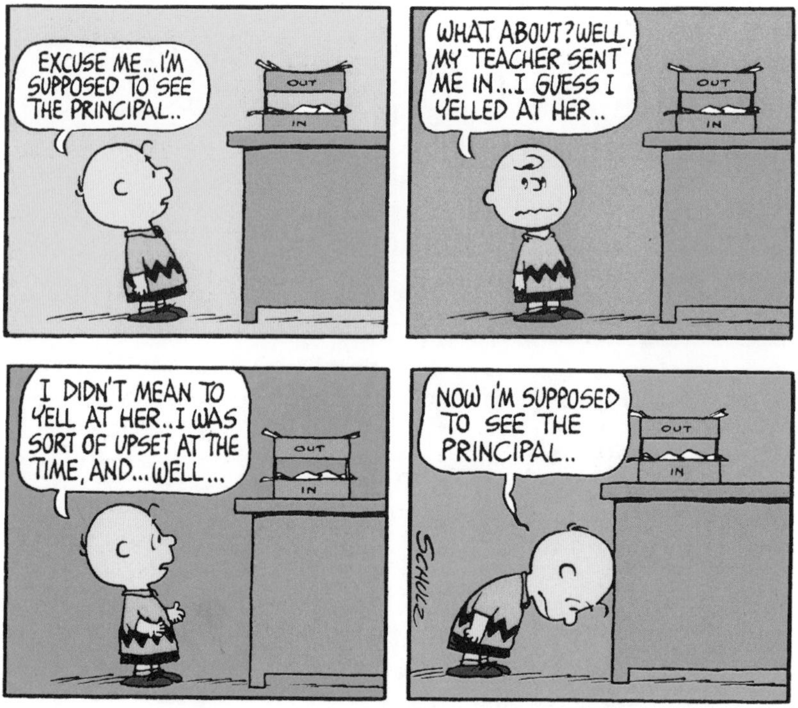
EXCUSE ME...I'M SUPPOSED TO SEE THE PRINCIPAL..
OUT
IN
WHAT ABOUT? WELL, MY TEACHER SENT ME IN...I GUESS I YELLED AT HER..
I DIDN'T MEAN TO YELL AT HER..I WAS SORT OF UPSET AT THE TIME, AND...WELL...
NOW I'M SUPPOSED TO SEE THE PRINCIPAL..
SCHULZ

AAUGH! AAUGH!

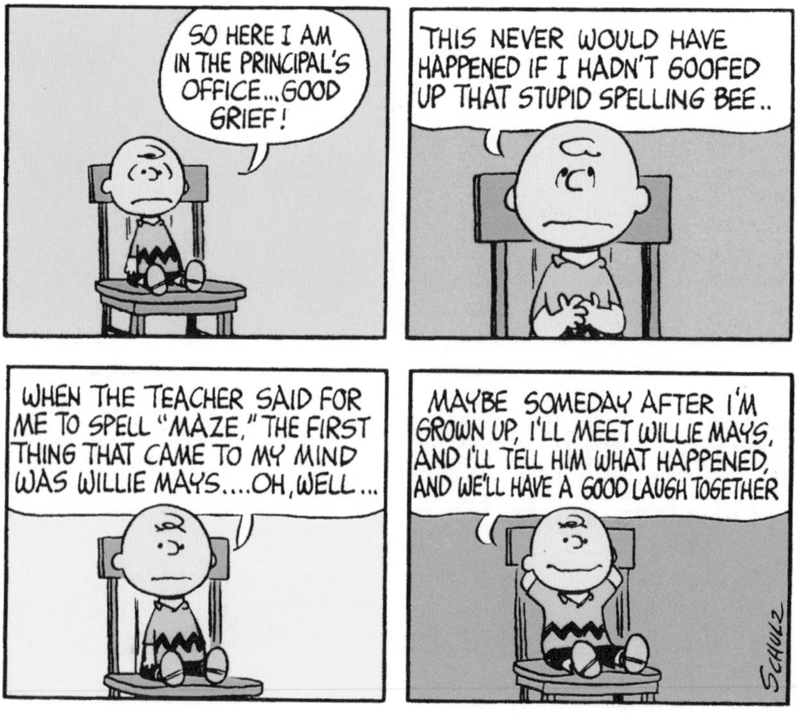
SO HERE I AM IN THE PRINCIPAL'S OFFICE...GOOD GRIEF!
THIS NEVER WOULD HAVE HAPPENED IF I HADN'T GOOFED UP THAT STUPID SPELLING BEE..
WHEN THE TEACHER SAID FOR ME TO SPELL "MAZE," THE FIRST THING THAT CAME TO MY MIND WAS WILLIE MAYS....OH, WELL...
MAYBE SOMEDAY AFTER I'M GROWN UP, I'LL MEET WILLIE MAYS, AND I'LL TELL HIM WHAT HAPPENED, AND WE'LL HAVE A GOOD LAUGH TOGETHER
SCHULZ

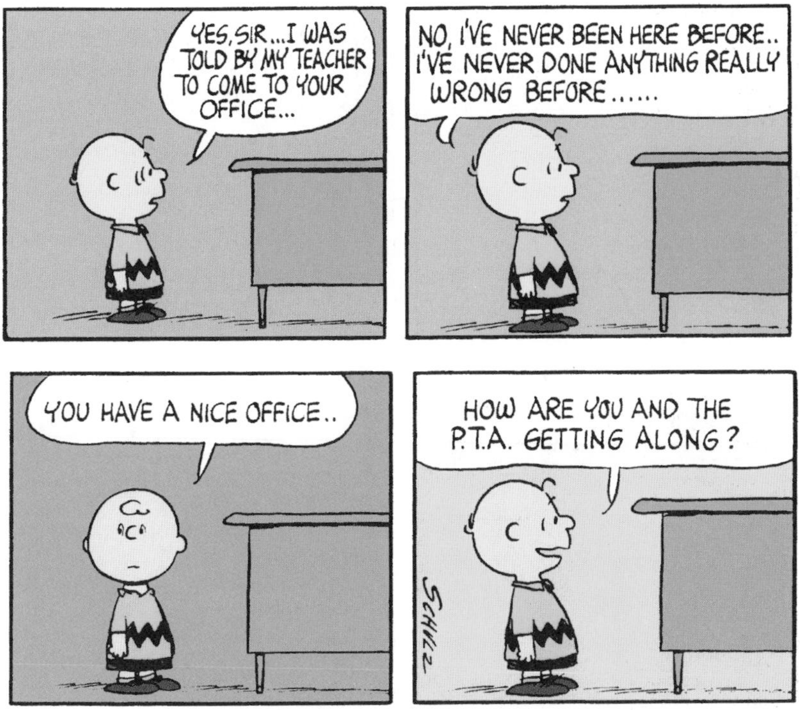
YES, SIR...I WAS TOLD BY MY TEACHER TO COME TO YOUR OFFICE...
NO, I'VE NEVER BEEN HERE BEFORE.. I'VE NEVER DONE ANYTHING REALLY WRONG BEFORE......
YOU HAVE A NICE OFFICE..
HOW ARE YOU AND THE P.T.A. GETTING ALONG?
SCHULZ

AAUGH! AAUGH!

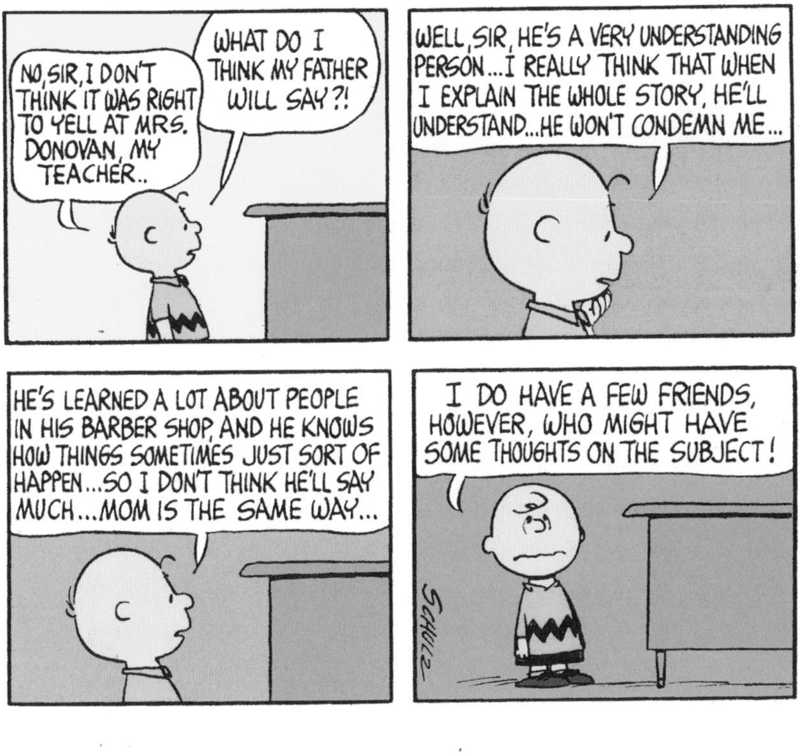
NO, SIR, I DON'T THINK IT WAS RIGHT TO YELL AT MRS. DONOVAN, MY TEACHER..
WHAT DO I THINK MY FATHER WILL SAY?!
WELL, SIR, HE'S A VERY UNDERSTANDING PERSON...I REALLY THINK THAT WHEN I EXPLAIN THE WHOLE STORY, HE'LL UNDERSTAND...HE WON'T CONDEMN ME...
HE'S LEARNED A LOT ABOUT PEOPLE IN HIS BARBER SHOP, AND HE KNOWS HOW THINGS SOMETIMES JUST SORT OF HAPPEN...SO I DON'T THINK HE'LL SAY MUCH...MOM IS THE SAME WAY...
I DO HAVE A FEW FRIENDS, HOWEVER, WHO MIGHT HAVE SOME THOUGHTS ON THE SUBJECT!
SCHULZ

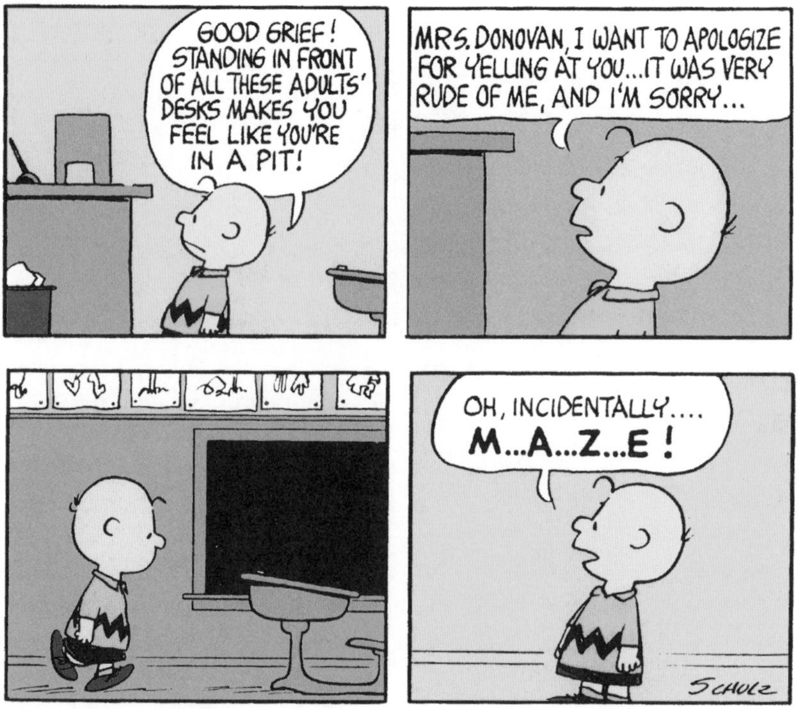
GOOD GRIEF! STANDING IN FRONT OF ALL THESE ADULTS' DESKS MAKES YOU FEEL LIKE YOU'RE IN A PIT!
MRS. DONOVAN, I WANT TO APOLOGIZE FOR YELLING AT YOU...IT WAS VERY RUDE OF ME, AND I'M SORRY...
OH, INCIDENTALLY....
M...A...Z...E!
SCHULZ

AAUGH! AAUGH!

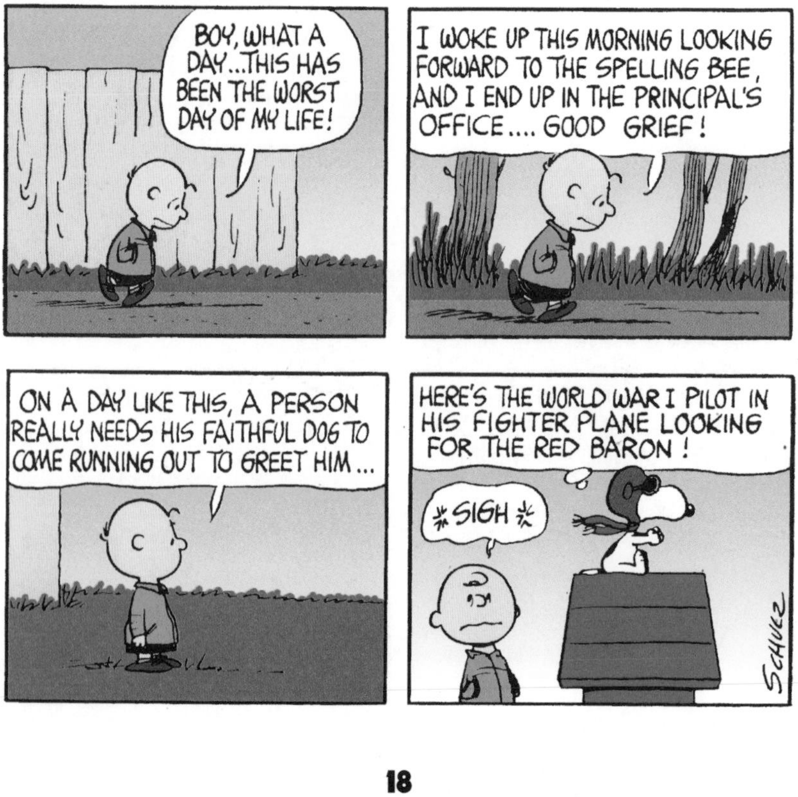
BOY, WHAT A DAY...THIS HAS BEEN THE WORST DAY OF MY LIFE!
I WOKE UP THIS MORNING LOOKING FORWARD TO THE SPELLING BEE, AND I END UP IN THE PRINCIPAL'S OFFICE.... GOOD GRIEF!
ON A DAY LIKE THIS, A PERSON REALLY NEEDS HIS FAITHFUL DOG TO COME RUNNING OUT TO GREET HIM...
HERE'S THE WORLD WAR I PILOT IN HIS FIGHTER PLANE LOOKING FOR THE RED BARON!
SIGH
SCHULZ

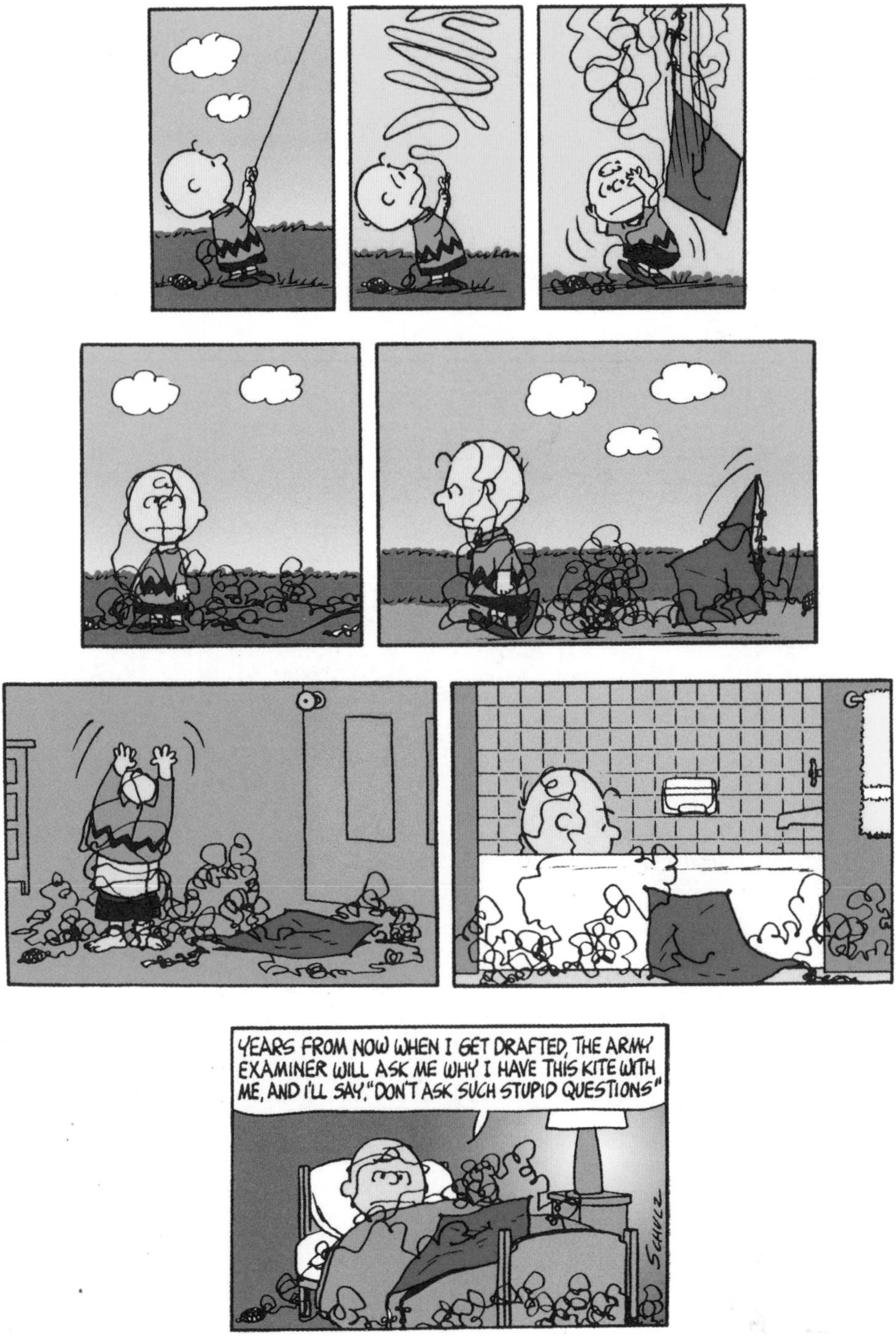
YEARS FROM NOW WHEN I GET DRAFTED, THE ARMY EXAMINER WILL ASK ME WHY I HAVE THIS KITE WITH ME, AND I'LL SAY, "DON'T ASK SUCH STUPID QUESTIONS"
SCHULZ

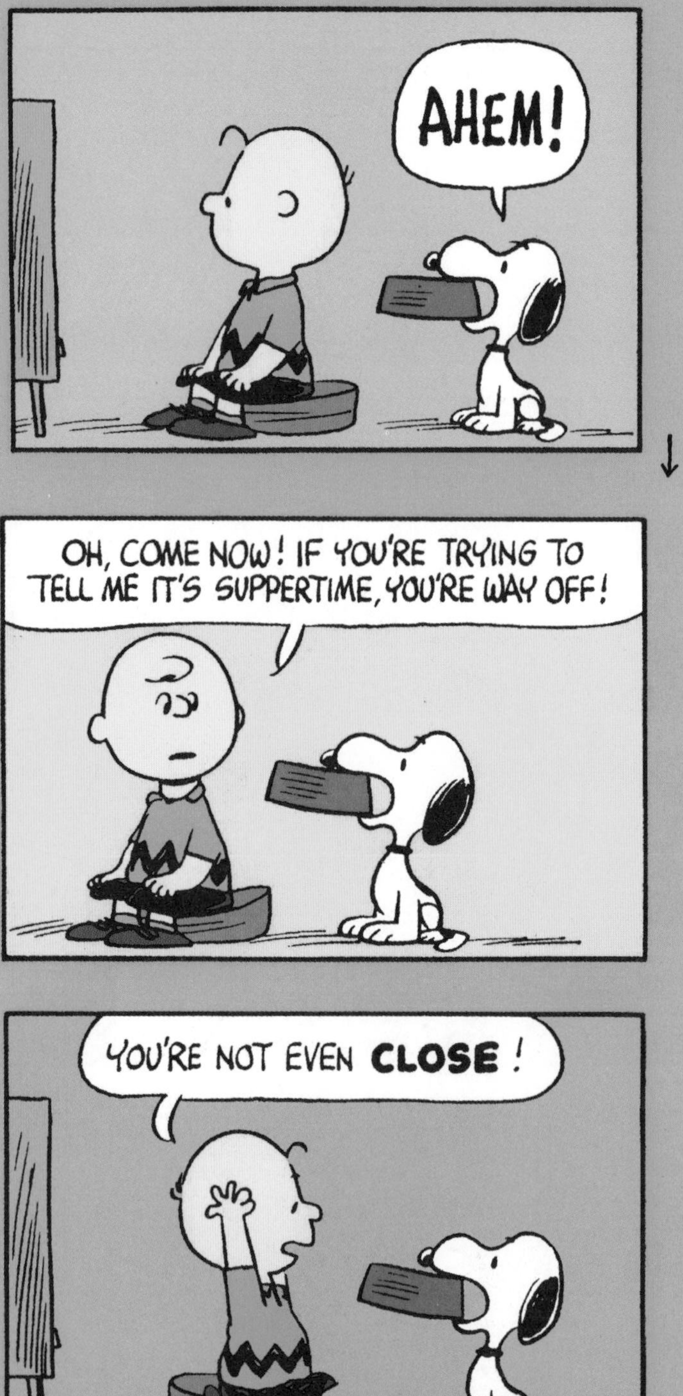
AHEM!
OH, COME NOW! IF YOU'RE TRYING TO TELL ME IT'S SUPPERTIME, YOU'RE WAY OFF!
YOU'RE NOT EVEN CLOSE!

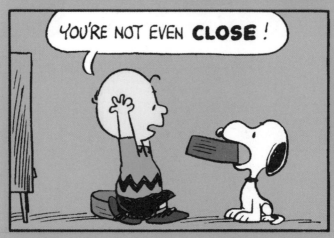

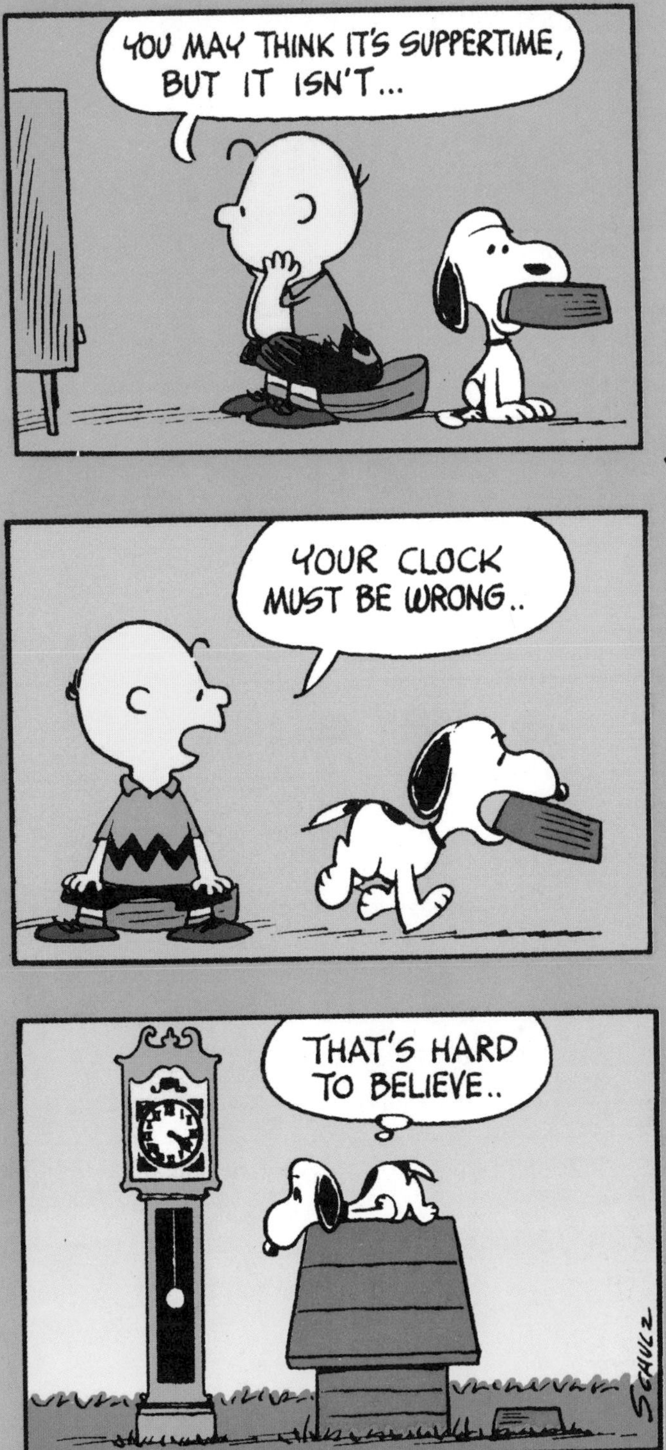
YOU MAY THINK IT'S SUPPERTIME, BUT IT ISN'T...
YOUR CLOCK MUST BE WRONG..
THAT'S HARD TO BELIEVE..
SCHULZ

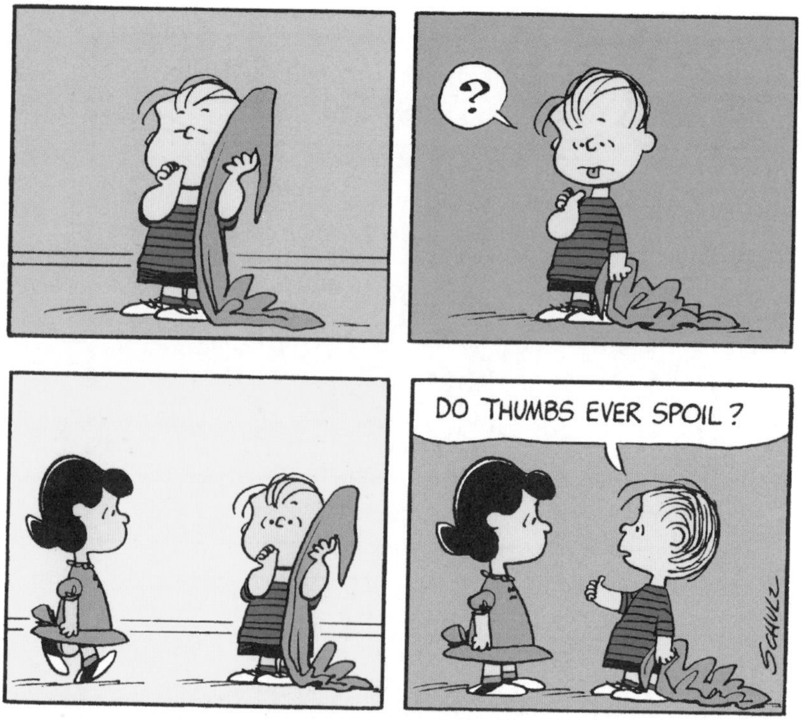

?
DO THUMBS EVER SPOIL?

AAUGH! AAUGH!

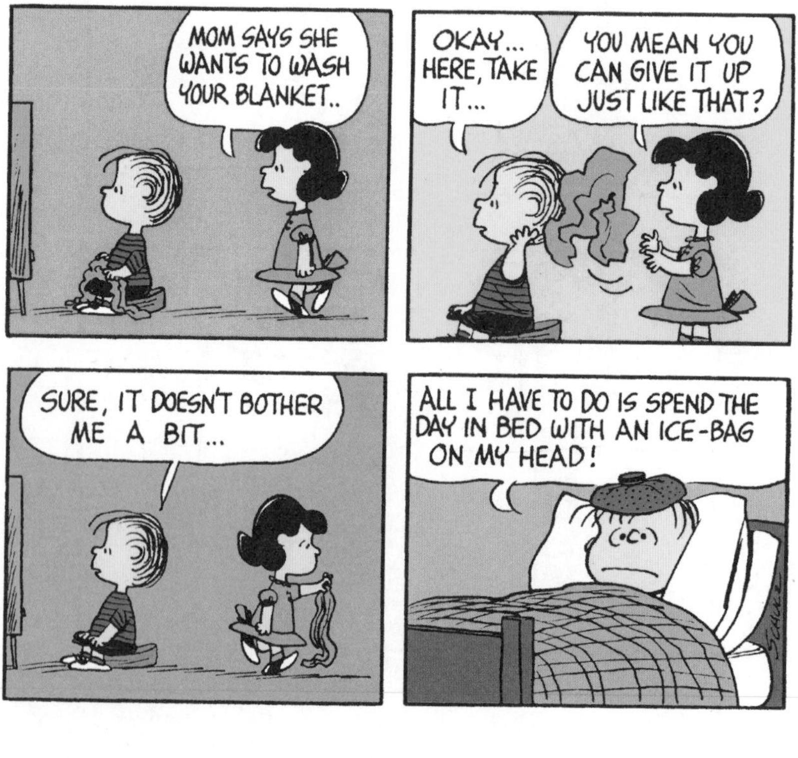

MOM SAYS SHE WANTS TO WASH YOUR BLANKET..
OKAY... HERE, TAKE IT...
YOU MEAN YOU CAN GIVE IT UP JUST LIKE THAT?
SURE, IT DOESN'T BOTHER ME A BIT...
ALL I HAVE TO DO IS SPEND THE DAY IN BED WITH AN ICE-BAG ON MY HEAD!

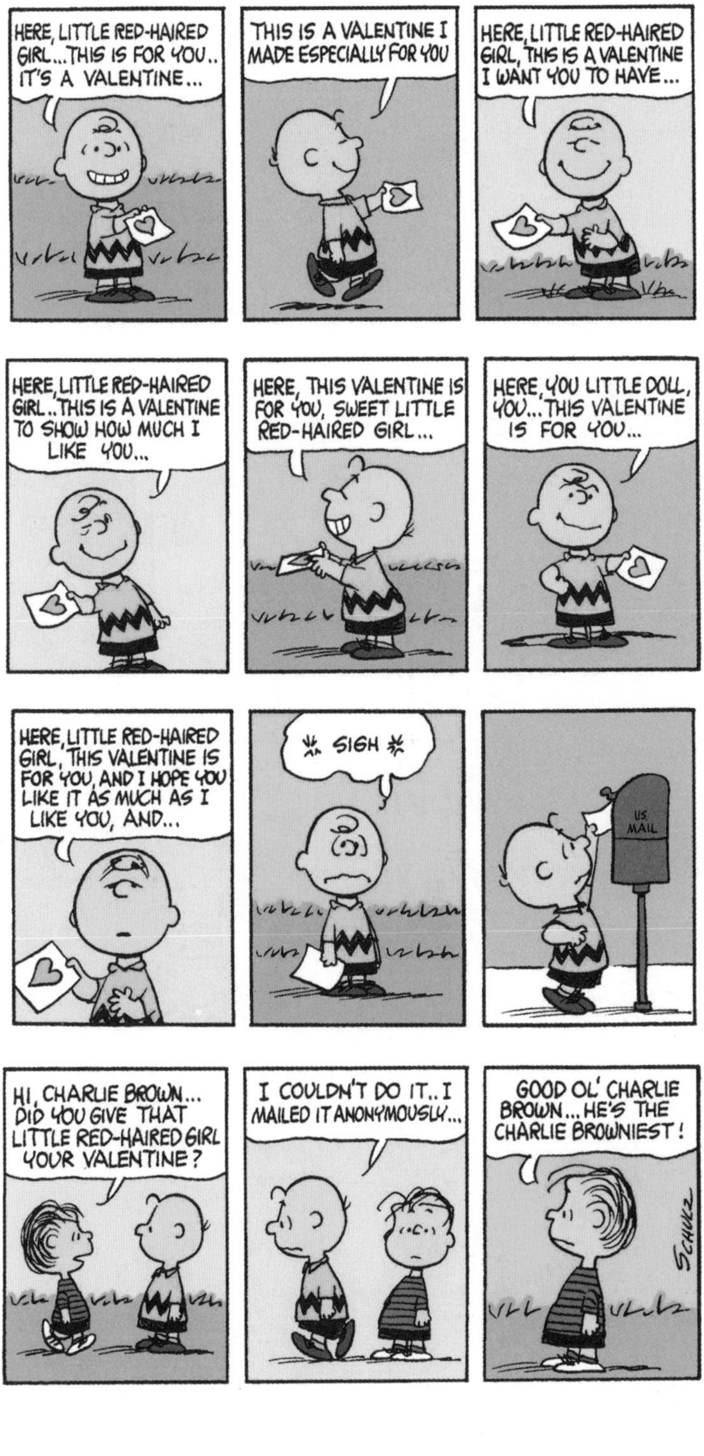
HERE, LITTLE RED-HAIRED GIRL...THIS IS FOR YOU.. IT'S A VALENTINE...
THIS IS A VALENTINE I MADE ESPECIALLY FOR YOU
HERE, LITTLE RED-HAIRED GIRL, THIS IS A VALENTINE I WANT YOU TO HAVE...
HERE, LITTLE RED-HAIRED GIRL..THIS IS A VALENTINE TO SHOW HOW MUCH I LIKE YOU...
HERE, THIS VALENTINE IS FOR YOU, SWEET LITTLE RED-HAIRED GIRL...
HERE, YOU LITTLE DOLL, YOU...THIS VALENTINE IS FOR YOU...
HERE, LITTLE RED-HAIRED GIRL, THIS VALENTINE IS FOR YOU, AND I HOPE YOU LIKE IT AS MUCH AS I LIKE YOU, AND...
SIGH
US MAIL
HI, CHARLIE BROWN... DID YOU GIVE THAT LITTLE RED-HAIRED GIRL YOUR VALENTINE?
I COULDN'T DO IT.. I MAILED IT ANONYMOUSLY...
GOOD OL' CHARLIE BROWN... HE'S THE CHARLIE BROWNIEST!
SCHULZ

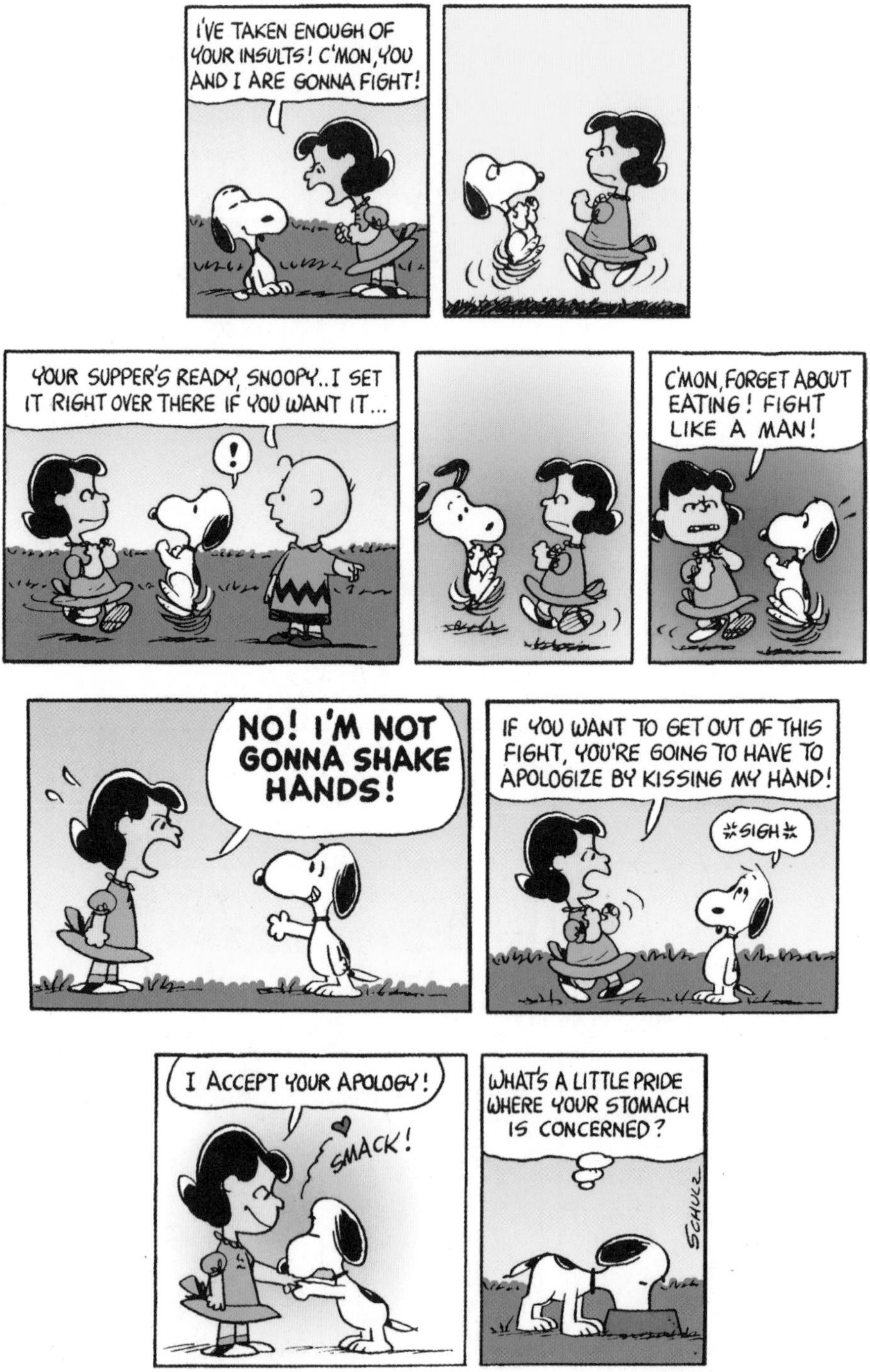
I'VE TAKEN ENOUGH OF YOUR INSULTS! C'MON, YOU AND I ARE GONNA FIGHT!
YOUR SUPPER'S READY, SNOOPY.. I SET IT RIGHT OVER THERE IF YOU WANT IT...
!
C'MON, FORGET ABOUT EATING! FIGHT LIKE A MAN!
NO! I'M NOT GONNA SHAKE HANDS!
IF YOU WANT TO GET OUT OF THIS FIGHT, YOU'RE GOING TO HAVE TO APOLOGIZE BY KISSING MY HAND!
SIGH
I ACCEPT YOUR APOLOGY!
SMACK!
WHAT'S A LITTLE PRIDE WHERE YOUR STOMACH IS CONCERNED?
SCHULZ

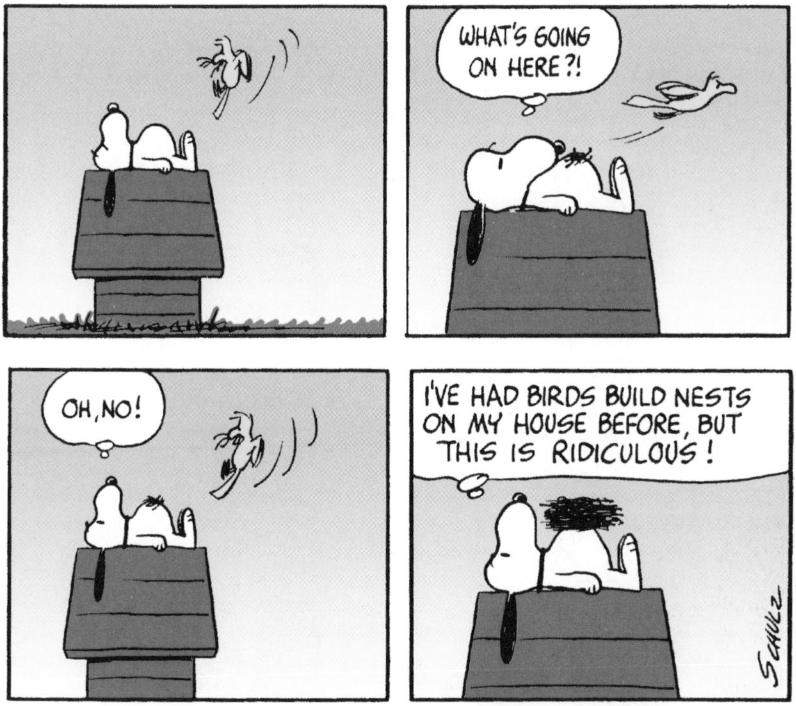
WHAT'S GOING ON HERE?!
OH, NO!
I'VE HAD BIRDS BUILD NESTS ON MY HOUSE BEFORE, BUT THIS IS RIDICULOUS!
SCHULZ

AAUGH! AAUGH!

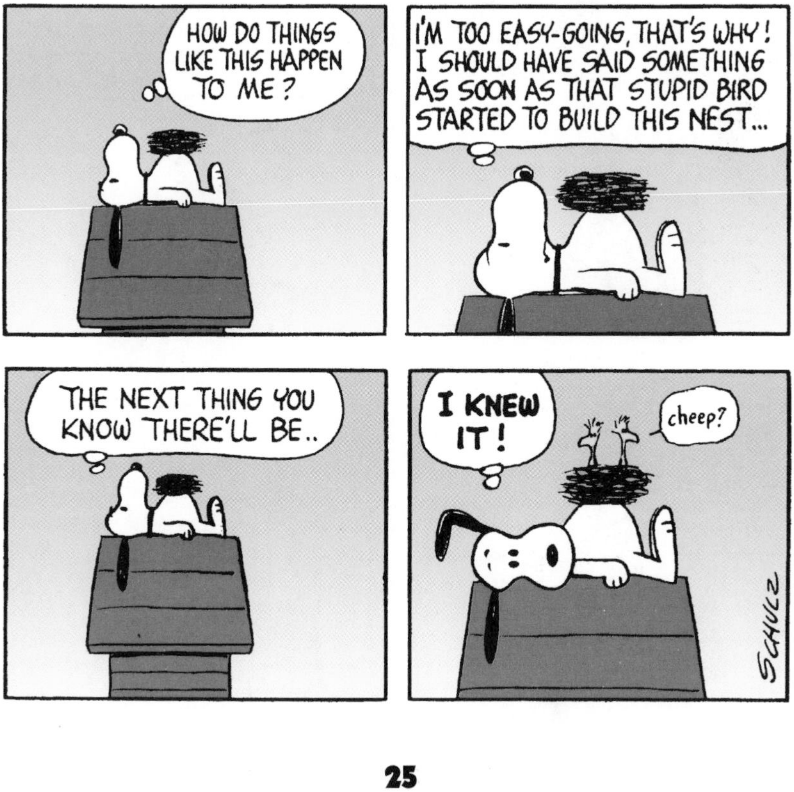
HOW DO THINGS LIKE THIS HAPPEN TO ME?
I'M TOO EASY-GOING, THAT'S WHY! I SHOULD HAVE SAID SOMETHING AS SOON AS THAT STUPID BIRD STARTED TO BUILD THIS NEST...
THE NEXT THING YOU KNOW THERE'LL BE..
I KNEW IT!
cheep?
SCHULZ

GOOD GRIEF! WHAT A PREDICAMENT!
MAYBE IF I BREATHE TO THE TUNE OF BRAHMS' LULLABY, THEY'LL GO TO SLEEP...
I BREATHE A GOOD LULLABY!
Z
SCHULZ

AAUGH! AAUGH!

THIS IS TERRIBLE!
IF THESE STUPID BIRDS DON'T LEARN TO FLY PRETTY SOON, I'LL BE LYING HERE FOR THE REST OF MY LIFE!
THAT'S IT... GET OUT OF THE NEST.... NOW, TAKE OFF...
OH, COME ON! FORGET THE FANCY STUFF.. JUST FLY!!
SCHULZ

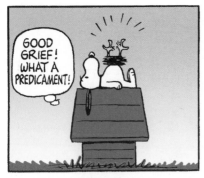

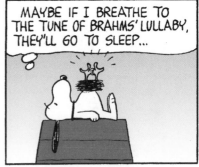

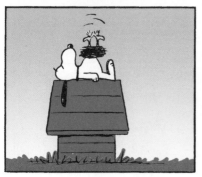

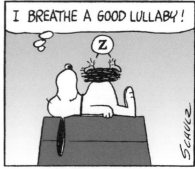

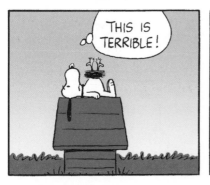

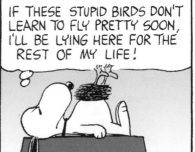

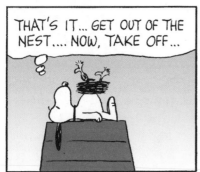

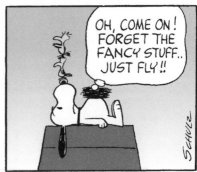

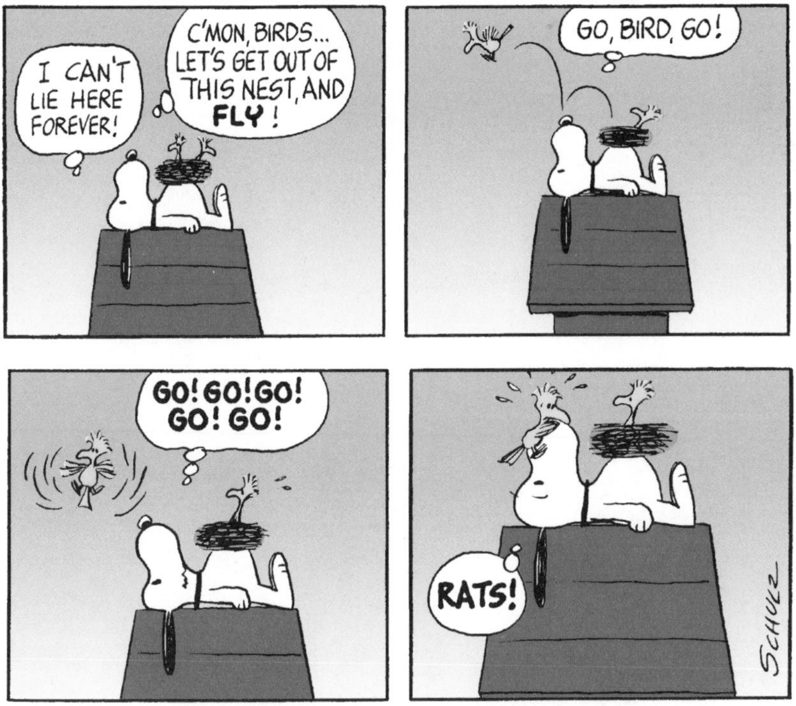
I CAN'T LIE HERE FOREVER!
C'MON, BIRDS... LET'S GET OUT OF THIS NEST, AND **FLY**!
GO, BIRD, GO!
GO! GO! GO! GO! GO!
RATS!
SCHULZ

AAUGH! AAUGH!

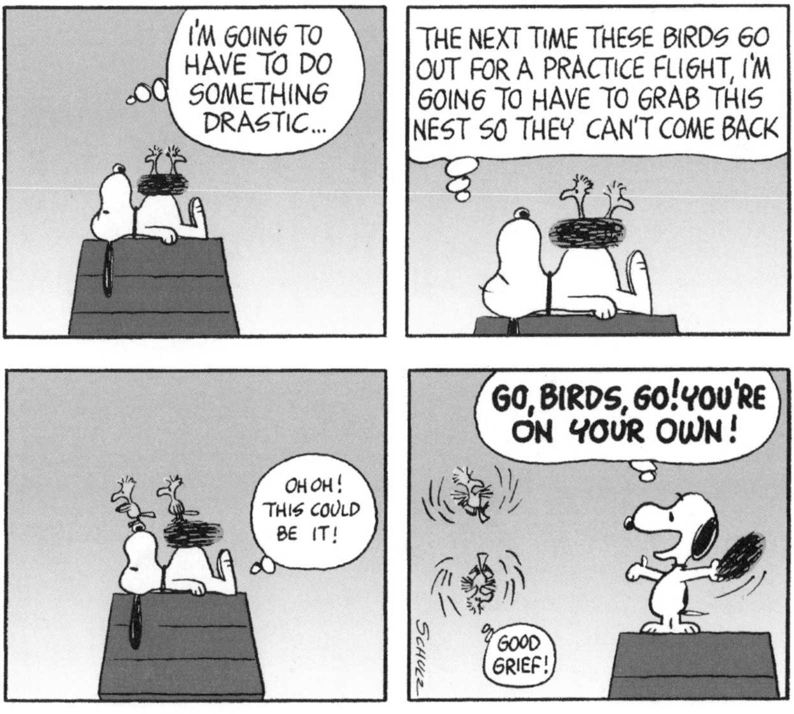
I'M GOING TO HAVE TO DO SOMETHING DRASTIC...
THE NEXT TIME THESE BIRDS GO OUT FOR A PRACTICE FLIGHT, I'M GOING TO HAVE TO GRAB THIS NEST SO THEY CAN'T COME BACK
OH OH! THIS COULD BE IT!
GO, BIRDS, GO! YOU'RE ON YOUR OWN!
GOOD GRIEF!
SCHULZ

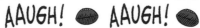

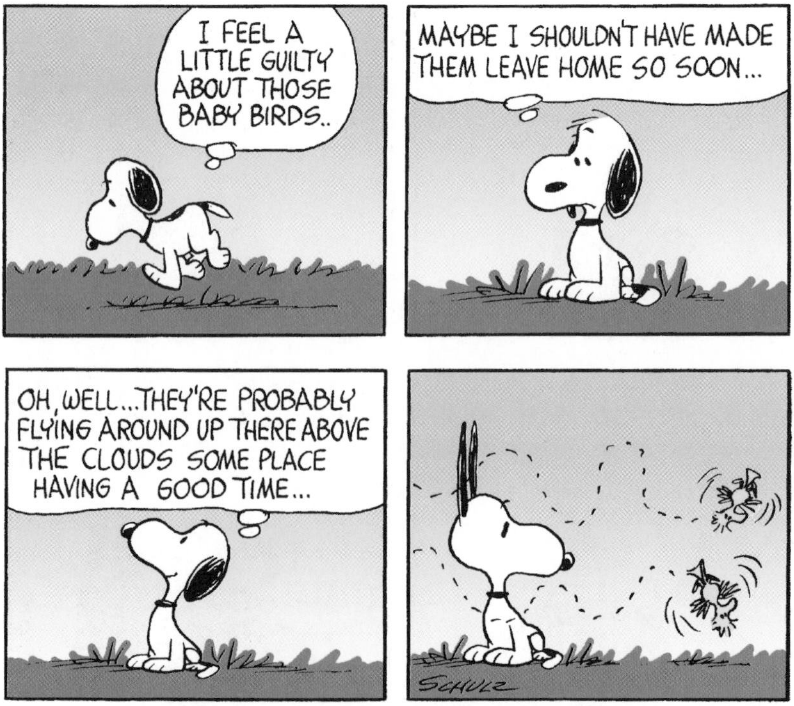
I FEEL A LITTLE GUILTY ABOUT THOSE BABY BIRDS..
MAYBE I SHOULDN'T HAVE MADE THEM LEAVE HOME SO SOON...
OH, WELL...THEY'RE PROBABLY FLYING AROUND UP THERE ABOVE THE CLOUDS SOME PLACE HAVING A GOOD TIME...
SCHULZ

AAUGH! AAUGH!

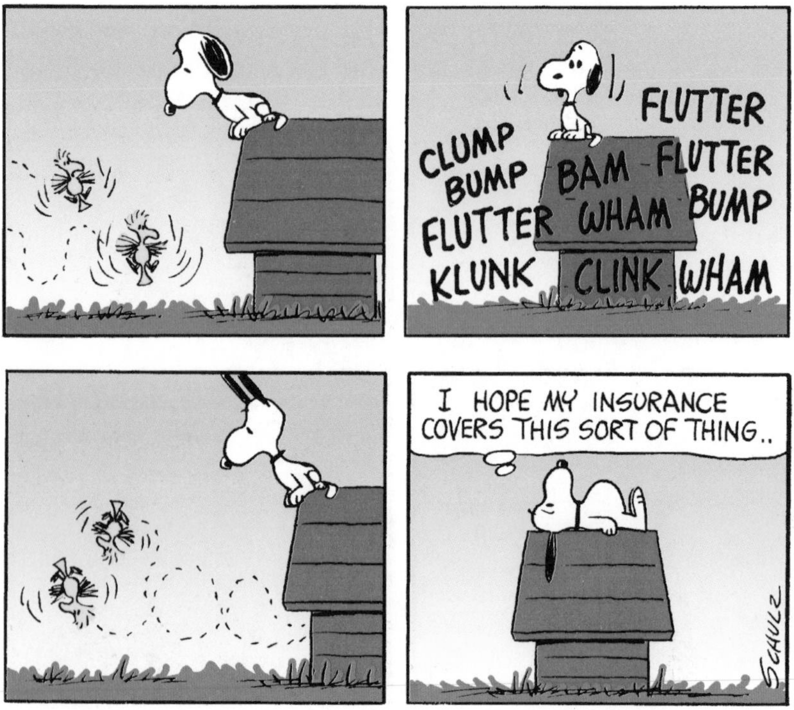
CLUMP
BUMP
FLUTTER
KLUNK
BAM
WHAM
CLINK
FLUTTER
FLUTTER
BUMP
WHAM
I HOPE MY INSURANCE COVERS THIS SORT OF THING..
SCHULZ

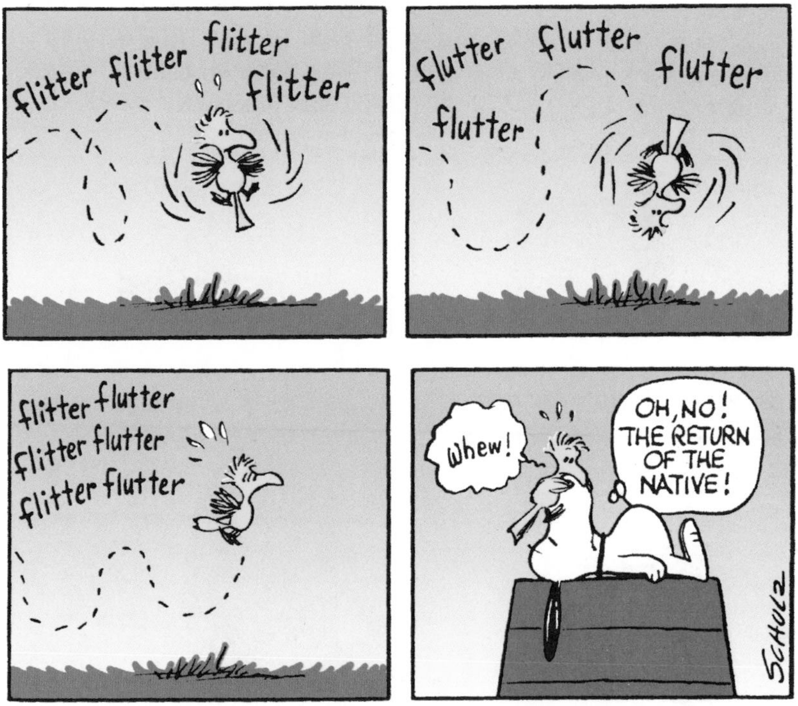
flitter flitter flitter flitter
flutter flutter flutter flutter
flitter flutter
flitter flutter
flitter flutter
Whew!
OH, NO! THE RETURN OF THE NATIVE!
SCHULZ

AAUGH! AAUGH!

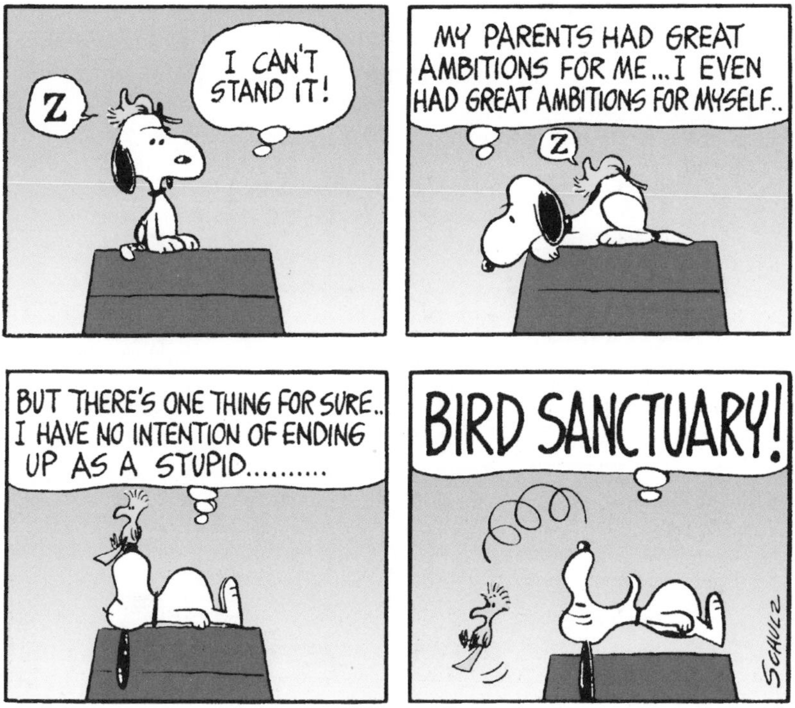
Z
I CAN'T STAND IT!
MY PARENTS HAD GREAT AMBITIONS FOR ME... I EVEN HAD GREAT AMBITIONS FOR MYSELF..
Z
BUT THERE'S ONE THING FOR SURE.. I HAVE NO INTENTION OF ENDING UP AS A STUPID.........
BIRD SANCTUARY!
SCHULZ

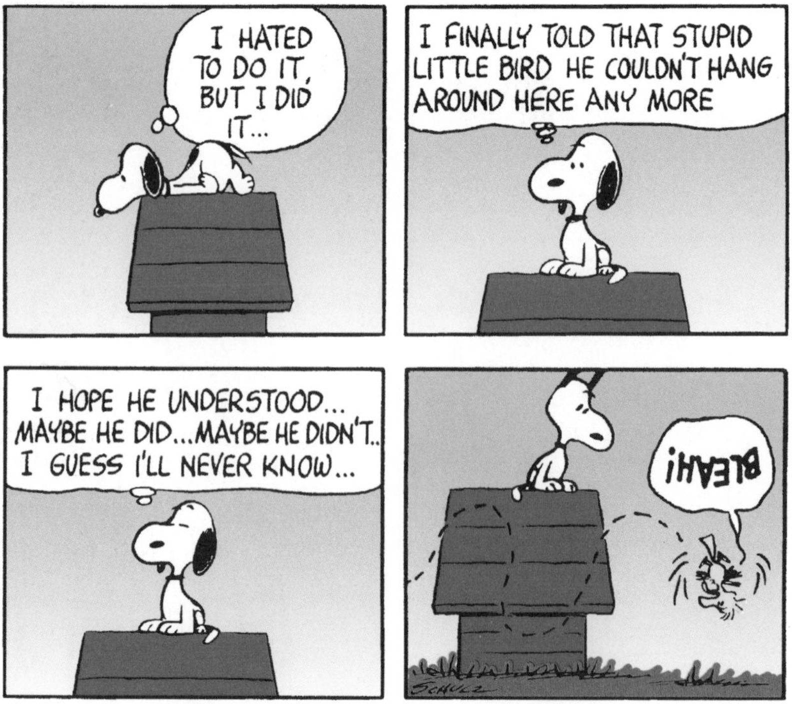
I HATED TO DO IT, BUT I DID IT...
I FINALLY TOLD THAT STUPID LITTLE BIRD HE COULDN'T HANG AROUND HERE ANY MORE
I HOPE HE UNDERSTOOD... MAYBE HE DID...MAYBE HE DIDN'T.. I GUESS I'LL NEVER KNOW...
BLEAH!
SCHULZ

AAUGH! AAUGH!

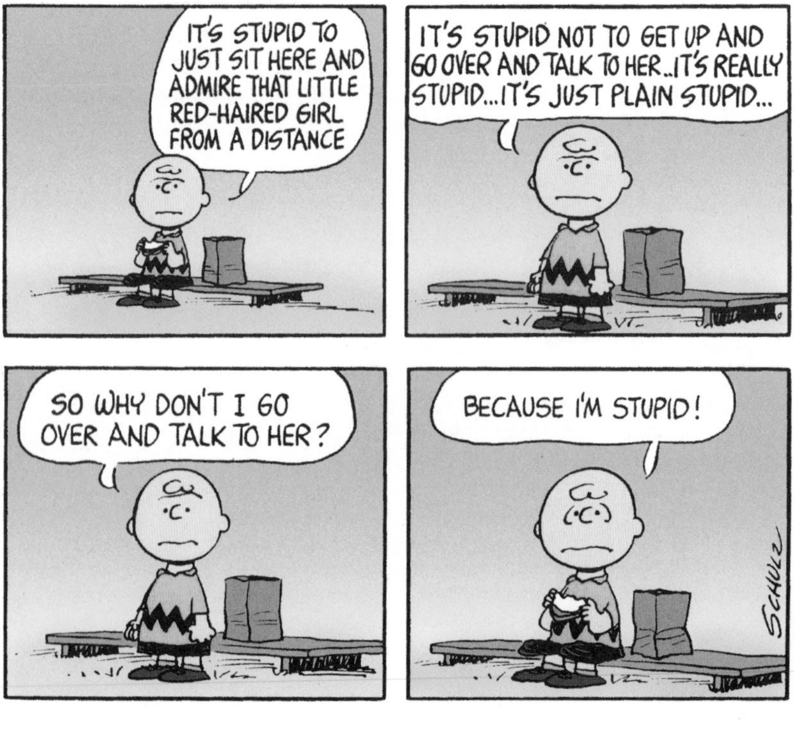
IT'S STUPID TO JUST SIT HERE AND ADMIRE THAT LITTLE RED-HAIRED GIRL FROM A DISTANCE
IT'S STUPID NOT TO GET UP AND GO OVER AND TALK TO HER..IT'S REALLY STUPID...IT'S JUST PLAIN STUPID...
SO WHY DON'T I GO OVER AND TALK TO HER?
BECAUSE I'M STUPID!
SCHULZ

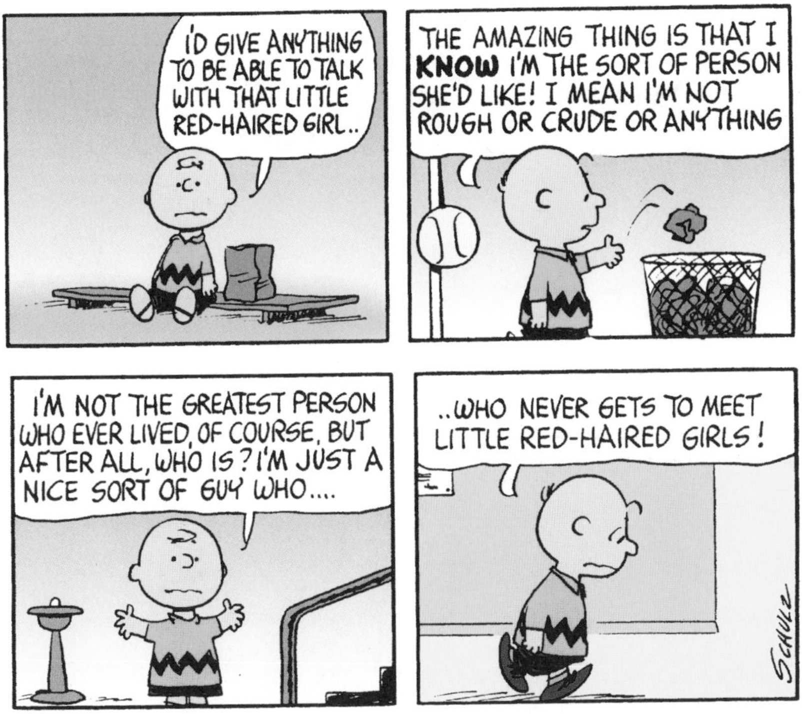
I'D GIVE ANYTHING TO BE ABLE TO TALK WITH THAT LITTLE RED-HAIRED GIRL..
THE AMAZING THING IS THAT I **KNOW** I'M THE SORT OF PERSON SHE'D LIKE! I MEAN I'M NOT ROUGH OR CRUDE OR ANYTHING
I'M NOT THE GREATEST PERSON WHO EVER LIVED, OF COURSE, BUT AFTER ALL, WHO IS? I'M JUST A NICE SORT OF GUY WHO....
..WHO NEVER GETS TO MEET LITTLE RED-HAIRED GIRLS!
SCHULZ

AAUGH! AAUGH!

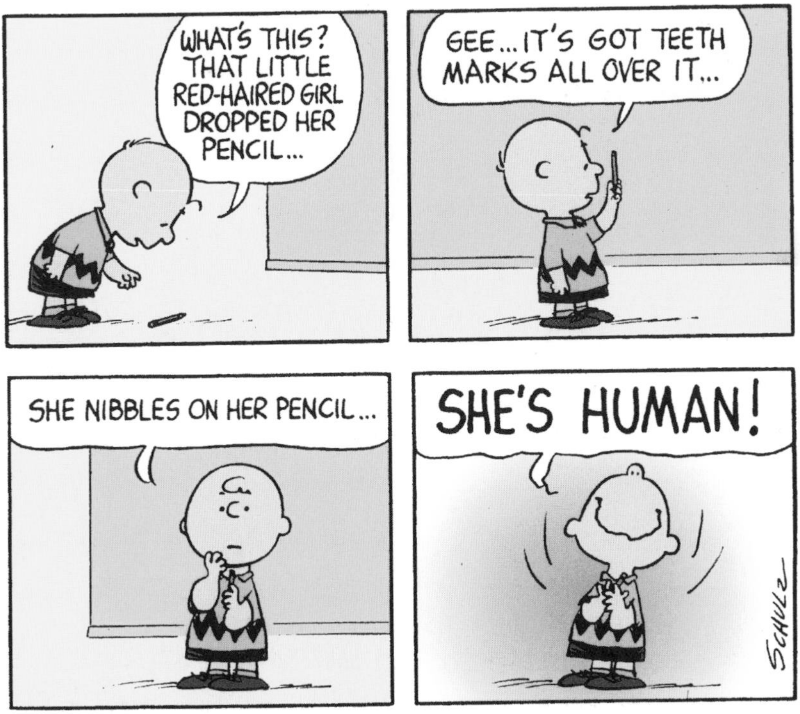
WHAT'S THIS? THAT LITTLE RED-HAIRED GIRL DROPPED HER PENCIL...
GEE...IT'S GOT TEETH MARKS ALL OVER IT...
SHE NIBBLES ON HER PENCIL...
SHE'S HUMAN!
SCHULZ

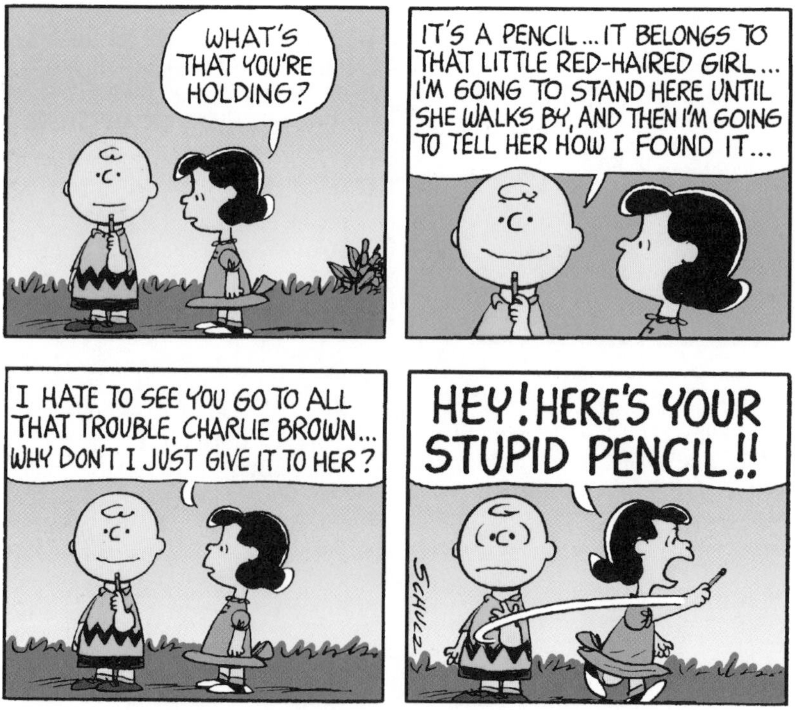
WHAT'S THAT YOU'RE HOLDING?
IT'S A PENCIL...IT BELONGS TO THAT LITTLE RED-HAIRED GIRL... I'M GOING TO STAND HERE UNTIL SHE WALKS BY, AND THEN I'M GOING TO TELL HER HOW I FOUND IT...
I HATE TO SEE YOU GO TO ALL THAT TROUBLE, CHARLIE BROWN... WHY DON'T I JUST GIVE IT TO HER?
HEY! HERE'S YOUR STUPID PENCIL!!
SCHULZ

AAUGH! AAUGH!

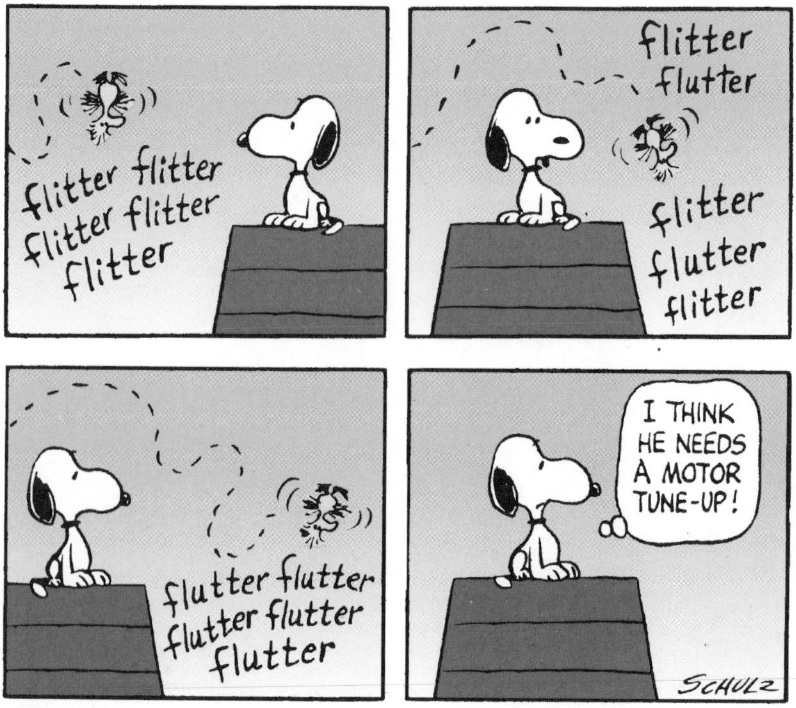
flitter flitter
flitter flitter
flitter
flitter
flutter
flitter
flutter
flitter
flutter flutter
flutter flutter
flutter
I THINK HE NEEDS A MOTOR TUNE-UP!
SCHULZ

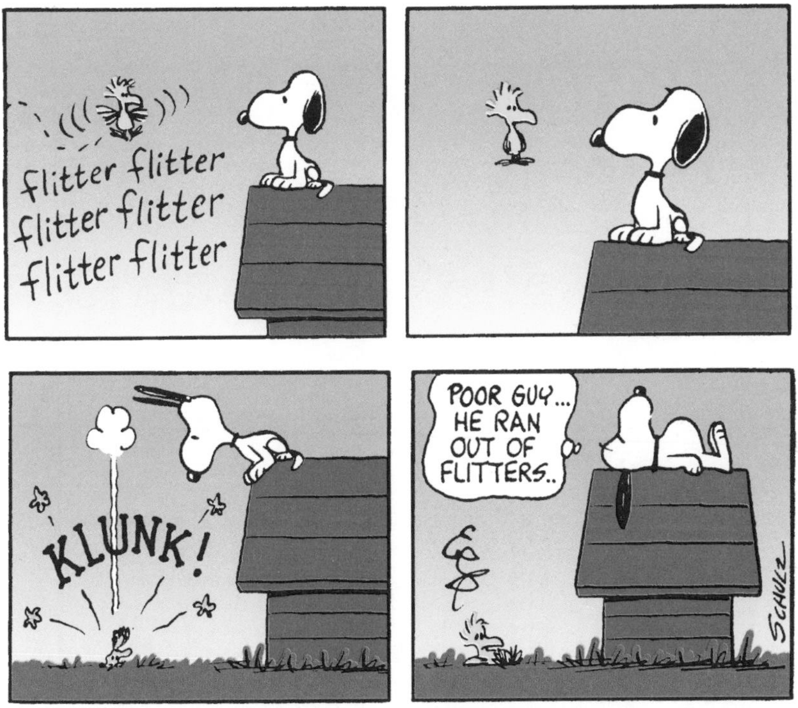
flitter flitter
flitter flitter
flitter flitter
KLUNK!
POOR GUY... HE RAN OUT OF FLITTERS..
SCHULZ

AAUGH! AAUGH!

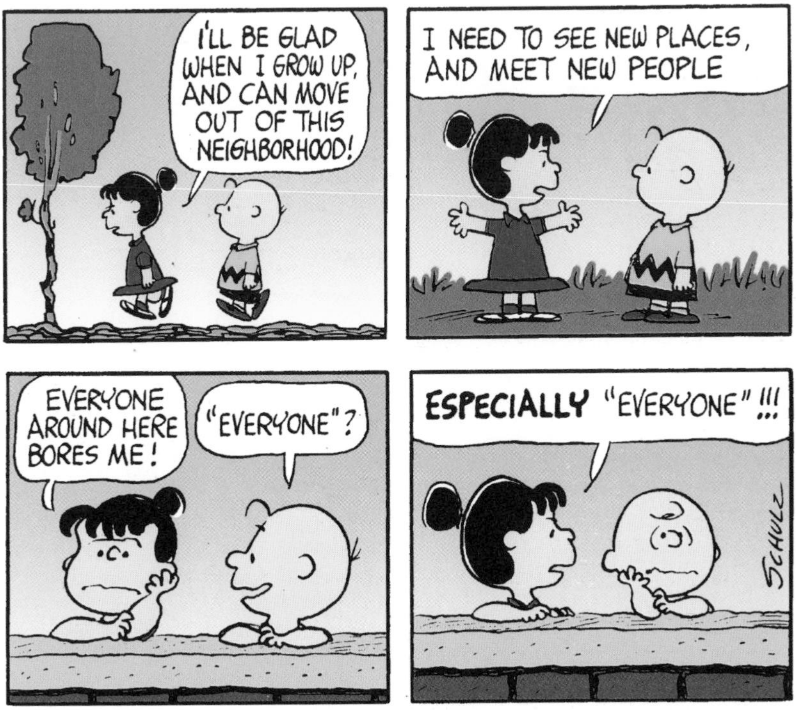
I'LL BE GLAD WHEN I GROW UP, AND CAN MOVE OUT OF THIS NEIGHBORHOOD!
I NEED TO SEE NEW PLACES, AND MEET NEW PEOPLE
EVERYONE AROUND HERE BORES ME!
"EVERYONE"?
ESPECIALLY "EVERYONE"!!!
SCHULZ

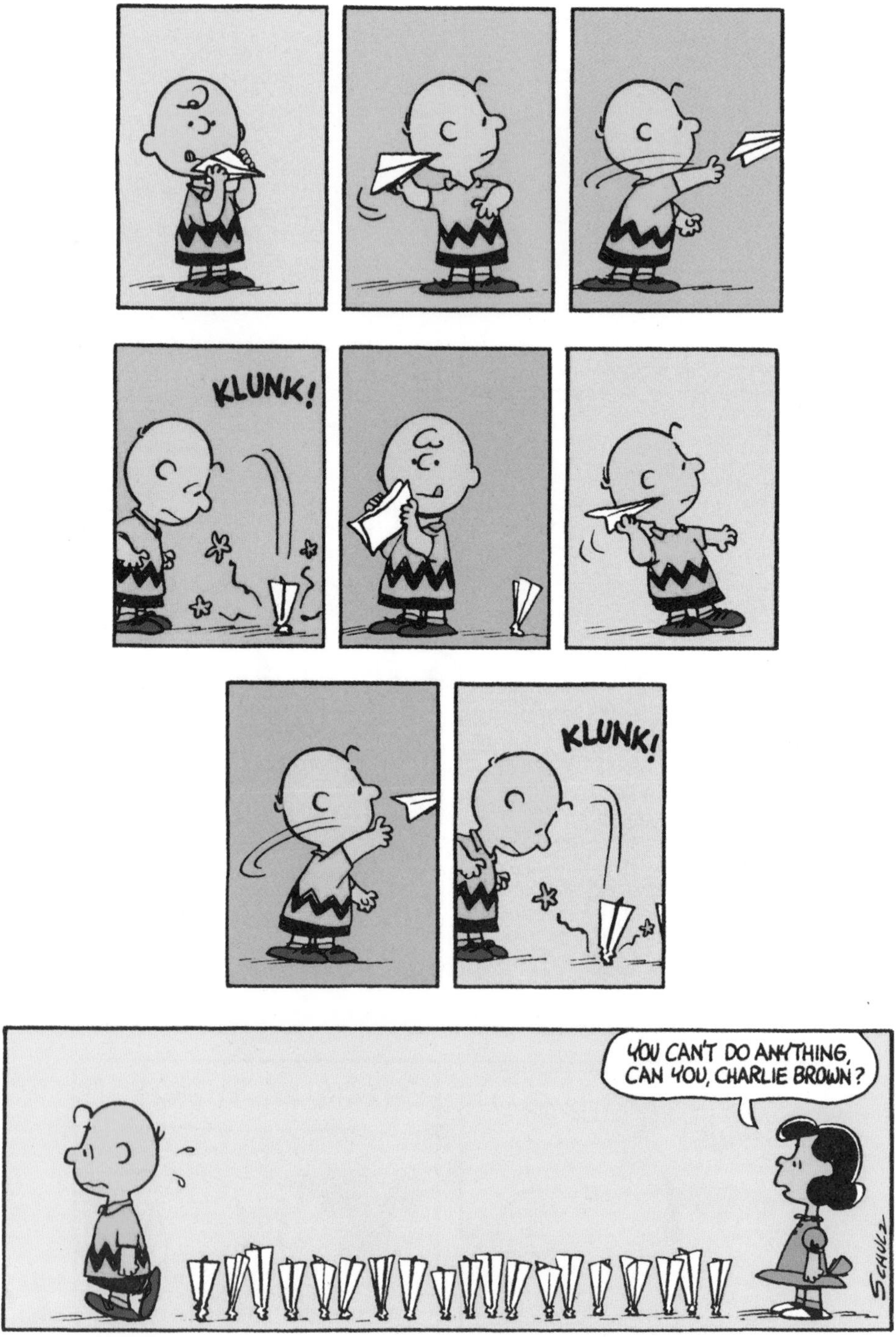
KLUNK!
KLUNK!
YOU CAN'T DO ANYTHING, CAN YOU, CHARLIE BROWN?
SCHULZ

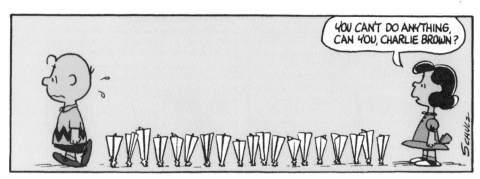

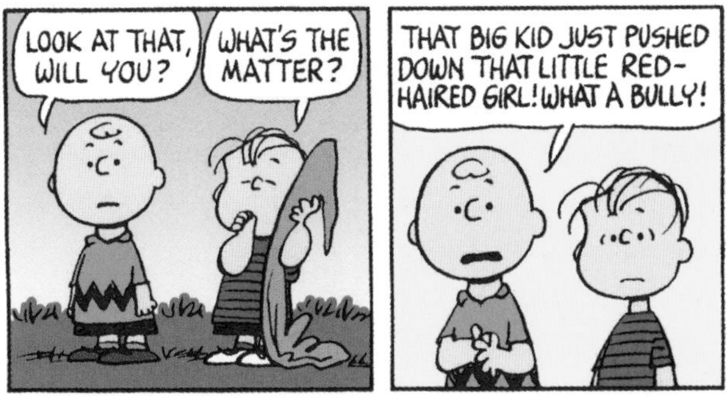
LOOK AT THAT, WILL YOU?
WHAT'S THE MATTER?
THAT BIG KID JUST PUSHED DOWN THAT LITTLE RED-HAIRED GIRL! WHAT A BULLY!

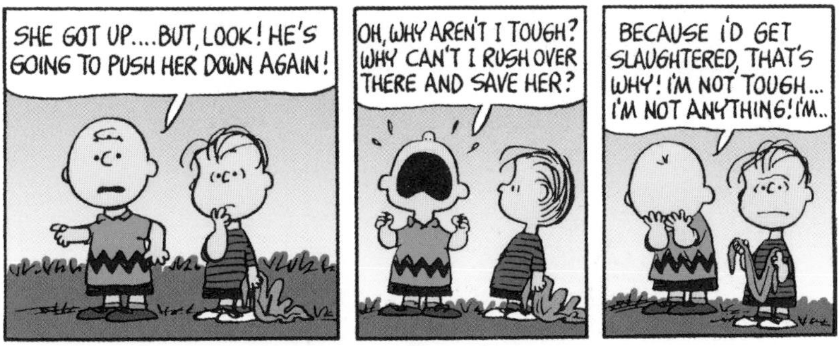
SHE GOT UP....BUT, LOOK! HE'S GOING TO PUSH HER DOWN AGAIN!
OH, WHY AREN'T I TOUGH? WHY CAN'T I RUSH OVER THERE AND SAVE HER?
BECAUSE I'D GET SLAUGHTERED, THAT'S WHY! I'M NOT TOUGH... I'M NOT ANYTHING! I'M..

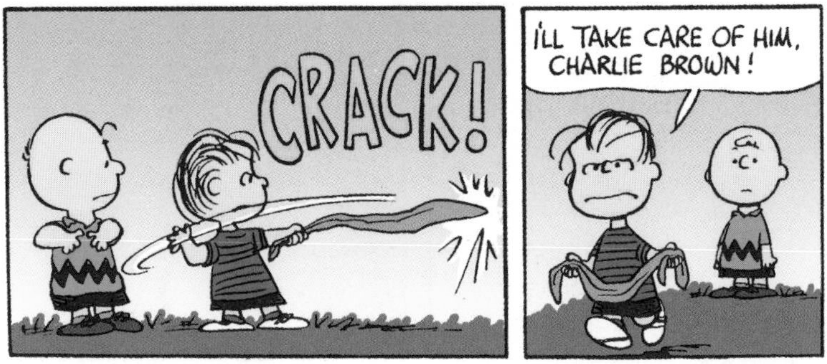
CRACK!
I'LL TAKE CARE OF HIM, CHARLIE BROWN!

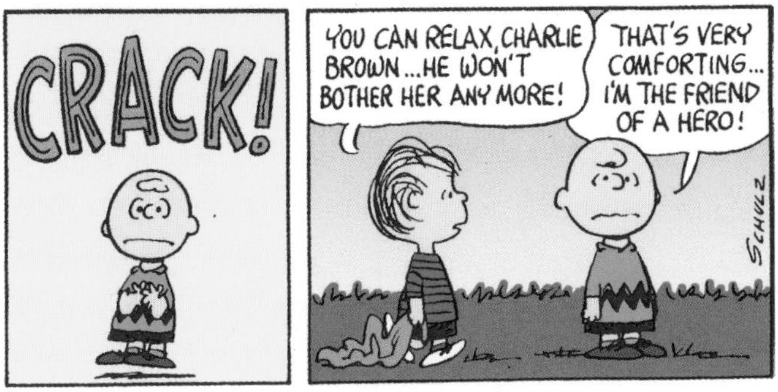
CRACK!
YOU CAN RELAX, CHARLIE BROWN...HE WON'T BOTHER HER ANY MORE!
THAT'S VERY COMFORTING... I'M THE FRIEND OF A HERO!
SCHULZ

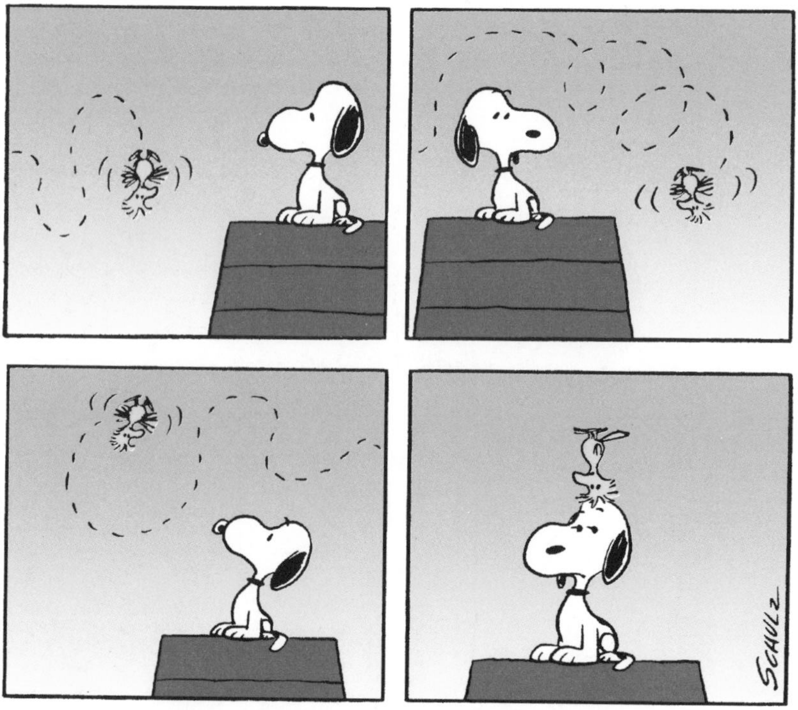
SCHULZ

AAUGH! AAUGH!

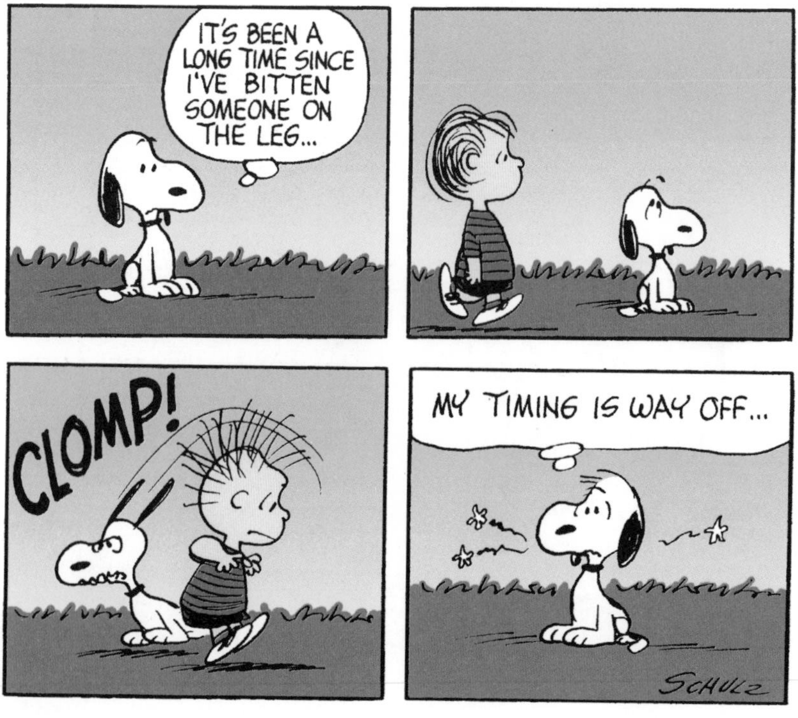
IT'S BEEN A LONG TIME SINCE I'VE BITTEN SOMEONE ON THE LEG...
CLOMP!
MY TIMING IS WAY OFF...
SCHULZ

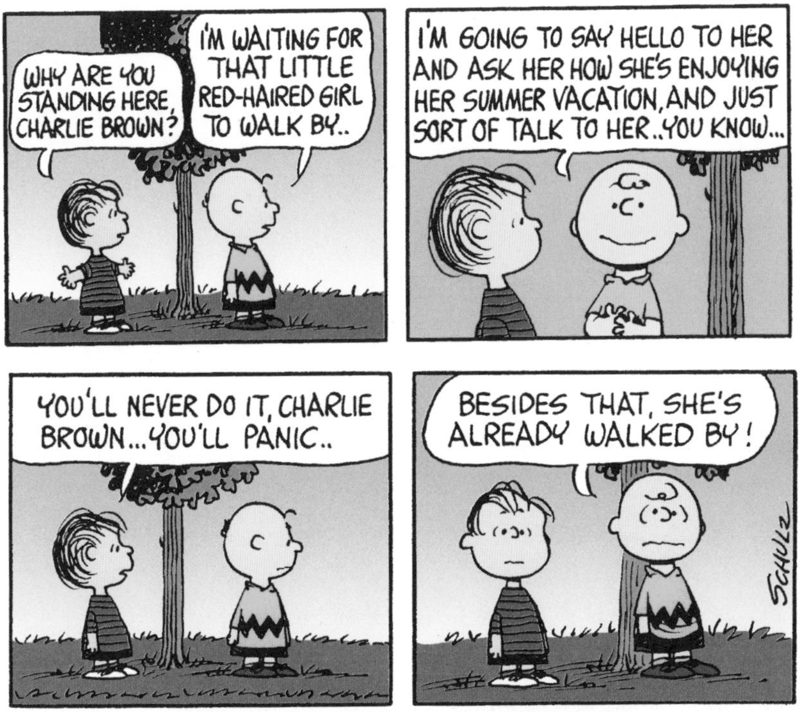
WHY ARE YOU STANDING HERE, CHARLIE BROWN?
I'M WAITING FOR THAT LITTLE RED-HAIRED GIRL TO WALK BY..
I'M GOING TO SAY HELLO TO HER AND ASK HER HOW SHE'S ENJOYING HER SUMMER VACATION, AND JUST SORT OF TALK TO HER..YOU KNOW...
YOU'LL NEVER DO IT, CHARLIE BROWN...YOU'LL PANIC..
BESIDES THAT, SHE'S ALREADY WALKED BY!
SCHULZ

AAUGH! AAUGH!

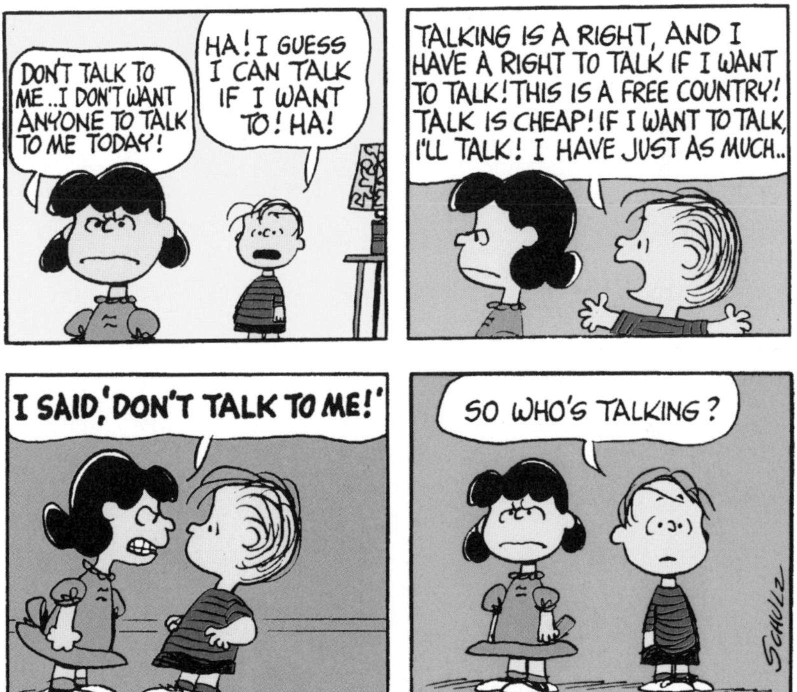
DON'T TALK TO ME..I DON'T WANT ANYONE TO TALK TO ME TODAY!
HA! I GUESS I CAN TALK IF I WANT TO! HA!
TALKING IS A RIGHT, AND I HAVE A RIGHT TO TALK IF I WANT TO TALK! THIS IS A FREE COUNTRY! TALK IS CHEAP! IF I WANT TO TALK, I'LL TALK! I HAVE JUST AS MUCH..
I SAID, 'DON'T TALK TO ME!'
SO WHO'S TALKING?
SCHULZ

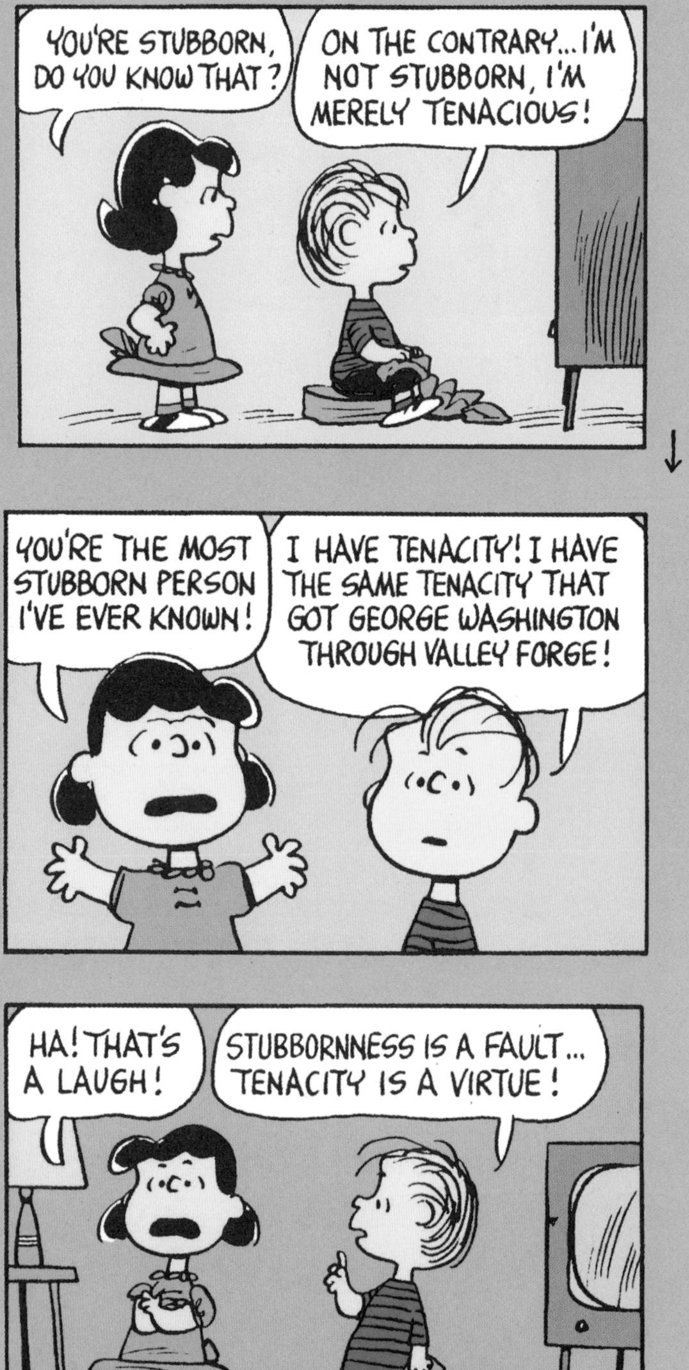
YOU'RE STUBBORN, DO YOU KNOW THAT?
ON THE CONTRARY...I'M NOT STUBBORN, I'M MERELY TENACIOUS!
YOU'RE THE MOST STUBBORN PERSON I'VE EVER KNOWN!
I HAVE TENACITY! I HAVE THE SAME TENACITY THAT GOT GEORGE WASHINGTON THROUGH VALLEY FORGE!
HA! THAT'S A LAUGH!
STUBBORNNESS IS A FAULT... TENACITY IS A VIRTUE!

YOU'RE SO STUBBORN YOU WON'T EVEN ADMIT YOU'RE STUBBORN!
I CLING TENACIOUSLY TO MY VERY VALID VIEW THAT I AM TENACIOUS...
POW!
ON THE OTHER HAND, PERHAPS I'LL ADMIT TO A LITTLE MULE-HEADEDNESS...
SCHULZ

 YOU KNOW WHAT YOUR TROUBLE IS? YOU JUST DON'T UNDERSTAND THE ADULT MIND..

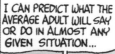 I CAN PREDICT WHAT THE AVERAGE ADULT WILL SAY OR DO IN ALMOST ANY GIVEN SITUATION...

 THIS IS A MUST IF YOU ARE GOING TO SURVIVE AS A CHILD!

 NOW, TAKE GRANDMA, FOR INSTANCE...I CAN PREDICT EXACTLY WHAT SHE WILL SAY IN THE FOLLOWING SITUATION....

 YOU DRAW A PICTURE AND I'LL DRAW A PICTURE...THEN YOU TAKE THE TWO PICTURES IN, AND SHOW THEM TO GRANDMA...

 ASK HER WHICH PICTURE SHE THINKS IS THE BETTER..I PREDICT THAT SHE WILL LOOK AT THEM AND SAY, "WHY, I THINK THEY'RE BOTH VERY NICE"

 GRANDMA, HERE ARE TWO PICTURES THAT LINUS AND I HAVE DRAWN..WHICH ONE DO YOU THINK IS THE BETTER?

 WHY, I THINK THEY'RE BOTH VERY NICE

 YOU JUST HAVE TO UNDERSTAND THE ADULT MIND!

40

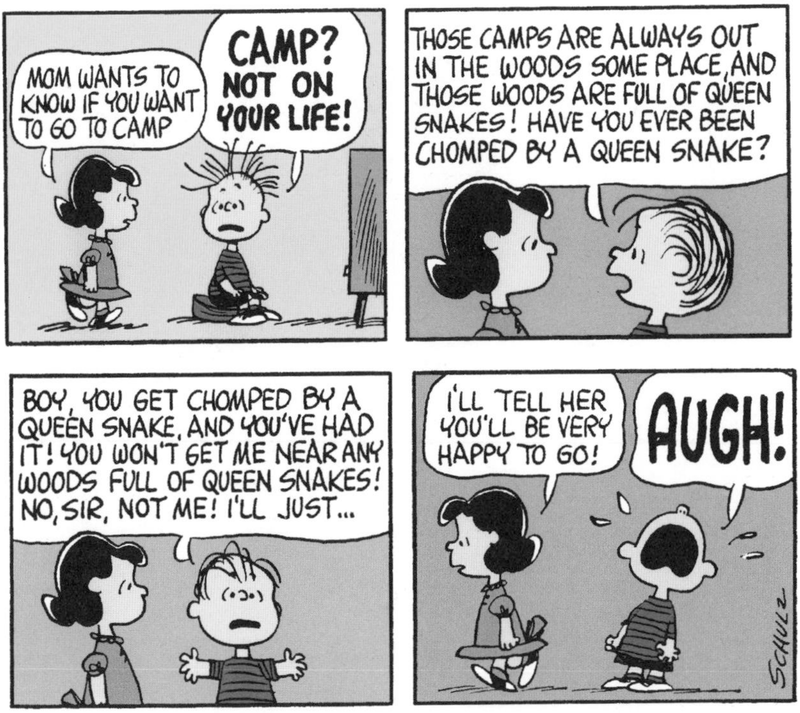
MOM WANTS TO KNOW IF YOU WANT TO GO TO CAMP
CAMP? NOT ON YOUR LIFE!
THOSE CAMPS ARE ALWAYS OUT IN THE WOODS SOME PLACE, AND THOSE WOODS ARE FULL OF QUEEN SNAKES! HAVE YOU EVER BEEN CHOMPED BY A QUEEN SNAKE?
BOY, YOU GET CHOMPED BY A QUEEN SNAKE, AND YOU'VE HAD IT! YOU WON'T GET ME NEAR ANY WOODS FULL OF QUEEN SNAKES! NO, SIR, NOT ME! I'LL JUST...
I'LL TELL HER YOU'LL BE VERY HAPPY TO GO!
AUGH!
SCHULZ

AAUGH! AAUGH!

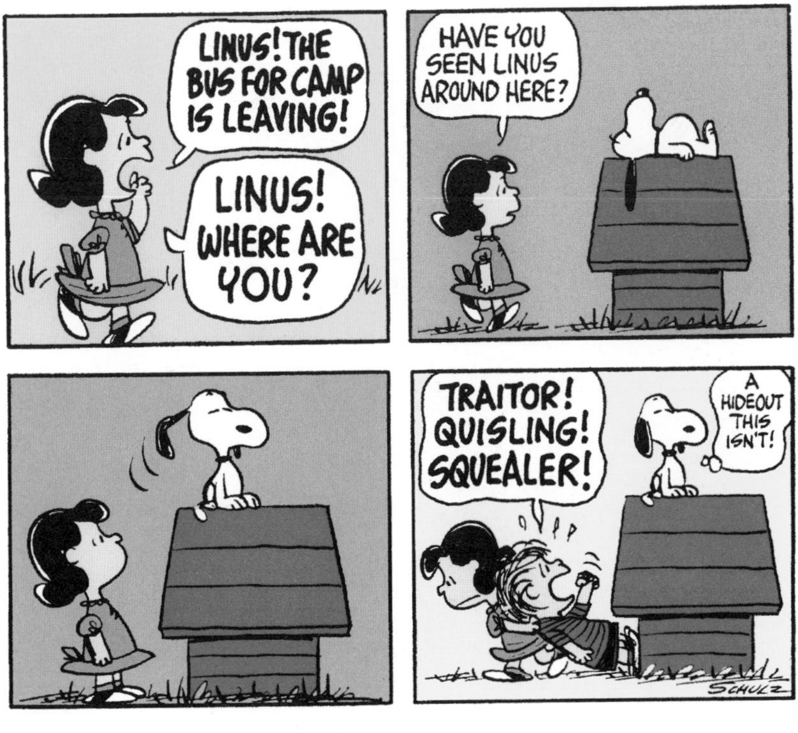
LINUS! THE BUS FOR CAMP IS LEAVING!
LINUS! WHERE ARE YOU?
HAVE YOU SEEN LINUS AROUND HERE?
TRAITOR! QUISLING! SQUEALER!
A HIDEOUT THIS ISN'T!
SCHULZ

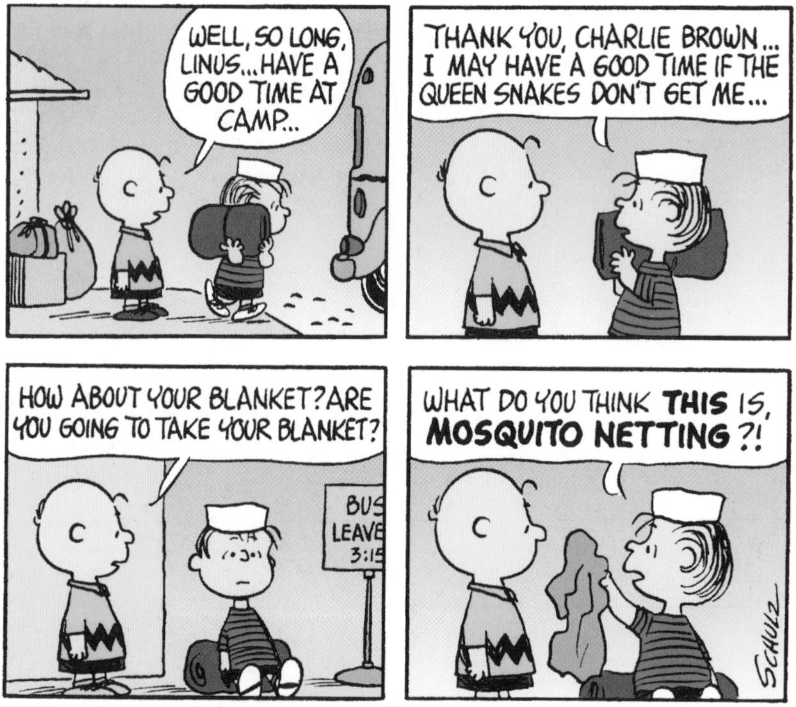
WELL, SO LONG, LINUS...HAVE A GOOD TIME AT CAMP...
THANK YOU, CHARLIE BROWN... I MAY HAVE A GOOD TIME IF THE QUEEN SNAKES DON'T GET ME...
HOW ABOUT YOUR BLANKET? ARE YOU GOING TO TAKE YOUR BLANKET?
BUS
LEAVE
3:15
WHAT DO YOU THINK **THIS** IS, **MOSQUITO NETTING** ?!
SCHULZ

AAUGH! AAUGH!

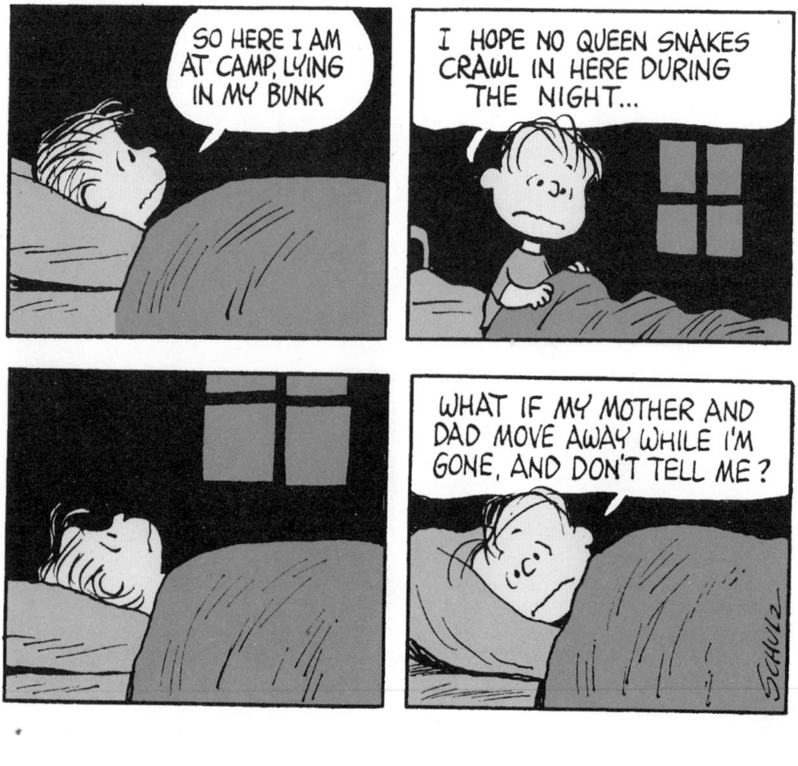
SO HERE I AM AT CAMP, LYING IN MY BUNK
I HOPE NO QUEEN SNAKES CRAWL IN HERE DURING THE NIGHT...
WHAT IF MY MOTHER AND DAD MOVE AWAY WHILE I'M GONE, AND DON'T TELL ME?
SCHULZ

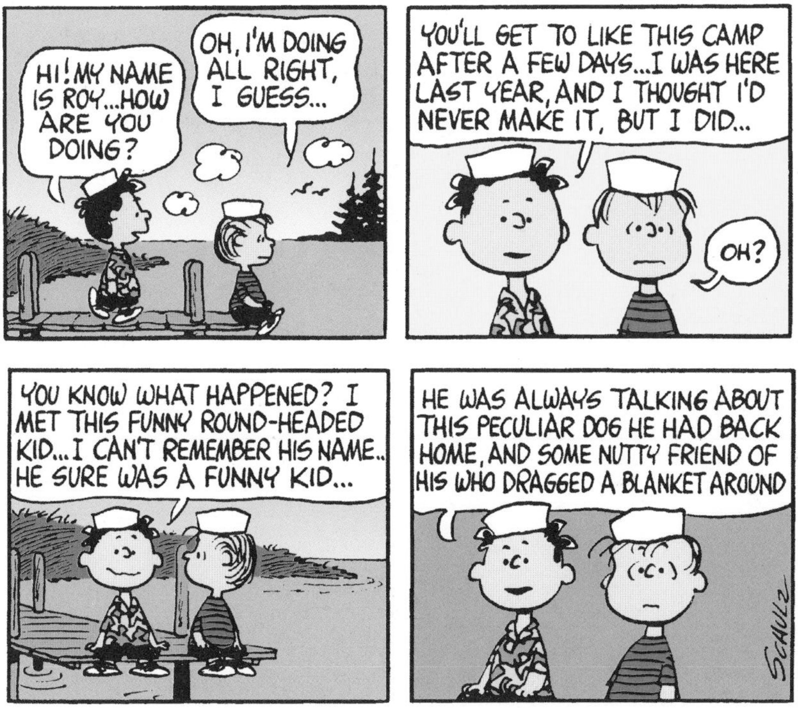
HI! MY NAME IS ROY...HOW ARE YOU DOING?
OH, I'M DOING ALL RIGHT, I GUESS...
YOU'LL GET TO LIKE THIS CAMP AFTER A FEW DAYS...I WAS HERE LAST YEAR, AND I THOUGHT I'D NEVER MAKE IT, BUT I DID...
OH?
YOU KNOW WHAT HAPPENED? I MET THIS FUNNY ROUND-HEADED KID...I CAN'T REMEMBER HIS NAME.. HE SURE WAS A FUNNY KID...
HE WAS ALWAYS TALKING ABOUT THIS PECULIAR DOG HE HAD BACK HOME, AND SOME NUTTY FRIEND OF HIS WHO DRAGGED A BLANKET AROUND
SCHULZ

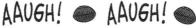

AAUGH! AAUGH!

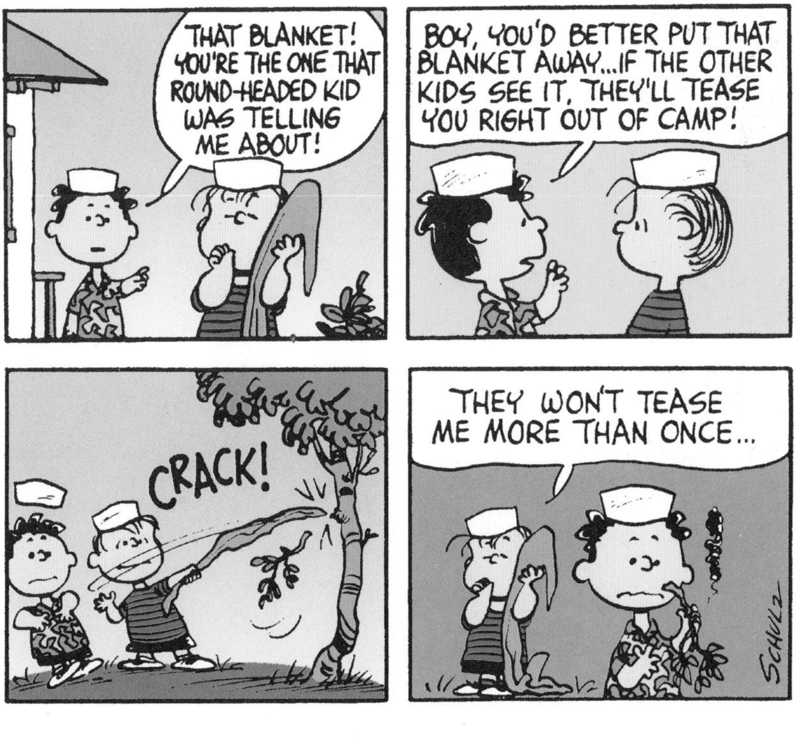
THAT BLANKET! YOU'RE THE ONE THAT ROUND-HEADED KID WAS TELLING ME ABOUT!
BOY, YOU'D BETTER PUT THAT BLANKET AWAY...IF THE OTHER KIDS SEE IT, THEY'LL TEASE YOU RIGHT OUT OF CAMP!
CRACK!
THEY WON'T TEASE ME MORE THAN ONCE...
SCHULZ

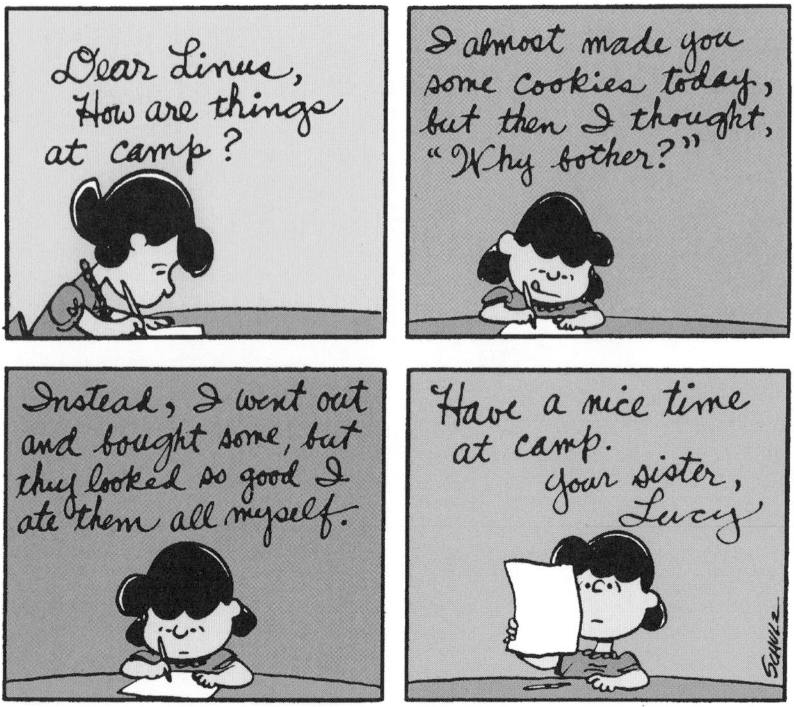
Dear Linus,
How are things at camp?
I almost made you some cookies today, but then I thought, "Why bother?"
Instead, I went out and bought some, but they looked so good I ate them all myself.
Have a nice time at camp.
Your sister,
Lucy
SCHULZ

AAUGH! AAUGH!

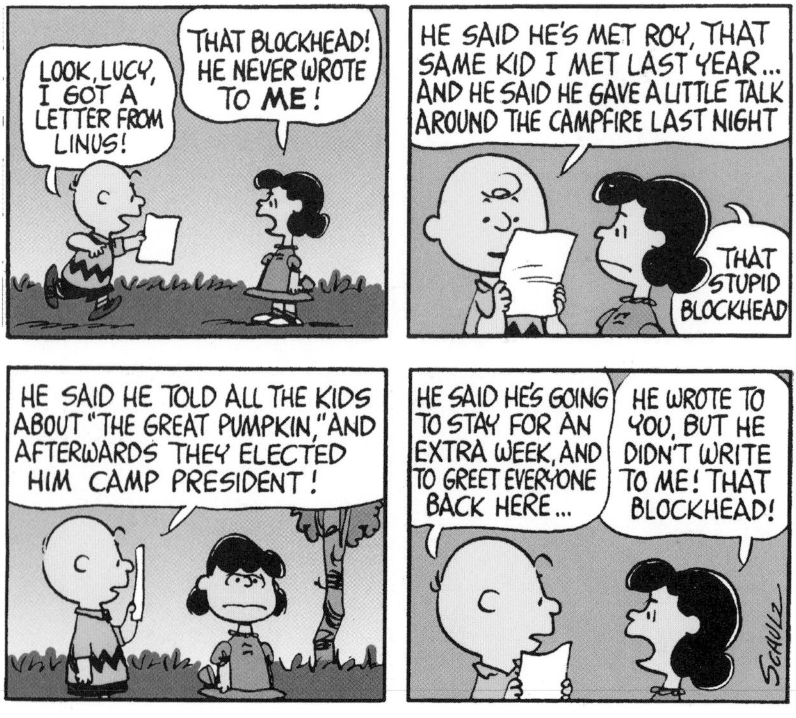
LOOK, LUCY, I GOT A LETTER FROM LINUS!
THAT BLOCKHEAD! HE NEVER WROTE TO ME!
HE SAID HE'S MET ROY, THAT SAME KID I MET LAST YEAR... AND HE SAID HE GAVE A LITTLE TALK AROUND THE CAMPFIRE LAST NIGHT
THAT STUPID BLOCKHEAD
HE SAID HE TOLD ALL THE KIDS ABOUT "THE GREAT PUMPKIN," AND AFTERWARDS THEY ELECTED HIM CAMP PRESIDENT!
HE SAID HE'S GOING TO STAY FOR AN EXTRA WEEK, AND TO GREET EVERYONE BACK HERE...
HE WROTE TO YOU, BUT HE DIDN'T WRITE TO ME! THAT BLOCKHEAD!
SCHULZ

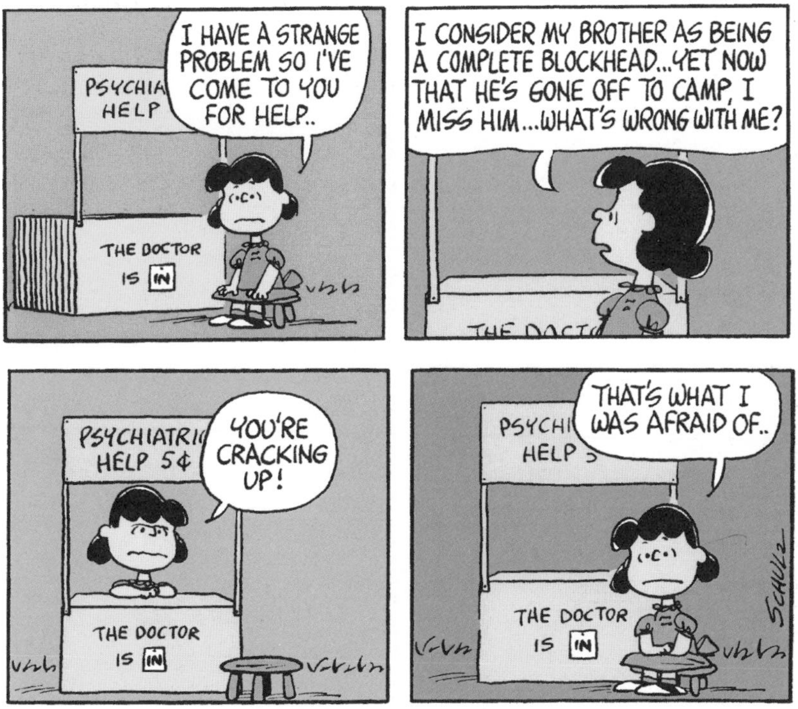
PSYCHIA HELP
I HAVE A STRANGE PROBLEM SO I'VE COME TO YOU FOR HELP..
THE DOCTOR IS IN
I CONSIDER MY BROTHER AS BEING A COMPLETE BLOCKHEAD...YET NOW THAT HE'S GONE OFF TO CAMP, I MISS HIM...WHAT'S WRONG WITH ME?
PSYCHIATRIC HELP 5¢
YOU'RE CRACKING UP!
THE DOCTOR IS IN
PSYCHI HELP
THAT'S WHAT I WAS AFRAID OF..
THE DOCTOR IS IN
SCHULZ

AAUGH! AAUGH!

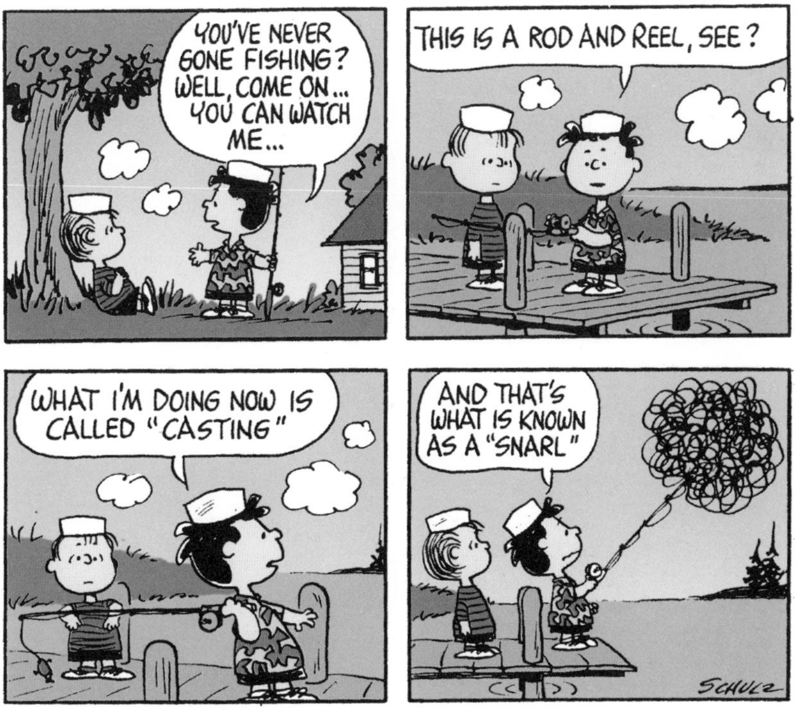
YOU'VE NEVER GONE FISHING? WELL, COME ON... YOU CAN WATCH ME...
THIS IS A ROD AND REEL, SEE?
WHAT I'M DOING NOW IS CALLED "CASTING"
AND THAT'S WHAT IS KNOWN AS A "SNARL"
SCHULZ

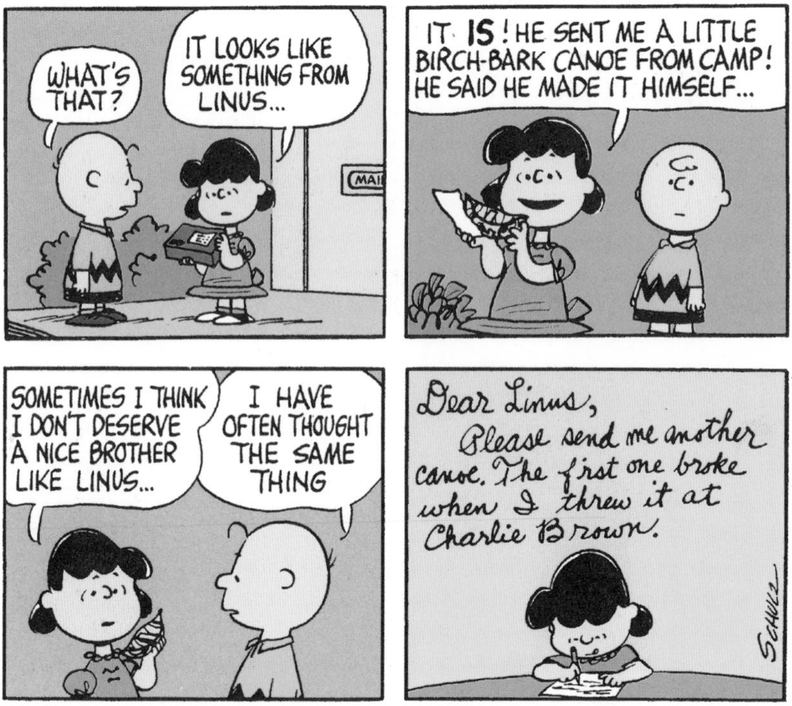
WHAT'S THAT?
IT LOOKS LIKE SOMETHING FROM LINUS...
MAIL
IT IS! HE SENT ME A LITTLE BIRCH-BARK CANOE FROM CAMP! HE SAID HE MADE IT HIMSELF...
SOMETIMES I THINK I DON'T DESERVE A NICE BROTHER LIKE LINUS...
I HAVE OFTEN THOUGHT THE SAME THING
Dear Linus,
Please send me another canoe. The first one broke when I threw it at Charlie Brown.
SCHULZ

AAUGH! AAUGH!

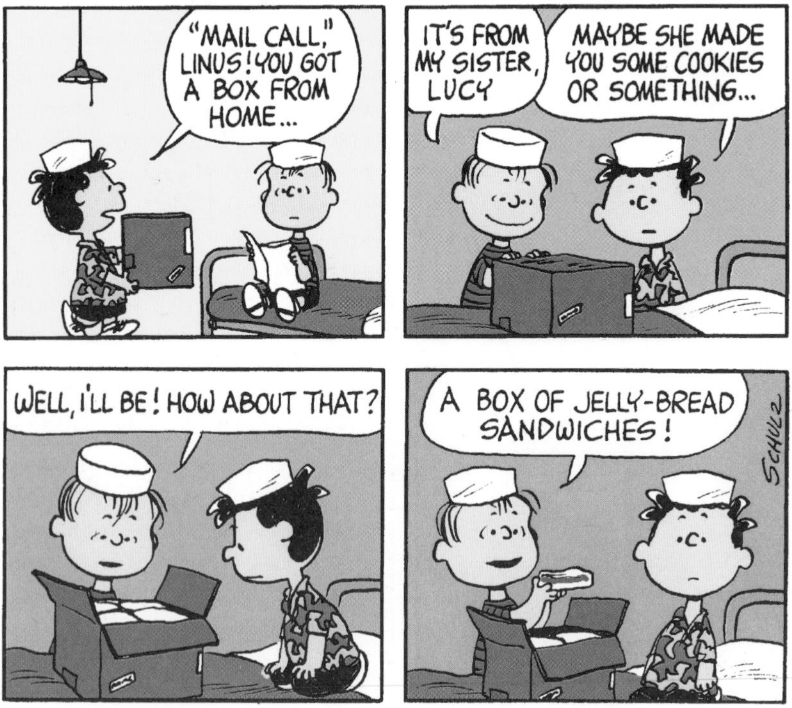
"MAIL CALL," LINUS! YOU GOT A BOX FROM HOME...
IT'S FROM MY SISTER, LUCY
MAYBE SHE MADE YOU SOME COOKIES OR SOMETHING...
WELL, I'LL BE! HOW ABOUT THAT?
A BOX OF JELLY-BREAD SANDWICHES!
SCHULZ

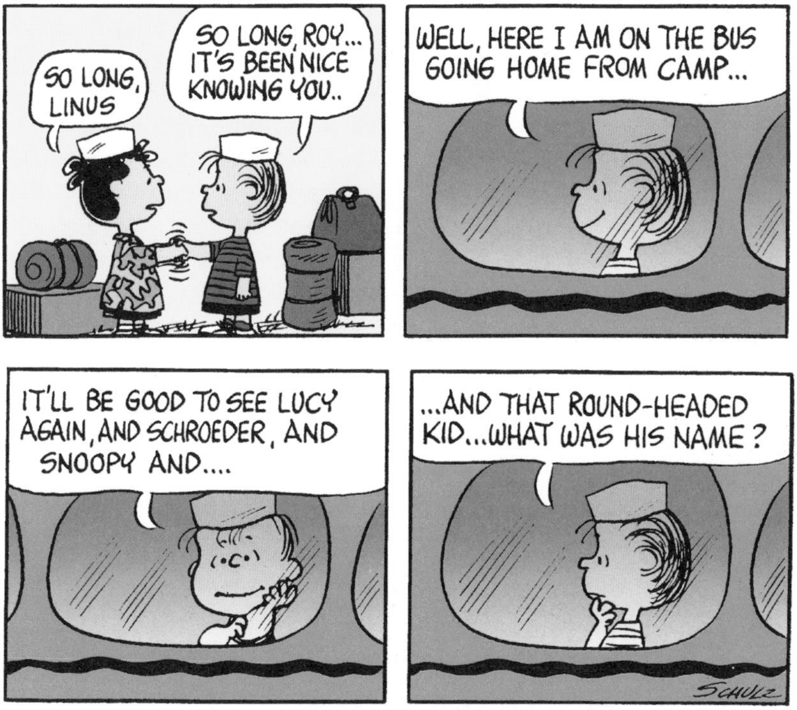
SO LONG, LINUS
SO LONG, ROY... IT'S BEEN NICE KNOWING YOU..
WELL, HERE I AM ON THE BUS GOING HOME FROM CAMP...
IT'LL BE GOOD TO SEE LUCY AGAIN, AND SCHROEDER, AND SNOOPY AND....
...AND THAT ROUND-HEADED KID...WHAT WAS HIS NAME?
SCHULZ

AAUGH! AAUGH!

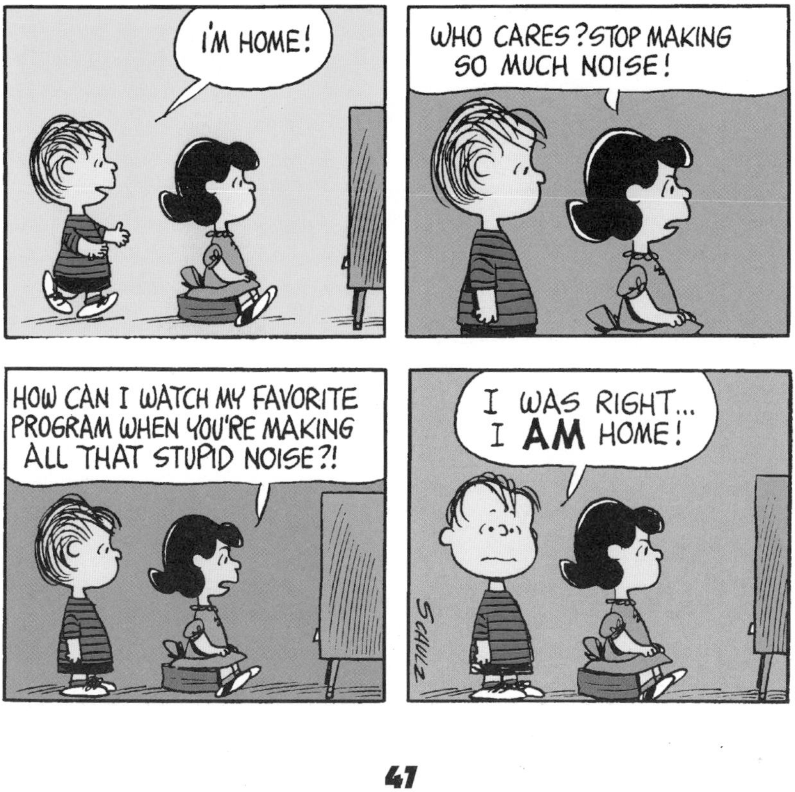
I'M HOME!
WHO CARES? STOP MAKING SO MUCH NOISE!
HOW CAN I WATCH MY FAVORITE PROGRAM WHEN YOU'RE MAKING ALL THAT STUPID NOISE?!
I WAS RIGHT... I **AM** HOME!
SCHULZ

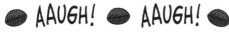

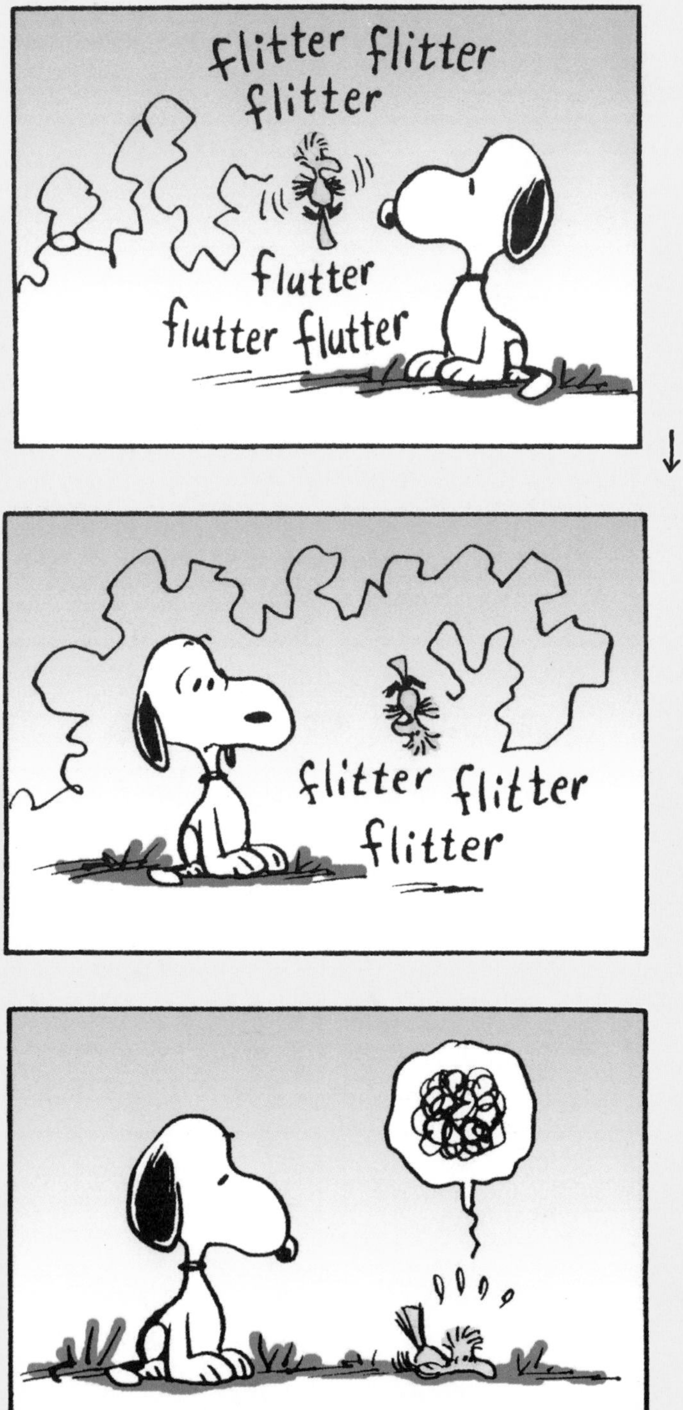
flitter flitter
flitter
flutter
flutter flutter
flitter flitter
flitter

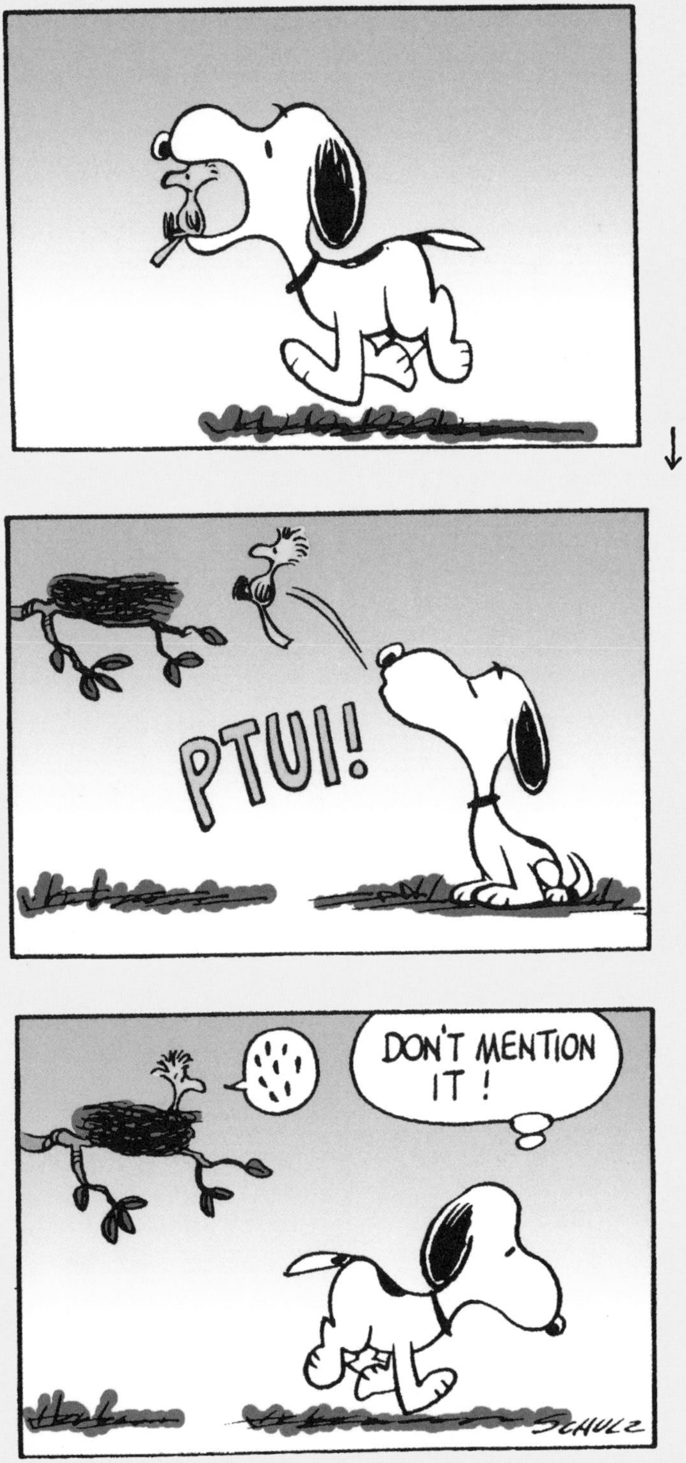
PTUI!
DON'T MENTION IT !
SCHULZ

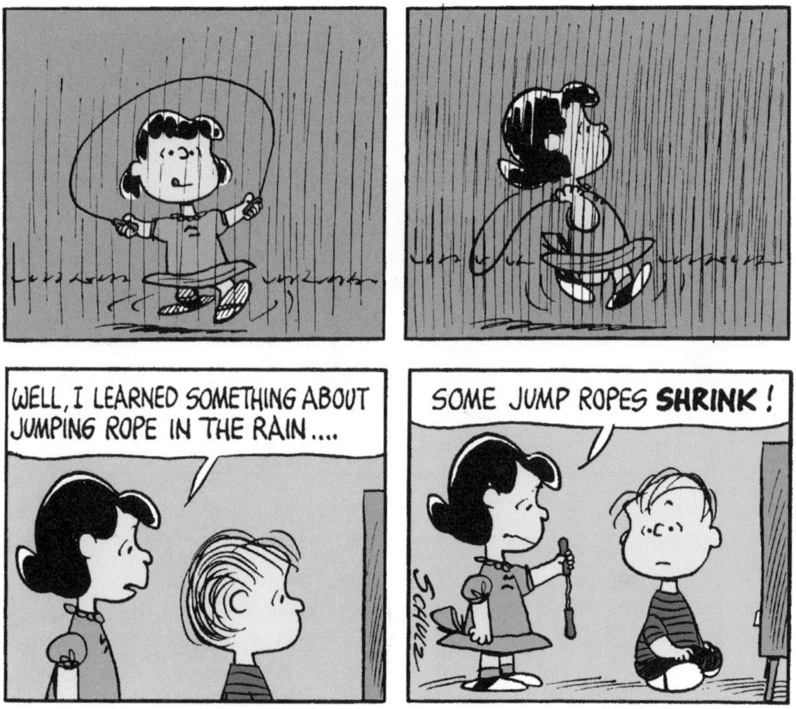
WELL, I LEARNED SOMETHING ABOUT JUMPING ROPE IN THE RAIN....
SOME JUMP ROPES **SHRINK**!
SCHULZ

AAUGH! AAUGH!

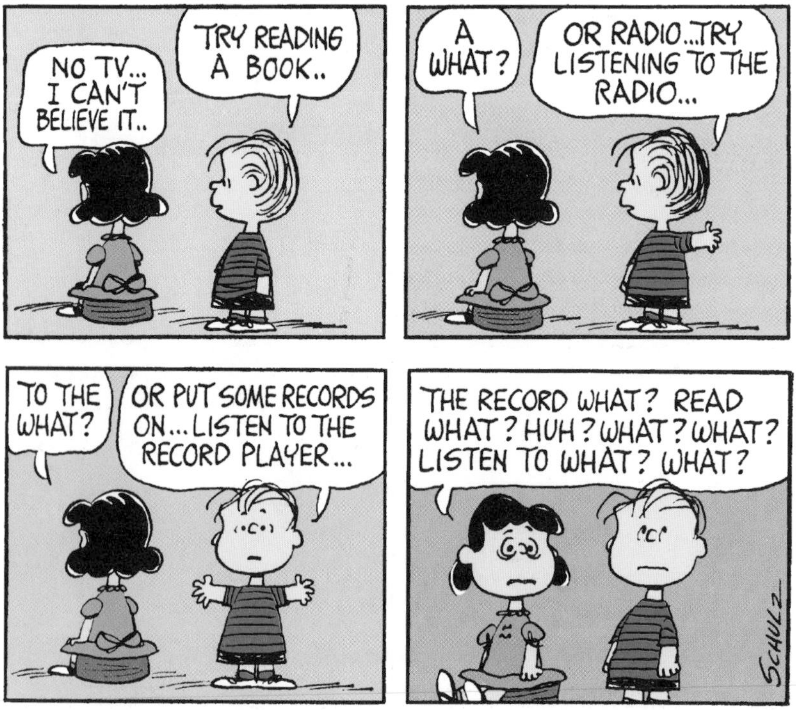
NO TV... I CAN'T BELIEVE IT..
TRY READING A BOOK..
A WHAT?
OR RADIO...TRY LISTENING TO THE RADIO...
TO THE WHAT?
OR PUT SOME RECORDS ON... LISTEN TO THE RECORD PLAYER...
THE RECORD WHAT? READ WHAT? HUH? WHAT? WHAT? LISTEN TO WHAT? WHAT?
SCHULZ

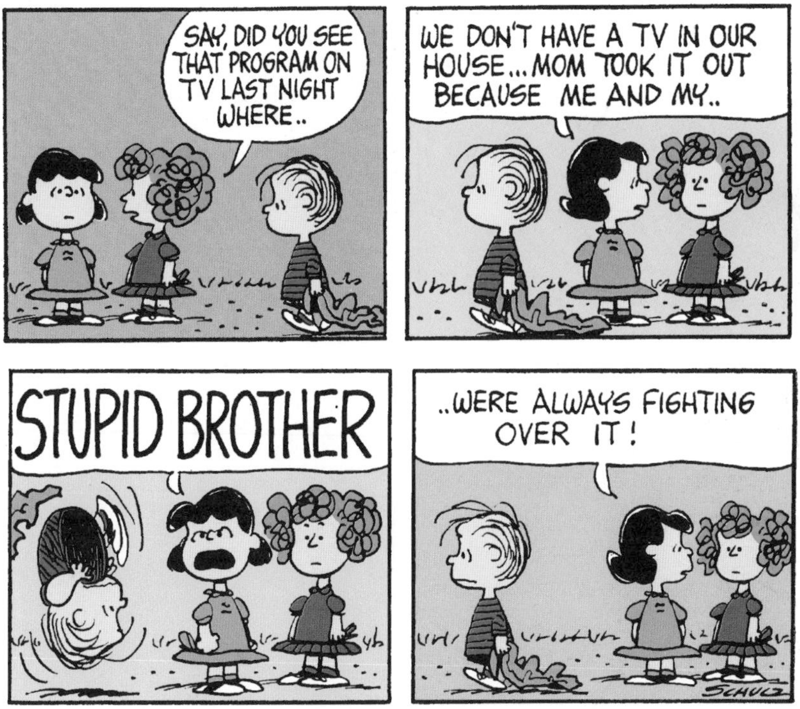
SAY, DID YOU SEE THAT PROGRAM ON TV LAST NIGHT WHERE..
WE DON'T HAVE A TV IN OUR HOUSE... MOM TOOK IT OUT BECAUSE ME AND MY..
STUPID BROTHER
..WERE ALWAYS FIGHTING OVER IT!
SCHULZ

AAUGH! AAUGH!

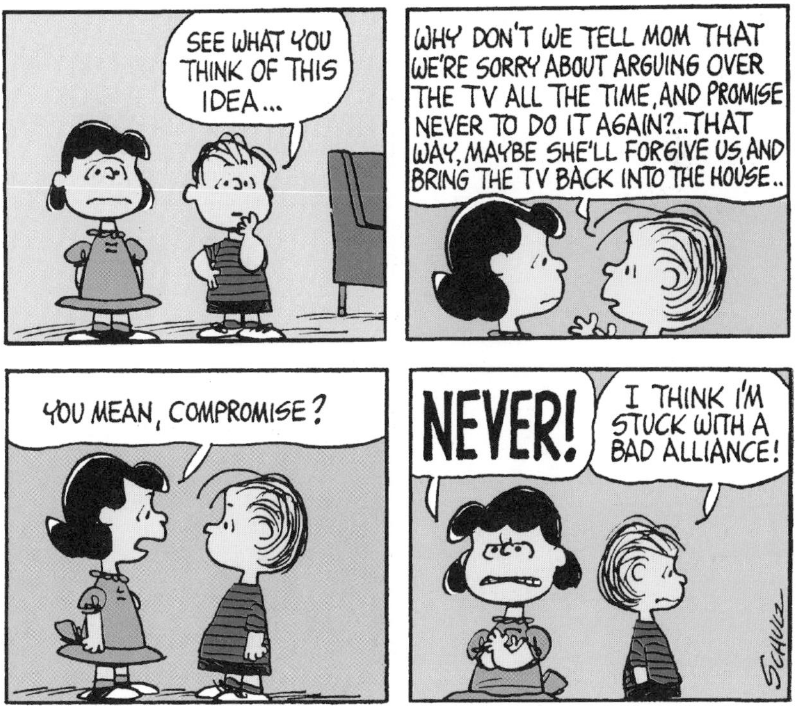
SEE WHAT YOU THINK OF THIS IDEA...
WHY DON'T WE TELL MOM THAT WE'RE SORRY ABOUT ARGUING OVER THE TV ALL THE TIME, AND PROMISE NEVER TO DO IT AGAIN?...THAT WAY, MAYBE SHE'LL FORGIVE US, AND BRING THE TV BACK INTO THE HOUSE..
YOU MEAN, COMPROMISE?
NEVER!
I THINK I'M STUCK WITH A BAD ALLIANCE!
SCHULZ

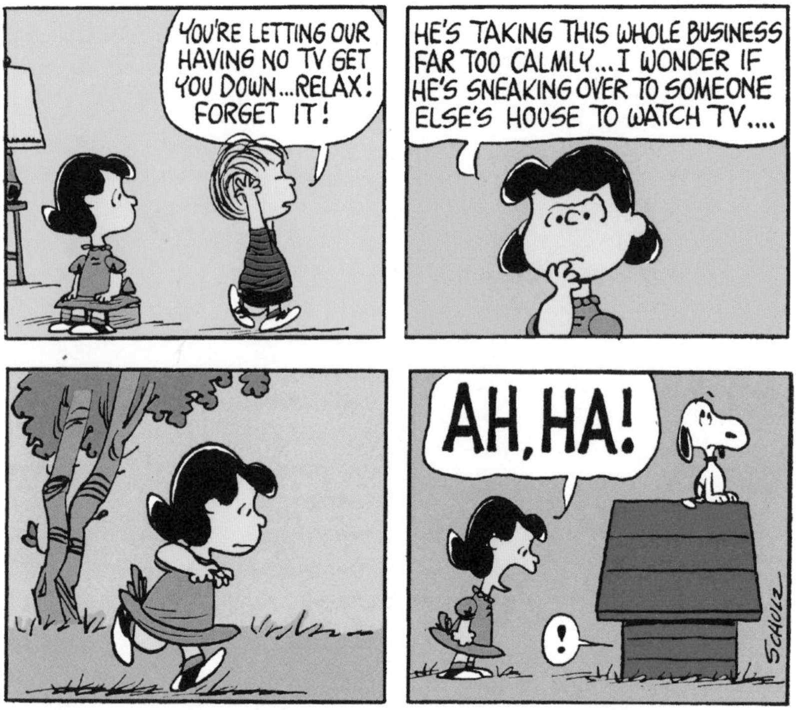
YOU'RE LETTING OUR HAVING NO TV GET YOU DOWN...RELAX! FORGET IT!
HE'S TAKING THIS WHOLE BUSINESS FAR TOO CALMLY... I WONDER IF HE'S SNEAKING OVER TO SOMEONE ELSE'S HOUSE TO WATCH TV....
AH, HA!
!
SCHULZ

AAUGH! AAUGH!

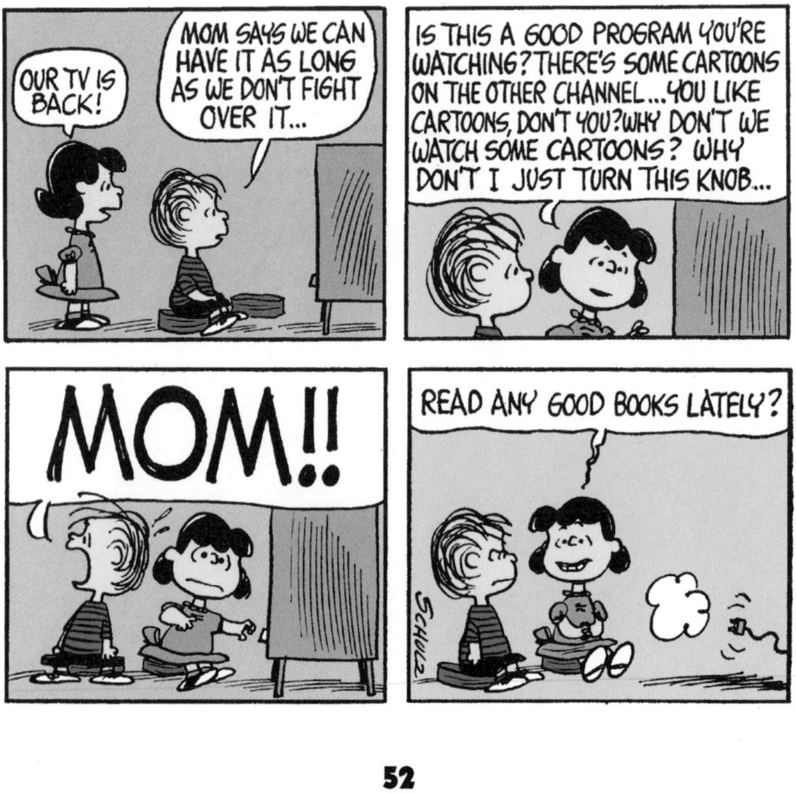
OUR TV IS BACK!
MOM SAYS WE CAN HAVE IT AS LONG AS WE DON'T FIGHT OVER IT...
IS THIS A GOOD PROGRAM YOU'RE WATCHING? THERE'S SOME CARTOONS ON THE OTHER CHANNEL...YOU LIKE CARTOONS, DON'T YOU? WHY DON'T WE WATCH SOME CARTOONS? WHY DON'T I JUST TURN THIS KNOB...
MOM!!
READ ANY GOOD BOOKS LATELY?
SCHULZ

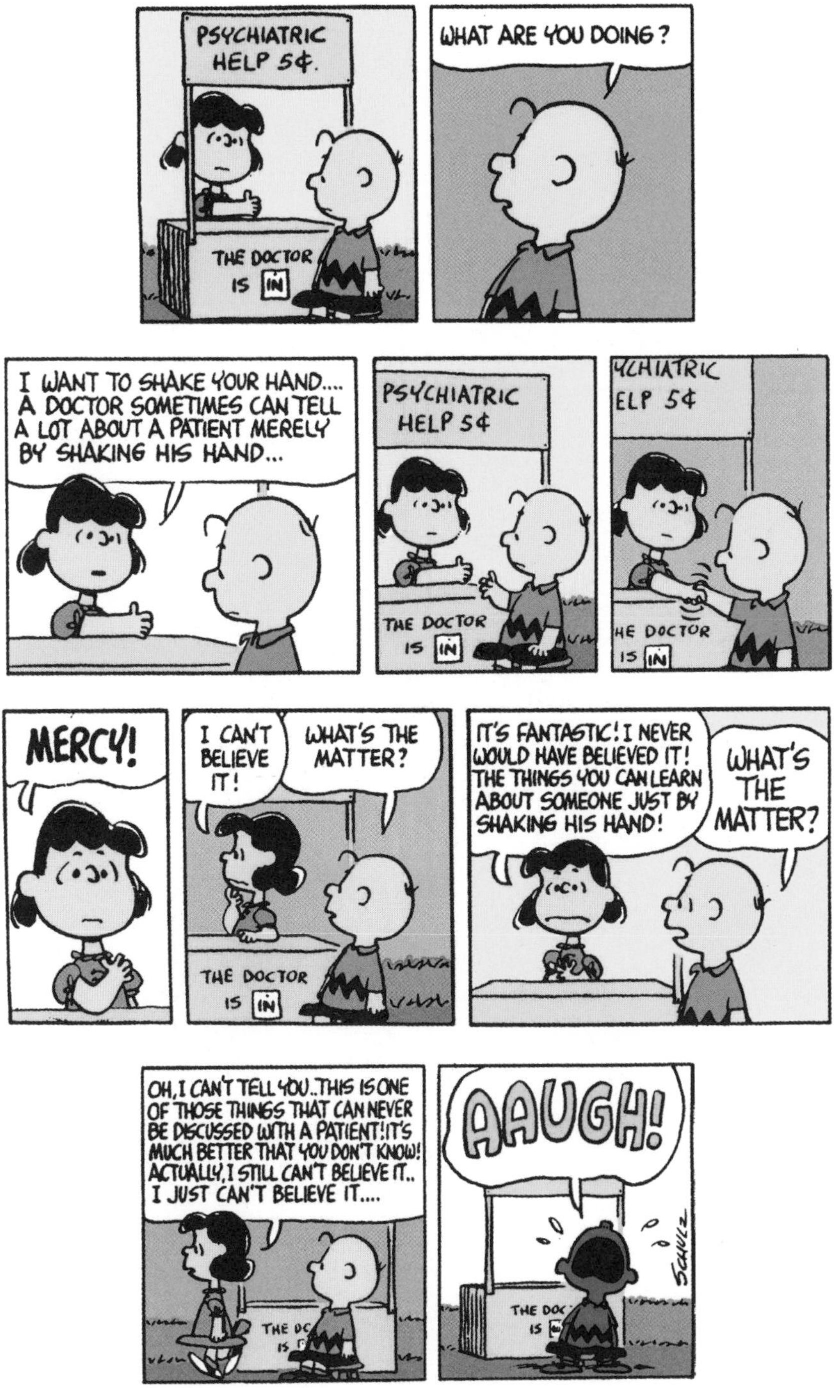
PSYCHIATRIC
HELP 5¢.
THE DOCTOR
IS IN
WHAT ARE YOU DOING?
I WANT TO SHAKE YOUR HAND.... A DOCTOR SOMETIMES CAN TELL A LOT ABOUT A PATIENT MERELY BY SHAKING HIS HAND...
PSYCHIATRIC
HELP 5¢
THE DOCTOR
IS IN
MERCY!
I CAN'T BELIEVE IT!
WHAT'S THE MATTER?
THE DOCTOR
IS IN
IT'S FANTASTIC! I NEVER WOULD HAVE BELIEVED IT! THE THINGS YOU CAN LEARN ABOUT SOMEONE JUST BY SHAKING HIS HAND!
WHAT'S THE MATTER?
OH, I CAN'T TELL YOU..THIS IS ONE OF THOSE THINGS THAT CAN NEVER BE DISCUSSED WITH A PATIENT! IT'S MUCH BETTER THAT YOU DON'T KNOW! ACTUALLY, I STILL CAN'T BELIEVE IT.. I JUST CAN'T BELIEVE IT....
AAUGH!
SCHULZ

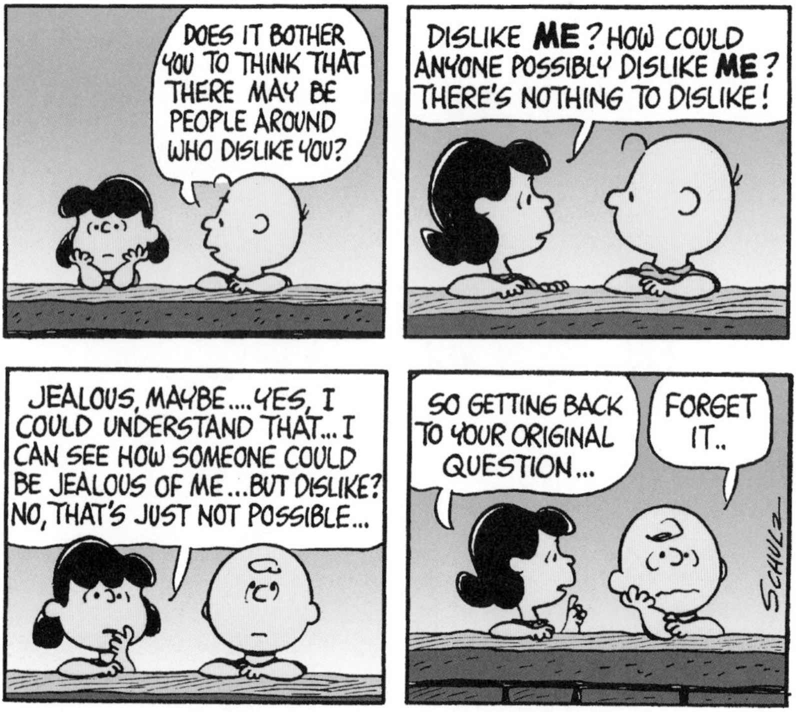
DOES IT BOTHER YOU TO THINK THAT THERE MAY BE PEOPLE AROUND WHO DISLIKE YOU?
DISLIKE **ME**? HOW COULD ANYONE POSSIBLY DISLIKE **ME**? THERE'S NOTHING TO DISLIKE!
JEALOUS, MAYBE.... YES, I COULD UNDERSTAND THAT... I CAN SEE HOW SOMEONE COULD BE JEALOUS OF ME... BUT DISLIKE? NO, THAT'S JUST NOT POSSIBLE...
SO GETTING BACK TO YOUR ORIGINAL QUESTION...
FORGET IT..
SCHULZ

AAUGH! AAUGH!

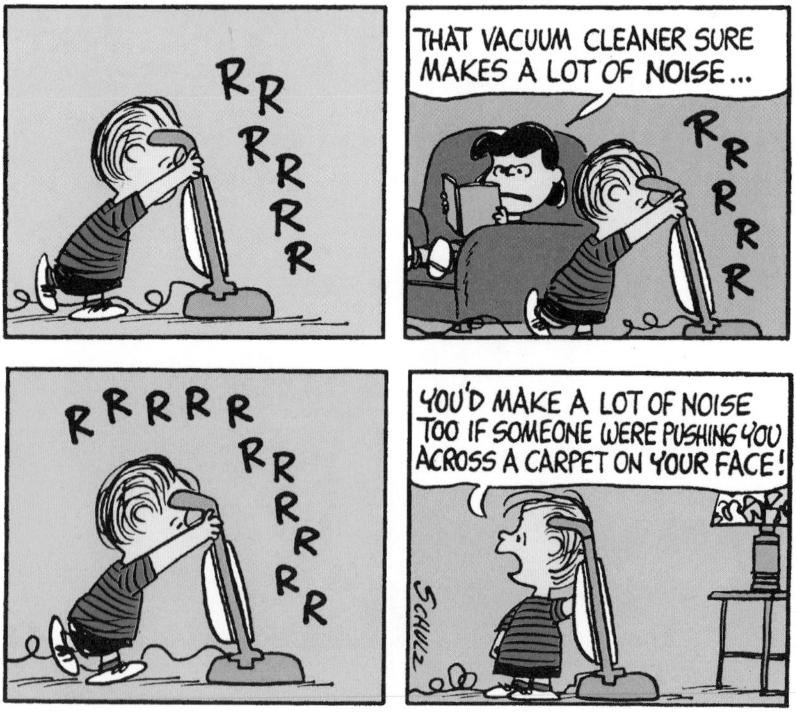
RRRRRRR
THAT VACUUM CLEANER SURE MAKES A LOT OF NOISE...
RRRRRR
RRRRRRRRRRRRR
YOU'D MAKE A LOT OF NOISE TOO IF SOMEONE WERE PUSHING YOU ACROSS A CARPET ON YOUR FACE!
SCHULZ

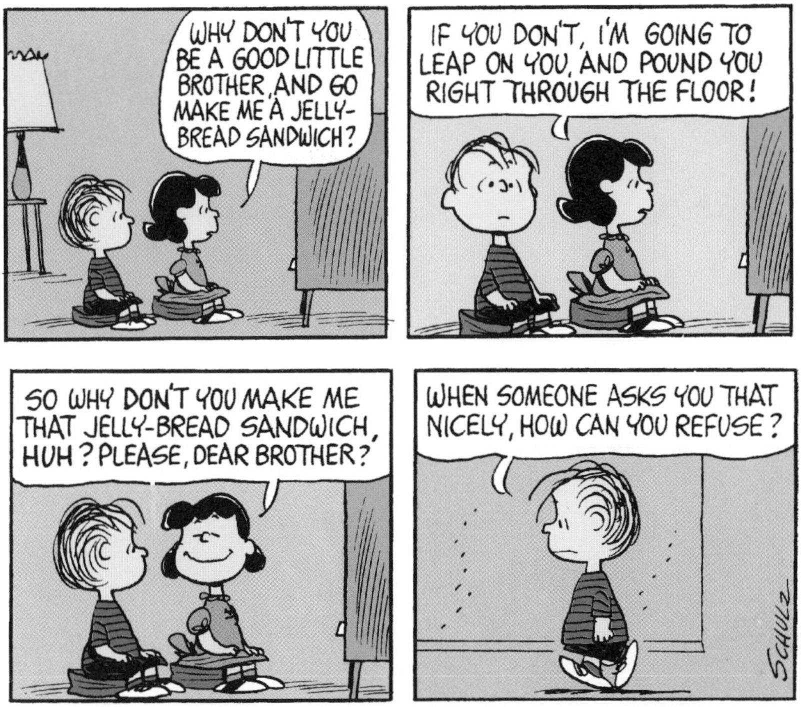
WHY DON'T YOU BE A GOOD LITTLE BROTHER, AND GO MAKE ME A JELLY-BREAD SANDWICH?
IF YOU DON'T, I'M GOING TO LEAP ON YOU, AND POUND YOU RIGHT THROUGH THE FLOOR!
SO WHY DON'T YOU MAKE ME THAT JELLY-BREAD SANDWICH, HUH? PLEASE, DEAR BROTHER?
WHEN SOMEONE ASKS YOU THAT NICELY, HOW CAN YOU REFUSE?
SCHULZ

AAUGH! AAUGH!

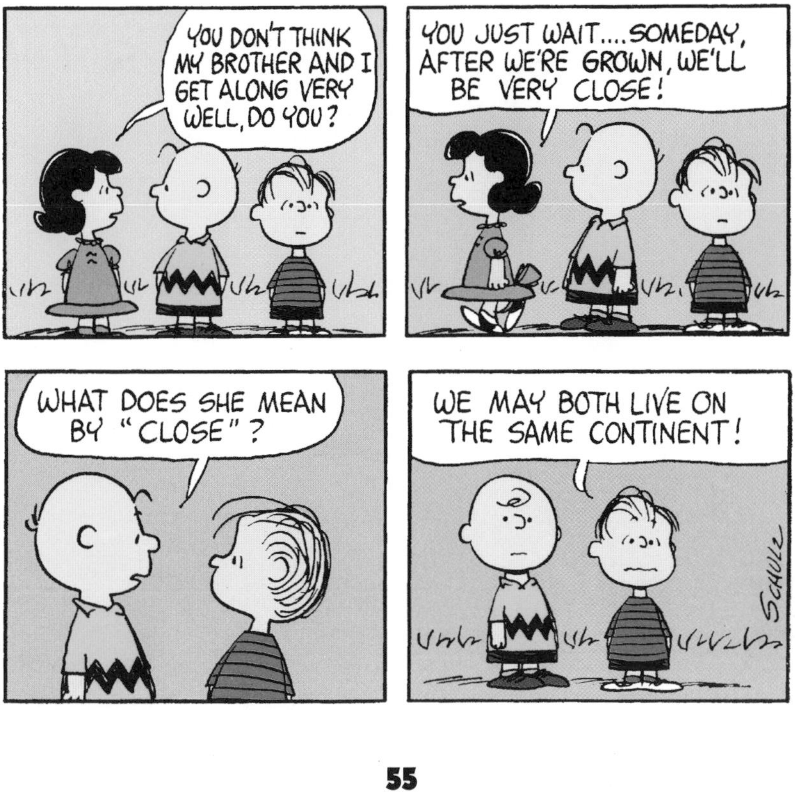
YOU DON'T THINK MY BROTHER AND I GET ALONG VERY WELL, DO YOU?
YOU JUST WAIT.... SOMEDAY, AFTER WE'RE GROWN, WE'LL BE VERY CLOSE!
WHAT DOES SHE MEAN BY "CLOSE"?
WE MAY BOTH LIVE ON THE SAME CONTINENT!
SCHULZ

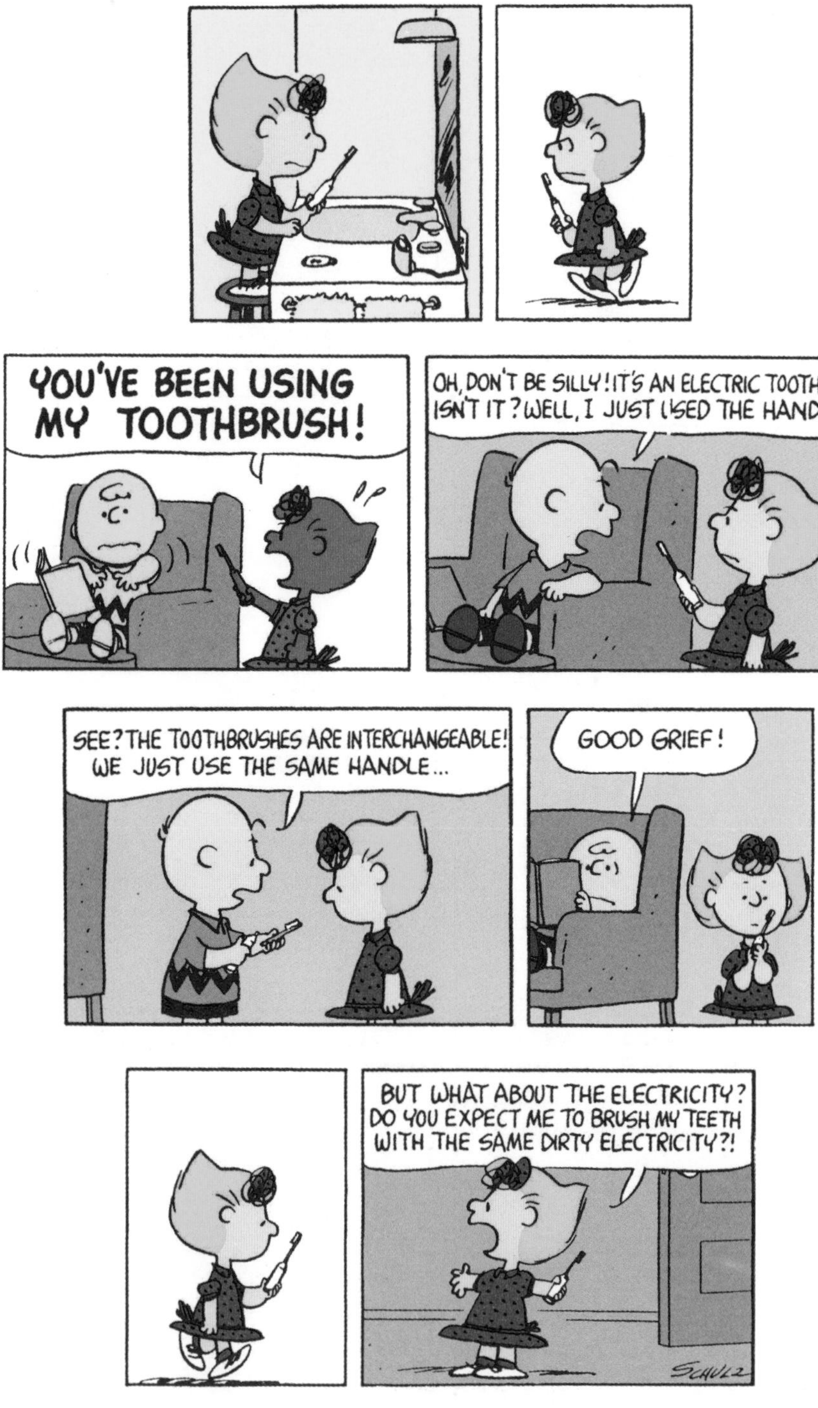

YOU'VE BEEN USING MY TOOTHBRUSH!
OH, DON'T BE SILLY! IT'S AN ELECTRIC TOOTHBRUSH, ISN'T IT? WELL, I JUST USED THE HANDLE!
SEE? THE TOOTHBRUSHES ARE INTERCHANGEABLE! WE JUST USE THE SAME HANDLE...
GOOD GRIEF!
BUT WHAT ABOUT THE ELECTRICITY? DO YOU EXPECT ME TO BRUSH MY TEETH WITH THE SAME DIRTY ELECTRICITY?!
SCHULZ

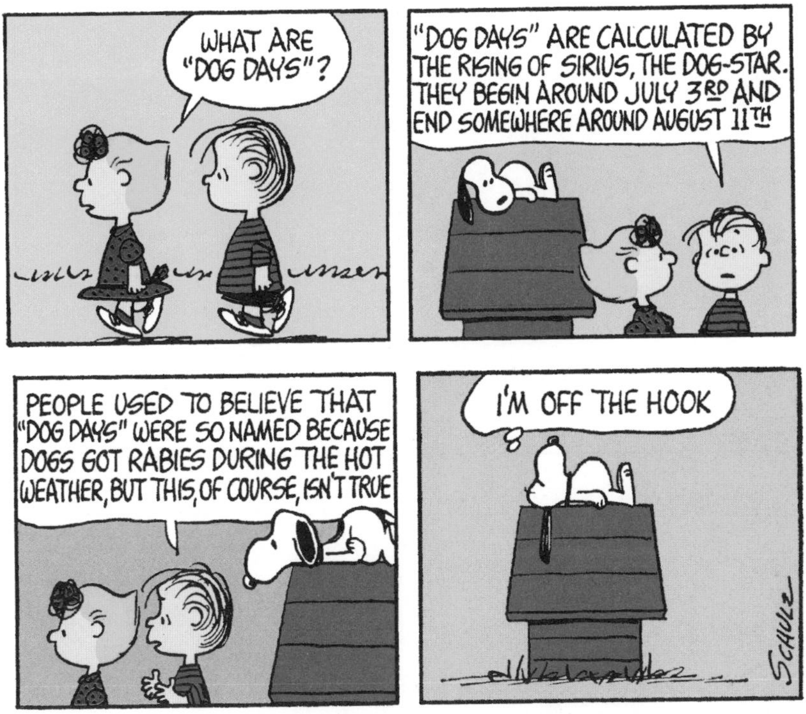
WHAT ARE "DOG DAYS"?
"DOG DAYS" ARE CALCULATED BY THE RISING OF SIRIUS, THE DOG-STAR. THEY BEGIN AROUND JULY 3RD AND END SOMEWHERE AROUND AUGUST 11TH
PEOPLE USED TO BELIEVE THAT "DOG DAYS" WERE SO NAMED BECAUSE DOGS GOT RABIES DURING THE HOT WEATHER, BUT THIS, OF COURSE, ISN'T TRUE
I'M OFF THE HOOK
SCHULZ

AAUGH! AAUGH!

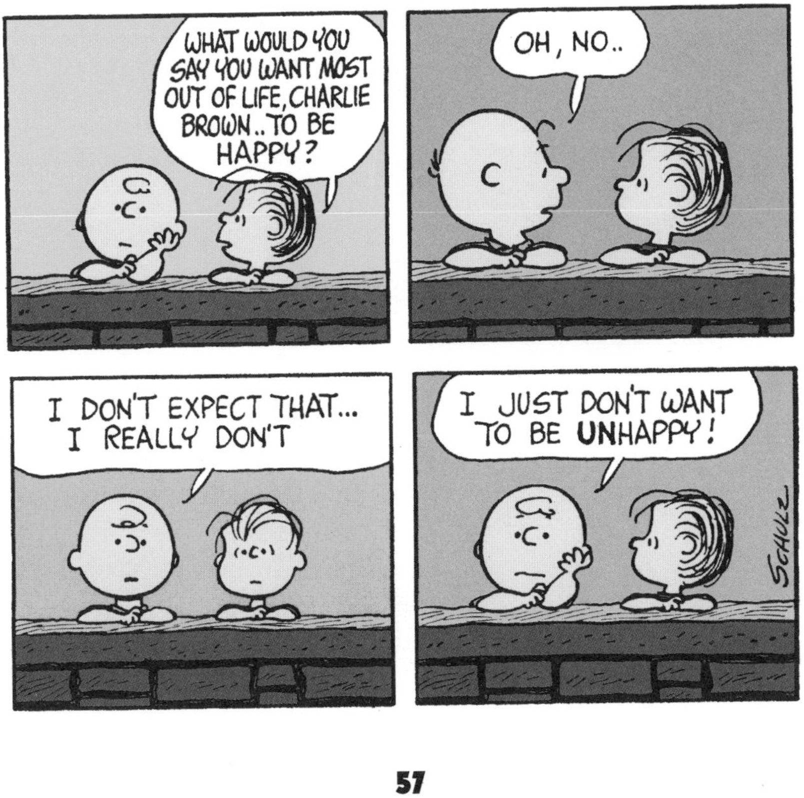
WHAT WOULD YOU SAY YOU WANT MOST OUT OF LIFE, CHARLIE BROWN.. TO BE HAPPY?
OH, NO..
I DON'T EXPECT THAT... I REALLY DON'T
I JUST DON'T WANT TO BE **UN**HAPPY!
SCHULZ

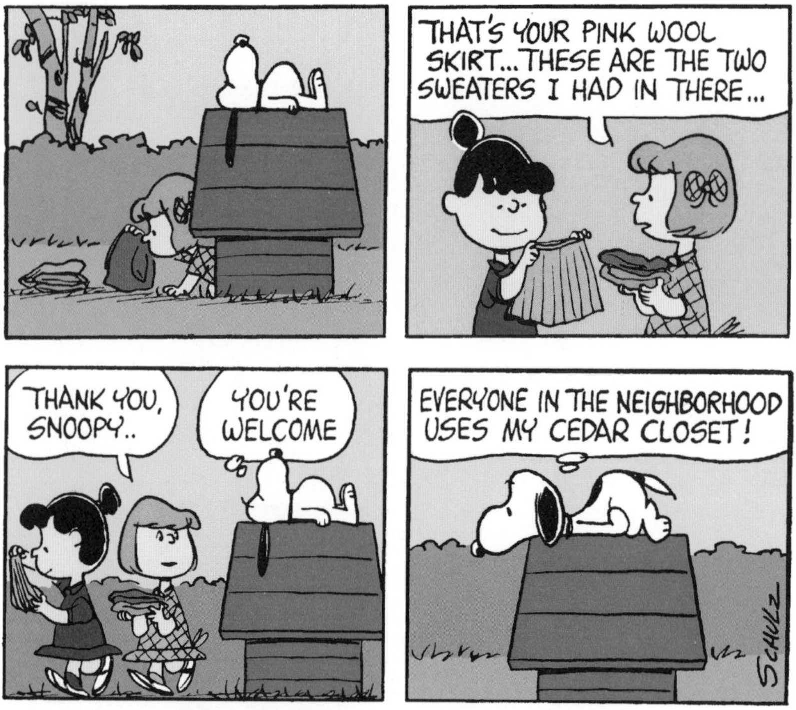
THAT'S YOUR PINK WOOL SKIRT... THESE ARE THE TWO SWEATERS I HAD IN THERE...
THANK YOU, SNOOPY..
YOU'RE WELCOME
EVERYONE IN THE NEIGHBORHOOD USES MY CEDAR CLOSET!
SCHULZ

AAUGH! AAUGH!

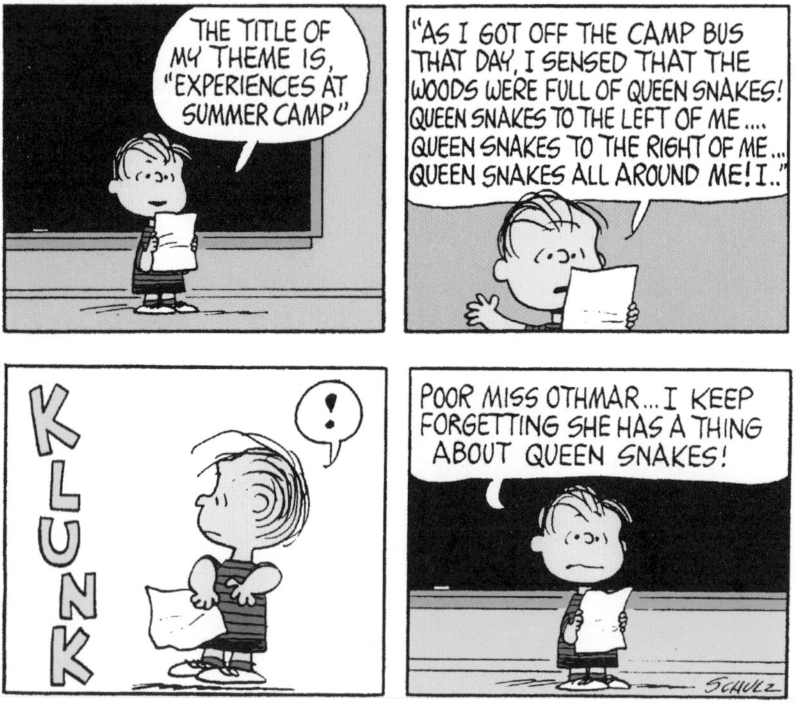
THE TITLE OF MY THEME IS, "EXPERIENCES AT SUMMER CAMP"
"AS I GOT OFF THE CAMP BUS THAT DAY, I SENSED THAT THE WOODS WERE FULL OF QUEEN SNAKES! QUEEN SNAKES TO THE LEFT OF ME.... QUEEN SNAKES TO THE RIGHT OF ME... QUEEN SNAKES ALL AROUND ME! I.."
KLUNK
!
POOR MISS OTHMAR... I KEEP FORGETTING SHE HAS A THING ABOUT QUEEN SNAKES!
SCHULZ

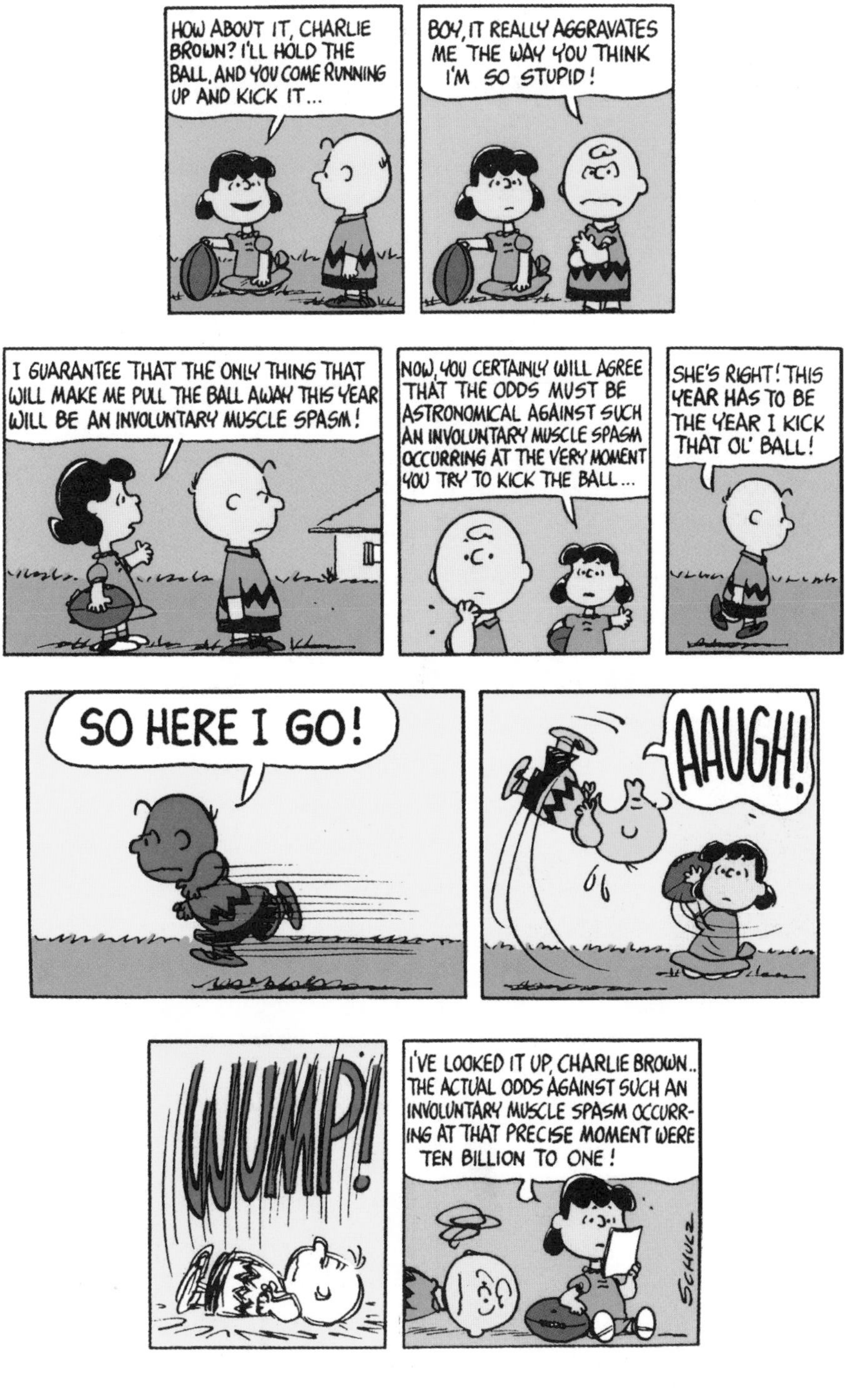
HOW ABOUT IT, CHARLIE BROWN? I'LL HOLD THE BALL, AND YOU COME RUNNING UP AND KICK IT...
BOY, IT REALLY AGGRAVATES ME THE WAY YOU THINK I'M SO STUPID!
I GUARANTEE THAT THE ONLY THING THAT WILL MAKE ME PULL THE BALL AWAY THIS YEAR WILL BE AN INVOLUNTARY MUSCLE SPASM!
NOW, YOU CERTAINLY WILL AGREE THAT THE ODDS MUST BE ASTRONOMICAL AGAINST SUCH AN INVOLUNTARY MUSCLE SPASM OCCURRING AT THE VERY MOMENT YOU TRY TO KICK THE BALL...
SHE'S RIGHT! THIS YEAR HAS TO BE THE YEAR I KICK THAT OL' BALL!
SO HERE I GO!
AAUGH!
WUMP!
I'VE LOOKED IT UP, CHARLIE BROWN.. THE ACTUAL ODDS AGAINST SUCH AN INVOLUNTARY MUSCLE SPASM OCCURR-ING AT THAT PRECISE MOMENT WERE TEN BILLION TO ONE!
SCHULZ

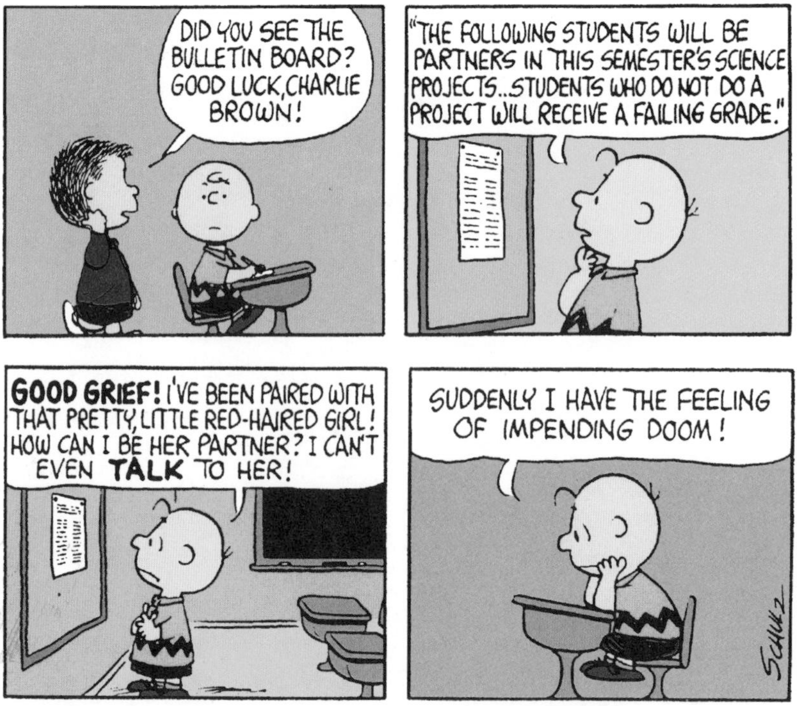
DID YOU SEE THE BULLETIN BOARD? GOOD LUCK, CHARLIE BROWN!
"THE FOLLOWING STUDENTS WILL BE PARTNERS IN THIS SEMESTER'S SCIENCE PROJECTS...STUDENTS WHO DO NOT DO A PROJECT WILL RECEIVE A FAILING GRADE."
GOOD GRIEF! I'VE BEEN PAIRED WITH THAT PRETTY, LITTLE RED-HAIRED GIRL! HOW CAN I BE HER PARTNER? I CAN'T EVEN TALK TO HER!
SUDDENLY I HAVE THE FEELING OF IMPENDING DOOM!
SCHULZ

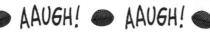

AAUGH! AAUGH!

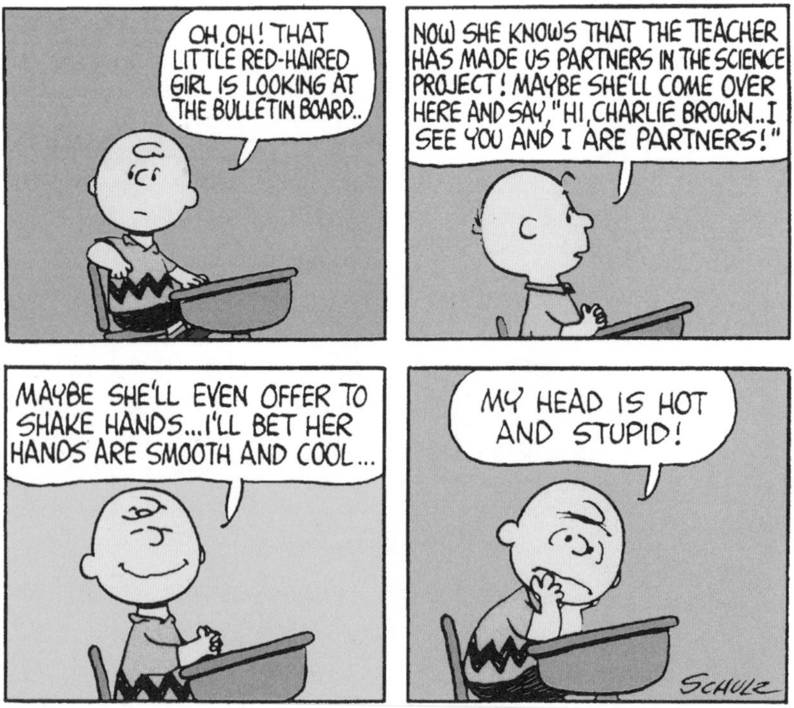
OH, OH! THAT LITTLE RED-HAIRED GIRL IS LOOKING AT THE BULLETIN BOARD..
NOW SHE KNOWS THAT THE TEACHER HAS MADE US PARTNERS IN THE SCIENCE PROJECT! MAYBE SHE'LL COME OVER HERE AND SAY, "HI, CHARLIE BROWN..I SEE YOU AND I ARE PARTNERS!"
MAYBE SHE'LL EVEN OFFER TO SHAKE HANDS...I'LL BET HER HANDS ARE SMOOTH AND COOL...
MY HEAD IS HOT AND STUPID!
SCHULZ

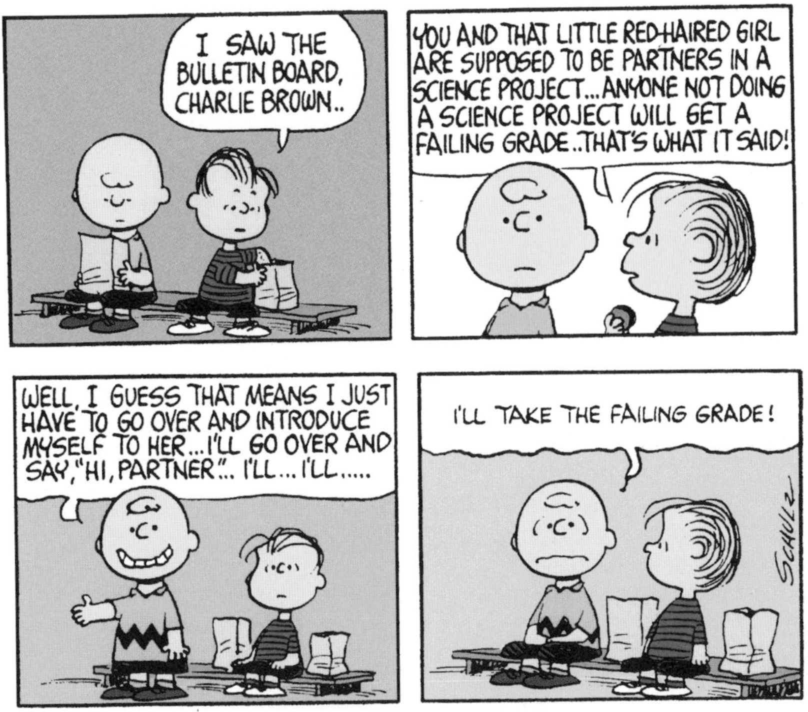
I SAW THE BULLETIN BOARD, CHARLIE BROWN..
YOU AND THAT LITTLE RED-HAIRED GIRL ARE SUPPOSED TO BE PARTNERS IN A SCIENCE PROJECT...ANYONE NOT DOING A SCIENCE PROJECT WILL GET A FAILING GRADE..THAT'S WHAT IT SAID!
WELL, I GUESS THAT MEANS I JUST HAVE TO GO OVER AND INTRODUCE MYSELF TO HER...I'LL GO OVER AND SAY, "HI, PARTNER"... I'LL... I'LL.....
I'LL TAKE THE FAILING GRADE!
SCHULZ

AAUGH! AAUGH!

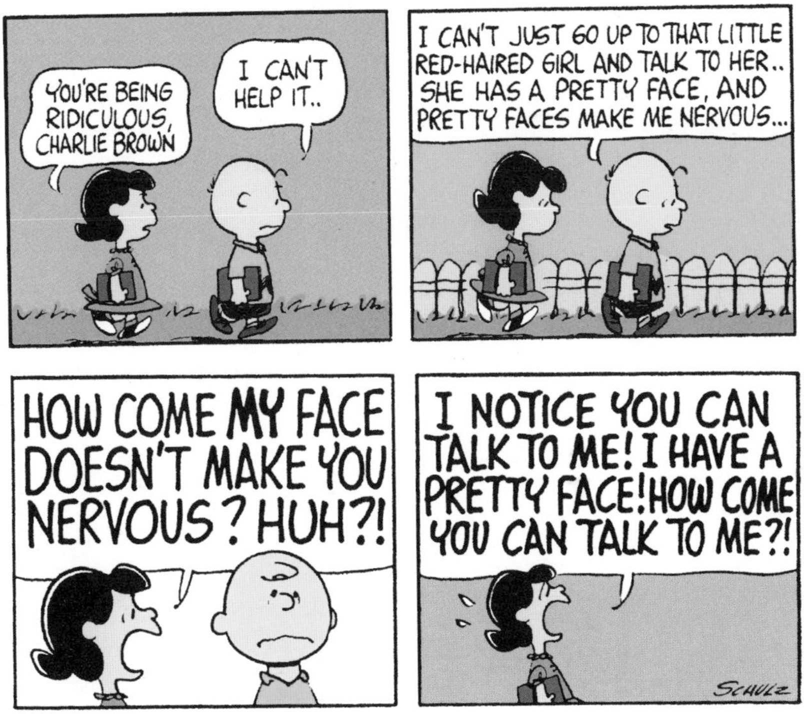
YOU'RE BEING RIDICULOUS, CHARLIE BROWN
I CAN'T HELP IT..
I CAN'T JUST GO UP TO THAT LITTLE RED-HAIRED GIRL AND TALK TO HER.. SHE HAS A PRETTY FACE, AND PRETTY FACES MAKE ME NERVOUS...
HOW COME MY FACE DOESN'T MAKE YOU NERVOUS? HUH?!
I NOTICE YOU CAN TALK TO ME! I HAVE A PRETTY FACE! HOW COME YOU CAN TALK TO ME?!
SCHULZ

TO THE OFFICE? YES, MA'AM..
I'VE BEEN CALLED TO THE OFFICE! WHY SHOULD I BE CALLED TO THE OFFICE? I HAVEN'T DONE ANYTHING WRONG! IT CAN'T BE ABOUT OUR SCIENCE PROJECT.. THAT ISN'T DUE FOR A WEEK
MAYBE SOMETHING HAPPENED AT HOME! MAYBE SOMEONE IS SICK...I USUALLY NEVER GET CALLED TO THE OFFICE... WHY SHOULD THEY CALL ME? WHY ME? I HAVEN'T DONE ANYTHING...
OFFICE, WHY DO YOU PERSECUTE ME?
OFFICE

AAUGH! AAUGH!

CHARLIE BROWN GOT SENT TO THE OFFICE..
HE DIDN'T GET "SENT."... HE WAS CALLED! THERE'S A BIG DIFFERENCE, YOU KNOW!
SHH! LOOK, HE'S COMING BACK.. CHARLIE BROWN IS COMING BACK FROM THE PRINCIPAL'S OFFICE...
MERCY!
?
WELL, I'LL BE!!
SCHULZ

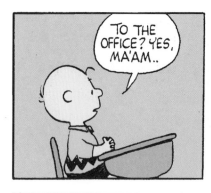

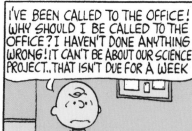

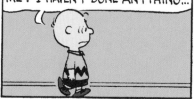

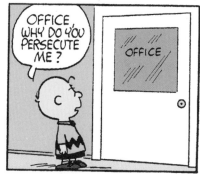

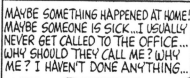

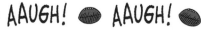

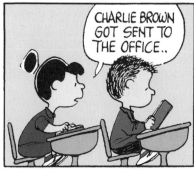

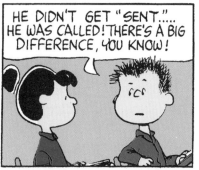

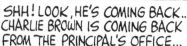

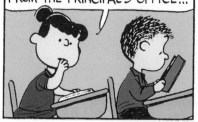

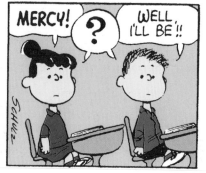

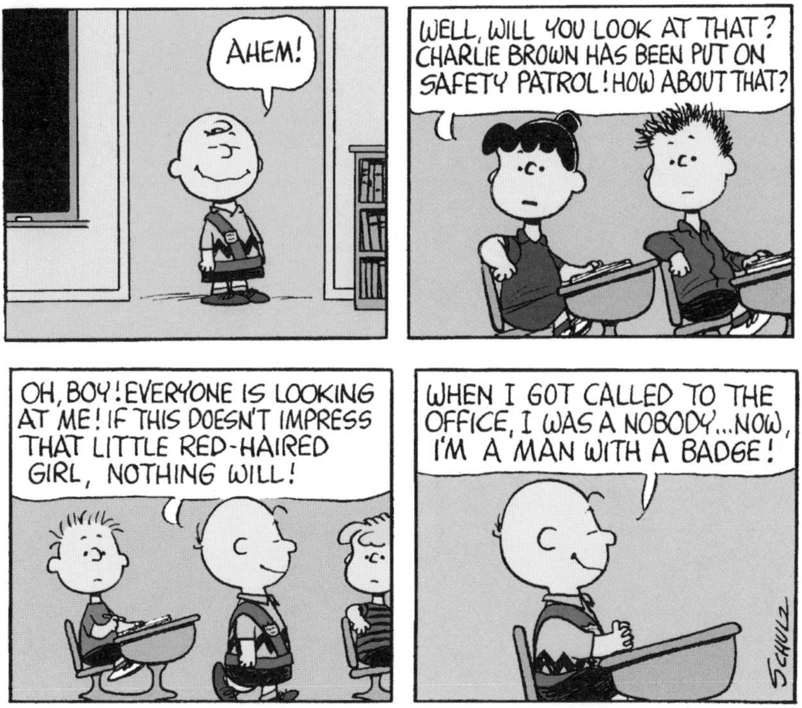
AHEM!
WELL, WILL YOU LOOK AT THAT? CHARLIE BROWN HAS BEEN PUT ON SAFETY PATROL! HOW ABOUT THAT?
OH, BOY! EVERYONE IS LOOKING AT ME! IF THIS DOESN'T IMPRESS THAT LITTLE RED-HAIRED GIRL, NOTHING WILL!
WHEN I GOT CALLED TO THE OFFICE, I WAS A NOBODY...NOW, I'M A MAN WITH A BADGE!
SCHULZ

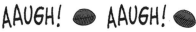

AAUGH! AAUGH!

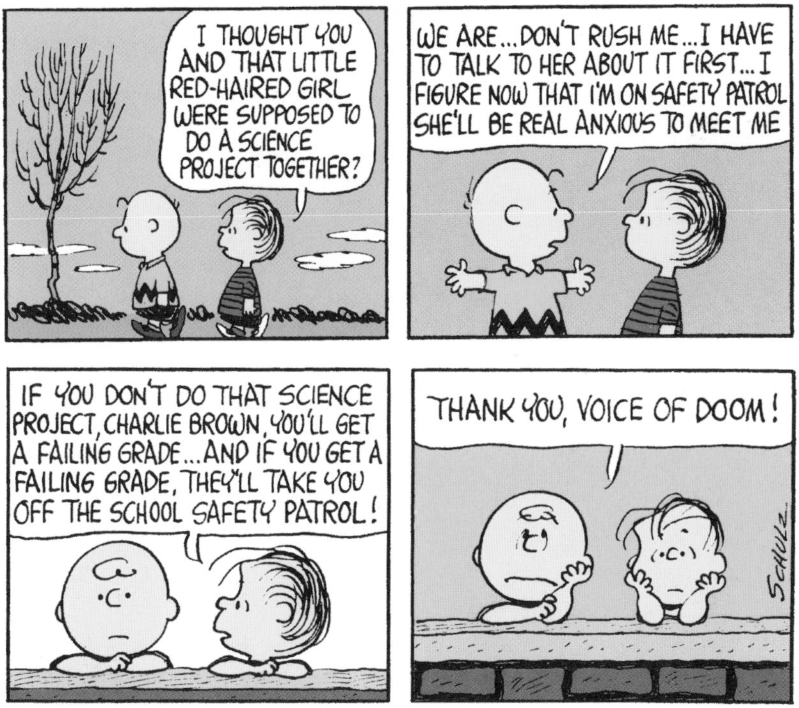
I THOUGHT YOU AND THAT LITTLE RED-HAIRED GIRL WERE SUPPOSED TO DO A SCIENCE PROJECT TOGETHER?
WE ARE...DON'T RUSH ME...I HAVE TO TALK TO HER ABOUT IT FIRST...I FIGURE NOW THAT I'M ON SAFETY PATROL SHE'LL BE REAL ANXIOUS TO MEET ME
IF YOU DON'T DO THAT SCIENCE PROJECT, CHARLIE BROWN, YOU'LL GET A FAILING GRADE...AND IF YOU GET A FAILING GRADE, THEY'LL TAKE YOU OFF THE SCHOOL SAFETY PATROL!
THANK YOU, VOICE OF DOOM!
SCHULZ

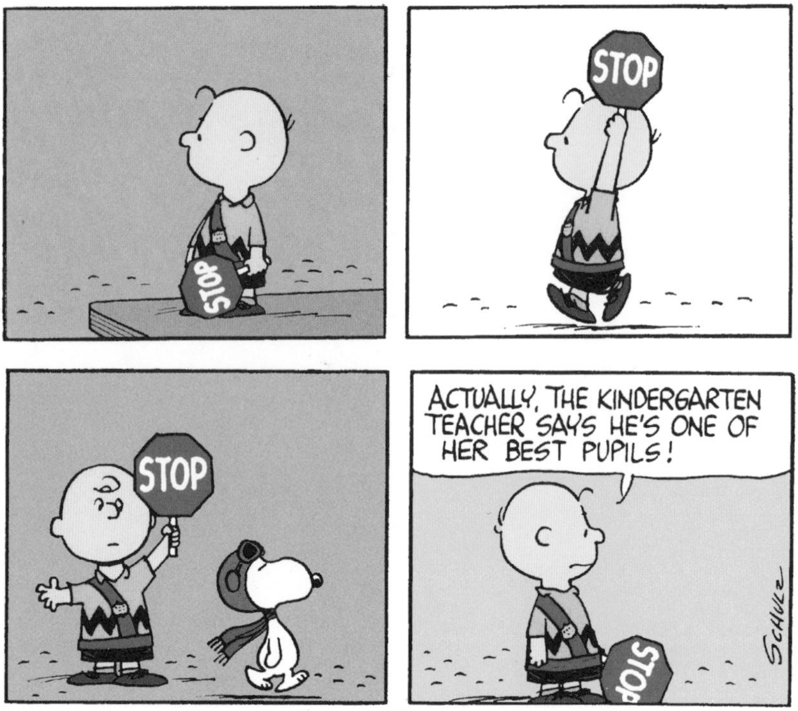
STOP
STOP
STOP
ACTUALLY, THE KINDERGARTEN TEACHER SAYS HE'S ONE OF HER BEST PUPILS!
STOP
SCHULZ

AAUGH! AAUGH!

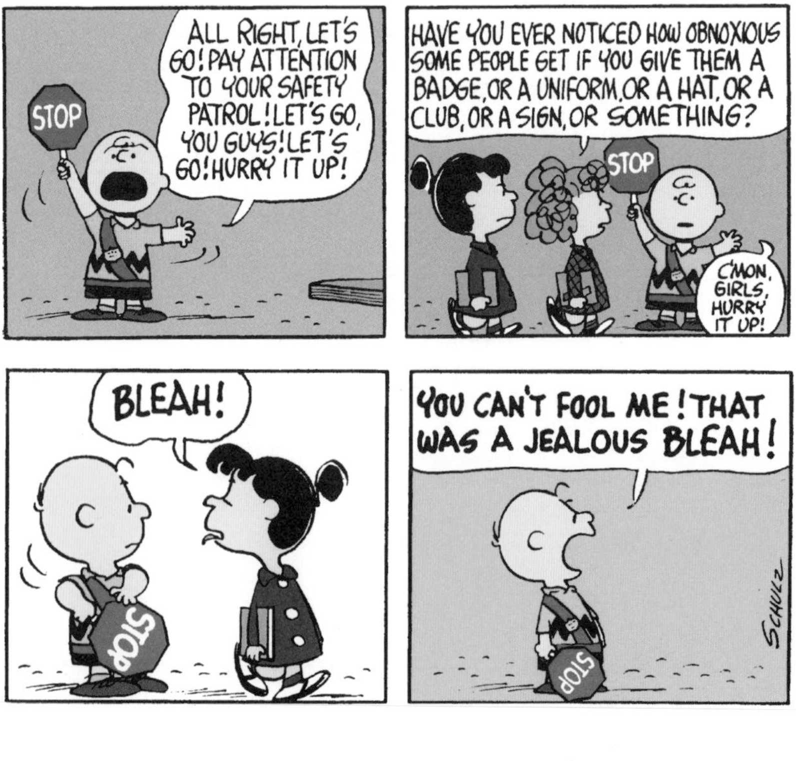
STOP
ALL RIGHT, LET'S GO! PAY ATTENTION TO YOUR SAFETY PATROL! LET'S GO, YOU GUYS! LET'S GO! HURRY IT UP!
HAVE YOU EVER NOTICED HOW OBNOXIOUS SOME PEOPLE GET IF YOU GIVE THEM A BADGE, OR A UNIFORM, OR A HAT, OR A CLUB, OR A SIGN, OR SOMETHING?
STOP
C'MON, GIRLS, HURRY IT UP!
BLEAH!
STOP
YOU CAN'T FOOL ME! THAT WAS A JEALOUS BLEAH!
STOP
SCHULZ

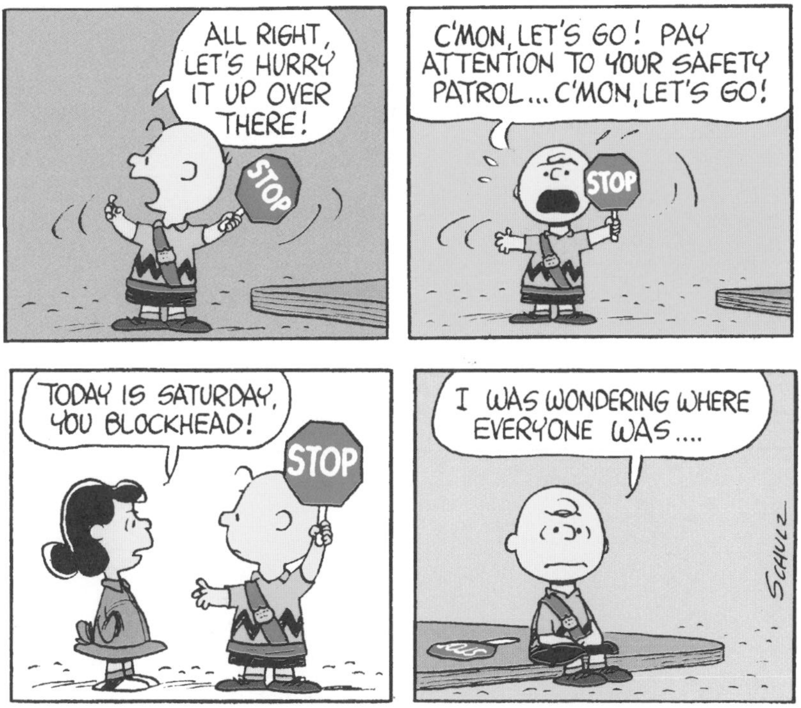
ALL RIGHT, LET'S HURRY IT UP OVER THERE!
STOP
C'MON, LET'S GO! PAY ATTENTION TO YOUR SAFETY PATROL... C'MON, LET'S GO!
STOP
TODAY IS SATURDAY, YOU BLOCKHEAD!
STOP
I WAS WONDERING WHERE EVERYONE WAS....
SCHULZ

AAUGH! AAUGH!

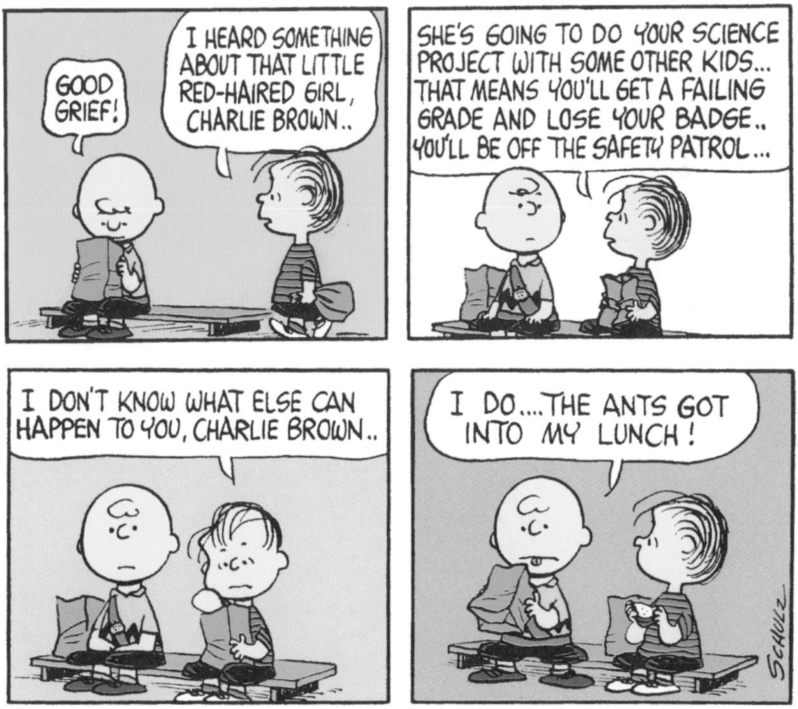
I HEARD SOMETHING ABOUT THAT LITTLE RED-HAIRED GIRL, CHARLIE BROWN..
GOOD GRIEF!
SHE'S GOING TO DO YOUR SCIENCE PROJECT WITH SOME OTHER KIDS... THAT MEANS YOU'LL GET A FAILING GRADE AND LOSE YOUR BADGE.. YOU'LL BE OFF THE SAFETY PATROL...
I DON'T KNOW WHAT ELSE CAN HAPPEN TO YOU, CHARLIE BROWN..
I DO....THE ANTS GOT INTO MY LUNCH!
SCHULZ

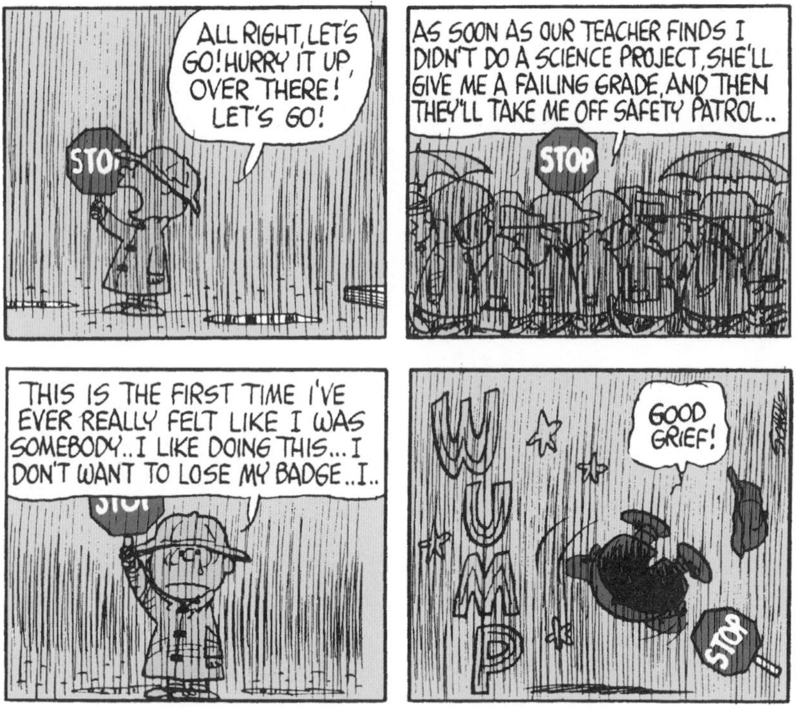
ALL RIGHT, LET'S GO! HURRY IT UP, OVER THERE! LET'S GO!
STOP
AS SOON AS OUR TEACHER FINDS I DIDN'T DO A SCIENCE PROJECT, SHE'LL GIVE ME A FAILING GRADE, AND THEN THEY'LL TAKE ME OFF SAFETY PATROL..
STOP
THIS IS THE FIRST TIME I'VE EVER REALLY FELT LIKE I WAS SOMEBODY..I LIKE DOING THIS...I DON'T WANT TO LOSE MY BADGE..I..
WUMP
GOOD GRIEF!
STOP

AAUGH! AAUGH!

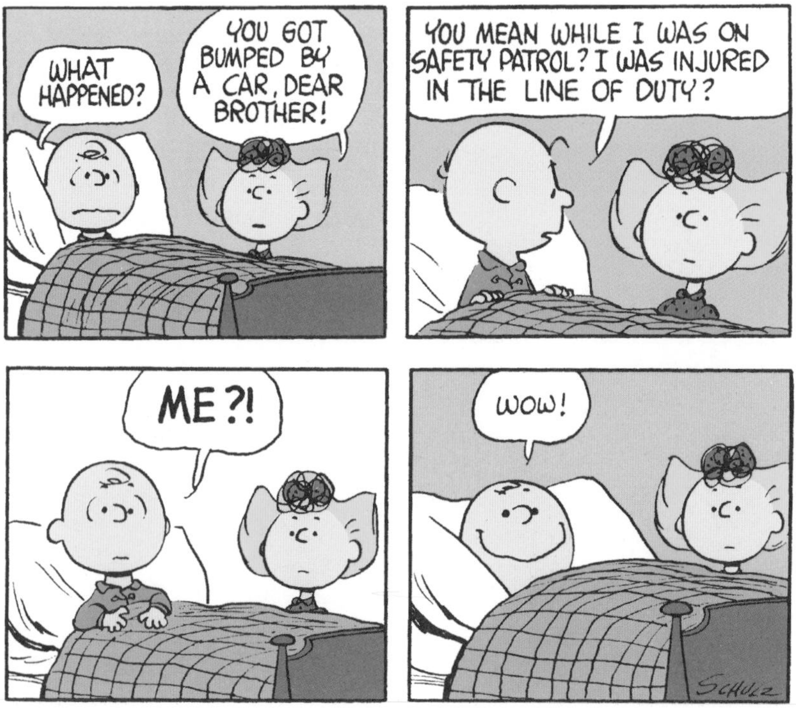
WHAT HAPPENED?
YOU GOT BUMPED BY A CAR, DEAR BROTHER!
YOU MEAN WHILE I WAS ON SAFETY PATROL? I WAS INJURED IN THE LINE OF DUTY?
ME?!
WOW!
SCHULZ

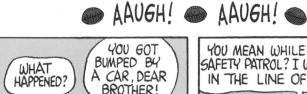

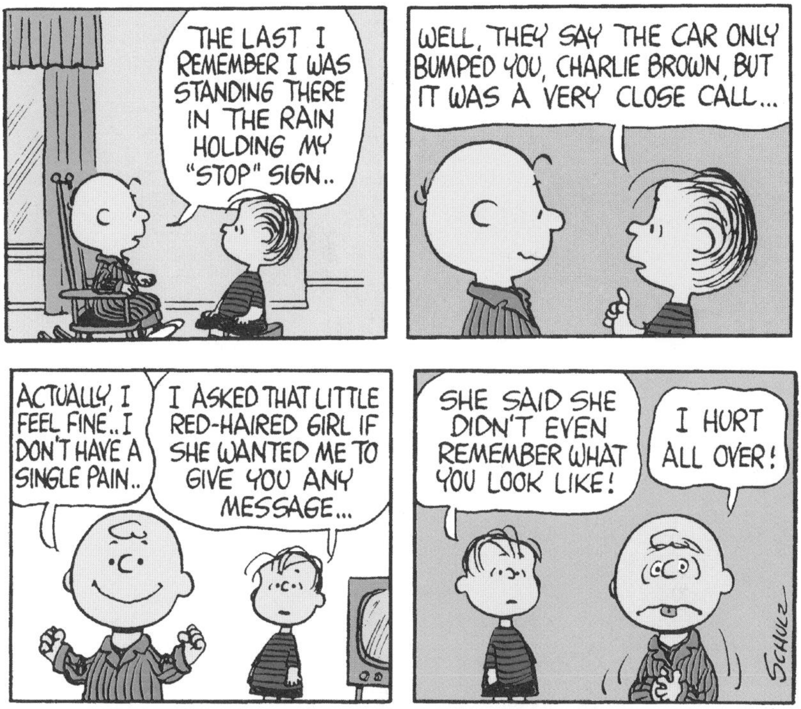
THE LAST I REMEMBER I WAS STANDING THERE IN THE RAIN HOLDING MY "STOP" SIGN..
WELL, THEY SAY THE CAR ONLY BUMPED YOU, CHARLIE BROWN, BUT IT WAS A VERY CLOSE CALL...
ACTUALLY, I FEEL FINE..I DON'T HAVE A SINGLE PAIN..
I ASKED THAT LITTLE RED-HAIRED GIRL IF SHE WANTED ME TO GIVE YOU ANY MESSAGE...
SHE SAID SHE DIDN'T EVEN REMEMBER WHAT YOU LOOK LIKE!
I HURT ALL OVER!
SCHULZ

AAUGH! AAUGH!

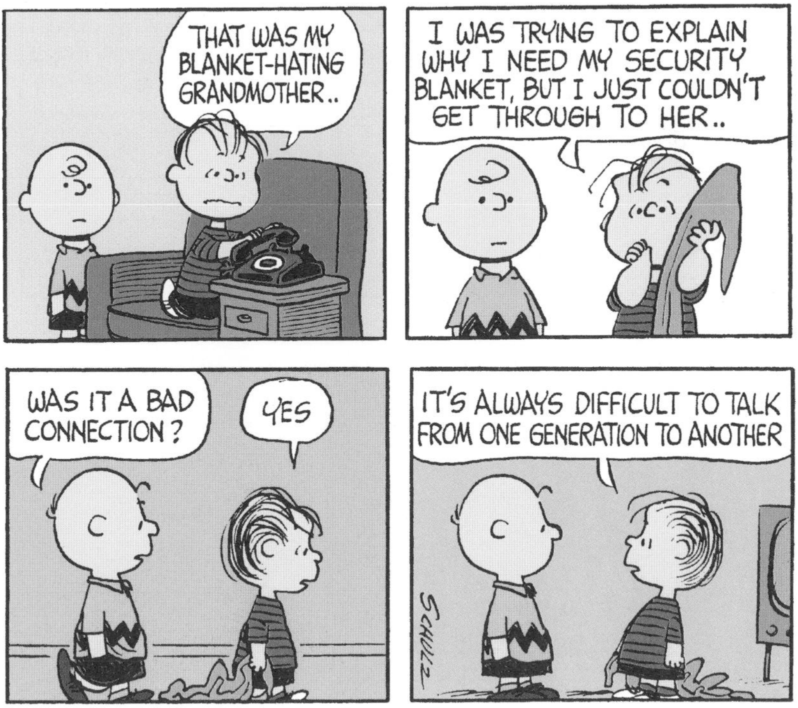
THAT WAS MY BLANKET-HATING GRANDMOTHER..
I WAS TRYING TO EXPLAIN WHY I NEED MY SECURITY BLANKET, BUT I JUST COULDN'T GET THROUGH TO HER..
WAS IT A BAD CONNECTION?
YES
IT'S ALWAYS DIFFICULT TO TALK FROM ONE GENERATION TO ANOTHER
SCHULZ

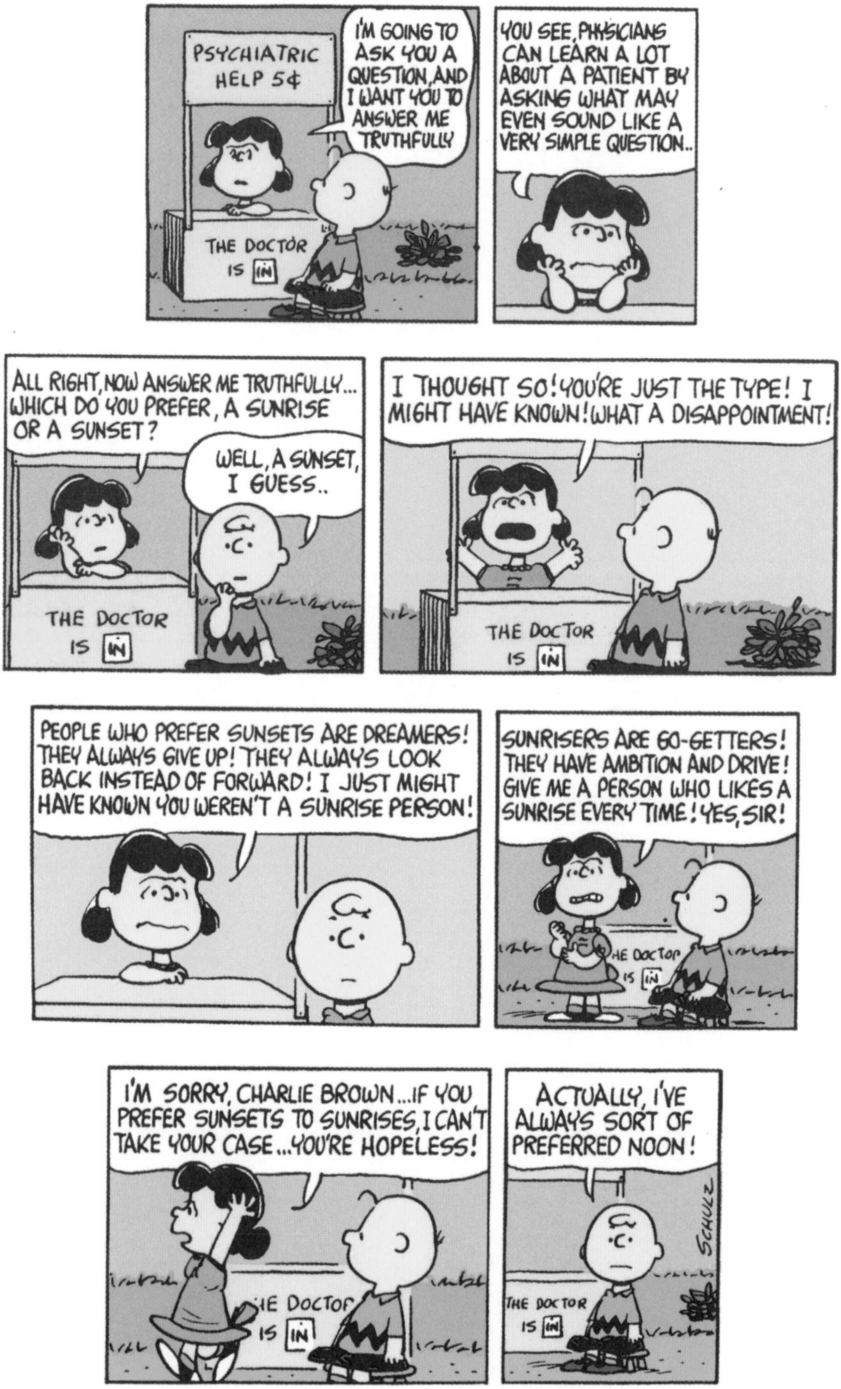
PSYCHIATRIC HELP 5¢
I'M GOING TO ASK YOU A QUESTION, AND I WANT YOU TO ANSWER ME TRUTHFULLY
THE DOCTOR IS IN
YOU SEE, PHYSICIANS CAN LEARN A LOT ABOUT A PATIENT BY ASKING WHAT MAY EVEN SOUND LIKE A VERY SIMPLE QUESTION..
ALL RIGHT, NOW ANSWER ME TRUTHFULLY... WHICH DO YOU PREFER, A SUNRISE OR A SUNSET?
WELL, A SUNSET, I GUESS..
THE DOCTOR IS IN
I THOUGHT SO! YOU'RE JUST THE TYPE! I MIGHT HAVE KNOWN! WHAT A DISAPPOINTMENT!
THE DOCTOR IS IN
PEOPLE WHO PREFER SUNSETS ARE DREAMERS! THEY ALWAYS GIVE UP! THEY ALWAYS LOOK BACK INSTEAD OF FORWARD! I JUST MIGHT HAVE KNOWN YOU WEREN'T A SUNRISE PERSON!
SUNRISERS ARE GO-GETTERS! THEY HAVE AMBITION AND DRIVE! GIVE ME A PERSON WHO LIKES A SUNRISE EVERY TIME! YES, SIR!
I'M SORRY, CHARLIE BROWN...IF YOU PREFER SUNSETS TO SUNRISES, I CAN'T TAKE YOUR CASE...YOU'RE HOPELESS!
ACTUALLY, I'VE ALWAYS SORT OF PREFERRED NOON!
SCHULZ
THE DOCTOR IS IN

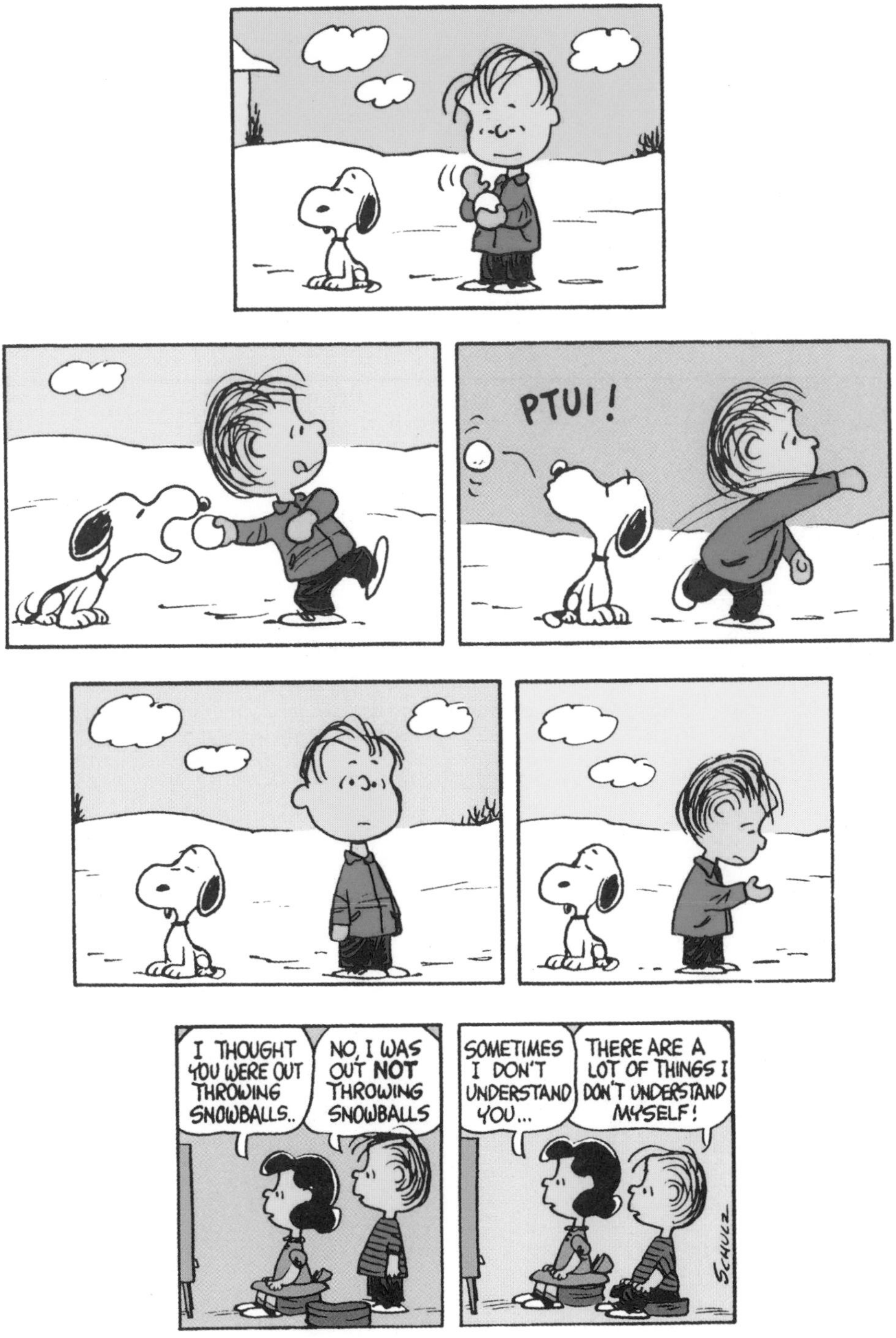
PTUI!
I THOUGHT YOU WERE OUT THROWING SNOWBALLS..
NO, I WAS OUT **NOT** THROWING SNOWBALLS
SOMETIMES I DON'T UNDERSTAND YOU...
THERE ARE A LOT OF THINGS I DON'T UNDERSTAND MYSELF!
SCHULZ

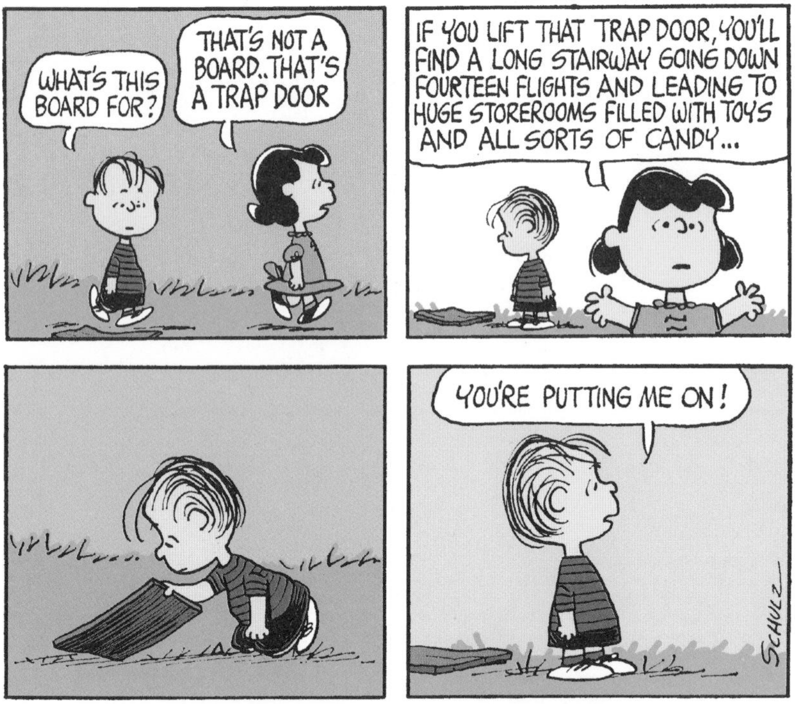
WHAT'S THIS BOARD FOR?
THAT'S NOT A BOARD..THAT'S A TRAP DOOR
IF YOU LIFT THAT TRAP DOOR, YOU'LL FIND A LONG STAIRWAY GOING DOWN FOURTEEN FLIGHTS AND LEADING TO HUGE STOREROOMS FILLED WITH TOYS AND ALL SORTS OF CANDY...
YOU'RE PUTTING ME ON!
SCHULZ

AAUGH! AAUGH!

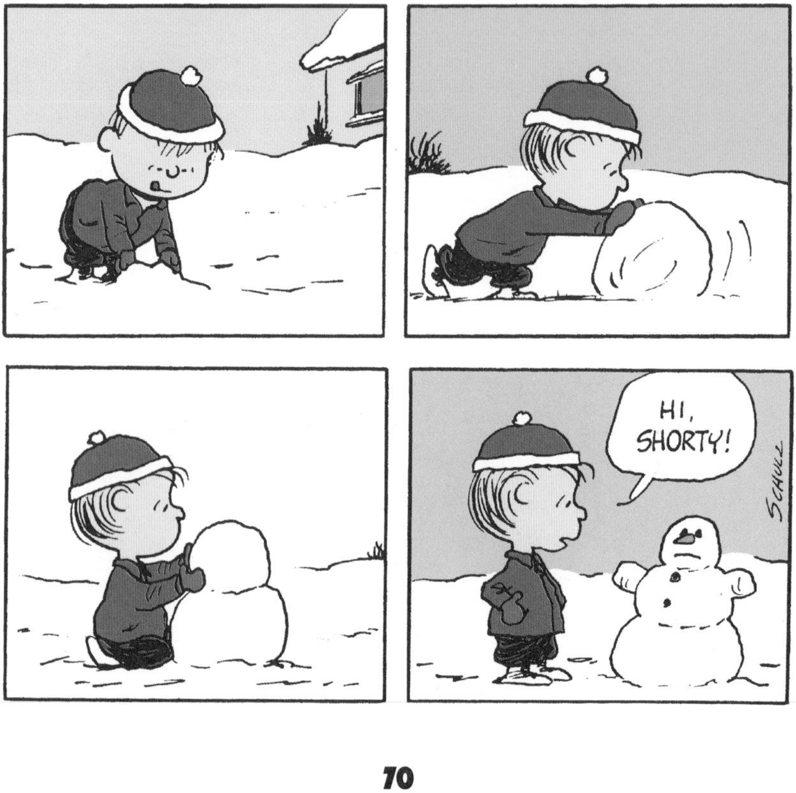
HI, SHORTY!
SCHULZ

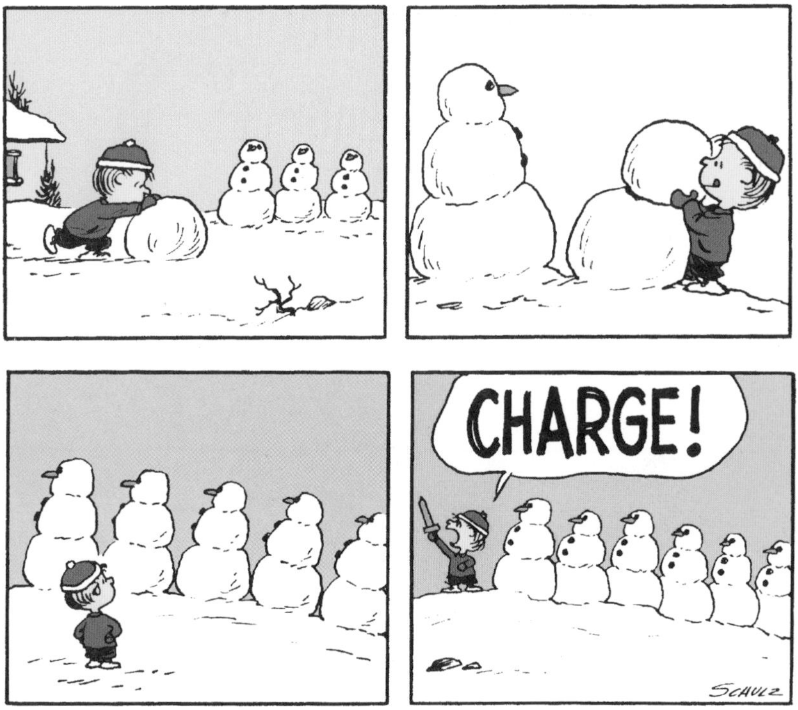
CHARGE!
SCHULZ

AAUGH! AAUGH!

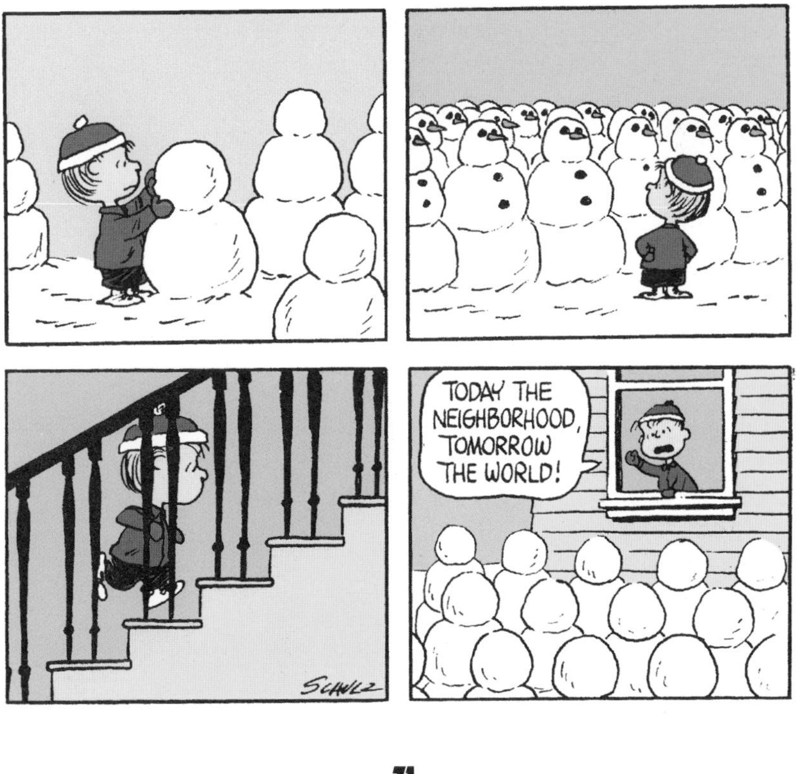
SCHULZ
TODAY THE NEIGHBORHOOD, TOMORROW THE WORLD!

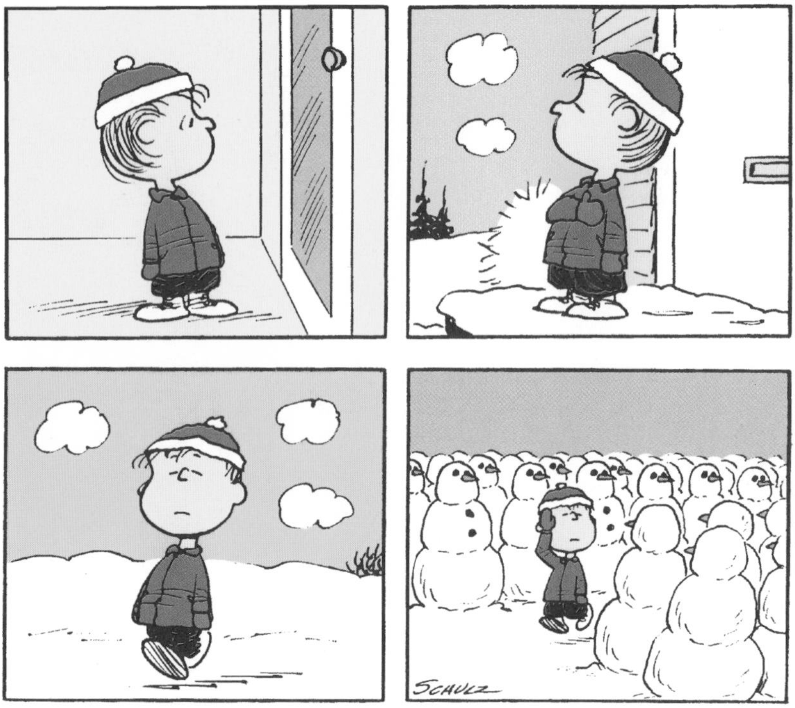
SCHULZ

AAUGH! AAUGH!

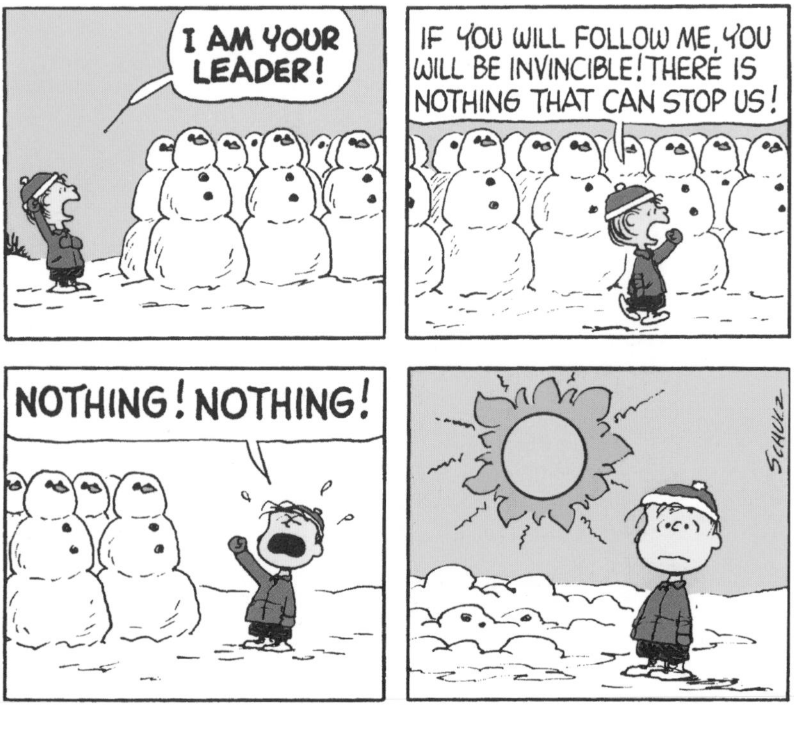
I AM YOUR LEADER!
IF YOU WILL FOLLOW ME, YOU WILL BE INVINCIBLE! THERE IS NOTHING THAT CAN STOP US!
NOTHING! NOTHING!
SCHULZ

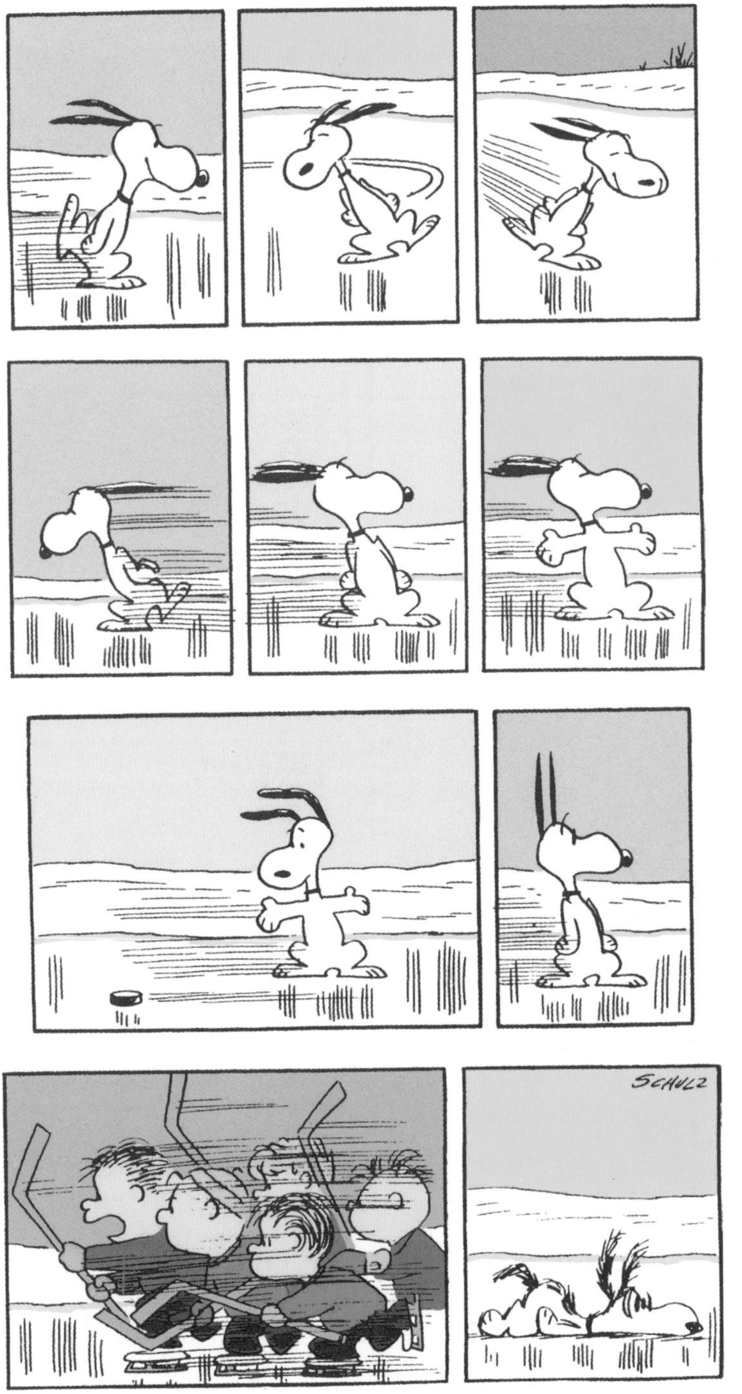
SCHULZ

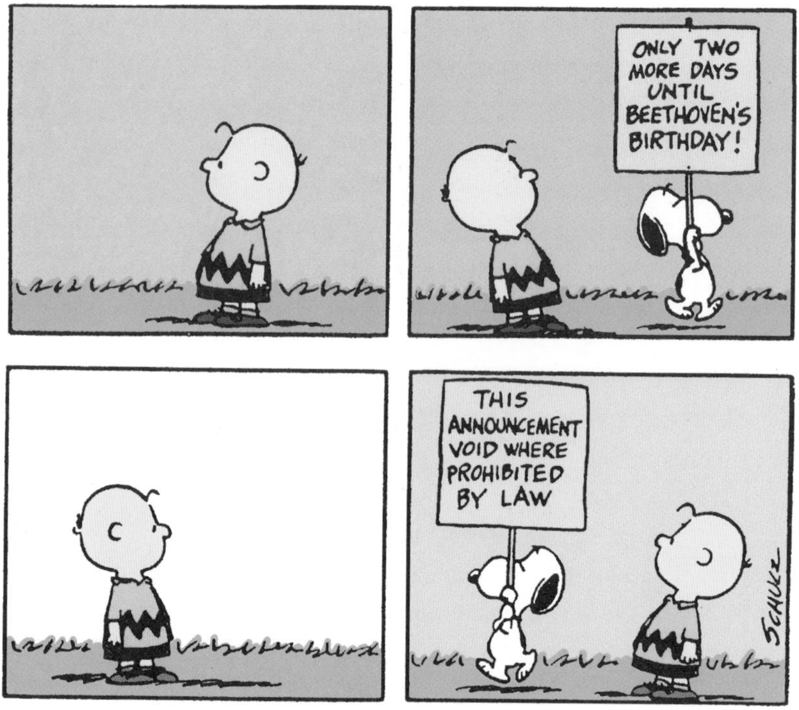
ONLY TWO MORE DAYS UNTIL BEETHOVEN'S BIRTHDAY!
THIS ANNOUNCEMENT VOID WHERE PROHIBITED BY LAW
SCHULZ

AAUGH! AAUGH!

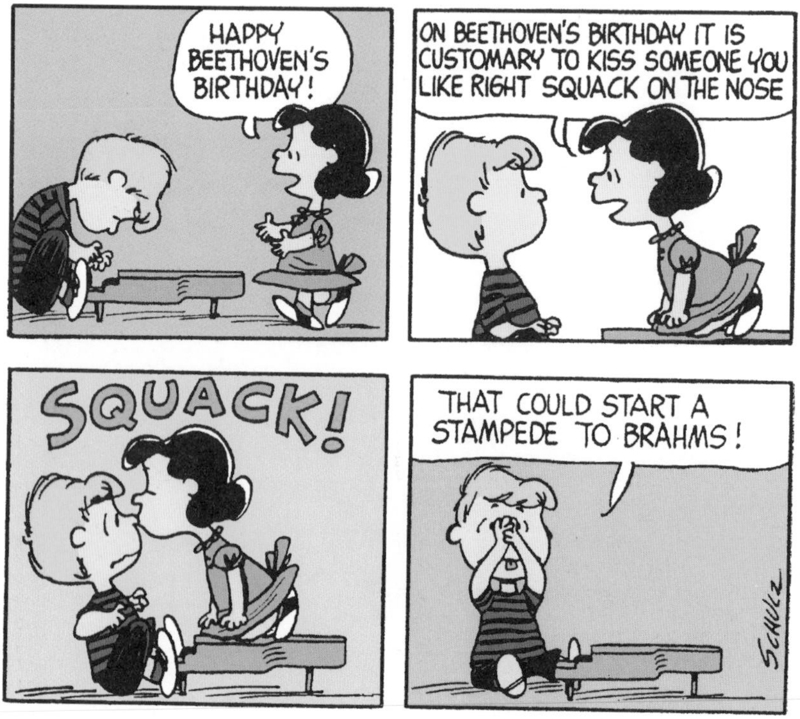
HAPPY BEETHOVEN'S BIRTHDAY!
ON BEETHOVEN'S BIRTHDAY IT IS CUSTOMARY TO KISS SOMEONE YOU LIKE RIGHT SQUACK ON THE NOSE
SQUACK!
THAT COULD START A STAMPEDE TO BRAHMS!
SCHULZ

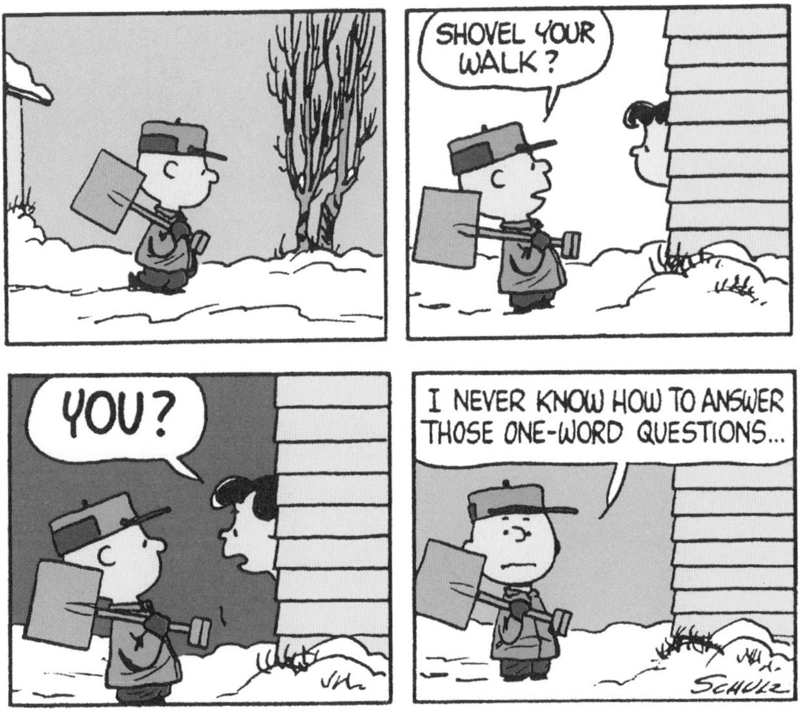
SHOVEL YOUR WALK?
YOU?
I NEVER KNOW HOW TO ANSWER THOSE ONE-WORD QUESTIONS...
SCHULZ

AAUGH! AAUGH!

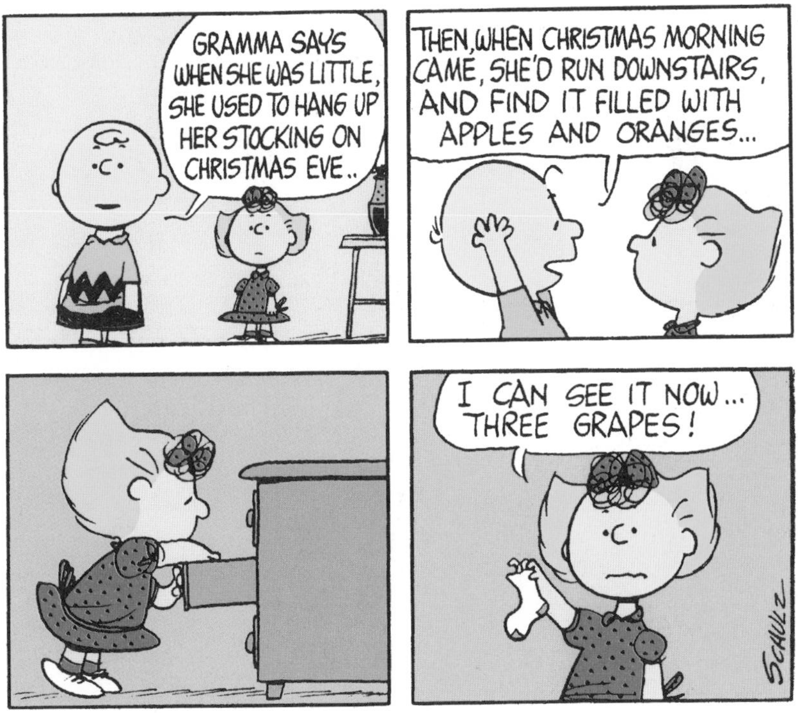
GRAMMA SAYS WHEN SHE WAS LITTLE, SHE USED TO HANG UP HER STOCKING ON CHRISTMAS EVE..
THEN, WHEN CHRISTMAS MORNING CAME, SHE'D RUN DOWNSTAIRS, AND FIND IT FILLED WITH APPLES AND ORANGES...
I CAN SEE IT NOW... THREE GRAPES!
SCHULZ

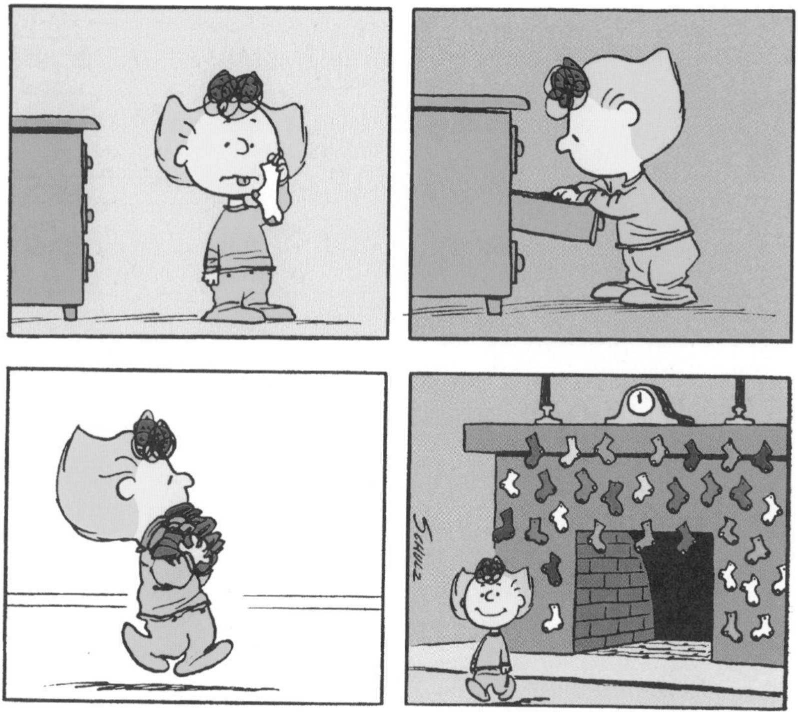
SCHULZ

AAUGH! AAUGH!

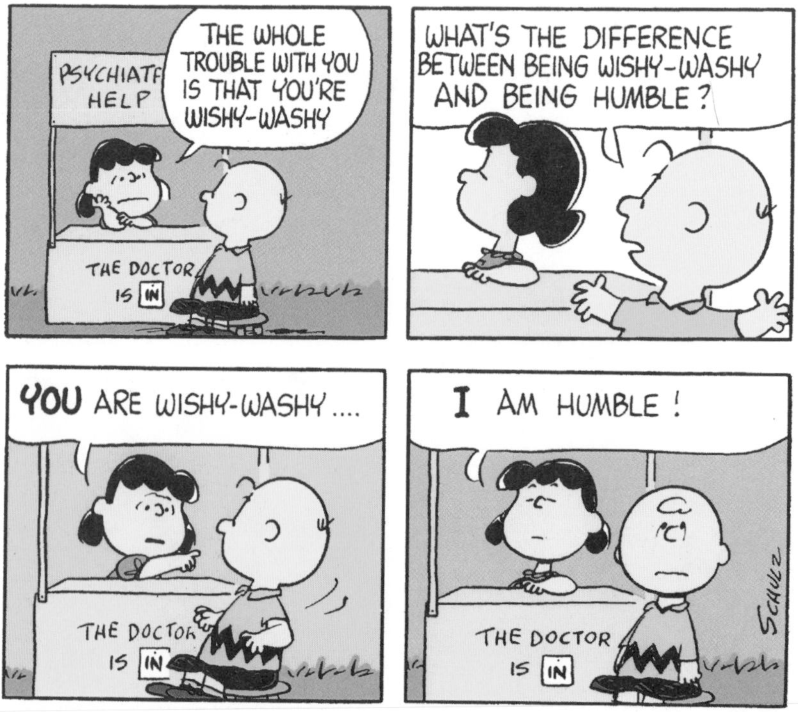
PSYCHIAT
HELP
THE WHOLE TROUBLE WITH YOU IS THAT YOU'RE WISHY-WASHY
THE DOCTOR IS IN
WHAT'S THE DIFFERENCE BETWEEN BEING WISHY-WASHY AND BEING HUMBLE ?
YOU ARE WISHY-WASHY ....
THE DOCTOR IS IN
I AM HUMBLE !
THE DOCTOR IS IN
SCHULZ

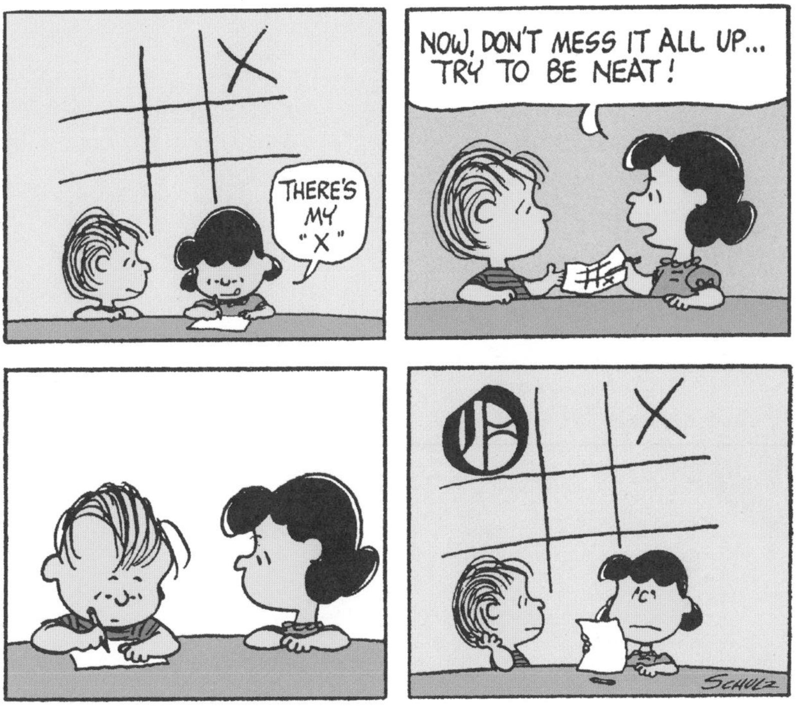
THERE'S MY "X"
NOW, DON'T MESS IT ALL UP... TRY TO BE NEAT!
SCHULZ

AAUGH! AAUGH!

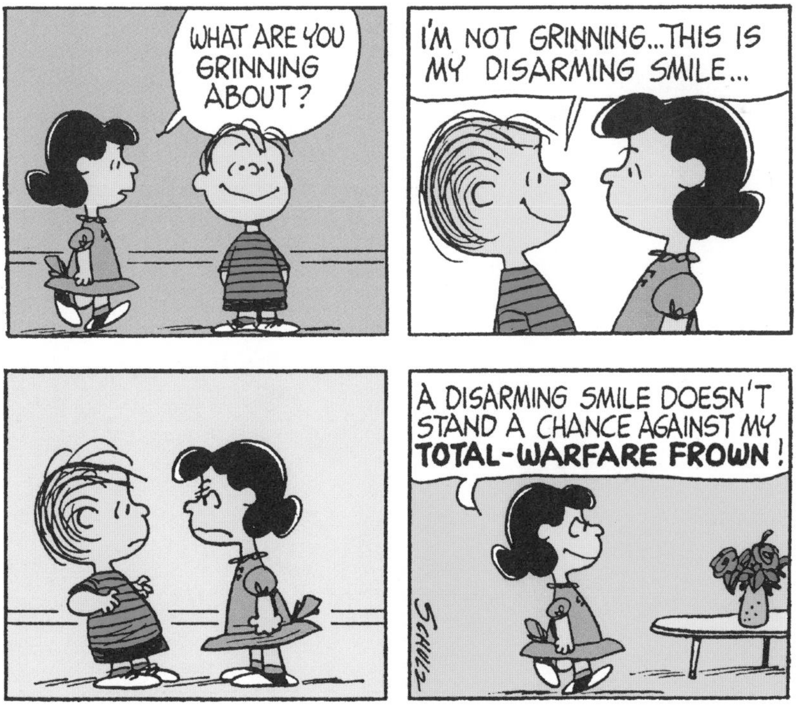
WHAT ARE YOU GRINNING ABOUT?
I'M NOT GRINNING...THIS IS MY DISARMING SMILE...
A DISARMING SMILE DOESN'T STAND A CHANCE AGAINST MY **TOTAL-WARFARE FROWN**!
SCHULZ

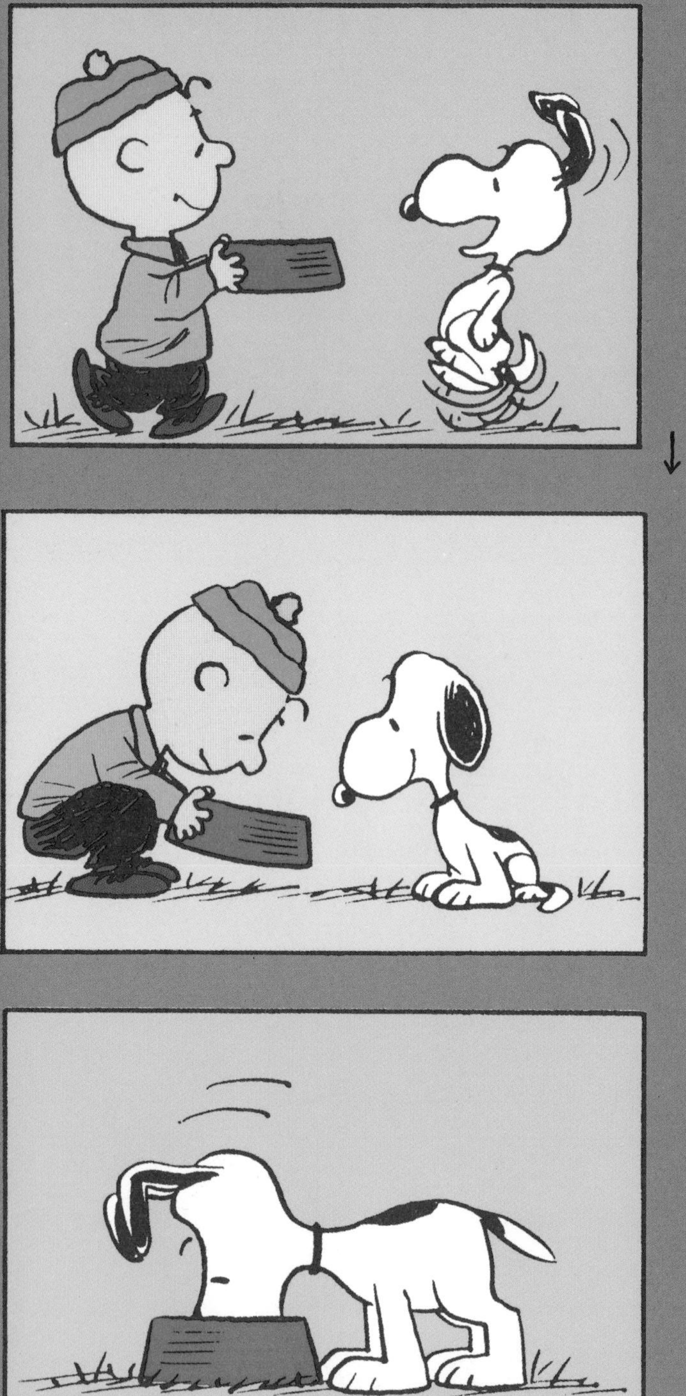

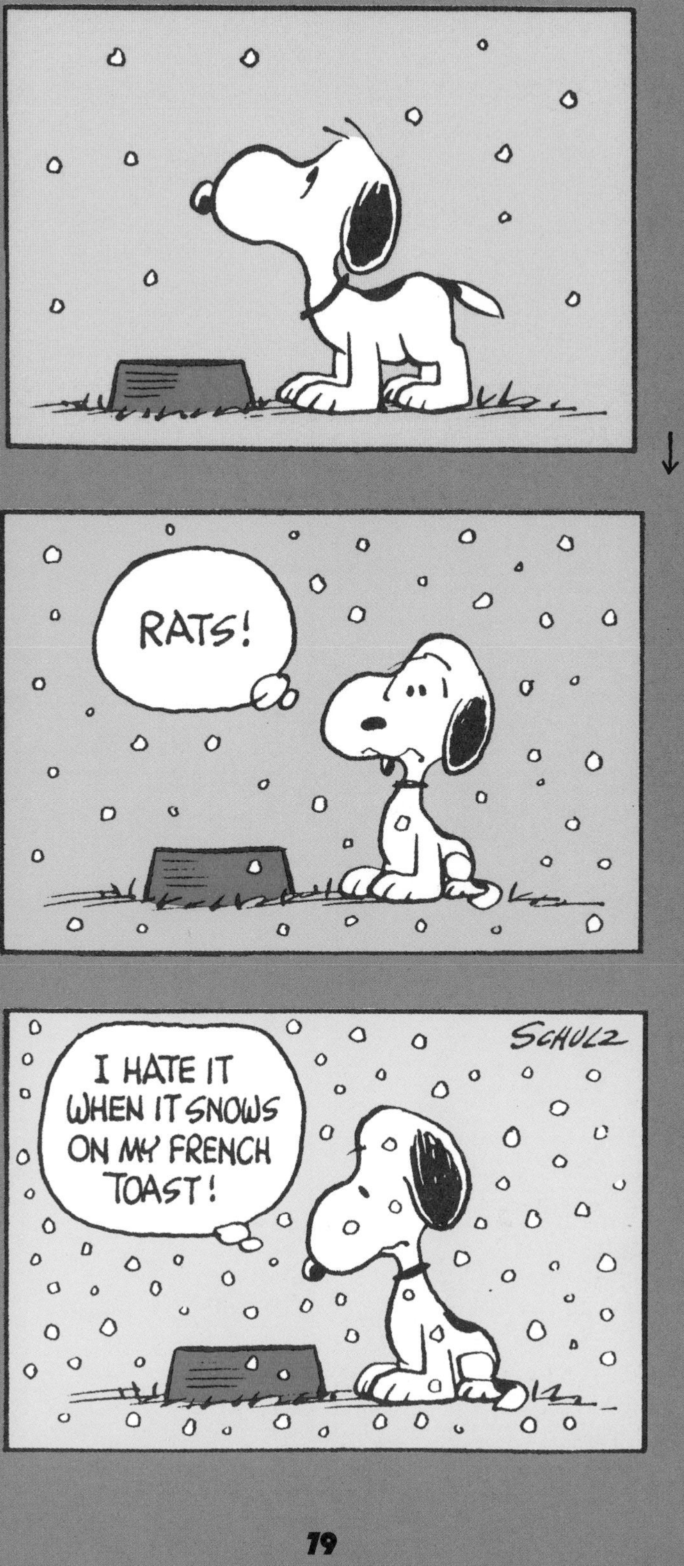
RATS!
I HATE IT WHEN IT SNOWS ON MY FRENCH TOAST!
SCHULZ

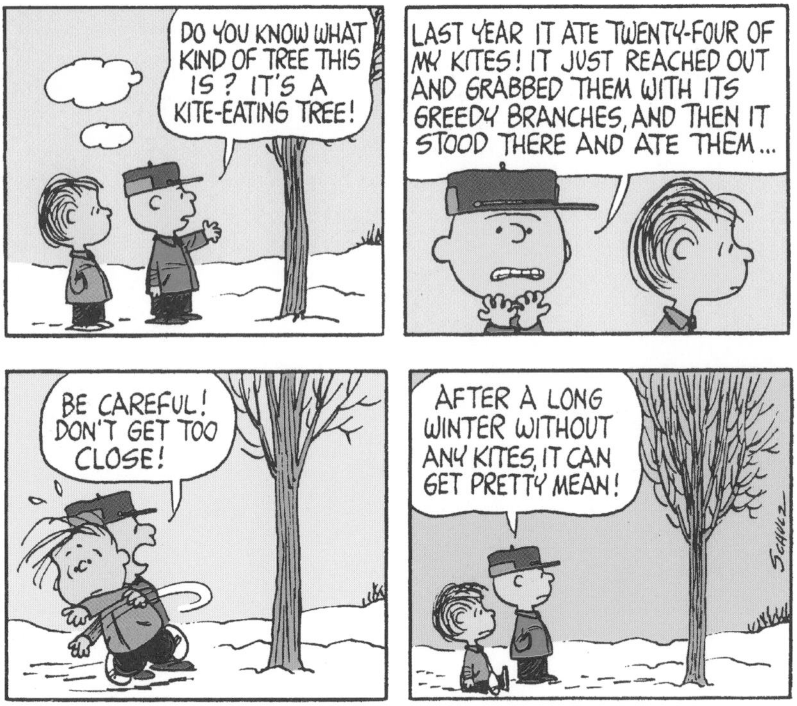
DO YOU KNOW WHAT KIND OF TREE THIS IS ? IT'S A KITE-EATING TREE!
LAST YEAR IT ATE TWENTY-FOUR OF MY KITES! IT JUST REACHED OUT AND GRABBED THEM WITH ITS GREEDY BRANCHES, AND THEN IT STOOD THERE AND ATE THEM...
BE CAREFUL! DON'T GET TOO CLOSE!
AFTER A LONG WINTER WITHOUT ANY KITES, IT CAN GET PRETTY MEAN!
SCHULZ

AAUGH! AAUGH!

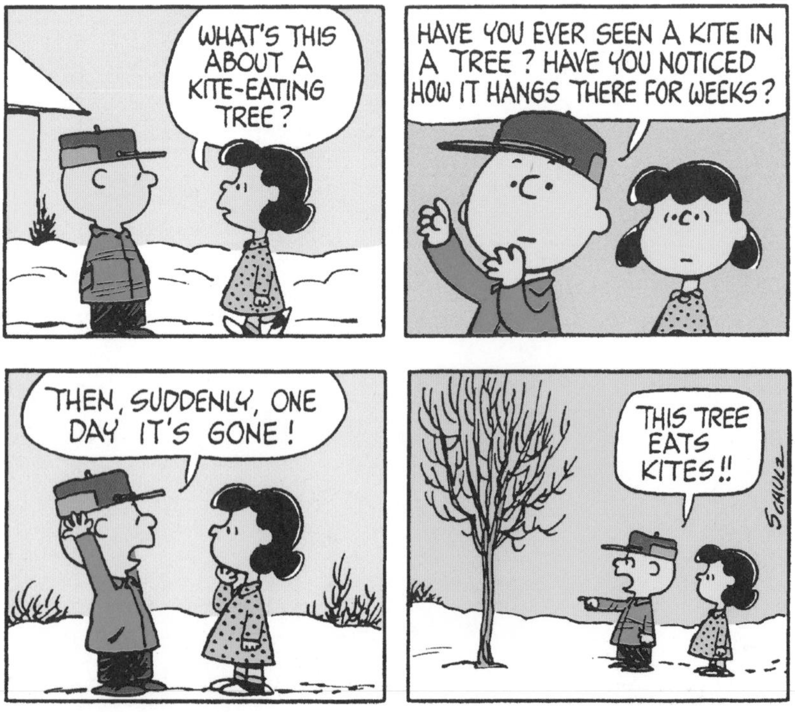
WHAT'S THIS ABOUT A KITE-EATING TREE ?
HAVE YOU EVER SEEN A KITE IN A TREE ? HAVE YOU NOTICED HOW IT HANGS THERE FOR WEEKS ?
THEN, SUDDENLY, ONE DAY IT'S GONE !
THIS TREE EATS KITES !!
SCHULZ

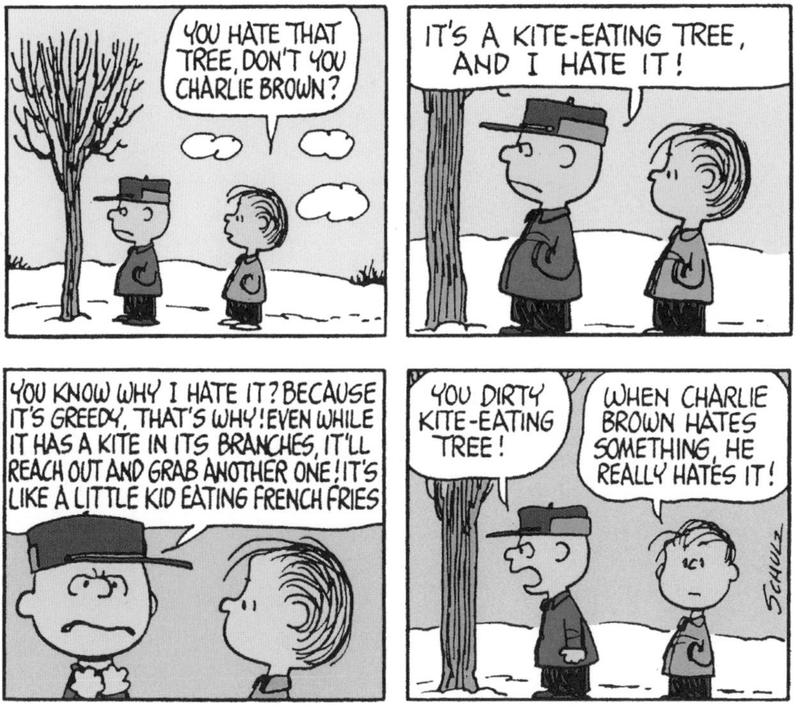
YOU HATE THAT TREE, DON'T YOU CHARLIE BROWN?
IT'S A KITE-EATING TREE, AND I HATE IT!
YOU KNOW WHY I HATE IT? BECAUSE IT'S GREEDY, THAT'S WHY! EVEN WHILE IT HAS A KITE IN ITS BRANCHES, IT'LL REACH OUT AND GRAB ANOTHER ONE! IT'S LIKE A LITTLE KID EATING FRENCH FRIES
YOU DIRTY KITE-EATING TREE!
WHEN CHARLIE BROWN HATES SOMETHING, HE REALLY HATES IT!
SCHULZ

AAUGH! AAUGH!

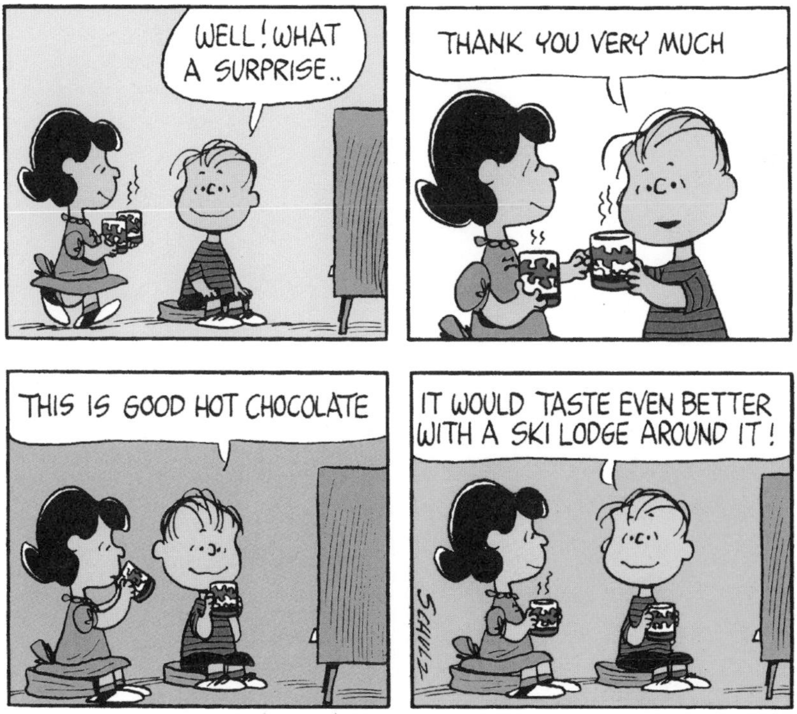
WELL! WHAT A SURPRISE..
THANK YOU VERY MUCH
THIS IS GOOD HOT CHOCOLATE
IT WOULD TASTE EVEN BETTER WITH A SKI LODGE AROUND IT!
SCHULZ

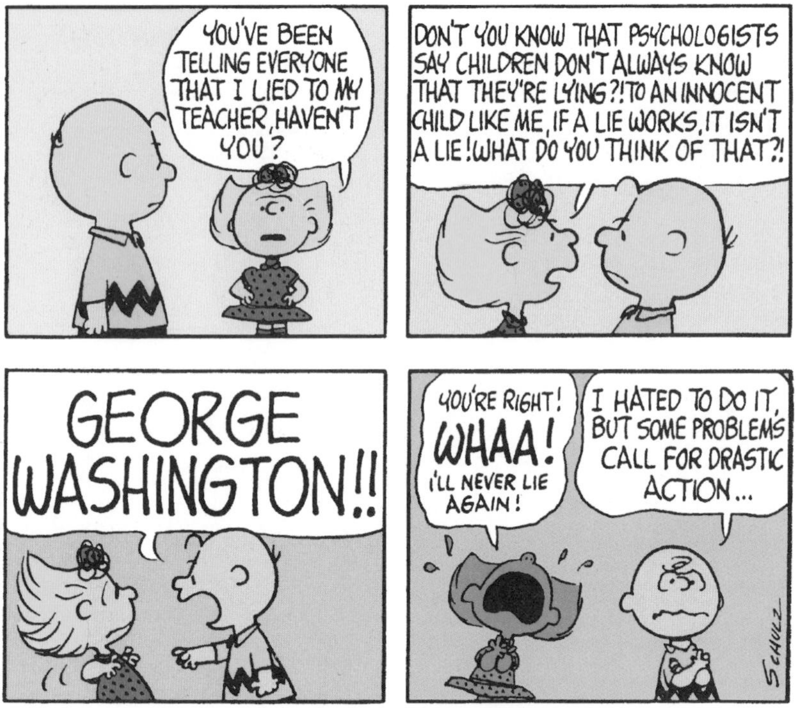
YOU'VE BEEN TELLING EVERYONE THAT I LIED TO MY TEACHER, HAVEN'T YOU?
DON'T YOU KNOW THAT PSYCHOLOGISTS SAY CHILDREN DON'T ALWAYS KNOW THAT THEY'RE LYING?! TO AN INNOCENT CHILD LIKE ME, IF A LIE WORKS, IT ISN'T A LIE! WHAT DO YOU THINK OF THAT?!
GEORGE WASHINGTON!!
YOU'RE RIGHT! WHAA! I'LL NEVER LIE AGAIN!
I HATED TO DO IT, BUT SOME PROBLEMS CALL FOR DRASTIC ACTION...
SCHULZ

AAUGH! AAUGH!

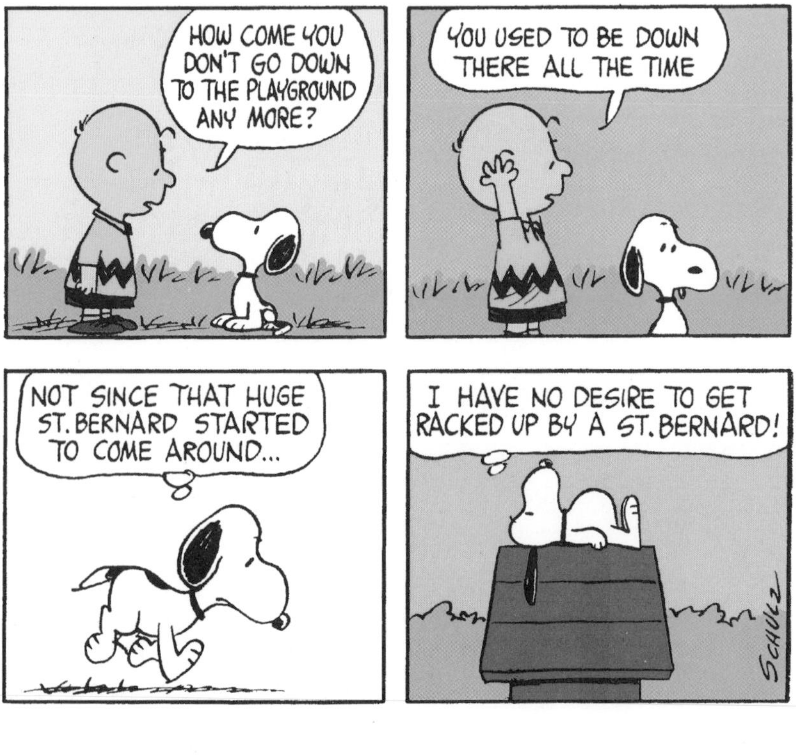
HOW COME YOU DON'T GO DOWN TO THE PLAYGROUND ANY MORE?
YOU USED TO BE DOWN THERE ALL THE TIME
NOT SINCE THAT HUGE ST. BERNARD STARTED TO COME AROUND...
I HAVE NO DESIRE TO GET RACKED UP BY A ST. BERNARD!
SCHULZ

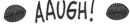

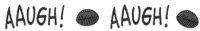

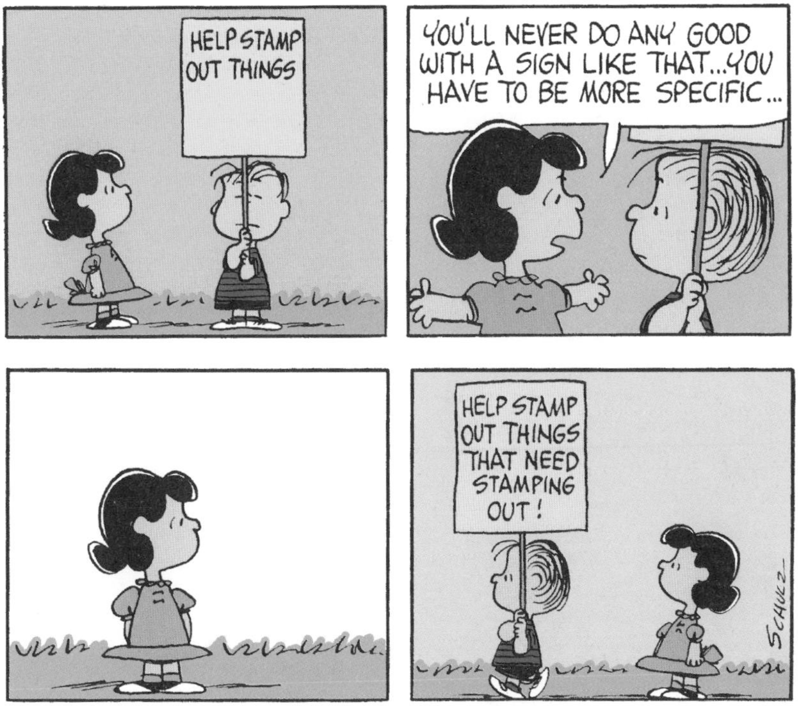
HELP STAMP OUT THINGS
YOU'LL NEVER DO ANY GOOD WITH A SIGN LIKE THAT...YOU HAVE TO BE MORE SPECIFIC...
HELP STAMP OUT THINGS THAT NEED STAMPING OUT!
SCHULZ

AAUGH! AAUGH!

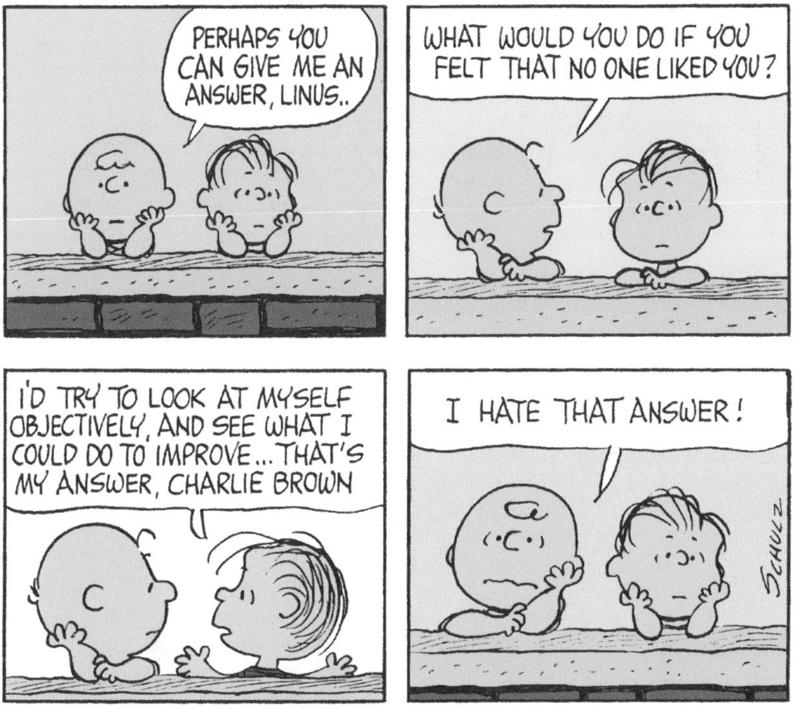
PERHAPS YOU CAN GIVE ME AN ANSWER, LINUS..
WHAT WOULD YOU DO IF YOU FELT THAT NO ONE LIKED YOU?
I'D TRY TO LOOK AT MYSELF OBJECTIVELY, AND SEE WHAT I COULD DO TO IMPROVE... THAT'S MY ANSWER, CHARLIE BROWN
I HATE THAT ANSWER!
SCHULZ

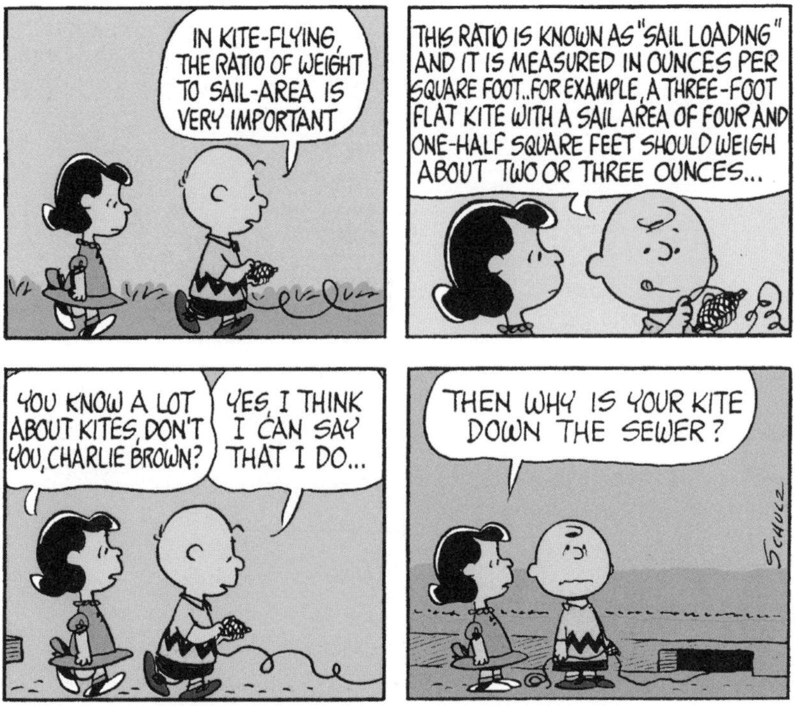
IN KITE-FLYING, THE RATIO OF WEIGHT TO SAIL-AREA IS VERY IMPORTANT
THIS RATIO IS KNOWN AS "SAIL LOADING" AND IT IS MEASURED IN OUNCES PER SQUARE FOOT..FOR EXAMPLE, A THREE-FOOT FLAT KITE WITH A SAIL AREA OF FOUR AND ONE-HALF SQUARE FEET SHOULD WEIGH ABOUT TWO OR THREE OUNCES...
YOU KNOW A LOT ABOUT KITES, DON'T YOU, CHARLIE BROWN?
YES, I THINK I CAN SAY THAT I DO...
THEN WHY IS YOUR KITE DOWN THE SEWER?
SCHULZ

AAUGH! AAUGH!

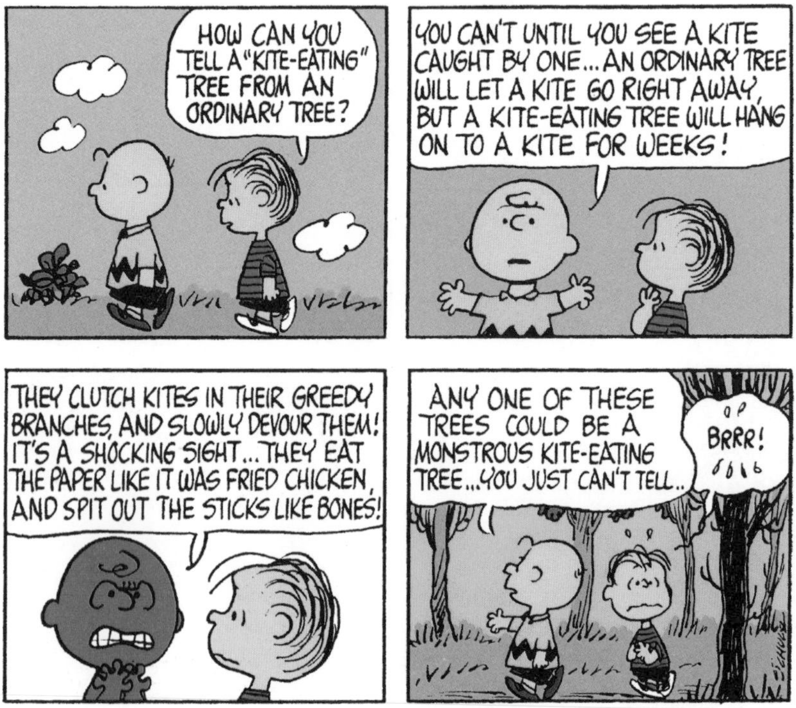
HOW CAN YOU TELL A "KITE-EATING" TREE FROM AN ORDINARY TREE?
YOU CAN'T UNTIL YOU SEE A KITE CAUGHT BY ONE... AN ORDINARY TREE WILL LET A KITE GO RIGHT AWAY, BUT A KITE-EATING TREE WILL HANG ON TO A KITE FOR WEEKS!
THEY CLUTCH KITES IN THEIR GREEDY BRANCHES, AND SLOWLY DEVOUR THEM! IT'S A SHOCKING SIGHT... THEY EAT THE PAPER LIKE IT WAS FRIED CHICKEN, AND SPIT OUT THE STICKS LIKE BONES!
ANY ONE OF THESE TREES COULD BE A MONSTROUS KITE-EATING TREE...YOU JUST CAN'T TELL..
BRRR!

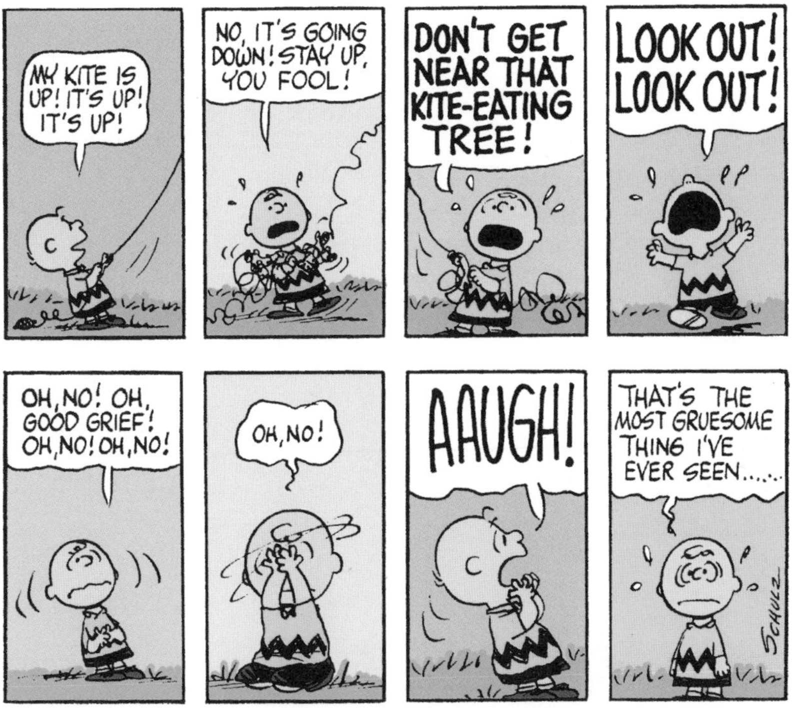
MY KITE IS UP! IT'S UP! IT'S UP!
NO, IT'S GOING DOWN! STAY UP, YOU FOOL!
DON'T GET NEAR THAT KITE-EATING TREE!
LOOK OUT! LOOK OUT!
OH, NO! OH, GOOD GRIEF! OH, NO! OH, NO!
OH, NO!
AAUGH!
THAT'S THE MOST GRUESOME THING I'VE EVER SEEN.......
SCHULZ

AAUGH! AAUGH!

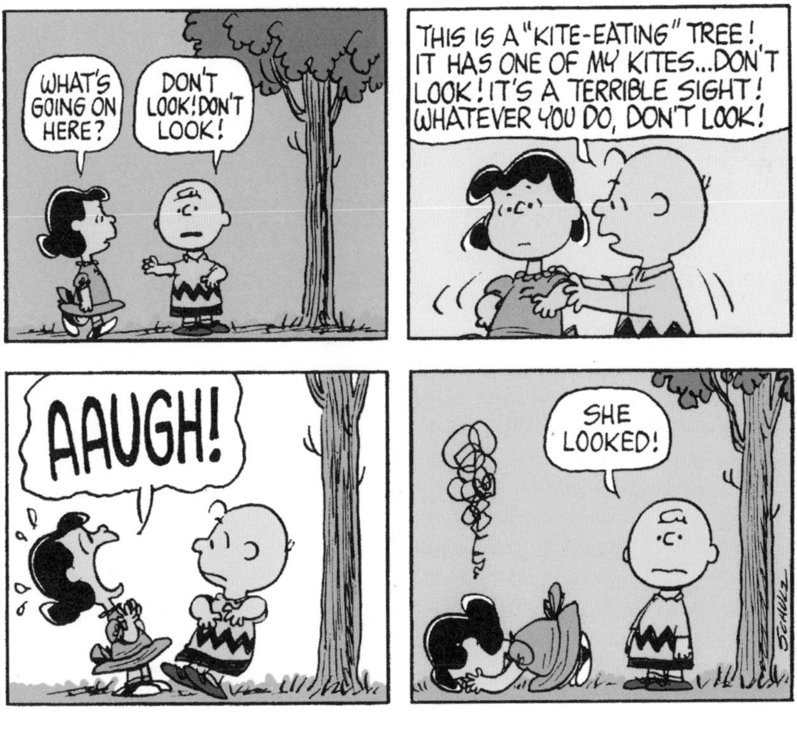
WHAT'S GOING ON HERE?
DON'T LOOK! DON'T LOOK!
THIS IS A "KITE-EATING" TREE! IT HAS ONE OF MY KITES...DON'T LOOK! IT'S A TERRIBLE SIGHT! WHATEVER YOU DO, DON'T LOOK!
AAUGH!
SHE LOOKED!
SCHULZ

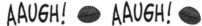

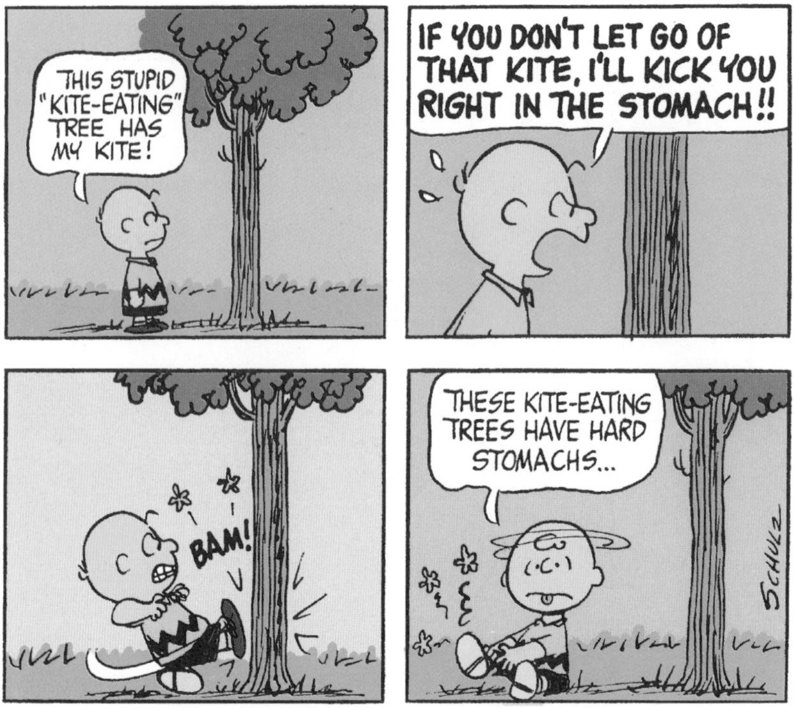
THIS STUPID "KITE-EATING" TREE HAS MY KITE!
IF YOU DON'T LET GO OF THAT KITE, I'LL KICK YOU RIGHT IN THE STOMACH!!
BAM!
THESE KITE-EATING TREES HAVE HARD STOMACHS...
SCHULZ

AAUGH! AAUGH!

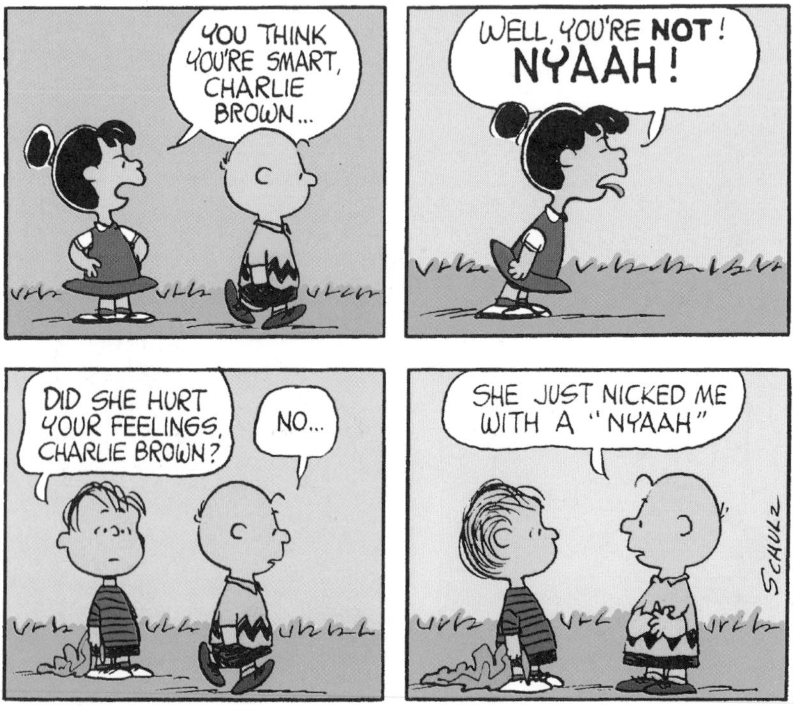
YOU THINK YOU'RE SMART, CHARLIE BROWN...
WELL, YOU'RE **NOT**! NYAAH!
DID SHE HURT YOUR FEELINGS, CHARLIE BROWN?
NO...
SHE JUST NICKED ME WITH A "NYAAH"
SCHULZ

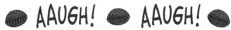

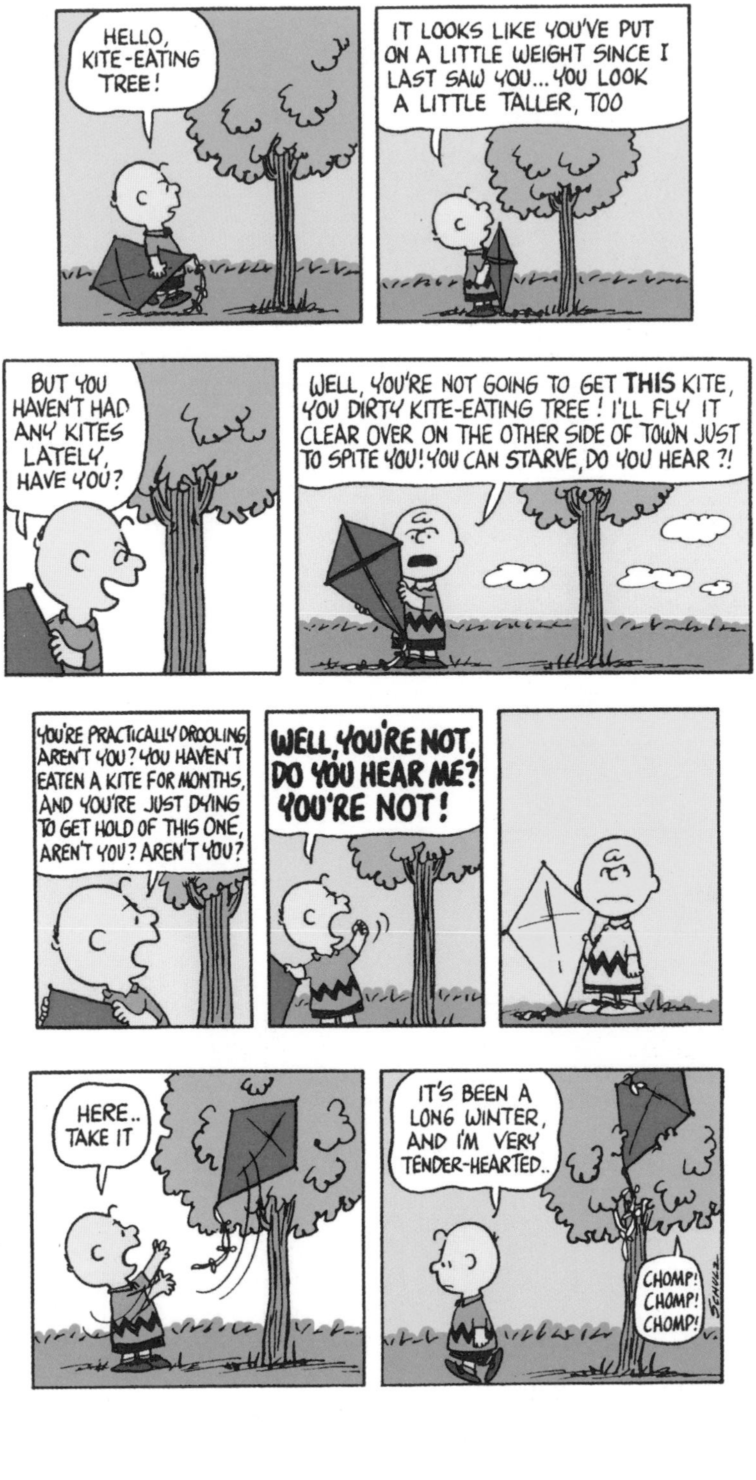
HELLO, KITE-EATING TREE!
IT LOOKS LIKE YOU'VE PUT ON A LITTLE WEIGHT SINCE I LAST SAW YOU... YOU LOOK A LITTLE TALLER, TOO
BUT YOU HAVEN'T HAD ANY KITES LATELY, HAVE YOU?
WELL, YOU'RE NOT GOING TO GET THIS KITE, YOU DIRTY KITE-EATING TREE! I'LL FLY IT CLEAR OVER ON THE OTHER SIDE OF TOWN JUST TO SPITE YOU! YOU CAN STARVE, DO YOU HEAR ?!
YOU'RE PRACTICALLY DROOLING, AREN'T YOU? YOU HAVEN'T EATEN A KITE FOR MONTHS, AND YOU'RE JUST DYING TO GET HOLD OF THIS ONE, AREN'T YOU? AREN'T YOU?
WELL, YOU'RE NOT, DO YOU HEAR ME? YOU'RE NOT!
HERE.. TAKE IT
IT'S BEEN A LONG WINTER, AND I'M VERY TENDER-HEARTED..
CHOMP! CHOMP! CHOMP!
SCHULZ

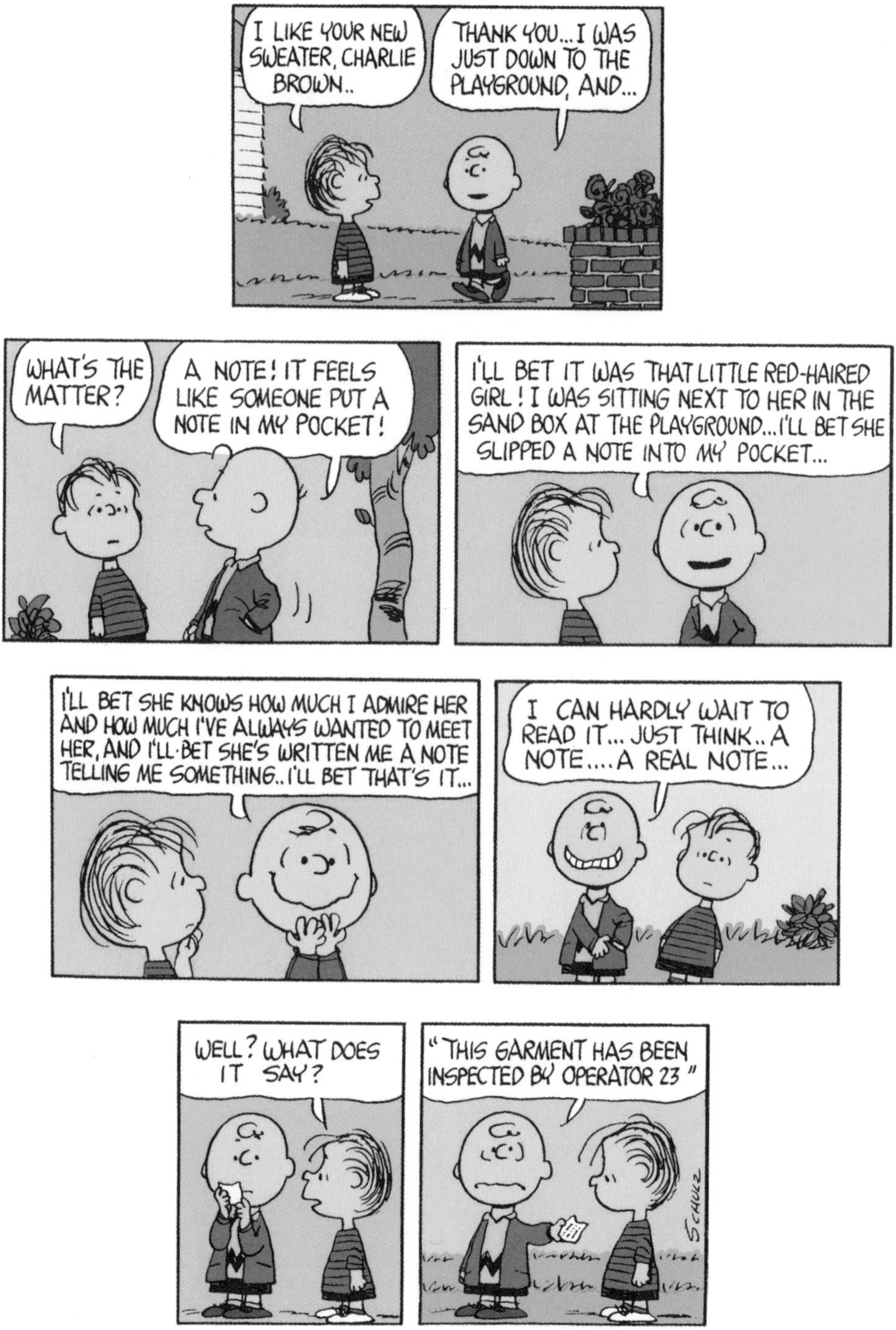
I LIKE YOUR NEW SWEATER, CHARLIE BROWN..
THANK YOU... I WAS JUST DOWN TO THE PLAYGROUND, AND...
WHAT'S THE MATTER?
A NOTE! IT FEELS LIKE SOMEONE PUT A NOTE IN MY POCKET!
I'LL BET IT WAS THAT LITTLE RED-HAIRED GIRL! I WAS SITTING NEXT TO HER IN THE SAND BOX AT THE PLAYGROUND... I'LL BET SHE SLIPPED A NOTE INTO MY POCKET...
I'LL BET SHE KNOWS HOW MUCH I ADMIRE HER AND HOW MUCH I'VE ALWAYS WANTED TO MEET HER, AND I'LL BET SHE'S WRITTEN ME A NOTE TELLING ME SOMETHING.. I'LL BET THAT'S IT...
I CAN HARDLY WAIT TO READ IT... JUST THINK.. A NOTE.... A REAL NOTE...
WELL? WHAT DOES IT SAY?
"THIS GARMENT HAS BEEN INSPECTED BY OPERATOR 23"
SCHULZ

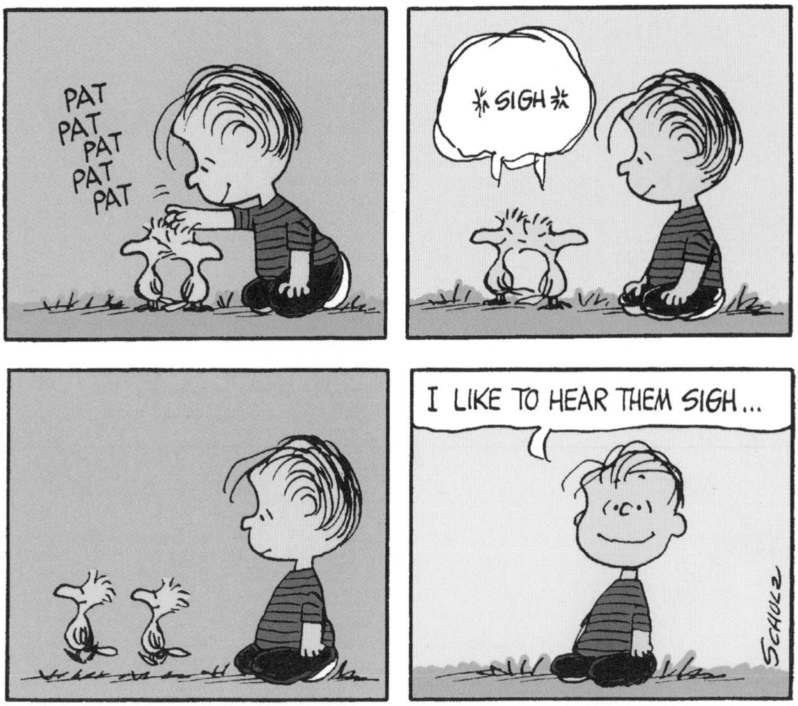
PAT PAT PAT PAT PAT
SIGH
I LIKE TO HEAR THEM SIGH...
SCHULZ

AAUGH! AAUGH!

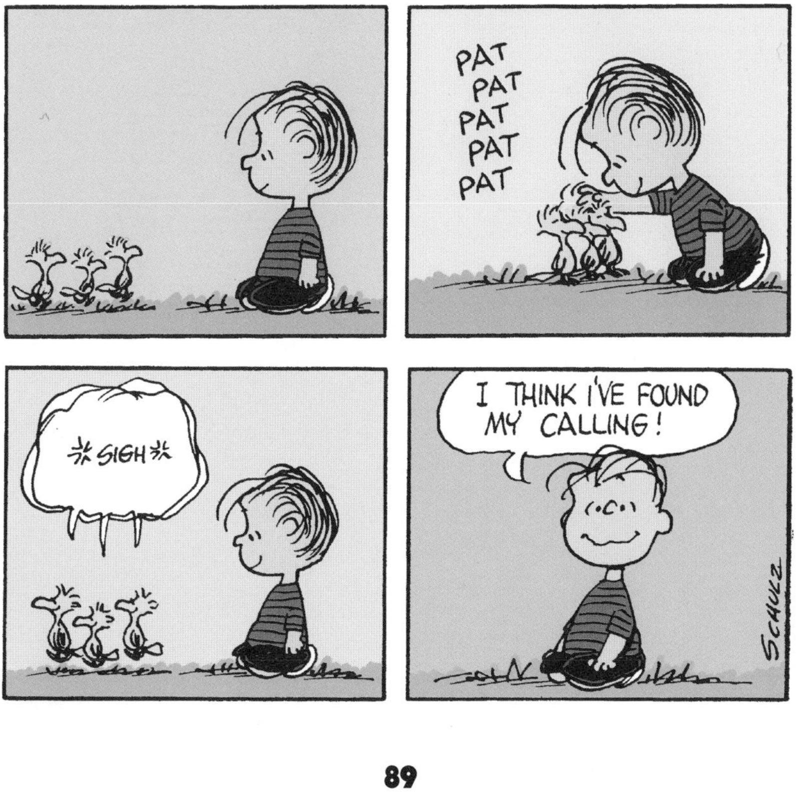
PAT PAT PAT PAT PAT
SIGH
I THINK I'VE FOUND MY CALLING!
SCHULZ

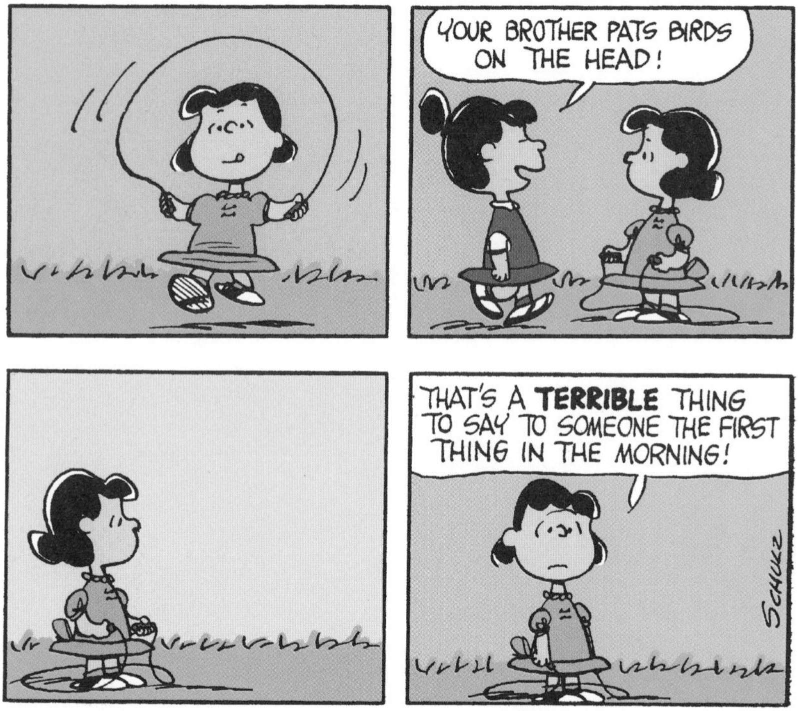
YOUR BROTHER PATS BIRDS ON THE HEAD!
THAT'S A **TERRIBLE** THING TO SAY TO SOMEONE THE FIRST THING IN THE MORNING!
SCHULZ

AAUGH! AAUGH!

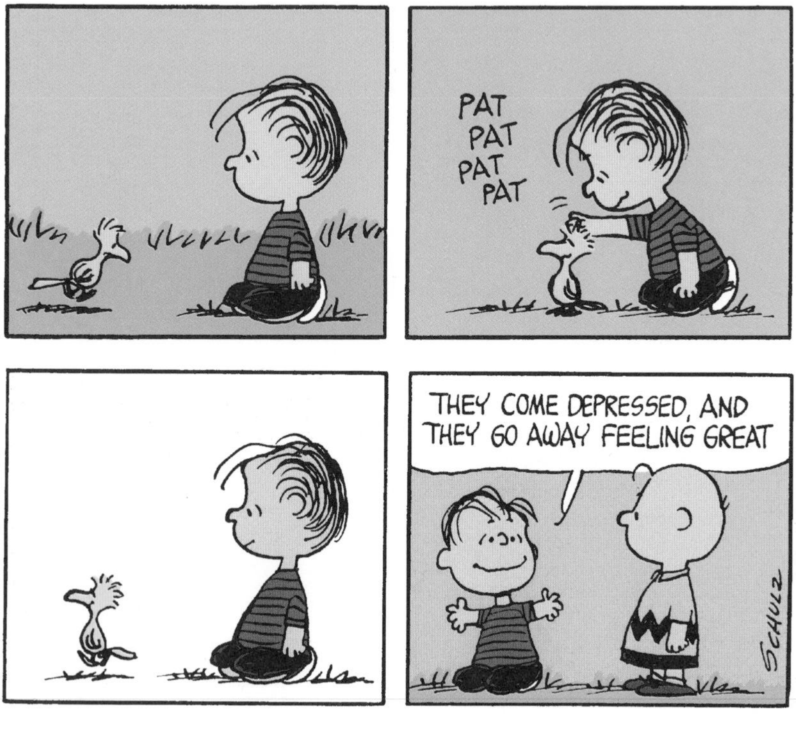
PAT PAT PAT PAT
THEY COME DEPRESSED, AND THEY GO AWAY FEELING GREAT
SCHULZ

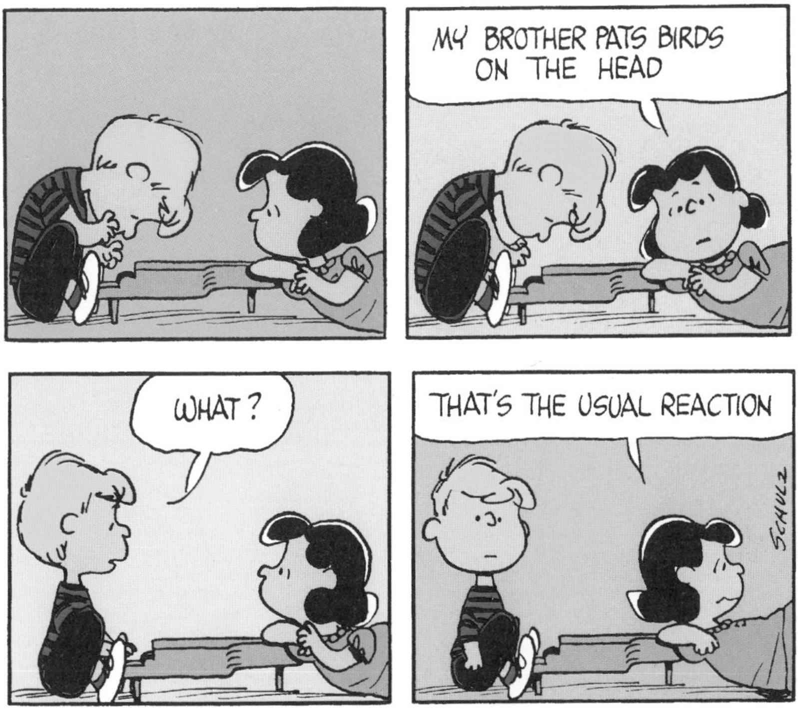
MY BROTHER PATS BIRDS ON THE HEAD
WHAT ?
THAT'S THE USUAL REACTION
SCHULZ

AAUGH! AAUGH!

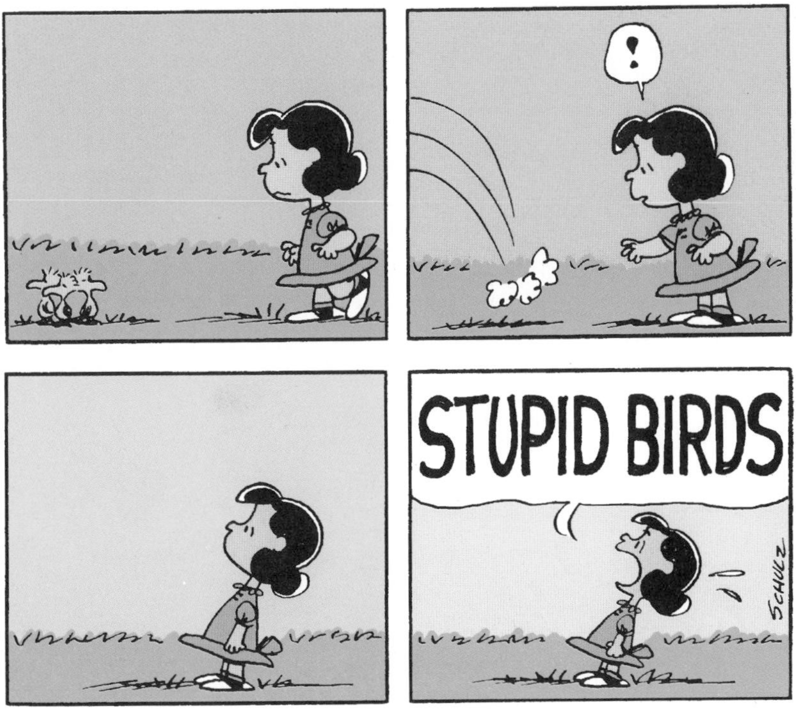
!
STUPID BIRDS
SCHULZ

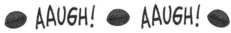

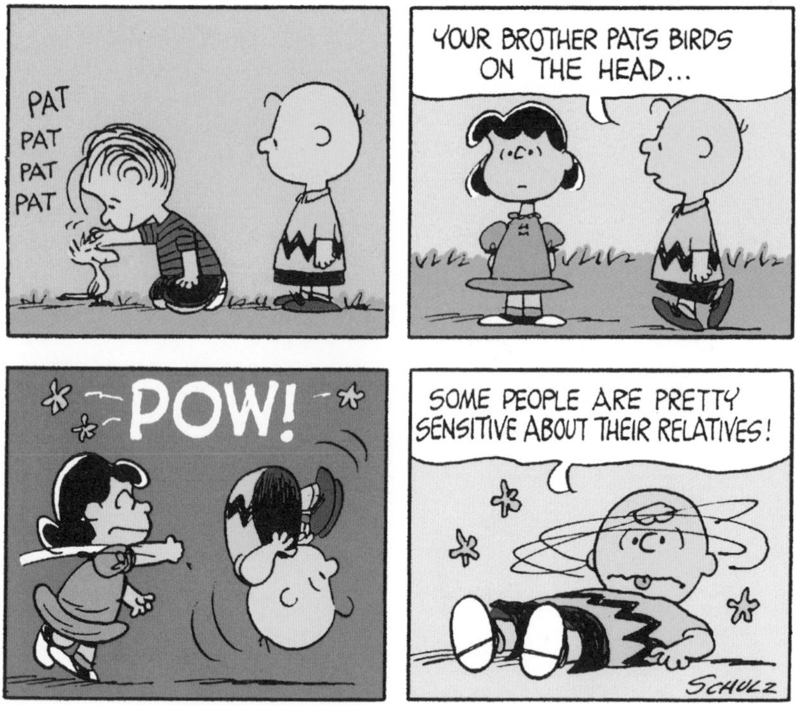
PAT
PAT
PAT
PAT
YOUR BROTHER PATS BIRDS ON THE HEAD...
POW!
SOME PEOPLE ARE PRETTY SENSITIVE ABOUT THEIR RELATIVES!
SCHULZ

AAUGH! AAUGH!

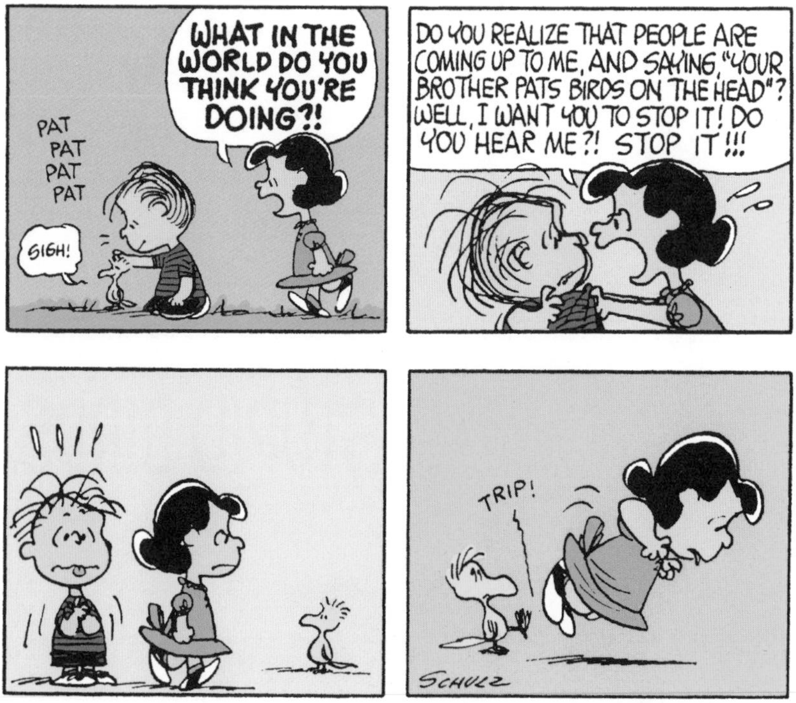
PAT
PAT
PAT
PAT
WHAT IN THE WORLD DO YOU THINK YOU'RE DOING?!
SIGH!
DO YOU REALIZE THAT PEOPLE ARE COMING UP TO ME, AND SAYING, "YOUR BROTHER PATS BIRDS ON THE HEAD"? WELL, I WANT YOU TO STOP IT! DO YOU HEAR ME?! STOP IT!!!
TRIP!
SCHULZ

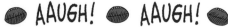

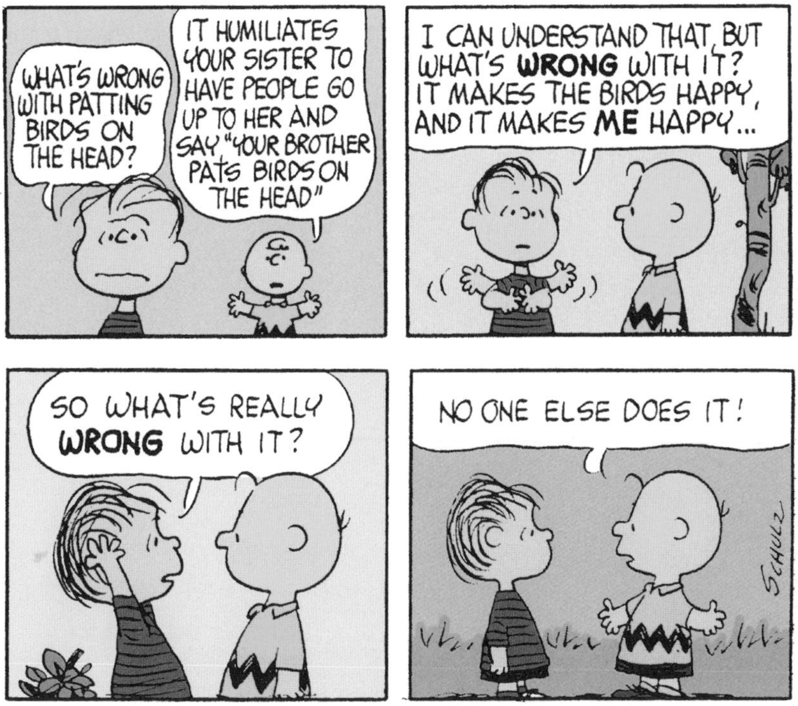
WHAT'S WRONG WITH PATTING BIRDS ON THE HEAD?
IT HUMILIATES YOUR SISTER TO HAVE PEOPLE GO UP TO HER AND SAY, "YOUR BROTHER PATS BIRDS ON THE HEAD"
I CAN UNDERSTAND THAT, BUT WHAT'S **WRONG** WITH IT? IT MAKES THE BIRDS HAPPY, AND IT MAKES **ME** HAPPY...
SO WHAT'S REALLY **WRONG** WITH IT?
NO ONE ELSE DOES IT!
SCHULZ

AAUGH! AAUGH!

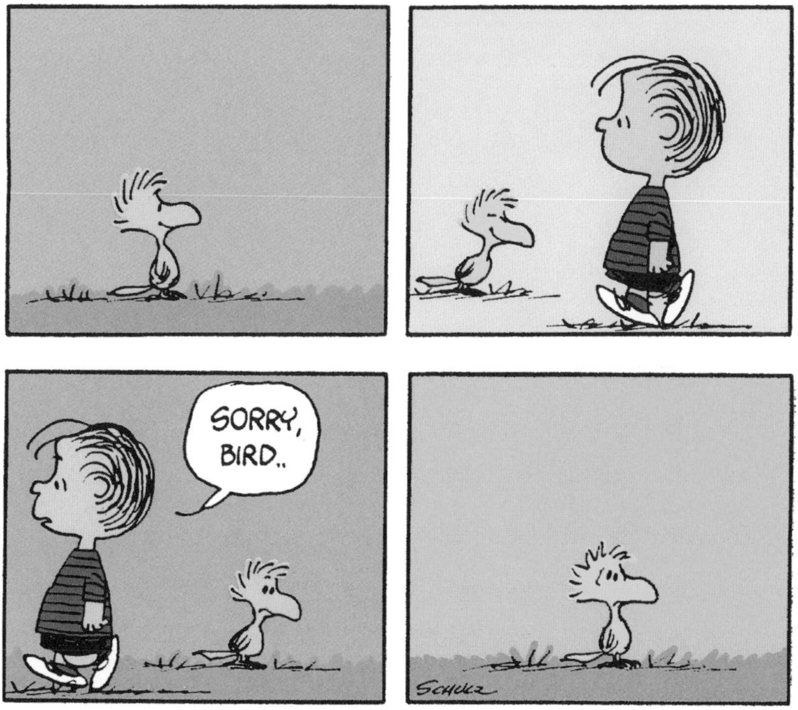
SORRY, BIRD..
SCHULZ

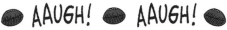

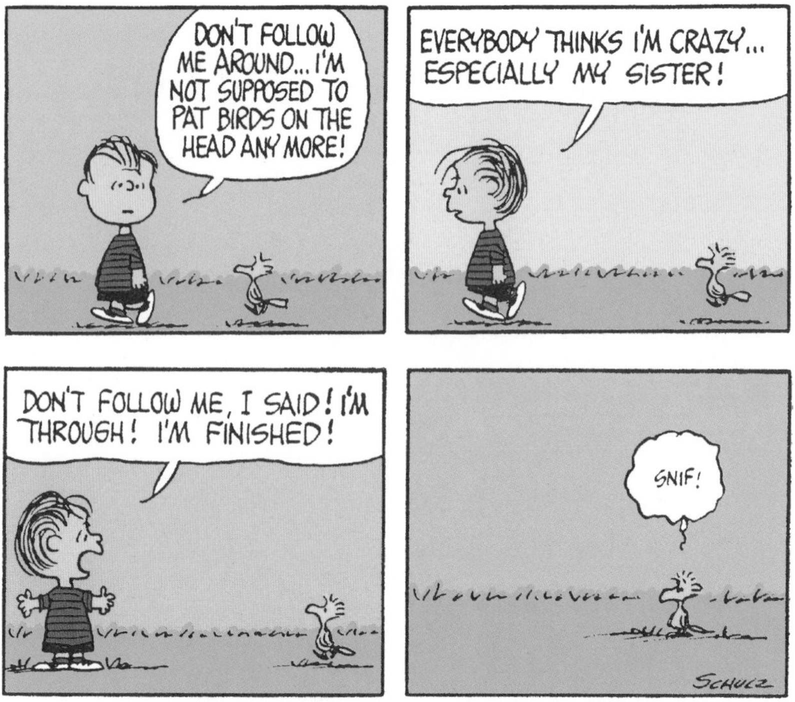
DON'T FOLLOW ME AROUND... I'M NOT SUPPOSED TO PAT BIRDS ON THE HEAD ANY MORE!
EVERYBODY THINKS I'M CRAZY... ESPECIALLY MY SISTER!
DON'T FOLLOW ME, I SAID! I'M THROUGH! I'M FINISHED!
SNIF!
SCHULZ

AAUGH! AAUGH!

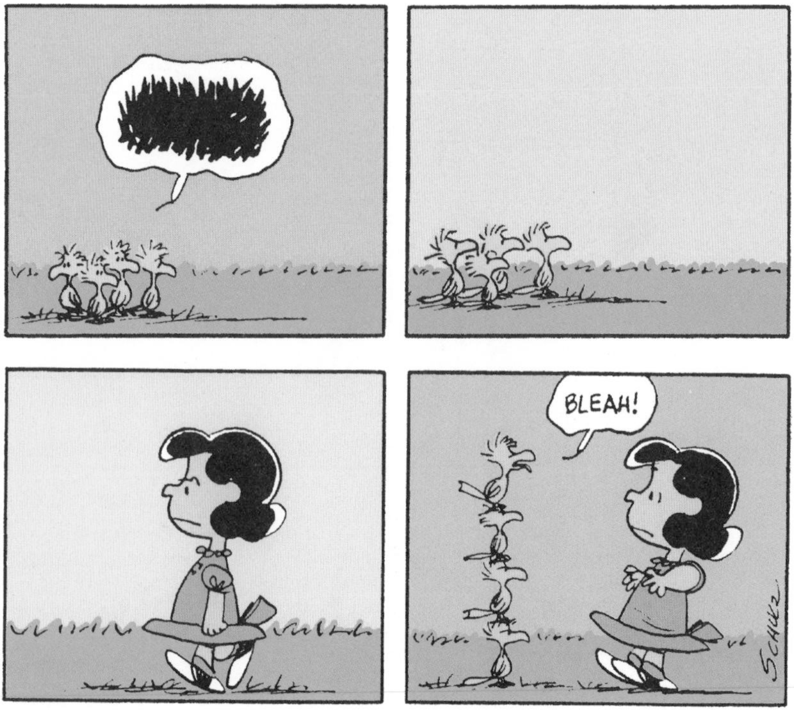
BLEAH!
SCHULZ

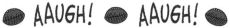

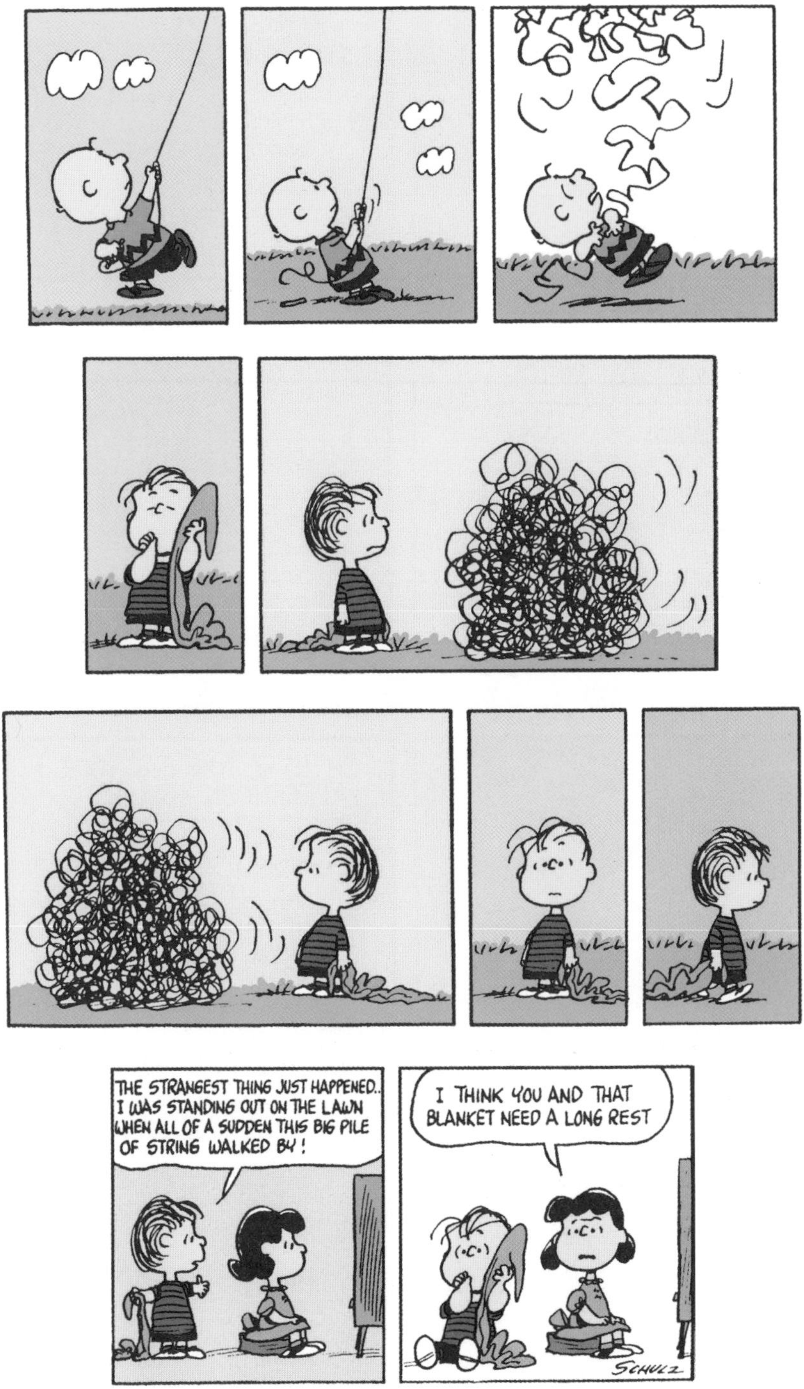
THE STRANGEST THING JUST HAPPENED.. I WAS STANDING OUT ON THE LAWN WHEN ALL OF A SUDDEN THIS BIG PILE OF STRING WALKED BY!
I THINK YOU AND THAT BLANKET NEED A LONG REST
SCHULZ

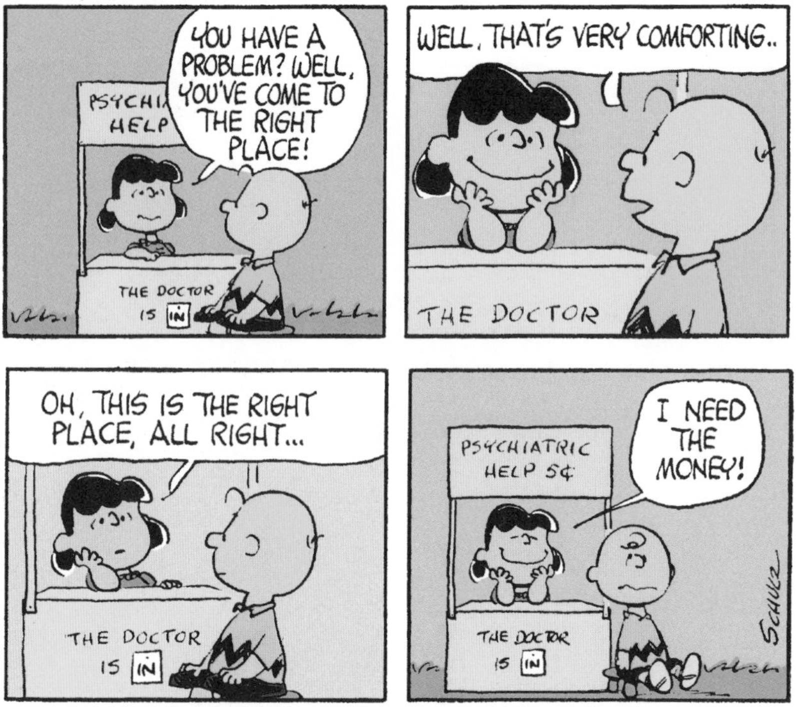
YOU HAVE A PROBLEM? WELL, YOU'VE COME TO THE RIGHT PLACE!
THE DOCTOR IS IN
WELL, THAT'S VERY COMFORTING..
THE DOCTOR
OH, THIS IS THE RIGHT PLACE, ALL RIGHT...
THE DOCTOR IS IN
PSYCHIATRIC HELP 5¢
I NEED THE MONEY!
THE DOCTOR IS IN
SCHULZ

AAUGH! AAUGH!

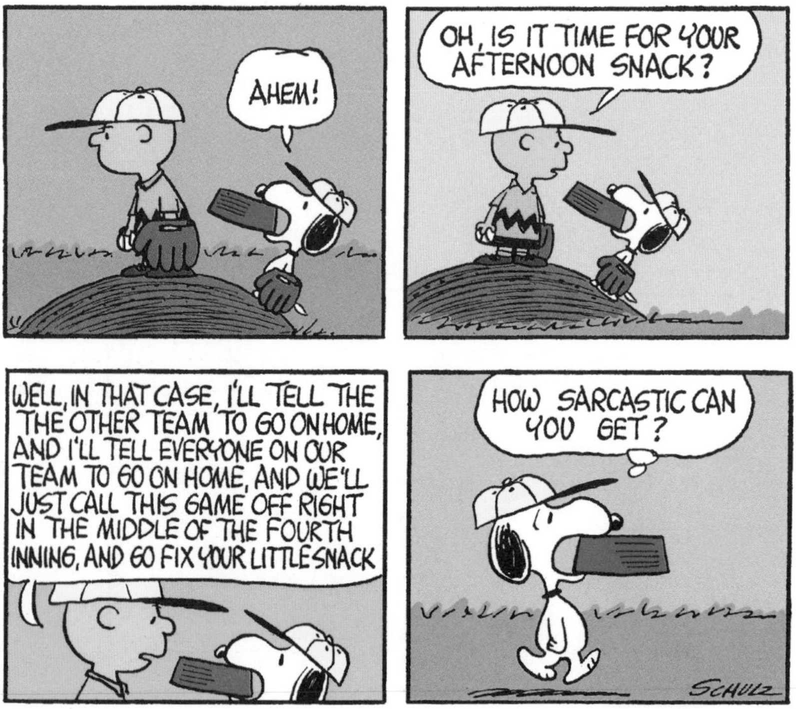
AHEM!
OH, IS IT TIME FOR YOUR AFTERNOON SNACK?
WELL, IN THAT CASE, I'LL TELL THE THE OTHER TEAM TO GO ON HOME, AND I'LL TELL EVERYONE ON OUR TEAM TO GO ON HOME, AND WE'LL JUST CALL THIS GAME OFF RIGHT IN THE MIDDLE OF THE FOURTH INNING, AND GO FIX YOUR LITTLE SNACK
HOW SARCASTIC CAN YOU GET?
SCHULZ

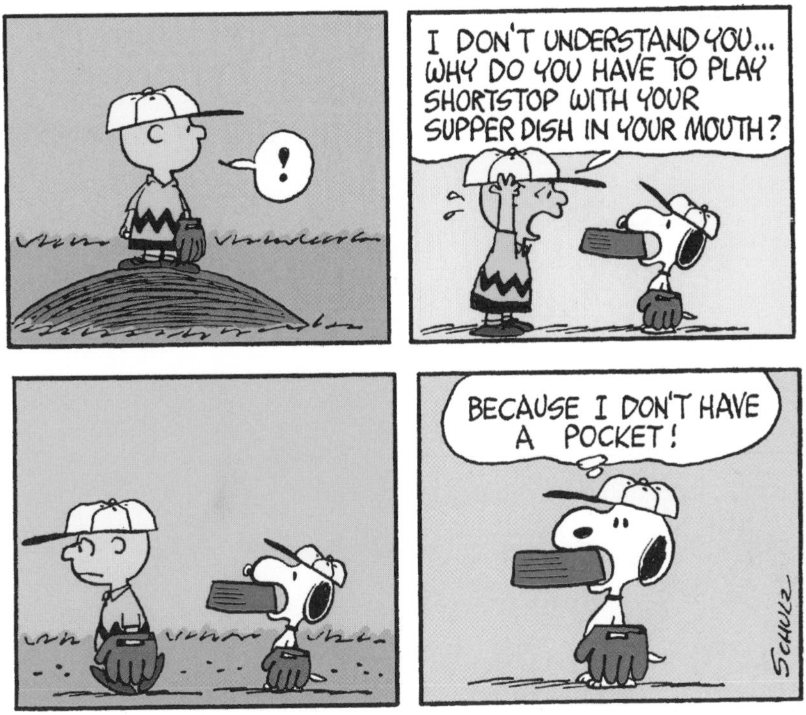
!
I DON'T UNDERSTAND YOU... WHY DO YOU HAVE TO PLAY SHORTSTOP WITH YOUR SUPPER DISH IN YOUR MOUTH?
BECAUSE I DON'T HAVE A POCKET!
SCHULZ

AAUGH! AAUGH!

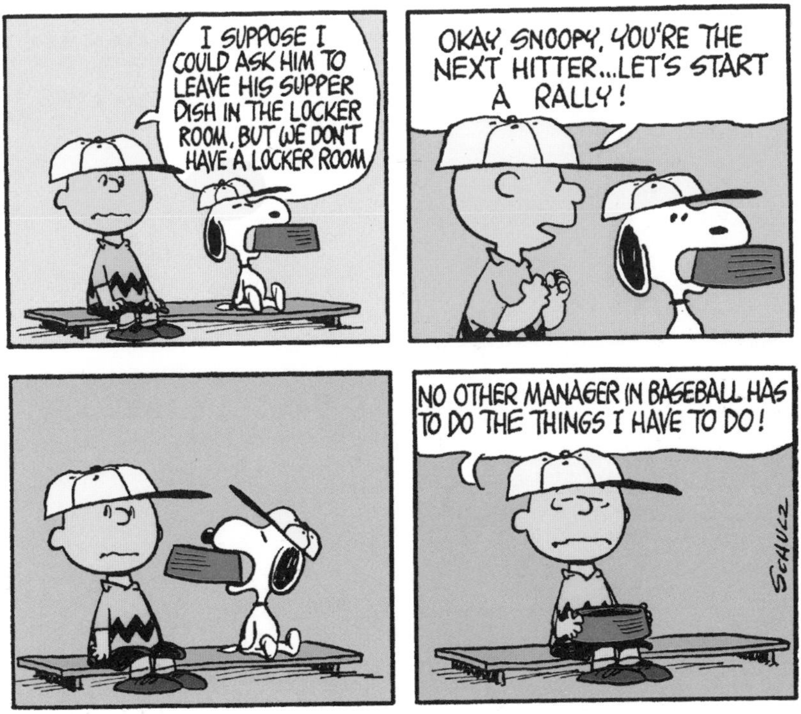
I SUPPOSE I COULD ASK HIM TO LEAVE HIS SUPPER DISH IN THE LOCKER ROOM, BUT WE DON'T HAVE A LOCKER ROOM
OKAY, SNOOPY, YOU'RE THE NEXT HITTER...LET'S START A RALLY!
NO OTHER MANAGER IN BASEBALL HAS TO DO THE THINGS I HAVE TO DO!
SCHULZ

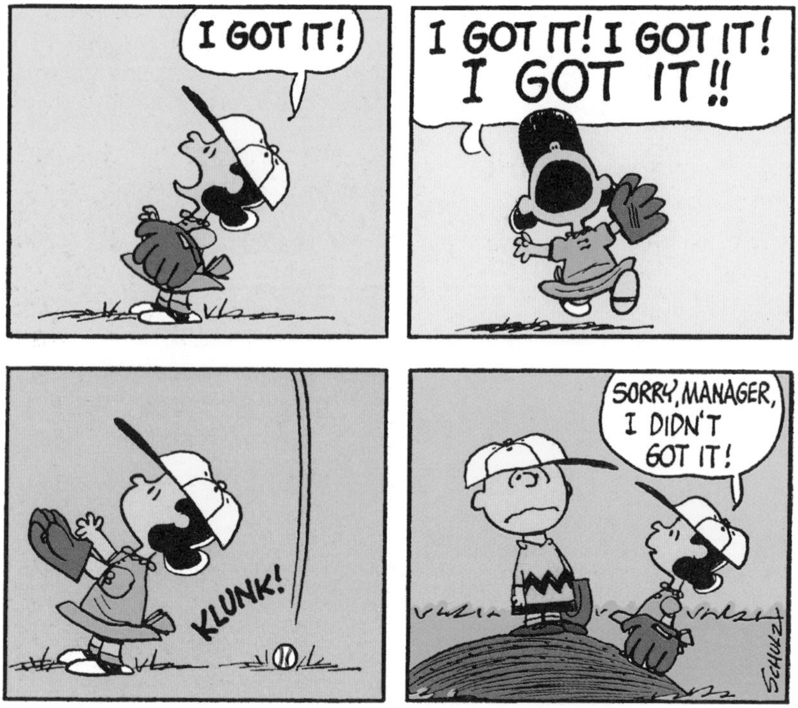
I GOT IT!
I GOT IT! I GOT IT! I GOT IT!!
KLUNK!
SORRY, MANAGER, I DIDN'T GOT IT!
SCHULZ

AAUGH! AAUGH!

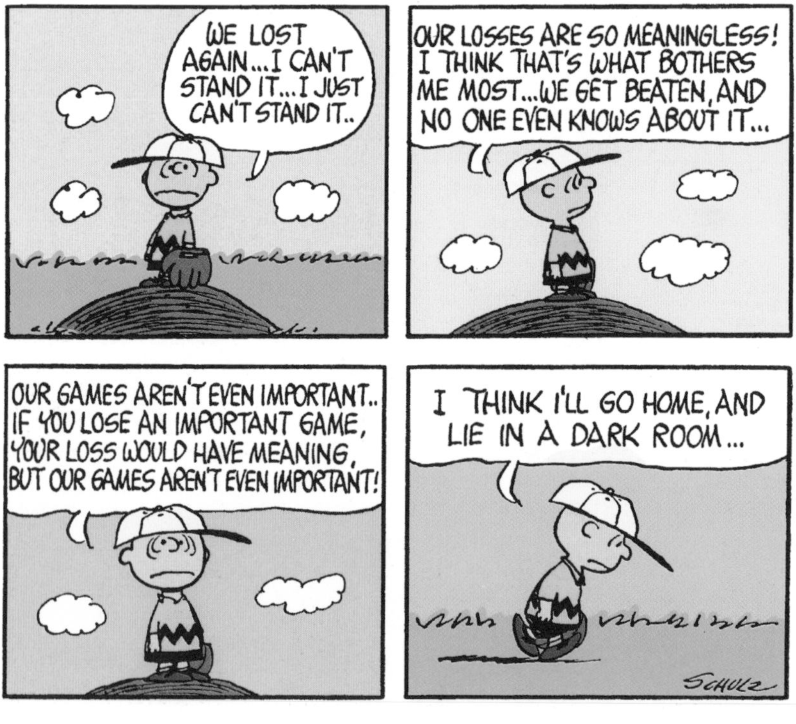
WE LOST AGAIN...I CAN'T STAND IT...I JUST CAN'T STAND IT..
OUR LOSSES ARE SO MEANINGLESS! I THINK THAT'S WHAT BOTHERS ME MOST...WE GET BEATEN, AND NO ONE EVEN KNOWS ABOUT IT...
OUR GAMES AREN'T EVEN IMPORTANT.. IF YOU LOSE AN IMPORTANT GAME, YOUR LOSS WOULD HAVE MEANING, BUT OUR GAMES AREN'T EVEN IMPORTANT!
I THINK I'LL GO HOME, AND LIE IN A DARK ROOM...
SCHULZ

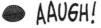

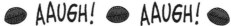

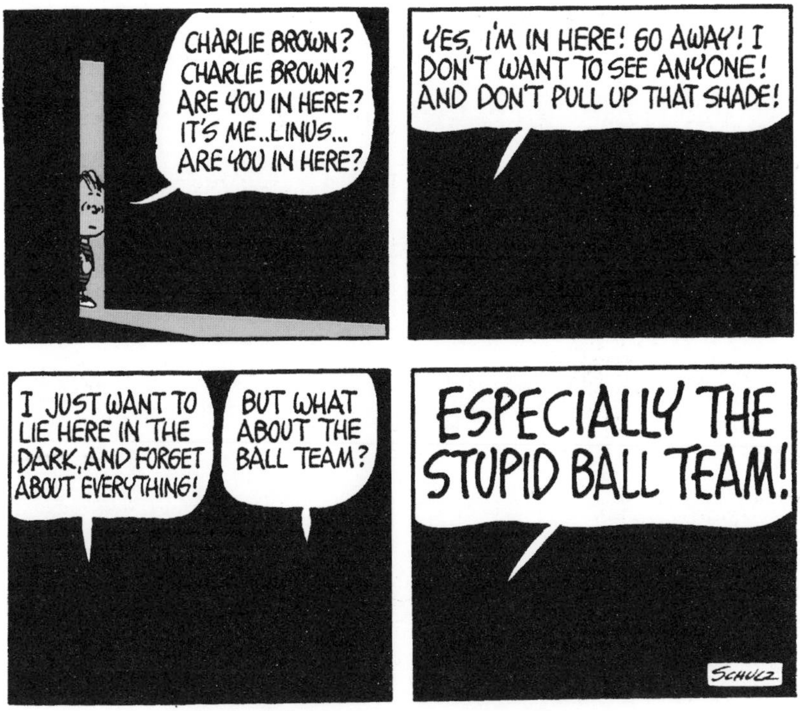
CHARLIE BROWN? CHARLIE BROWN? ARE YOU IN HERE? IT'S ME..LINUS... ARE YOU IN HERE?
YES, I'M IN HERE! GO AWAY! I DON'T WANT TO SEE ANYONE! AND DON'T PULL UP THAT SHADE!
I JUST WANT TO LIE HERE IN THE DARK, AND FORGET ABOUT EVERYTHING!
BUT WHAT ABOUT THE BALL TEAM?
ESPECIALLY THE STUPID BALL TEAM!
SCHULZ

AAUGH! AAUGH!

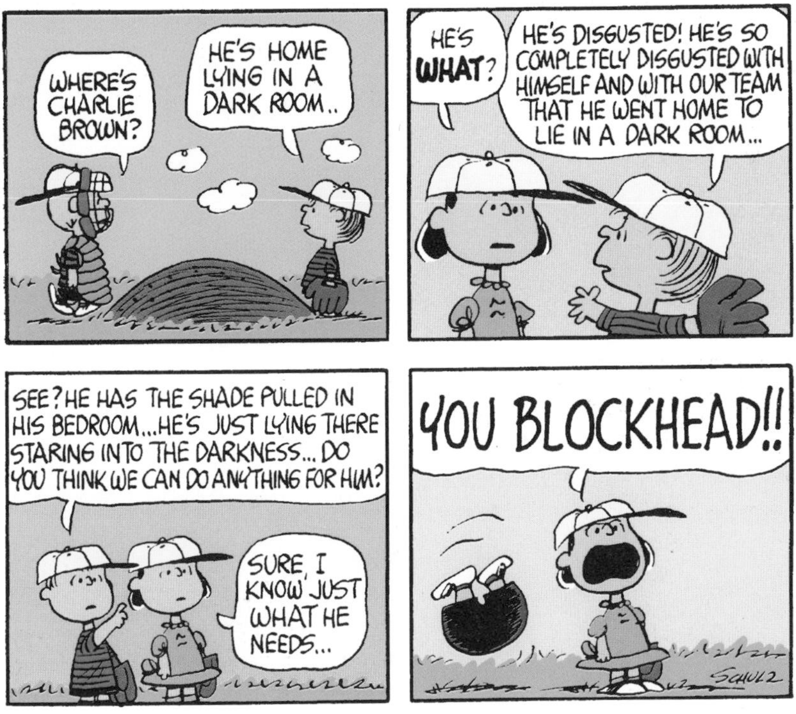
WHERE'S CHARLIE BROWN?
HE'S HOME LYING IN A DARK ROOM..
HE'S WHAT?
HE'S DISGUSTED! HE'S SO COMPLETELY DISGUSTED WITH HIMSELF AND WITH OUR TEAM THAT HE WENT HOME TO LIE IN A DARK ROOM...
SEE? HE HAS THE SHADE PULLED IN HIS BEDROOM...HE'S JUST LYING THERE STARING INTO THE DARKNESS... DO YOU THINK WE CAN DO ANYTHING FOR HIM?
SURE, I KNOW JUST WHAT HE NEEDS...
YOU BLOCKHEAD!!
SCHULZ

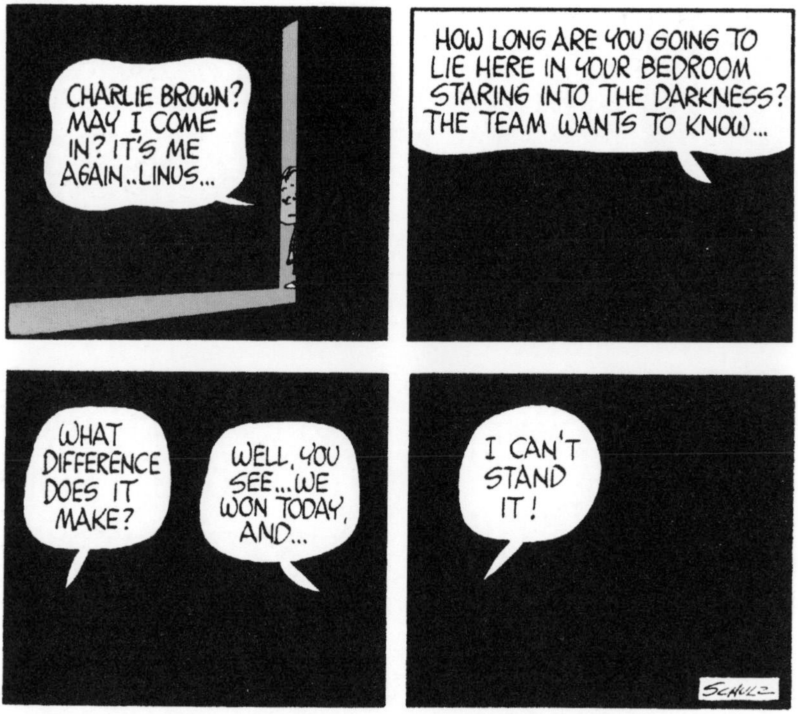
CHARLIE BROWN? MAY I COME IN? IT'S ME AGAIN..LINUS...
HOW LONG ARE YOU GOING TO LIE HERE IN YOUR BEDROOM STARING INTO THE DARKNESS? THE TEAM WANTS TO KNOW...
WHAT DIFFERENCE DOES IT MAKE?
WELL, YOU SEE...WE WON TODAY, AND...
I CAN'T STAND IT!
SCHULZ

AAUGH! AAUGH!

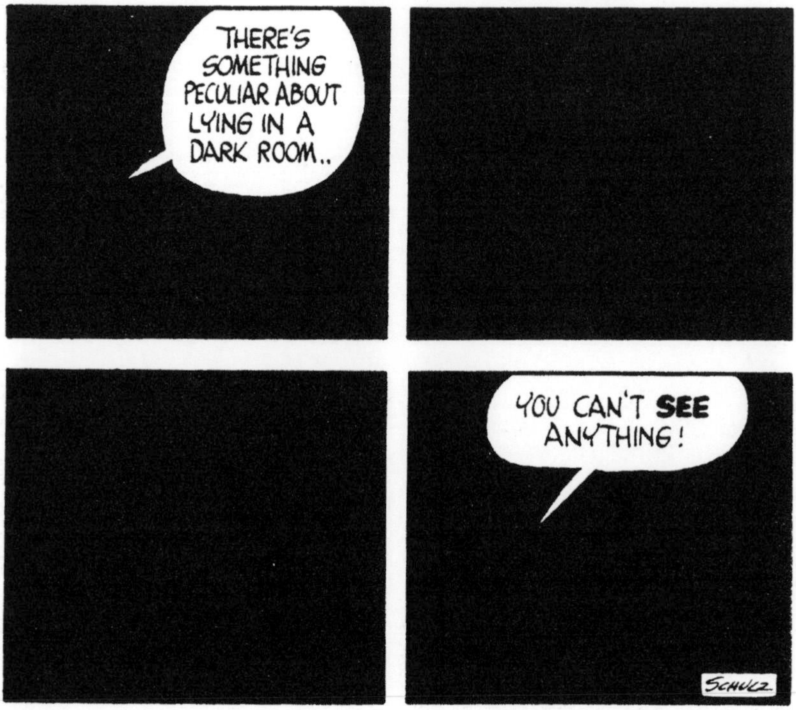
THERE'S SOMETHING PECULIAR ABOUT LYING IN A DARK ROOM..
YOU CAN'T **SEE** ANYTHING!
SCHULZ

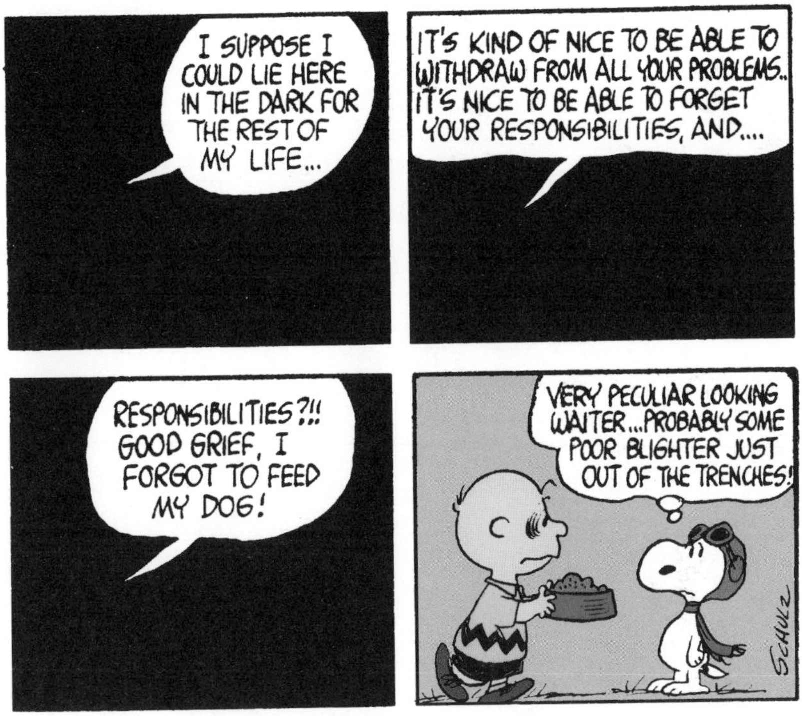
I SUPPOSE I COULD LIE HERE IN THE DARK FOR THE REST OF MY LIFE...
IT'S KIND OF NICE TO BE ABLE TO WITHDRAW FROM ALL YOUR PROBLEMS.. IT'S NICE TO BE ABLE TO FORGET YOUR RESPONSIBILITIES, AND....
RESPONSIBILITIES?!! GOOD GRIEF, I FORGOT TO FEED MY DOG!
VERY PECULIAR LOOKING WAITER...PROBABLY SOME POOR BLIGHTER JUST OUT OF THE TRENCHES!
SCHULZ

AAUGH! AAUGH!

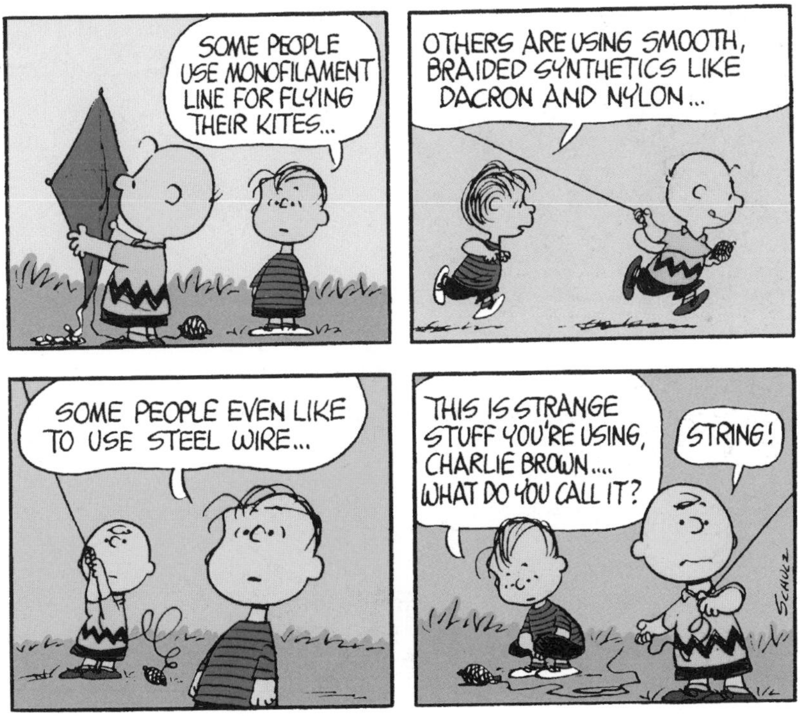
SOME PEOPLE USE MONOFILAMENT LINE FOR FLYING THEIR KITES...
OTHERS ARE USING SMOOTH, BRAIDED SYNTHETICS LIKE DACRON AND NYLON...
SOME PEOPLE EVEN LIKE TO USE STEEL WIRE...
THIS IS STRANGE STUFF YOU'RE USING, CHARLIE BROWN.... WHAT DO YOU CALL IT?
STRING!
SCHULZ

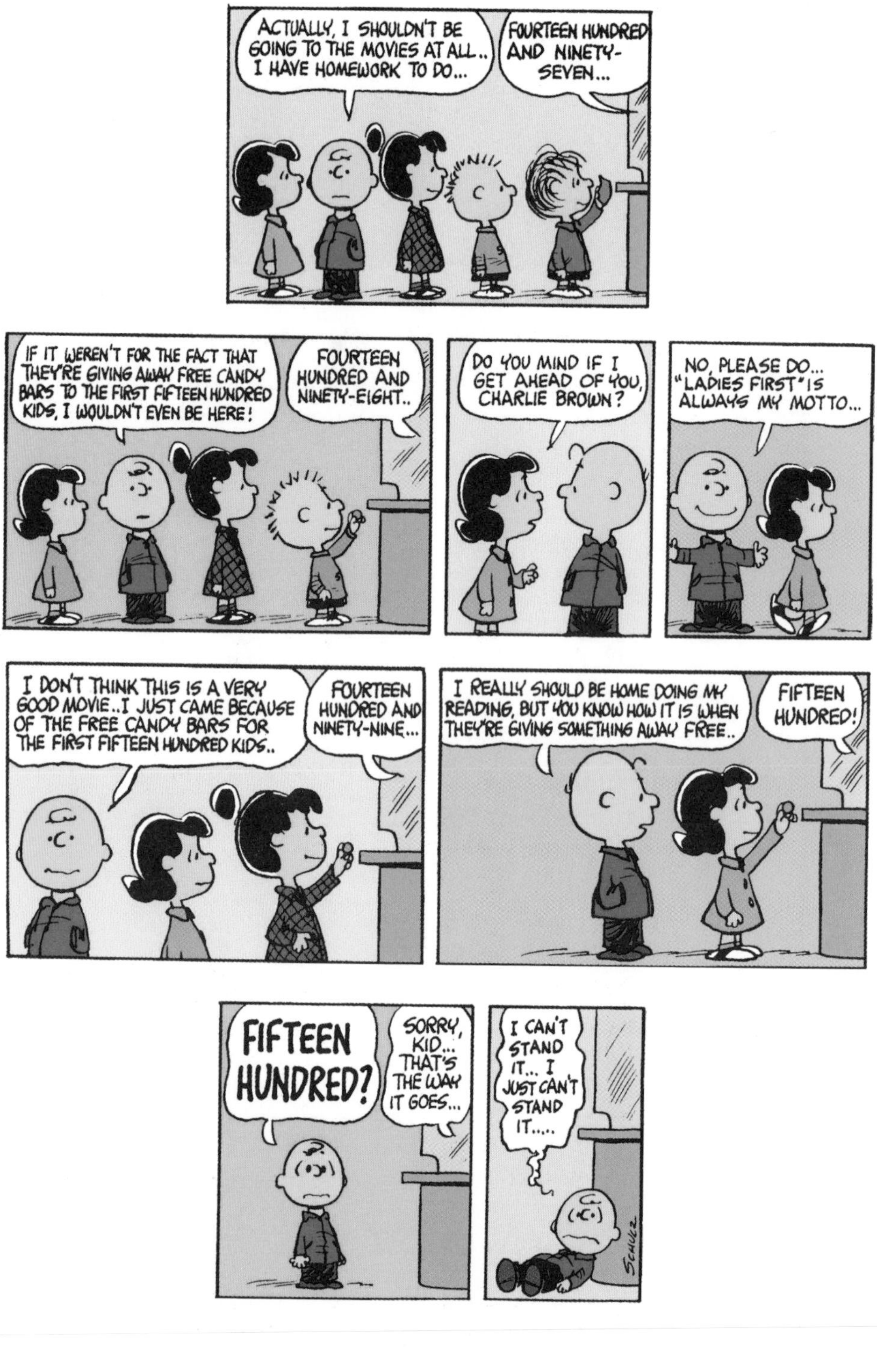
ACTUALLY, I SHOULDN'T BE GOING TO THE MOVIES AT ALL.. I HAVE HOMEWORK TO DO...
FOURTEEN HUNDRED AND NINETY-SEVEN...
IF IT WEREN'T FOR THE FACT THAT THEY'RE GIVING AWAY FREE CANDY BARS TO THE FIRST FIFTEEN HUNDRED KIDS, I WOULDN'T EVEN BE HERE!
FOURTEEN HUNDRED AND NINETY-EIGHT..
DO YOU MIND IF I GET AHEAD OF YOU, CHARLIE BROWN?
NO, PLEASE DO... "LADIES FIRST" IS ALWAYS MY MOTTO...
I DON'T THINK THIS IS A VERY GOOD MOVIE..I JUST CAME BECAUSE OF THE FREE CANDY BARS FOR THE FIRST FIFTEEN HUNDRED KIDS..
FOURTEEN HUNDRED AND NINETY-NINE...
I REALLY SHOULD BE HOME DOING MY READING, BUT YOU KNOW HOW IT IS WHEN THEY'RE GIVING SOMETHING AWAY FREE..
FIFTEEN HUNDRED!
FIFTEEN HUNDRED?
SORRY, KID... THAT'S THE WAY IT GOES...
I CAN'T STAND IT... I JUST CAN'T STAND IT.....
SCHULZ

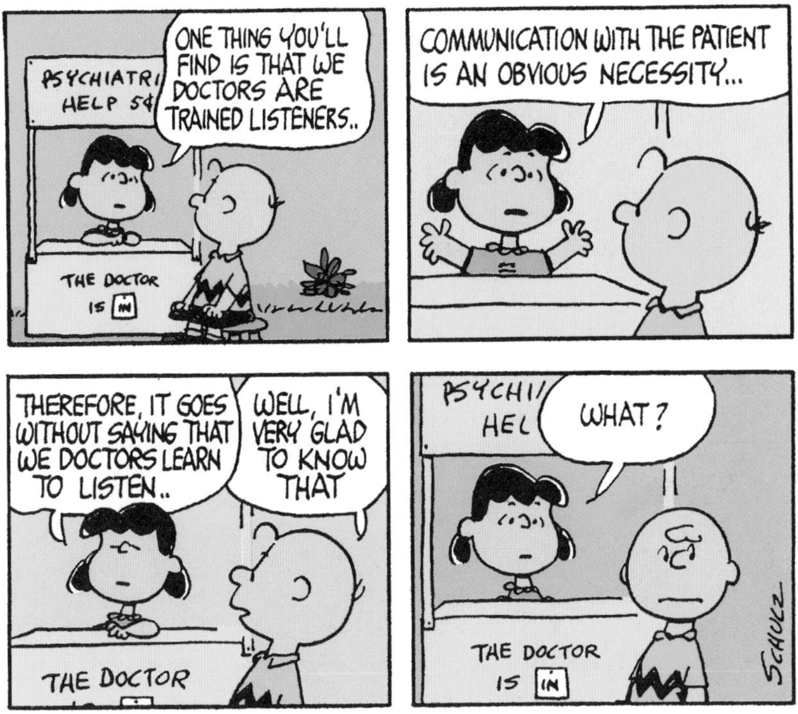
PSYCHIATRI
HELP 5¢
ONE THING YOU'LL FIND IS THAT WE DOCTORS ARE TRAINED LISTENERS..
THE DOCTOR IS IN
COMMUNICATION WITH THE PATIENT IS AN OBVIOUS NECESSITY...
THEREFORE, IT GOES WITHOUT SAYING THAT WE DOCTORS LEARN TO LISTEN..
WELL, I'M VERY GLAD TO KNOW THAT
THE DOCTOR
PSYCHI
HEL
WHAT?
THE DOCTOR IS IN
SCHULZ

AAUGH! AAUGH!

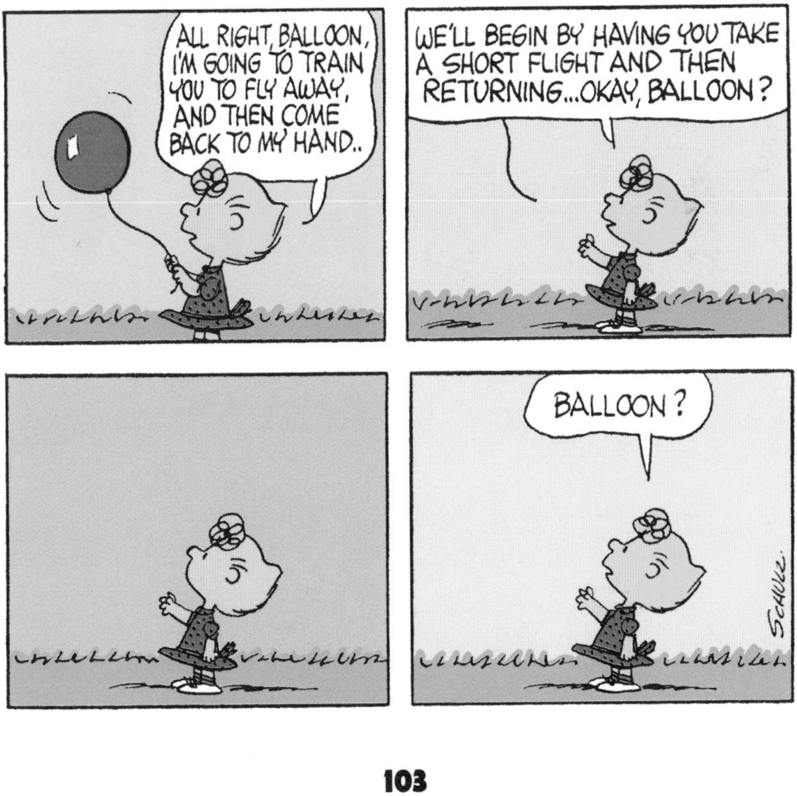
ALL RIGHT, BALLOON, I'M GOING TO TRAIN YOU TO FLY AWAY, AND THEN COME BACK TO MY HAND..
WE'LL BEGIN BY HAVING YOU TAKE A SHORT FLIGHT AND THEN RETURNING...OKAY, BALLOON?
BALLOON?
SCHULZ

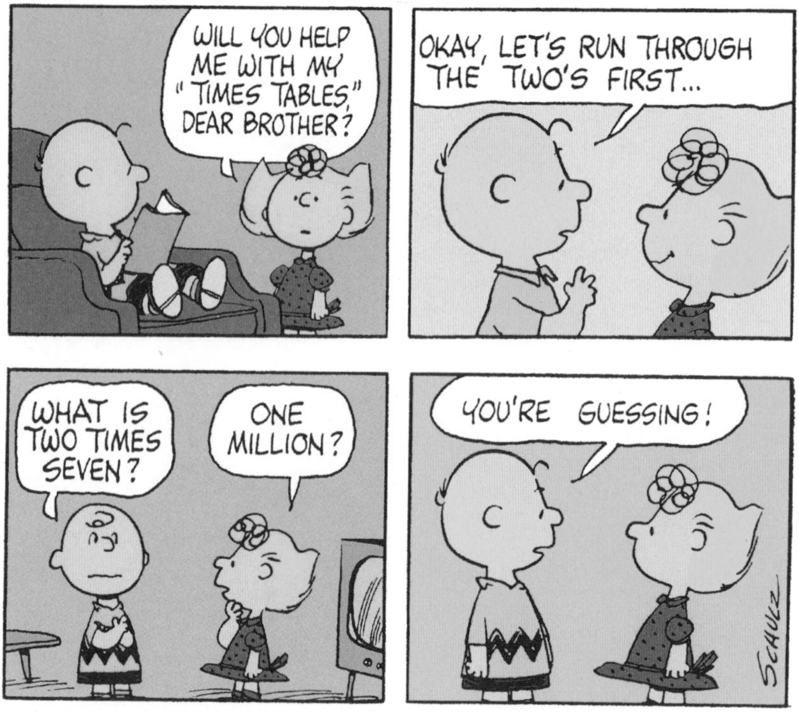
WILL YOU HELP ME WITH MY "TIMES TABLES," DEAR BROTHER?
OKAY, LET'S RUN THROUGH THE TWO'S FIRST...
WHAT IS TWO TIMES SEVEN?
ONE MILLION?
YOU'RE GUESSING!
SCHULZ

AAUGH! AAUGH!

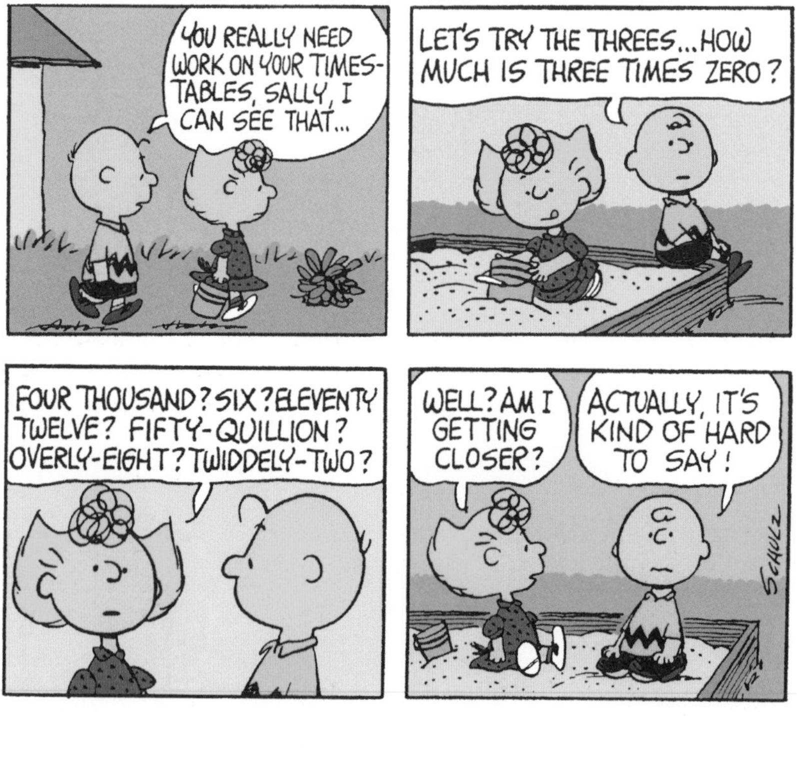
YOU REALLY NEED WORK ON YOUR TIMES-TABLES, SALLY, I CAN SEE THAT...
LET'S TRY THE THREES...HOW MUCH IS THREE TIMES ZERO?
FOUR THOUSAND? SIX? ELEVENTY TWELVE? FIFTY-QUILLION? OVERLY-EIGHT? TWIDDELY-TWO?
WELL? AM I GETTING CLOSER?
ACTUALLY, IT'S KIND OF HARD TO SAY!
SCHULZ

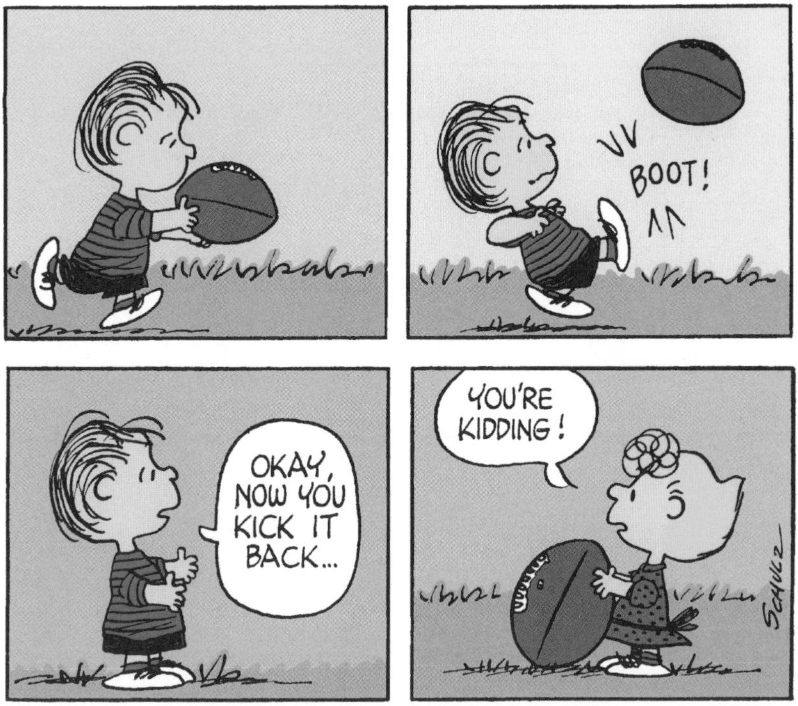
BOOT!
OKAY, NOW YOU KICK IT BACK...
YOU'RE KIDDING!
SCHULZ

AAUGH! AAUGH!

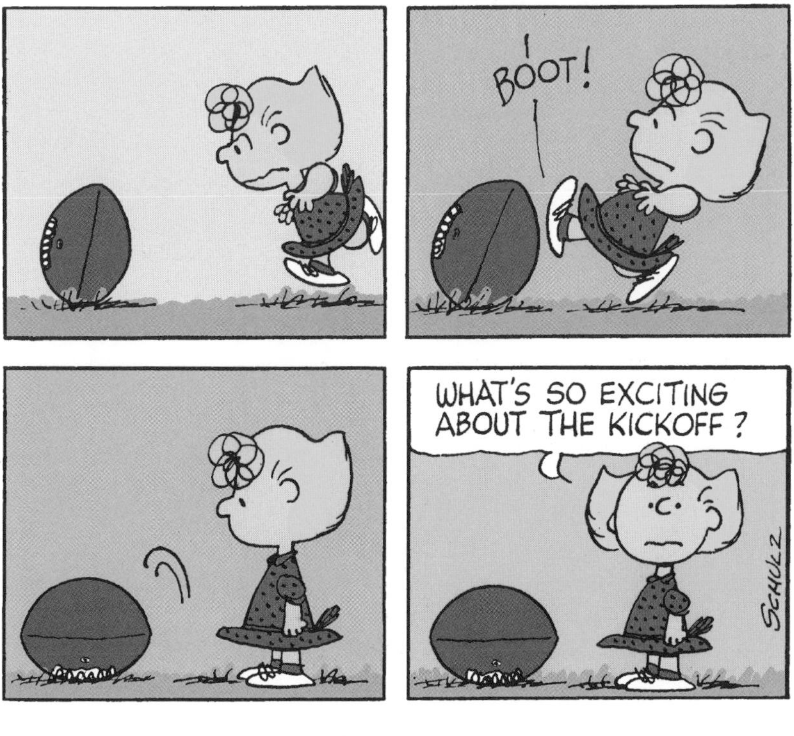
BOOT!
WHAT'S SO EXCITING ABOUT THE KICKOFF?
SCHULZ

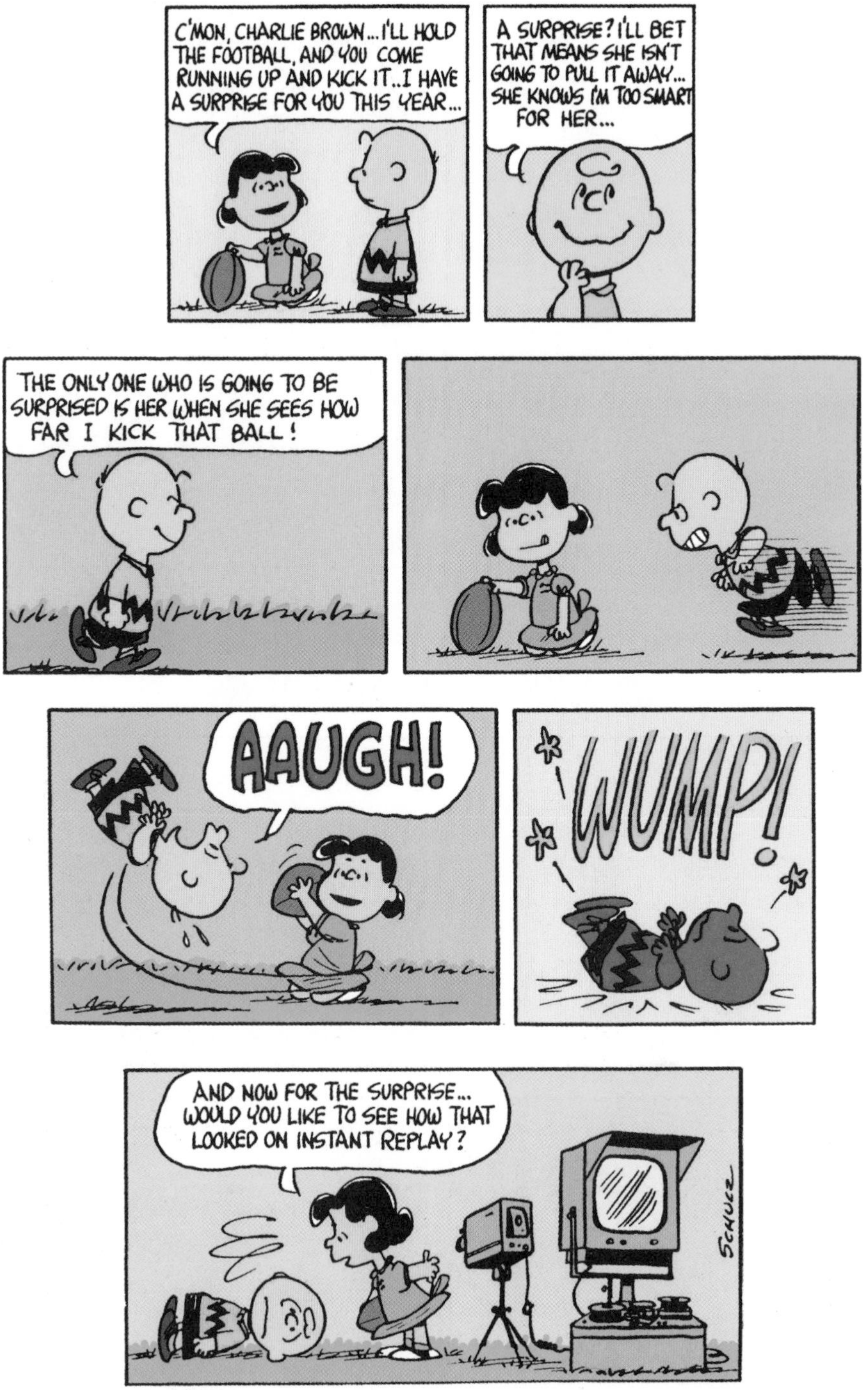
C'MON, CHARLIE BROWN... I'LL HOLD THE FOOTBALL, AND YOU COME RUNNING UP AND KICK IT.. I HAVE A SURPRISE FOR YOU THIS YEAR...
A SURPRISE? I'LL BET THAT MEANS SHE ISN'T GOING TO PULL IT AWAY... SHE KNOWS I'M TOO SMART FOR HER...
THE ONLY ONE WHO IS GOING TO BE SURPRISED IS HER WHEN SHE SEES HOW FAR I KICK THAT BALL!
AAUGH!
WUMP!
AND NOW FOR THE SURPRISE... WOULD YOU LIKE TO SEE HOW THAT LOOKED ON INSTANT REPLAY?
SCHULZ

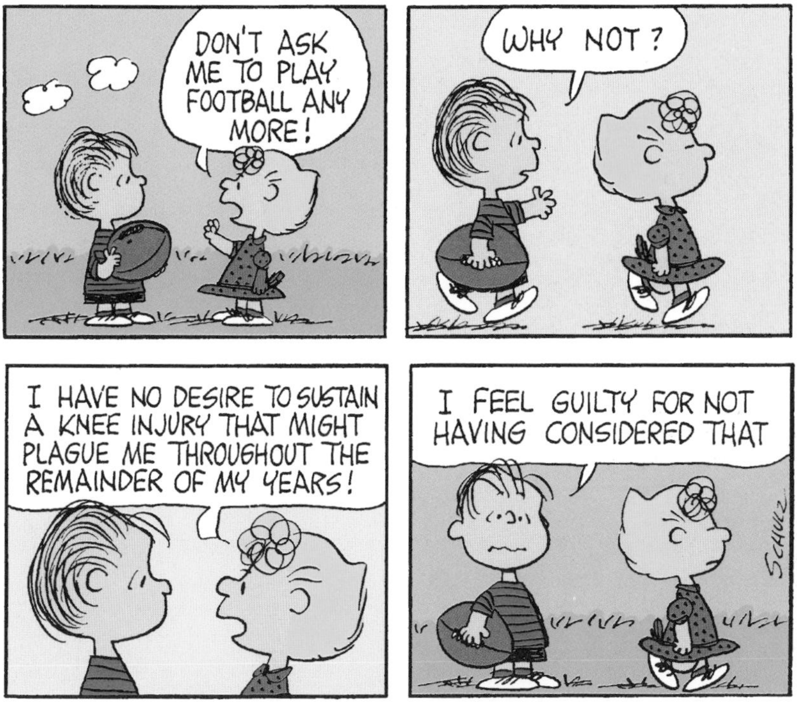
DON'T ASK ME TO PLAY FOOTBALL ANY MORE!
WHY NOT?
I HAVE NO DESIRE TO SUSTAIN A KNEE INJURY THAT MIGHT PLAGUE ME THROUGHOUT THE REMAINDER OF MY YEARS!
I FEEL GUILTY FOR NOT HAVING CONSIDERED THAT
SCHULZ

AAUGH! AAUGH!

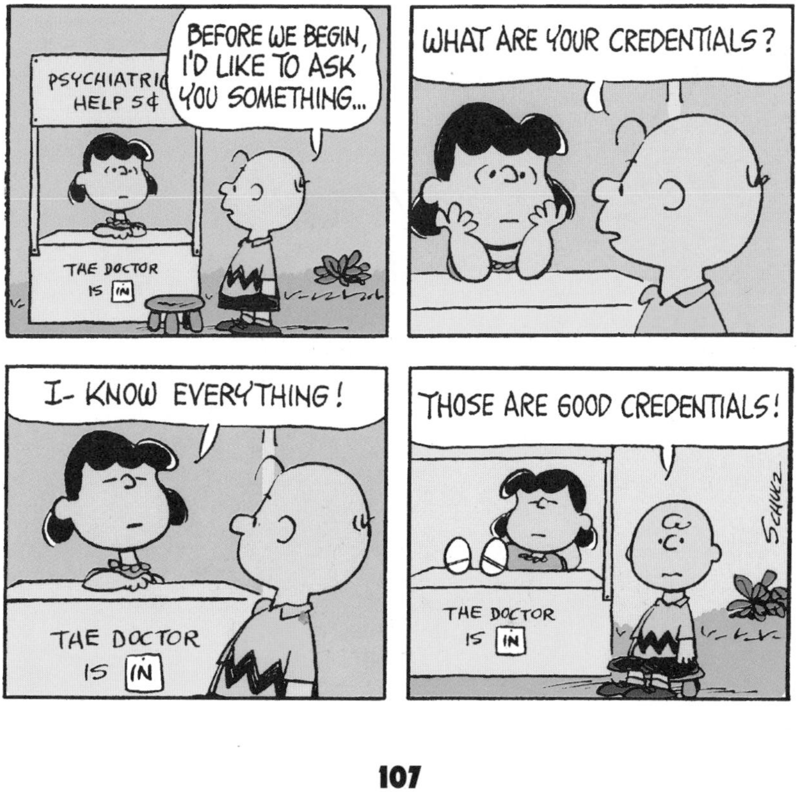
PSYCHIATRIC HELP 5¢
THE DOCTOR IS IN
BEFORE WE BEGIN, I'D LIKE TO ASK YOU SOMETHING...
WHAT ARE YOUR CREDENTIALS?
I- KNOW EVERYTHING!
THE DOCTOR IS IN
THOSE ARE GOOD CREDENTIALS!
THE DOCTOR IS IN
SCHULZ

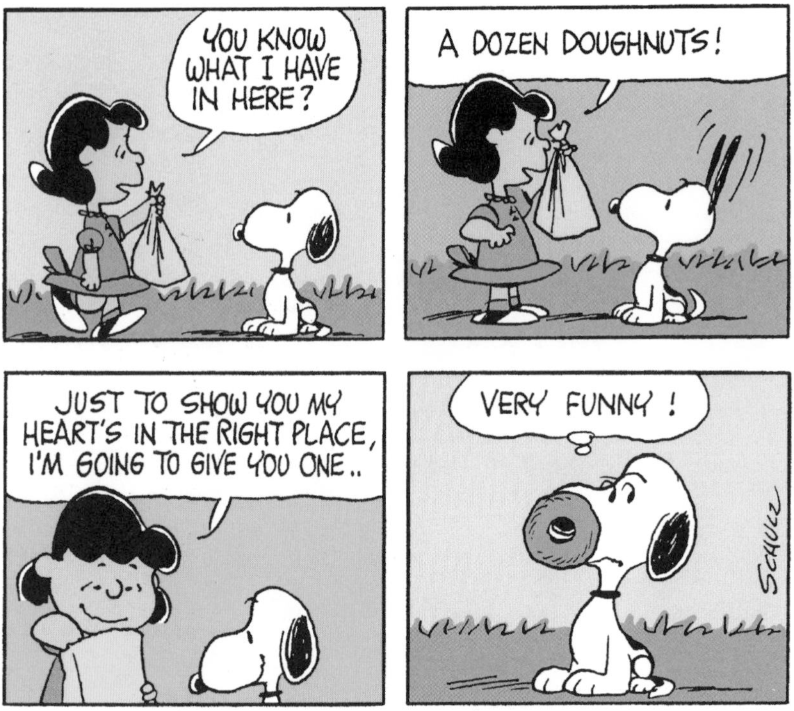
YOU KNOW WHAT I HAVE IN HERE?
A DOZEN DOUGHNUTS!
JUST TO SHOW YOU MY HEART'S IN THE RIGHT PLACE, I'M GOING TO GIVE YOU ONE..
VERY FUNNY!
SCHULZ

AAUGH! AAUGH!

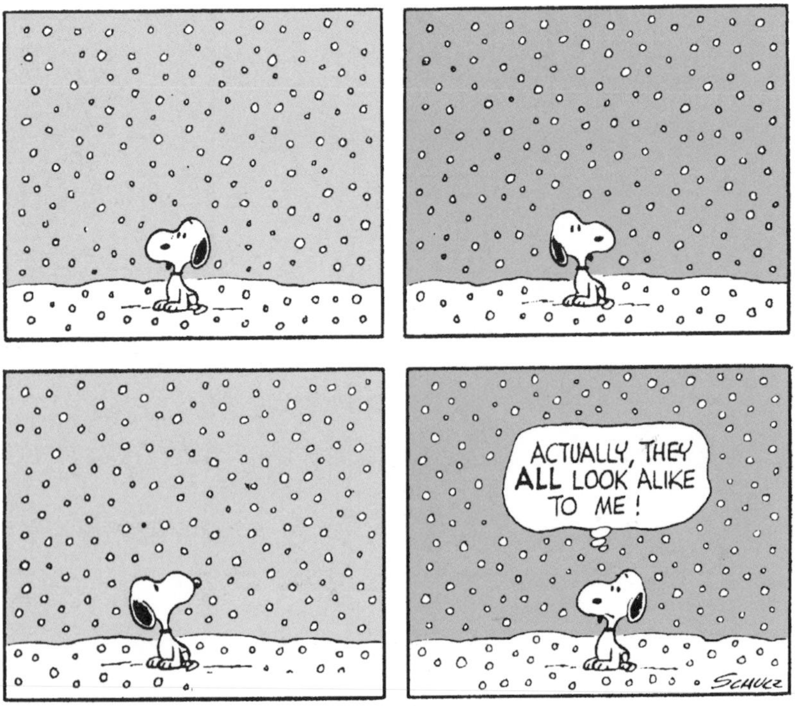
ACTUALLY, THEY **ALL** LOOK ALIKE TO ME!
SCHULZ

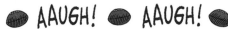

IF YOU HIT ME WITH THAT SNOWBALL, YOU'RE GONNA BE SORRY!

WOP!

OH, I'M SORRY! YOU'RE RIGHT.. I'M VERY SORRY! I HIT MY OWN SISTER WITH A SNOWBALL, AND NOW I'M REAL SORRY... I'M SO SORRY!

YOU WERE REALLY RIGHT! HOW DID YOU KNOW I'D BE SO SORRY? I'M REALLY SORRY!

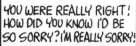

POW!

HOW SORRY CAN YOU GET?

SCHULZ

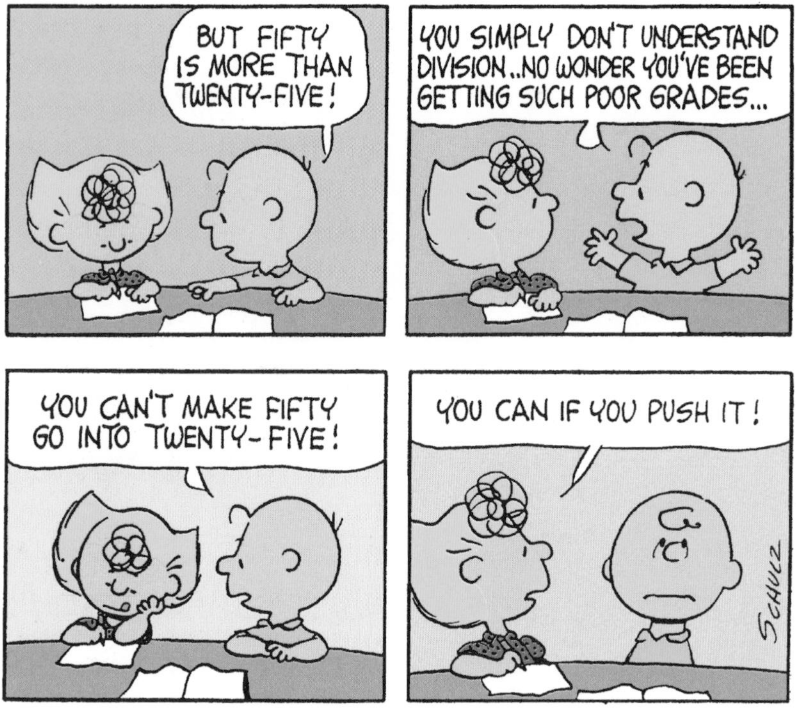
BUT FIFTY IS MORE THAN TWENTY-FIVE!
YOU SIMPLY DON'T UNDERSTAND DIVISION..NO WONDER YOU'VE BEEN GETTING SUCH POOR GRADES...
YOU CAN'T MAKE FIFTY GO INTO TWENTY-FIVE!
YOU CAN IF YOU PUSH IT!
SCHULZ

AAUGH! AAUGH!

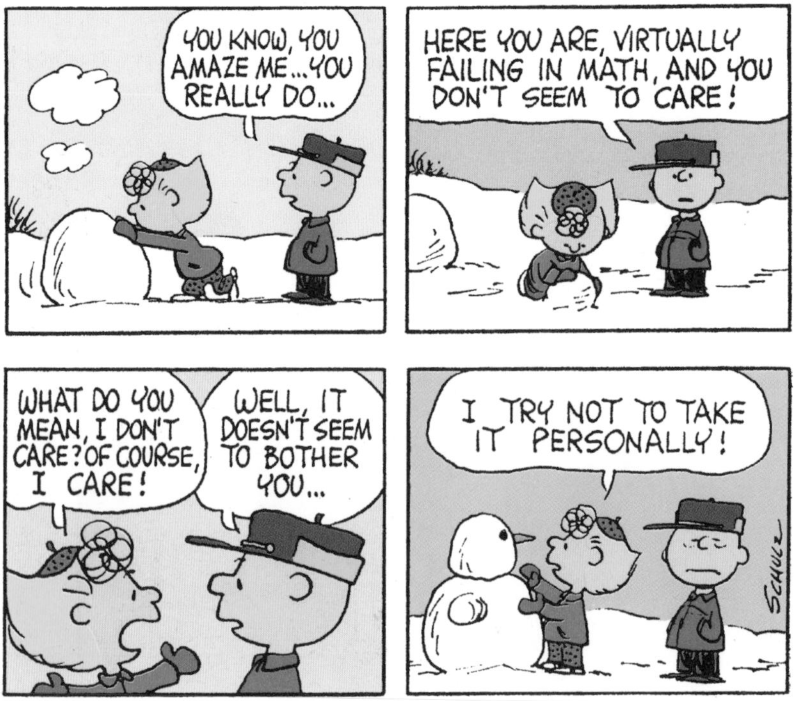
YOU KNOW, YOU AMAZE ME...YOU REALLY DO...
HERE YOU ARE, VIRTUALLY FAILING IN MATH, AND YOU DON'T SEEM TO CARE!
WHAT DO YOU MEAN, I DON'T CARE? OF COURSE, I CARE!
WELL, IT DOESN'T SEEM TO BOTHER YOU...
I TRY NOT TO TAKE IT PERSONALLY!
SCHULZ

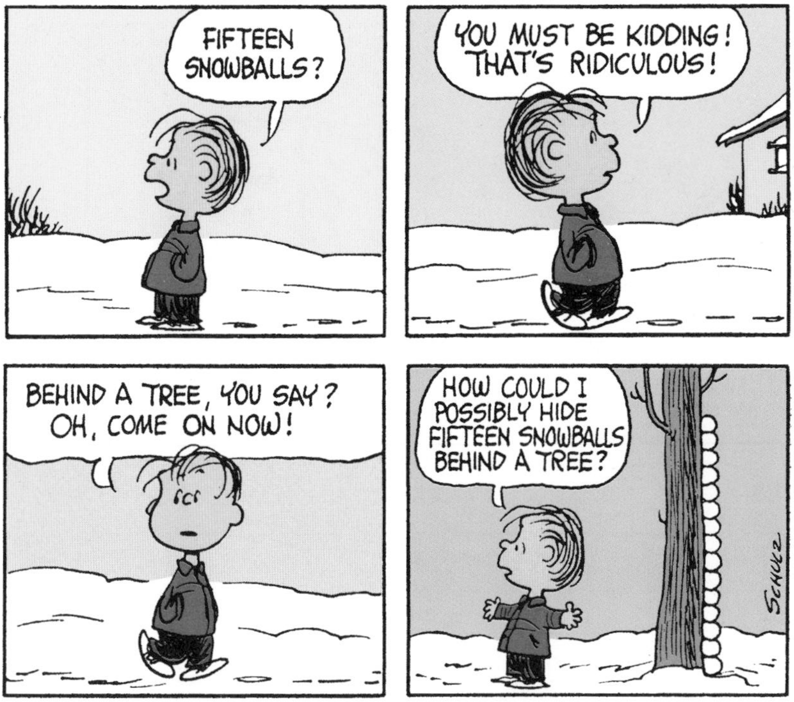
FIFTEEN SNOWBALLS?
YOU MUST BE KIDDING! THAT'S RIDICULOUS!
BEHIND A TREE, YOU SAY? OH, COME ON NOW!
HOW COULD I POSSIBLY HIDE FIFTEEN SNOWBALLS BEHIND A TREE?
SCHULZ

AAUGH! AAUGH!

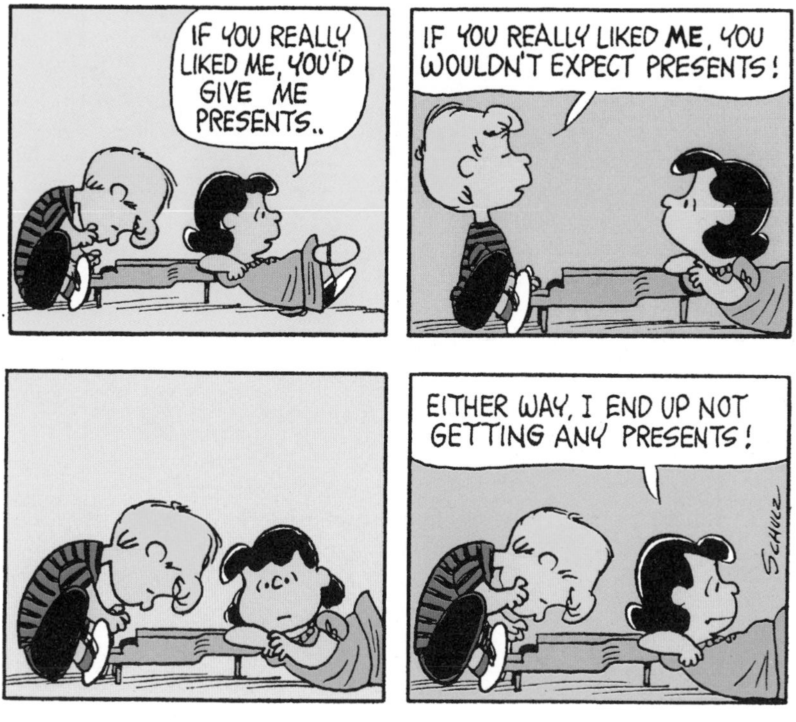
IF YOU REALLY LIKED ME, YOU'D GIVE ME PRESENTS..
IF YOU REALLY LIKED **ME**, YOU WOULDN'T EXPECT PRESENTS!
EITHER WAY, I END UP NOT GETTING ANY PRESENTS!
SCHULZ

VALENTINES!
WOW!

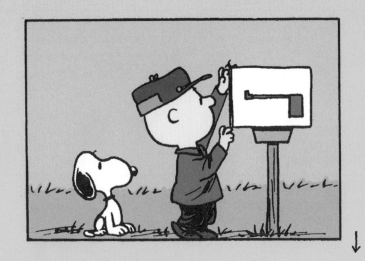

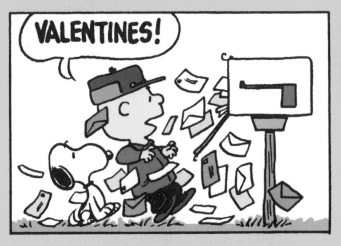

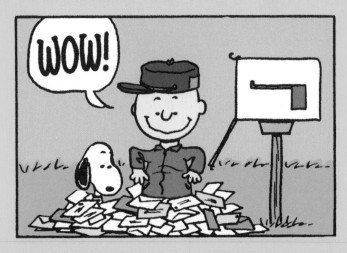

HERE YOU ARE, SNOOPY...THERE'S EVEN ONE FOR YOU...HOW ABOUT THAT? WELL! HERE'S ANOTHER ONE FOR YOU...THIS IS YOUR LUCKY DAY....
AND ONE MORE FOR YOU, AND ONE MORE, AND ONE MORE, AND ONE MORE, AND ONE MORE, AND..
I CAN'T STAND IT.. I JUST CAN'T STAND IT...
SCHULZ

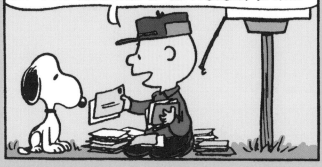

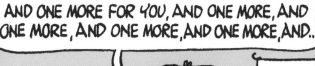

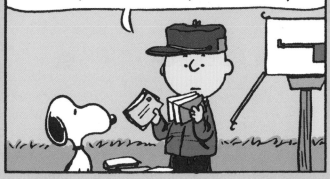

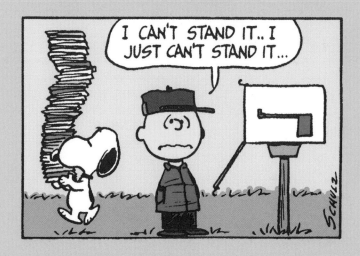

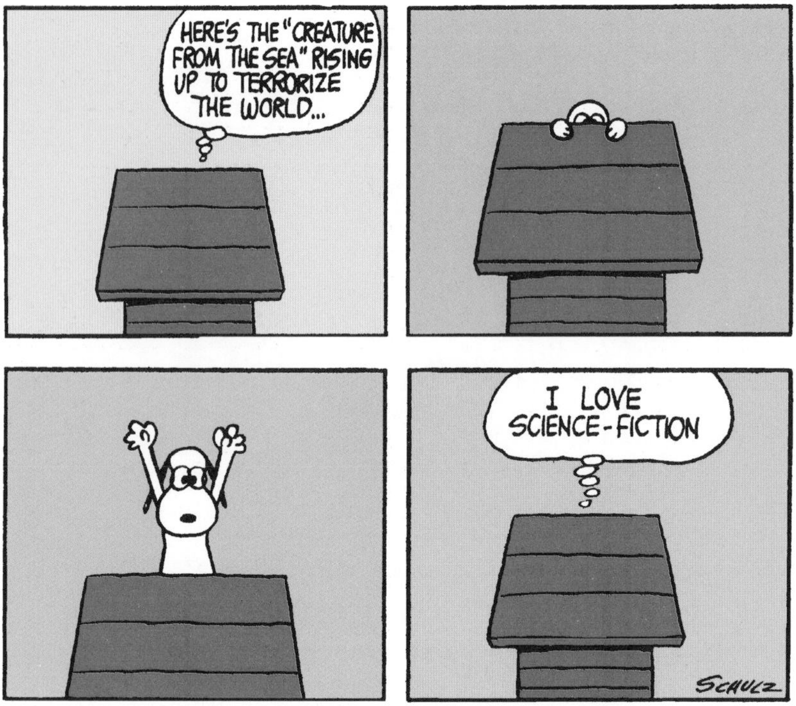
HERE'S THE "CREATURE FROM THE SEA" RISING UP TO TERRORIZE THE WORLD...
I LOVE SCIENCE-FICTION
SCHULZ

AAUGH! AAUGH!

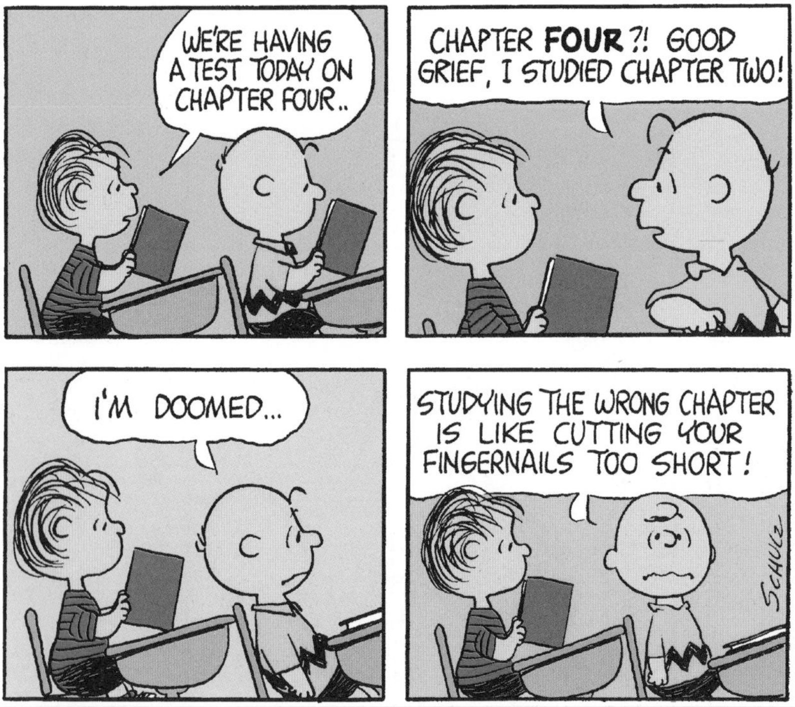
WE'RE HAVING A TEST TODAY ON CHAPTER FOUR..
CHAPTER **FOUR**?! GOOD GRIEF, I STUDIED CHAPTER TWO!
I'M DOOMED...
STUDYING THE WRONG CHAPTER IS LIKE CUTTING YOUR FINGERNAILS TOO SHORT!
SCHULZ

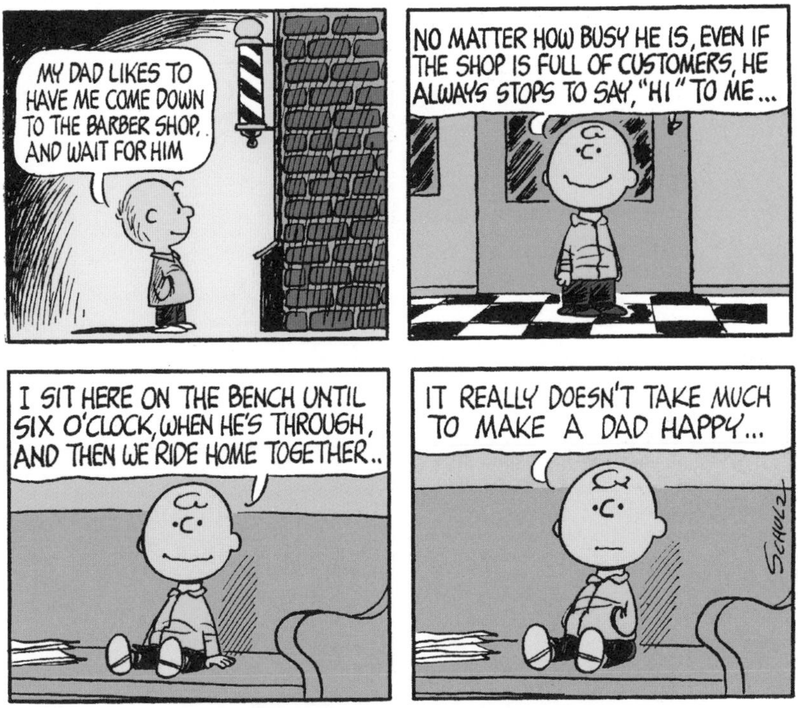
MY DAD LIKES TO HAVE ME COME DOWN TO THE BARBER SHOP, AND WAIT FOR HIM
NO MATTER HOW BUSY HE IS, EVEN IF THE SHOP IS FULL OF CUSTOMERS, HE ALWAYS STOPS TO SAY, "HI" TO ME...
I SIT HERE ON THE BENCH UNTIL SIX O'CLOCK, WHEN HE'S THROUGH, AND THEN WE RIDE HOME TOGETHER..
IT REALLY DOESN'T TAKE MUCH TO MAKE A DAD HAPPY...
SCHULZ

AAUGH! AAUGH!

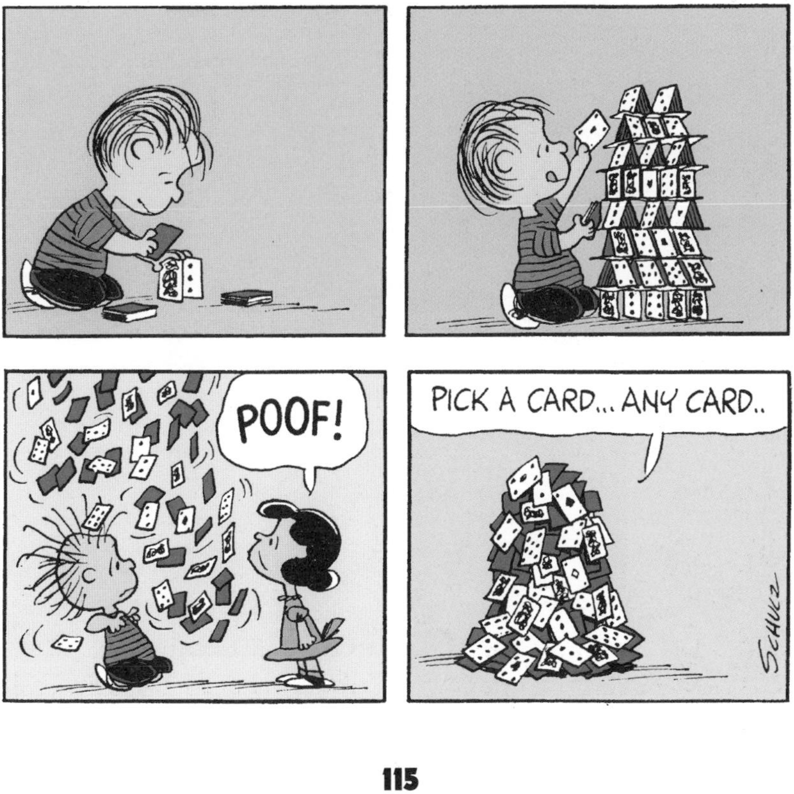
POOF!
PICK A CARD... ANY CARD..
SCHULZ

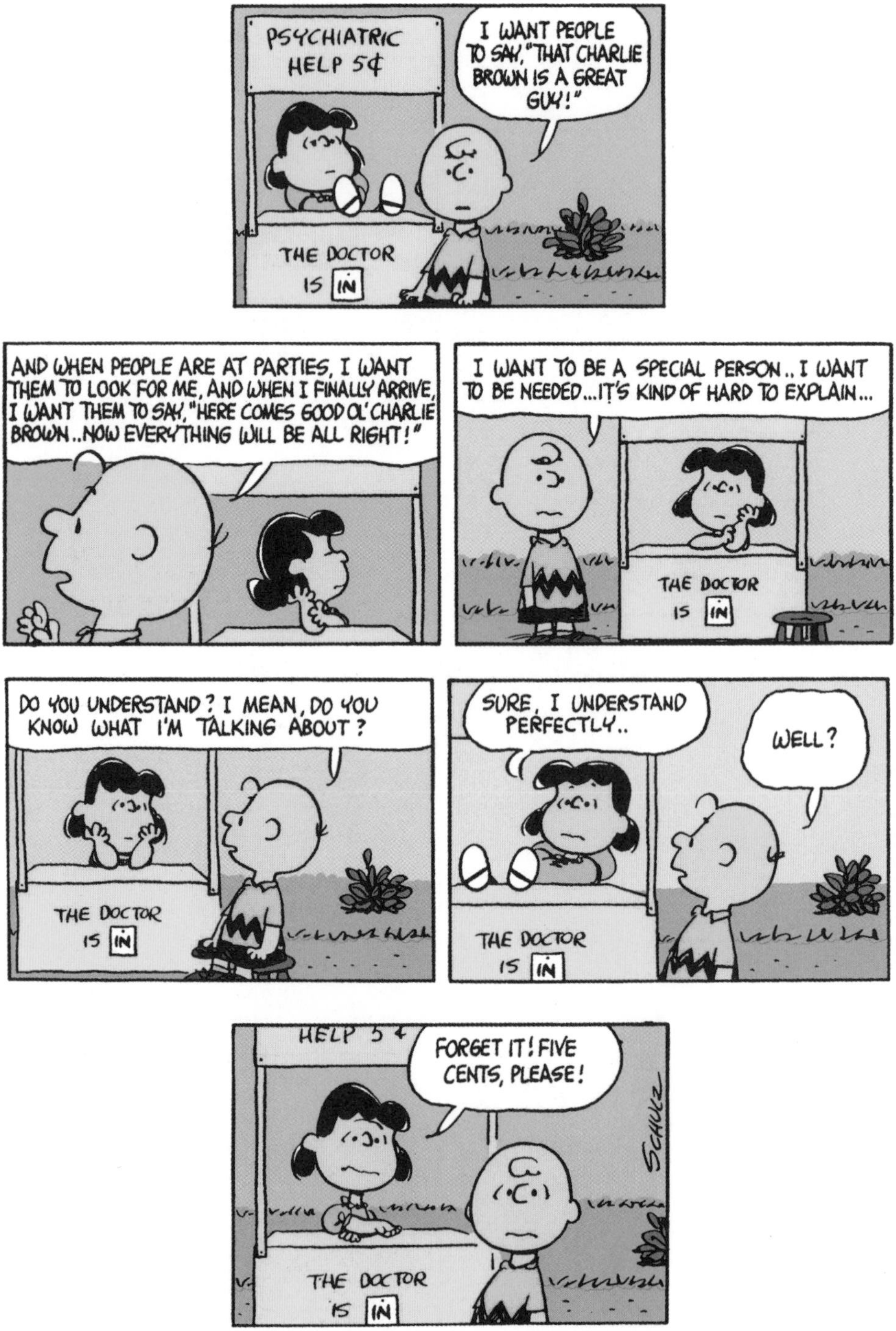
PSYCHIATRIC HELP 5¢
I WANT PEOPLE TO SAY, "THAT CHARLIE BROWN IS A GREAT GUY!"
THE DOCTOR IS IN
AND WHEN PEOPLE ARE AT PARTIES, I WANT THEM TO LOOK FOR ME, AND WHEN I FINALLY ARRIVE, I WANT THEM TO SAY, "HERE COMES GOOD OL' CHARLIE BROWN..NOW EVERYTHING WILL BE ALL RIGHT!"
I WANT TO BE A SPECIAL PERSON.. I WANT TO BE NEEDED...IT'S KIND OF HARD TO EXPLAIN...
THE DOCTOR IS IN
DO YOU UNDERSTAND? I MEAN, DO YOU KNOW WHAT I'M TALKING ABOUT?
THE DOCTOR IS IN
SURE, I UNDERSTAND PERFECTLY..
WELL?
THE DOCTOR IS IN
HELP 5¢
FORGET IT! FIVE CENTS, PLEASE!
SCHULZ
THE DOCTOR IS IN

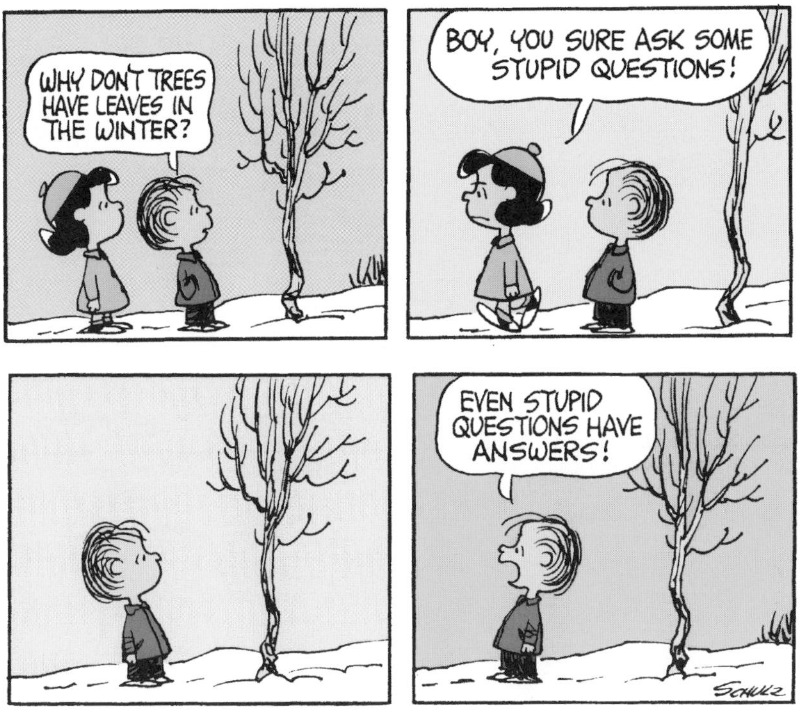
WHY DON'T TREES HAVE LEAVES IN THE WINTER?
BOY, YOU SURE ASK SOME STUPID QUESTIONS!
EVEN STUPID QUESTIONS HAVE ANSWERS!

AAUGH! AAUGH!

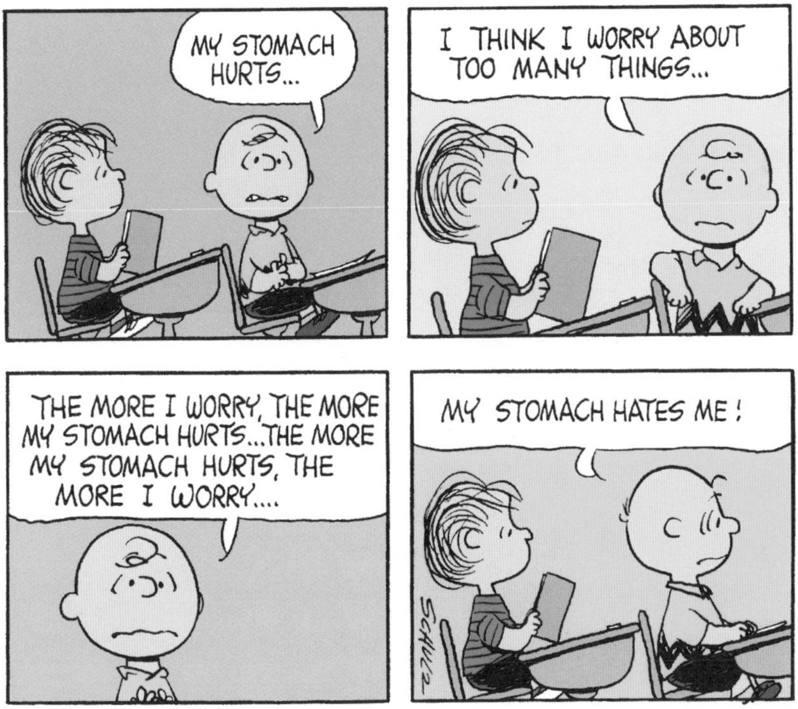
MY STOMACH HURTS...
I THINK I WORRY ABOUT TOO MANY THINGS...
THE MORE I WORRY, THE MORE MY STOMACH HURTS...THE MORE MY STOMACH HURTS, THE MORE I WORRY....
MY STOMACH HATES ME!

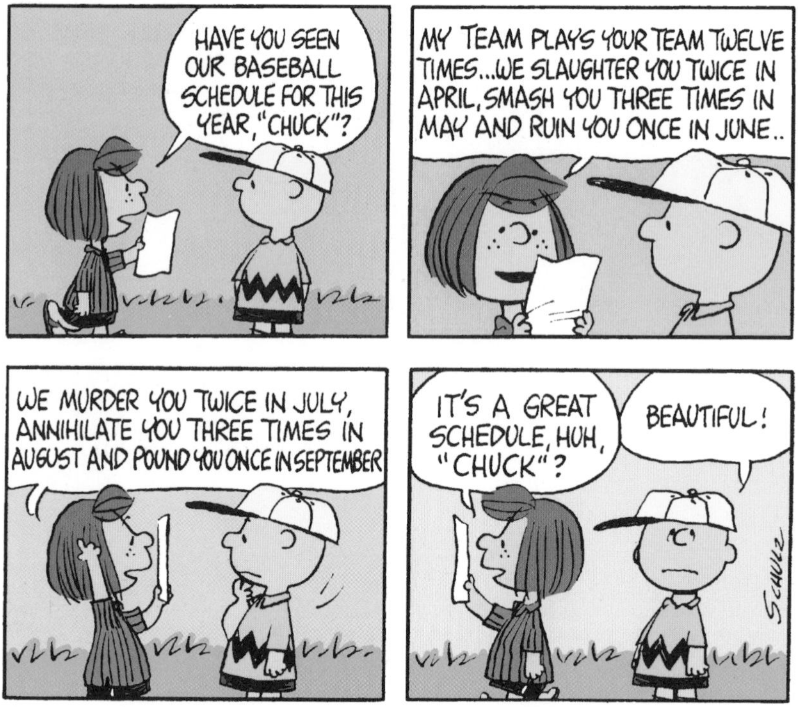
HAVE YOU SEEN OUR BASEBALL SCHEDULE FOR THIS YEAR, "CHUCK"?
MY TEAM PLAYS YOUR TEAM TWELVE TIMES...WE SLAUGHTER YOU TWICE IN APRIL, SMASH YOU THREE TIMES IN MAY AND RUIN YOU ONCE IN JUNE..
WE MURDER YOU TWICE IN JULY, ANNIHILATE YOU THREE TIMES IN AUGUST AND POUND YOU ONCE IN SEPTEMBER
IT'S A GREAT SCHEDULE, HUH, "CHUCK"?
BEAUTIFUL!
SCHULZ

AAUGH! AAUGH!

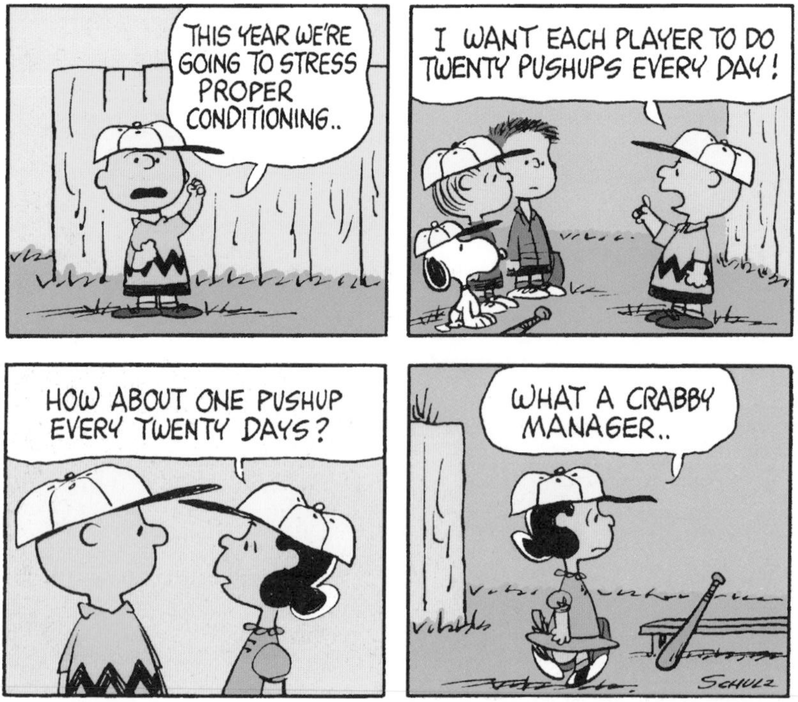
THIS YEAR WE'RE GOING TO STRESS PROPER CONDITIONING..
I WANT EACH PLAYER TO DO TWENTY PUSHUPS EVERY DAY!
HOW ABOUT ONE PUSHUP EVERY TWENTY DAYS?
WHAT A CRABBY MANAGER..
SCHULZ

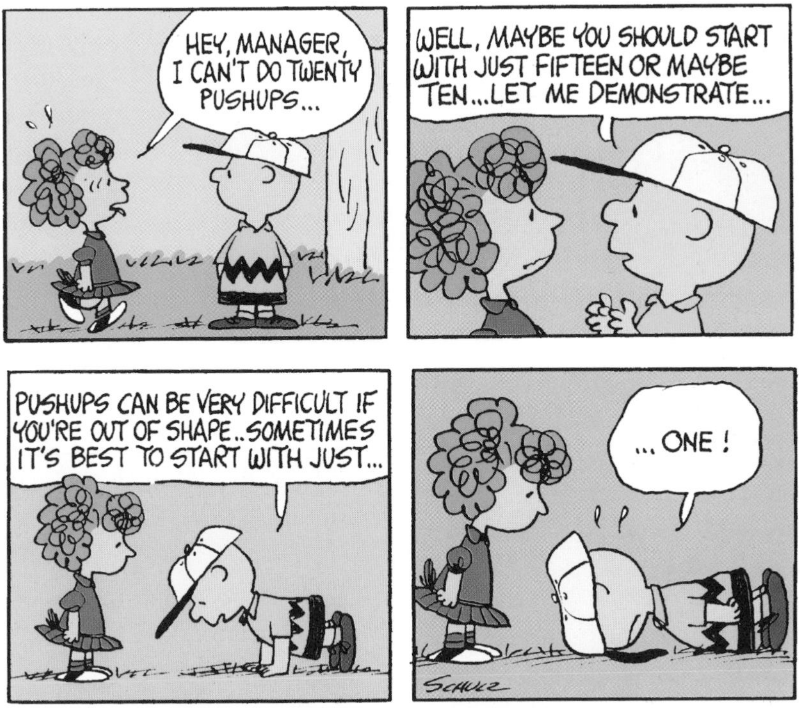
HEY, MANAGER, I CAN'T DO TWENTY PUSHUPS...
WELL, MAYBE YOU SHOULD START WITH JUST FIFTEEN OR MAYBE TEN...LET ME DEMONSTRATE...
PUSHUPS CAN BE VERY DIFFICULT IF YOU'RE OUT OF SHAPE..SOMETIMES IT'S BEST TO START WITH JUST...
...ONE!
SCHULZ

AAUGH! AAUGH!

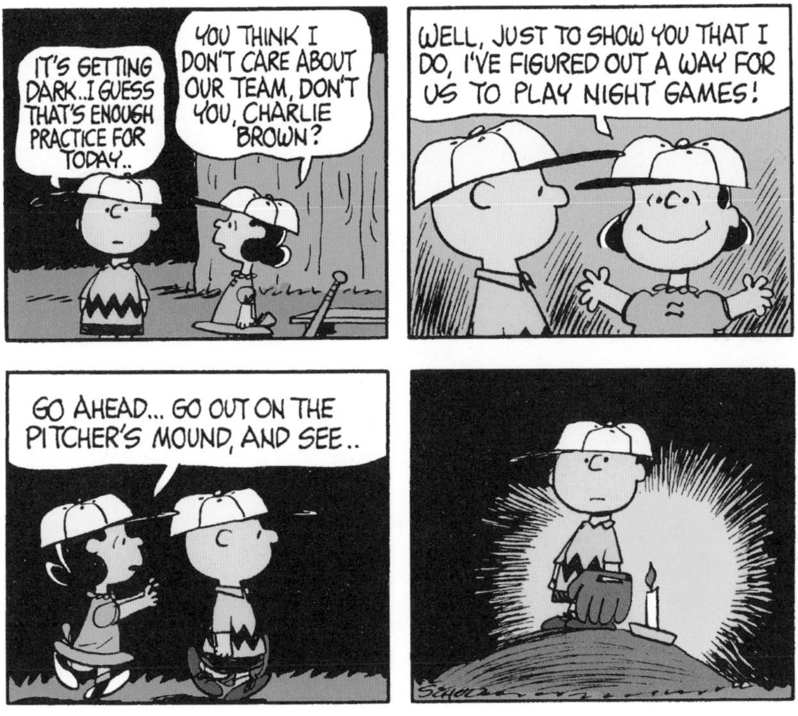
IT'S GETTING DARK..I GUESS THAT'S ENOUGH PRACTICE FOR TODAY..
YOU THINK I DON'T CARE ABOUT OUR TEAM, DON'T YOU, CHARLIE BROWN?
WELL, JUST TO SHOW YOU THAT I DO, I'VE FIGURED OUT A WAY FOR US TO PLAY NIGHT GAMES!
GO AHEAD... GO OUT ON THE PITCHER'S MOUND, AND SEE..
SCHULZ

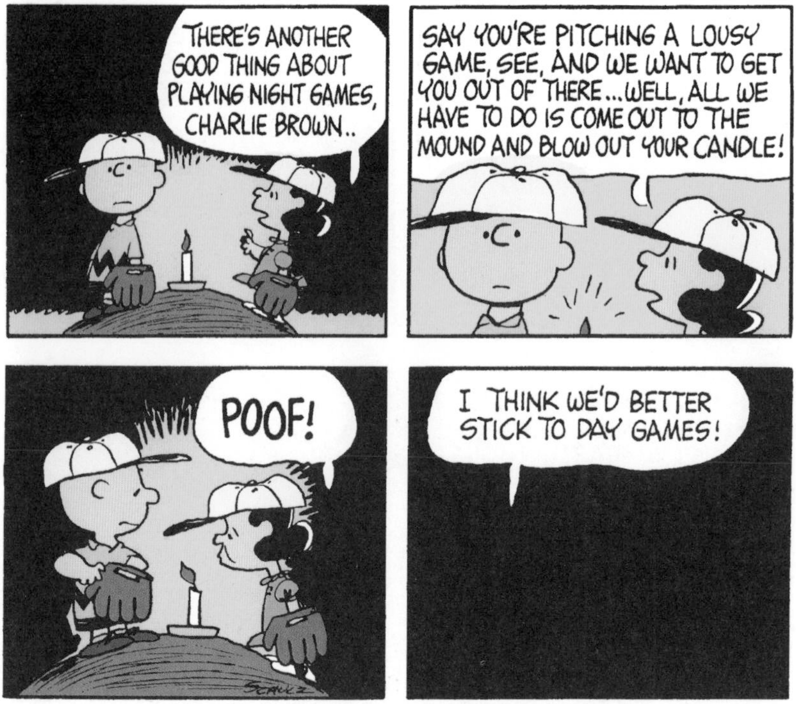
THERE'S ANOTHER GOOD THING ABOUT PLAYING NIGHT GAMES, CHARLIE BROWN..
SAY YOU'RE PITCHING A LOUSY GAME, SEE, AND WE WANT TO GET YOU OUT OF THERE...WELL, ALL WE HAVE TO DO IS COME OUT TO THE MOUND AND BLOW OUT YOUR CANDLE!
POOF!
I THINK WE'D BETTER STICK TO DAY GAMES!

AAUGH! AAUGH!

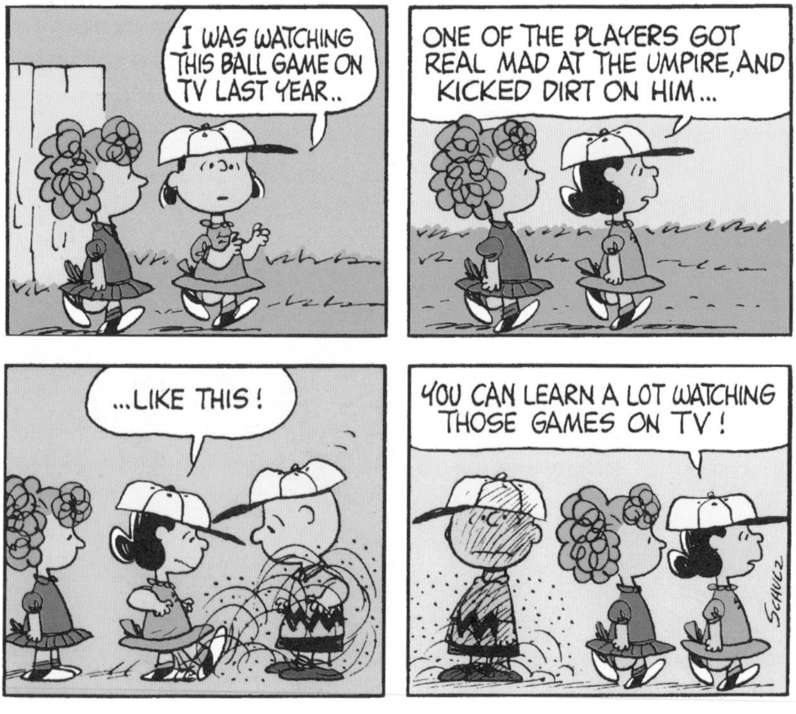
I WAS WATCHING THIS BALL GAME ON TV LAST YEAR..
ONE OF THE PLAYERS GOT REAL MAD AT THE UMPIRE, AND KICKED DIRT ON HIM...
...LIKE THIS!
YOU CAN LEARN A LOT WATCHING THOSE GAMES ON TV!

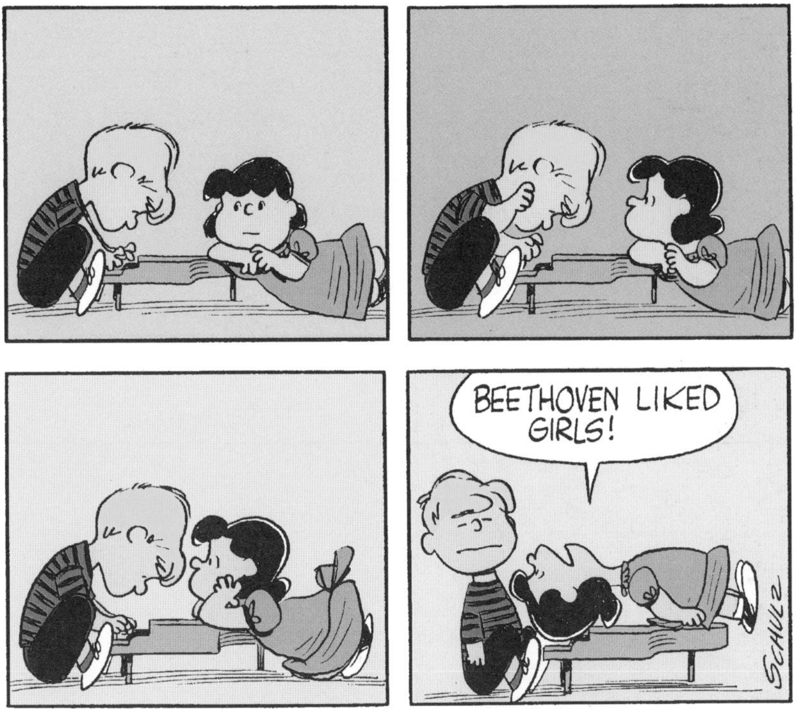
BEETHOVEN LIKED GIRLS!
SCHULZ

AAUGH! AAUGH!

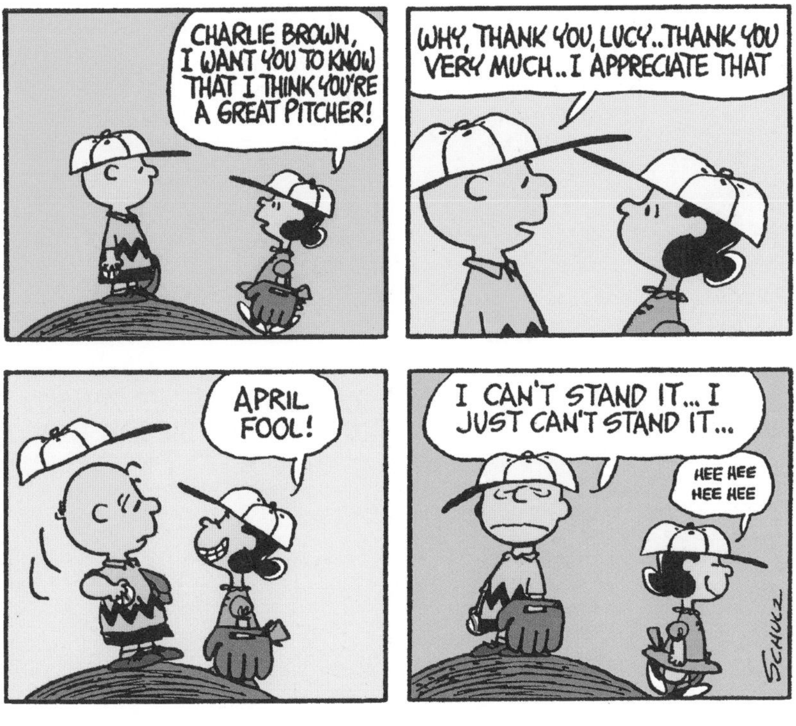
CHARLIE BROWN, I WANT YOU TO KNOW THAT I THINK YOU'RE A GREAT PITCHER!
WHY, THANK YOU, LUCY..THANK YOU VERY MUCH..I APPRECIATE THAT
APRIL FOOL!
I CAN'T STAND IT... I JUST CAN'T STAND IT...
HEE HEE HEE HEE
SCHULZ

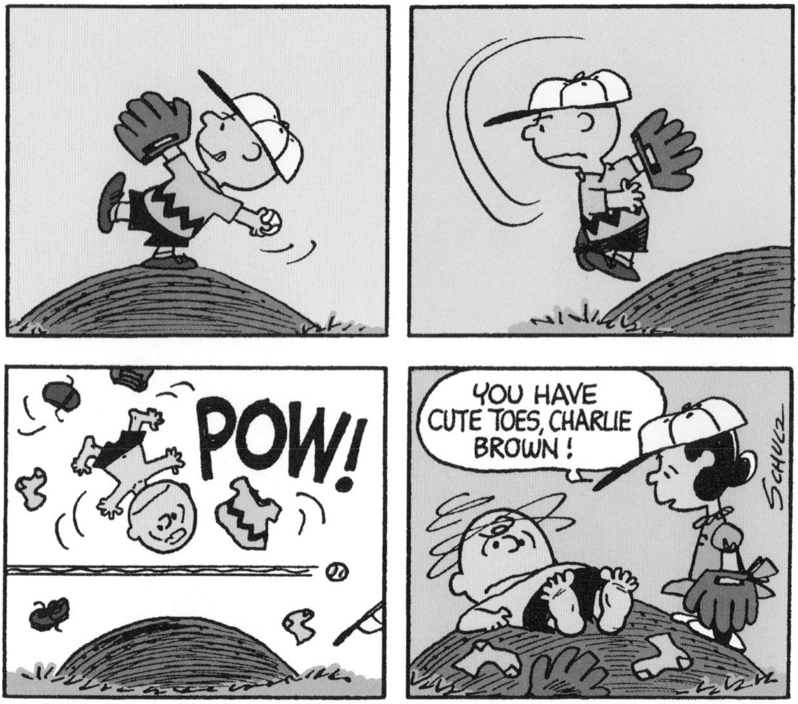
POW!
YOU HAVE CUTE TOES, CHARLIE BROWN!

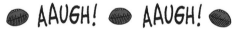

AAUGH! AAUGH!

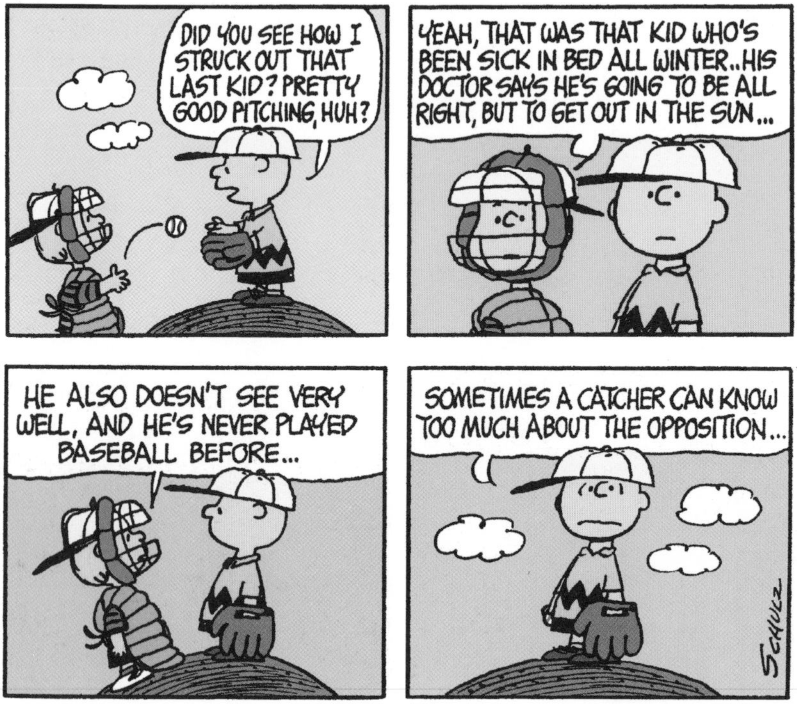
DID YOU SEE HOW I STRUCK OUT THAT LAST KID? PRETTY GOOD PITCHING, HUH?
YEAH, THAT WAS THAT KID WHO'S BEEN SICK IN BED ALL WINTER..HIS DOCTOR SAYS HE'S GOING TO BE ALL RIGHT, BUT TO GET OUT IN THE SUN...
HE ALSO DOESN'T SEE VERY WELL, AND HE'S NEVER PLAYED BASEBALL BEFORE...
SOMETIMES A CATCHER CAN KNOW TOO MUCH ABOUT THE OPPOSITION...

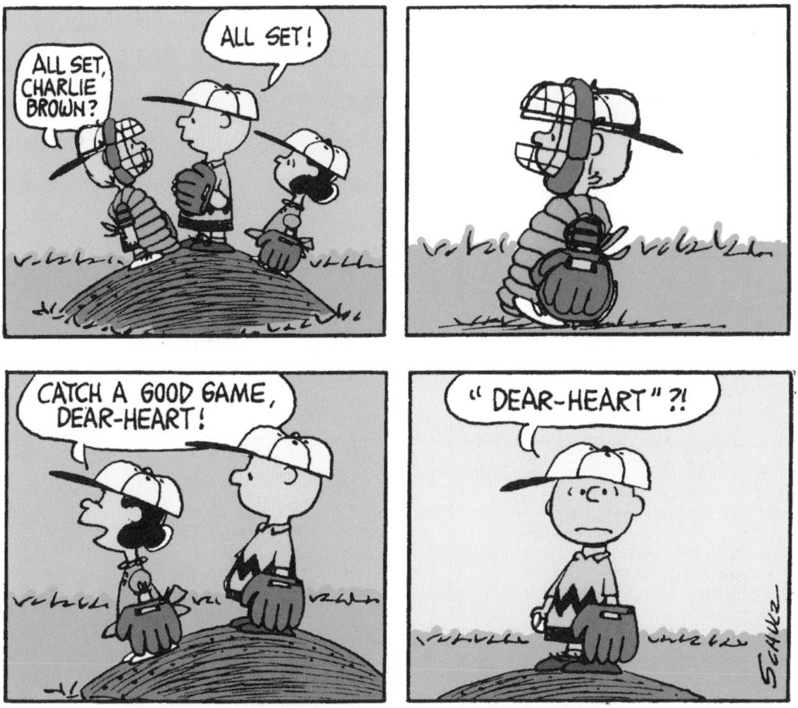
ALL SET, CHARLIE BROWN?
ALL SET!
CATCH A GOOD GAME, DEAR-HEART!
" DEAR-HEART " ?!
SCHULZ

AAUGH! AAUGH!

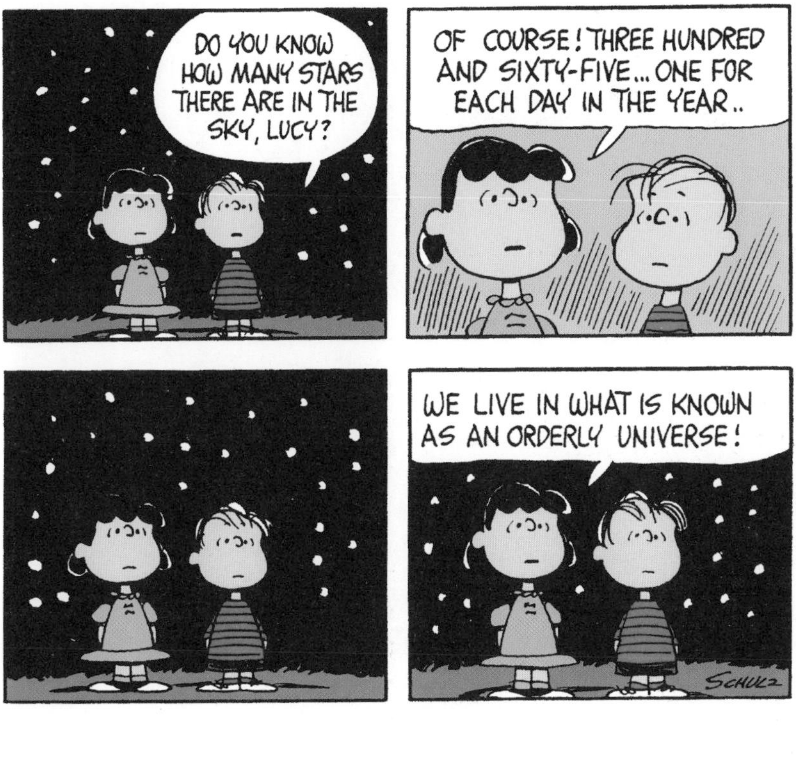
DO YOU KNOW HOW MANY STARS THERE ARE IN THE SKY, LUCY?
OF COURSE! THREE HUNDRED AND SIXTY-FIVE... ONE FOR EACH DAY IN THE YEAR..
WE LIVE IN WHAT IS KNOWN AS AN ORDERLY UNIVERSE!
SCHULZ

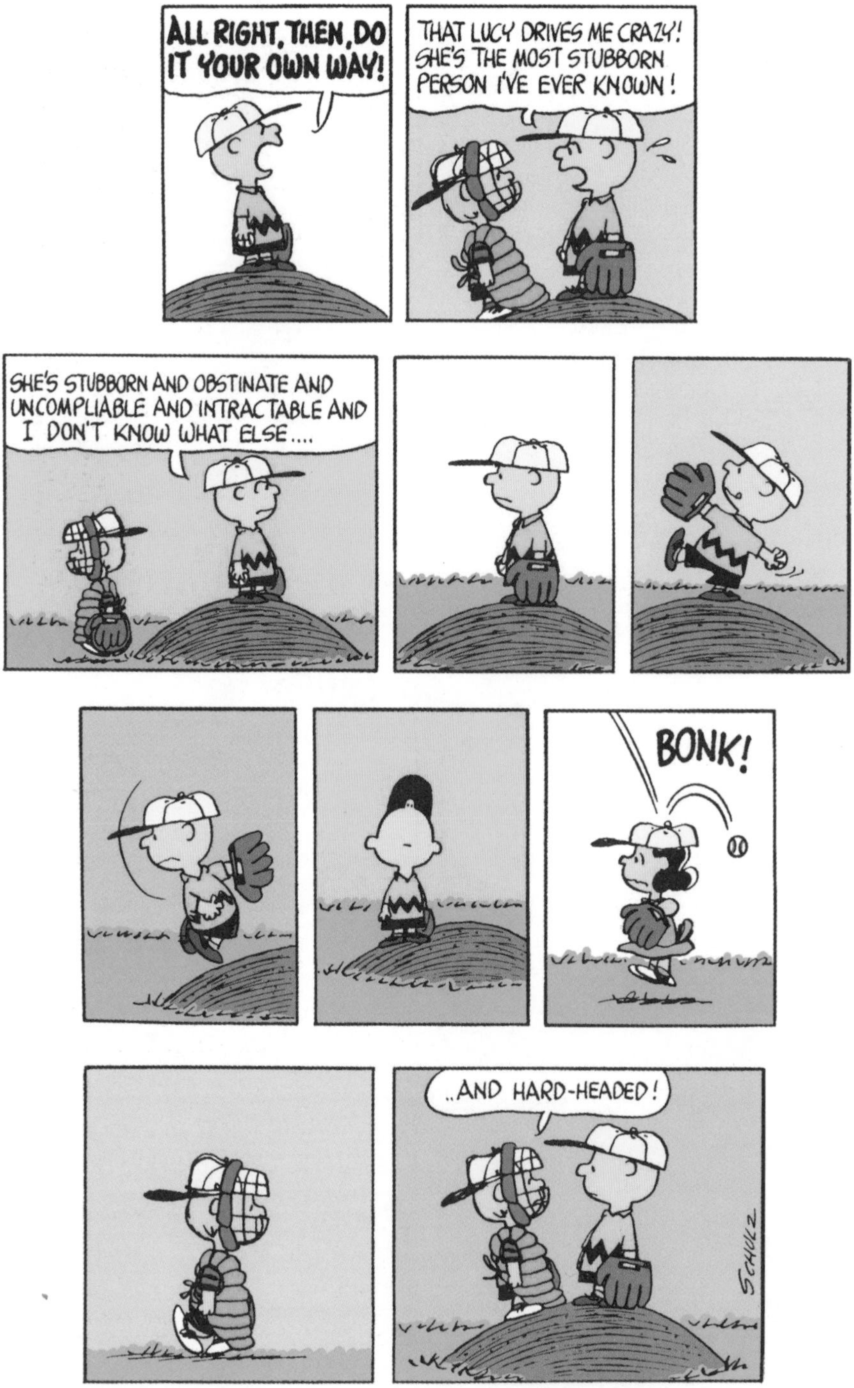
ALL RIGHT, THEN, DO IT YOUR OWN WAY!
THAT LUCY DRIVES ME CRAZY! SHE'S THE MOST STUBBORN PERSON I'VE EVER KNOWN!
SHE'S STUBBORN AND OBSTINATE AND UNCOMPLIABLE AND INTRACTABLE AND I DON'T KNOW WHAT ELSE....
BONK!
..AND HARD-HEADED!
SCHULZ

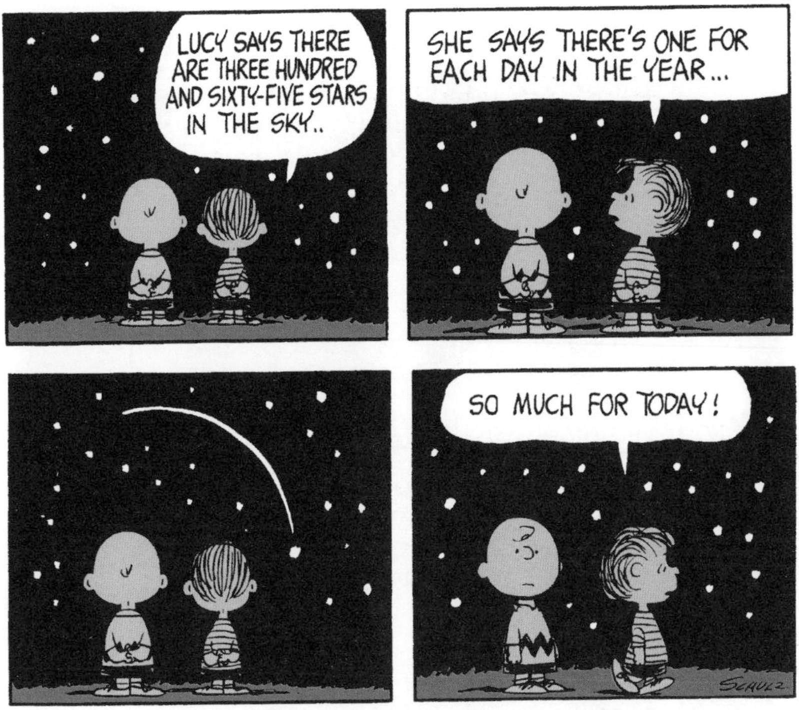
LUCY SAYS THERE ARE THREE HUNDRED AND SIXTY-FIVE STARS IN THE SKY..
SHE SAYS THERE'S ONE FOR EACH DAY IN THE YEAR...
SO MUCH FOR TODAY!
SCHULZ

AAUGH! AAUGH!

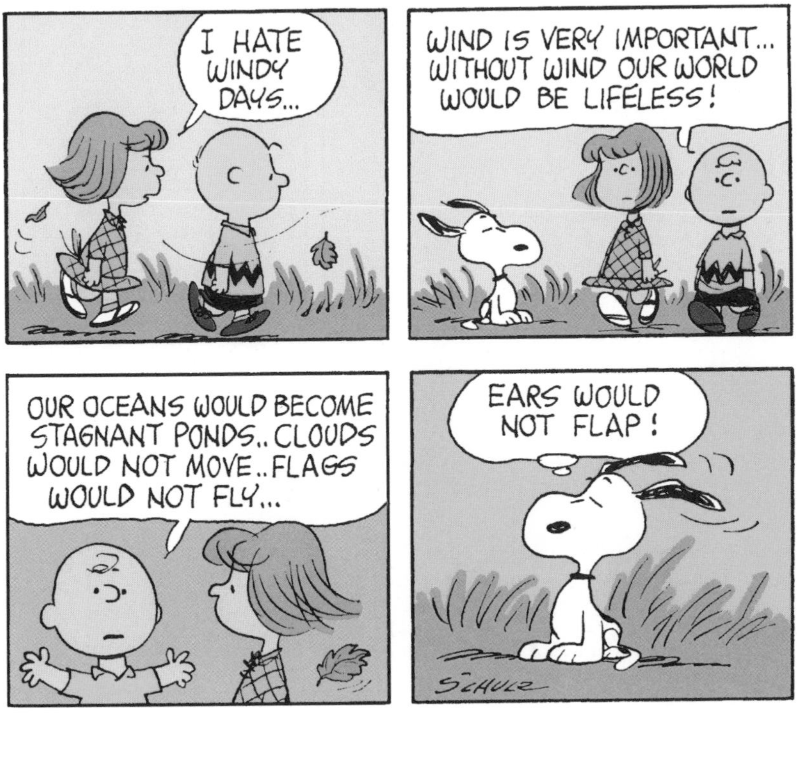
I HATE WINDY DAYS...
WIND IS VERY IMPORTANT... WITHOUT WIND OUR WORLD WOULD BE LIFELESS!
OUR OCEANS WOULD BECOME STAGNANT PONDS.. CLOUDS WOULD NOT MOVE.. FLAGS WOULD NOT FLY...
EARS WOULD NOT FLAP!
SCHULZ

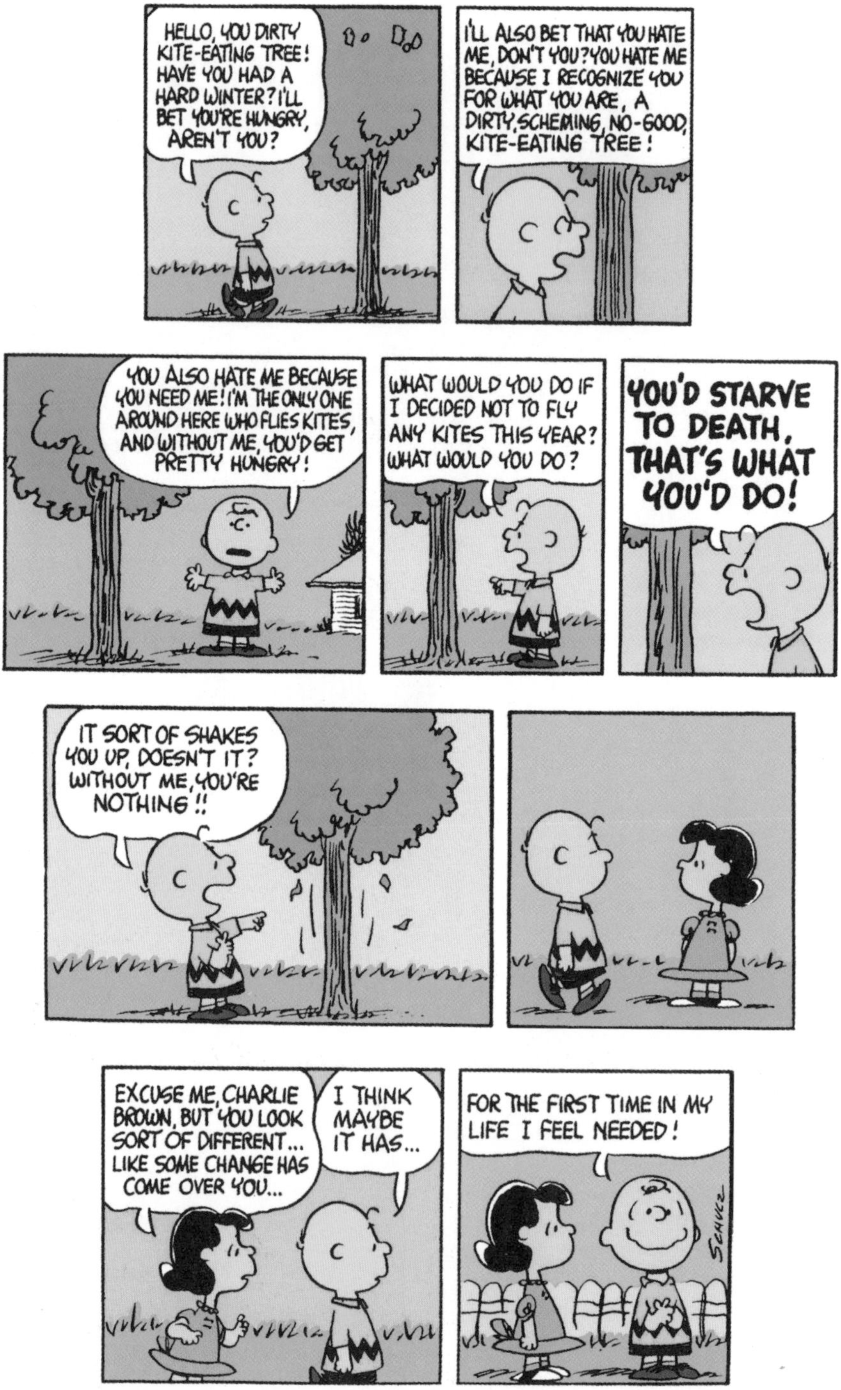
HELLO, YOU DIRTY KITE-EATING TREE! HAVE YOU HAD A HARD WINTER? I'LL BET YOU'RE HUNGRY, AREN'T YOU?
I'LL ALSO BET THAT YOU HATE ME, DON'T YOU? YOU HATE ME BECAUSE I RECOGNIZE YOU FOR WHAT YOU ARE, A DIRTY, SCHEMING, NO-GOOD, KITE-EATING TREE!
YOU ALSO HATE ME BECAUSE YOU NEED ME! I'M THE ONLY ONE AROUND HERE WHO FLIES KITES, AND WITHOUT ME, YOU'D GET PRETTY HUNGRY!
WHAT WOULD YOU DO IF I DECIDED NOT TO FLY ANY KITES THIS YEAR? WHAT WOULD YOU DO?
YOU'D STARVE TO DEATH, THAT'S WHAT YOU'D DO!
IT SORT OF SHAKES YOU UP, DOESN'T IT? WITHOUT ME, YOU'RE NOTHING!!
EXCUSE ME, CHARLIE BROWN, BUT YOU LOOK SORT OF DIFFERENT... LIKE SOME CHANGE HAS COME OVER YOU...
I THINK MAYBE IT HAS...
FOR THE FIRST TIME IN MY LIFE I FEEL NEEDED!
SCHULZ

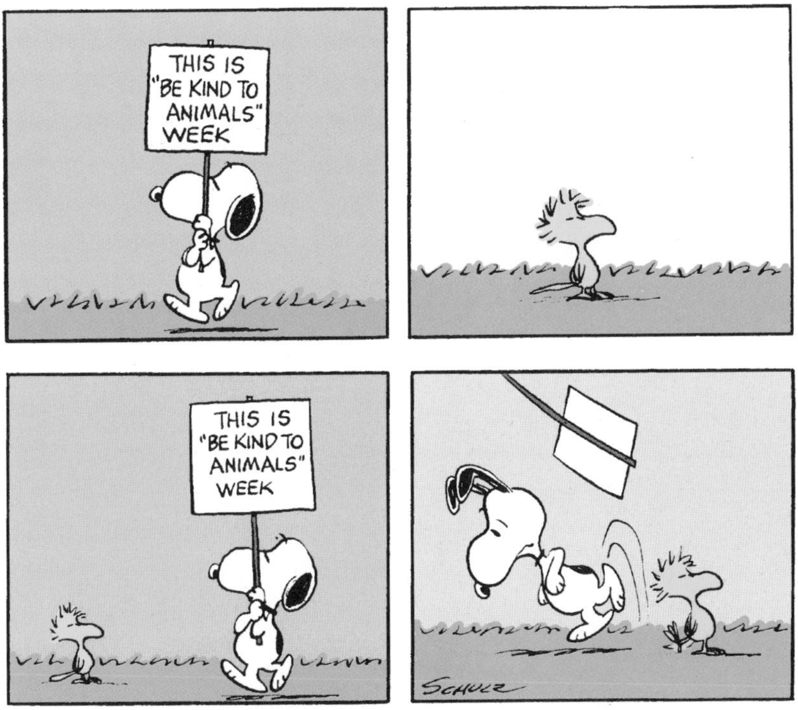
THIS IS "BE KIND TO ANIMALS" WEEK
THIS IS "BE KIND TO ANIMALS" WEEK

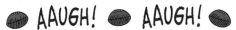

AAUGH! AAUGH!

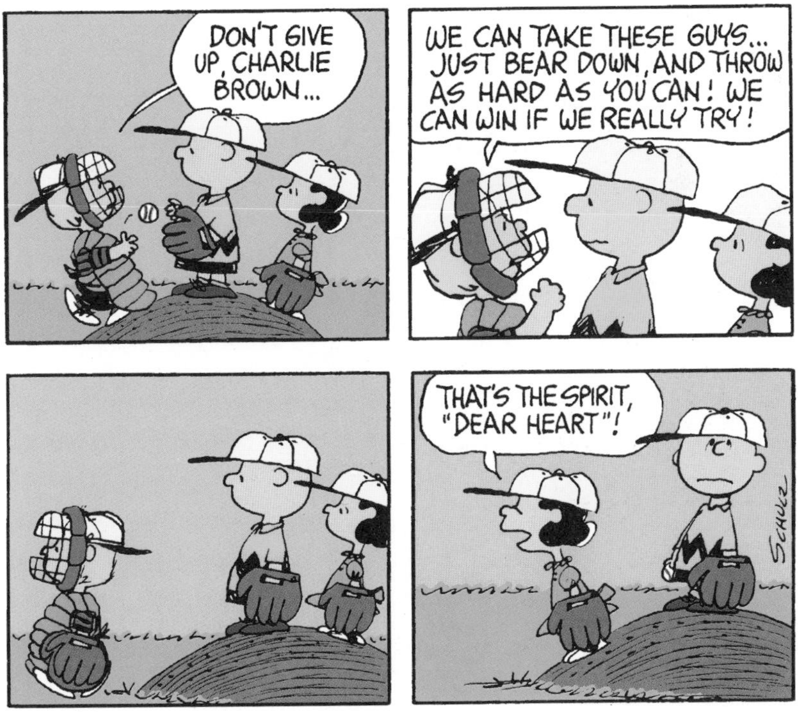
DON'T GIVE UP, CHARLIE BROWN...
WE CAN TAKE THESE GUYS... JUST BEAR DOWN, AND THROW AS HARD AS YOU CAN! WE CAN WIN IF WE REALLY TRY!
THAT'S THE SPIRIT, "DEAR HEART"!

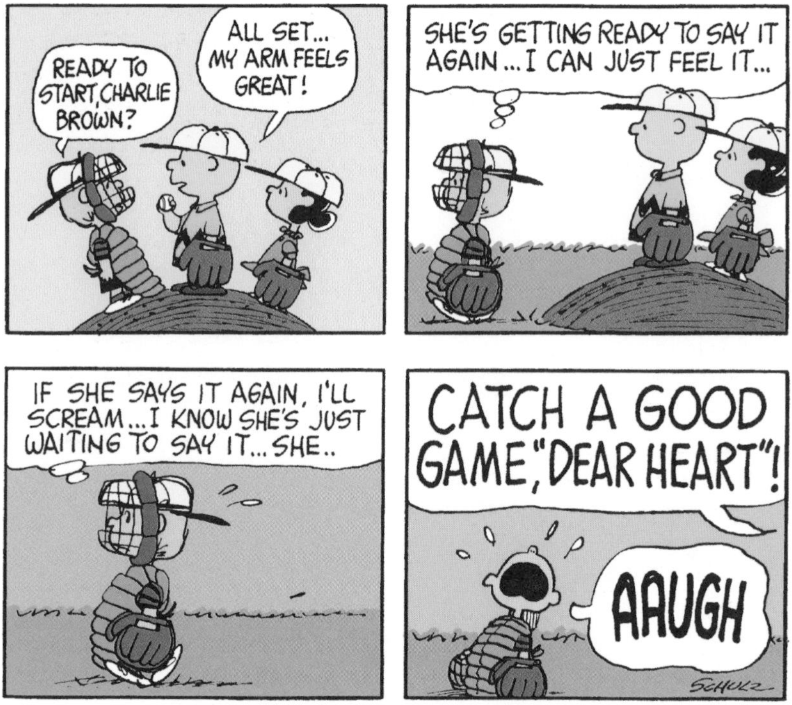
READY TO START, CHARLIE BROWN?
ALL SET... MY ARM FEELS GREAT!
SHE'S GETTING READY TO SAY IT AGAIN... I CAN JUST FEEL IT...
IF SHE SAYS IT AGAIN, I'LL SCREAM... I KNOW SHE'S JUST WAITING TO SAY IT... SHE..
CATCH A GOOD GAME, "DEAR HEART"!
AAUGH
SCHULZ

AAUGH! AAUGH!

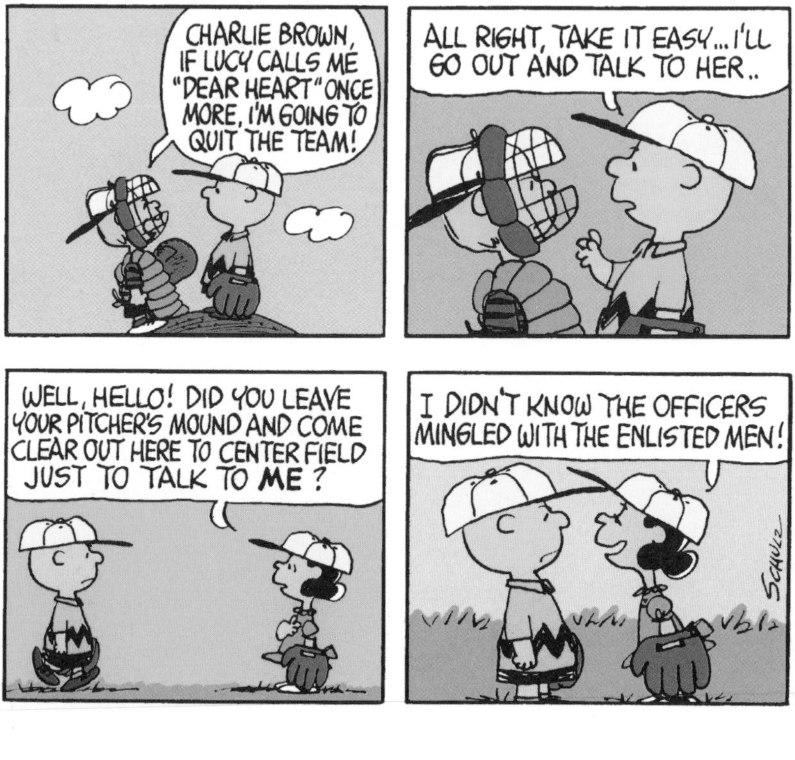
CHARLIE BROWN, IF LUCY CALLS ME "DEAR HEART" ONCE MORE, I'M GOING TO QUIT THE TEAM!
ALL RIGHT, TAKE IT EASY... I'LL GO OUT AND TALK TO HER..
WELL, HELLO! DID YOU LEAVE YOUR PITCHER'S MOUND AND COME CLEAR OUT HERE TO CENTER FIELD JUST TO TALK TO ME?
I DIDN'T KNOW THE OFFICERS MINGLED WITH THE ENLISTED MEN!
SCHULZ

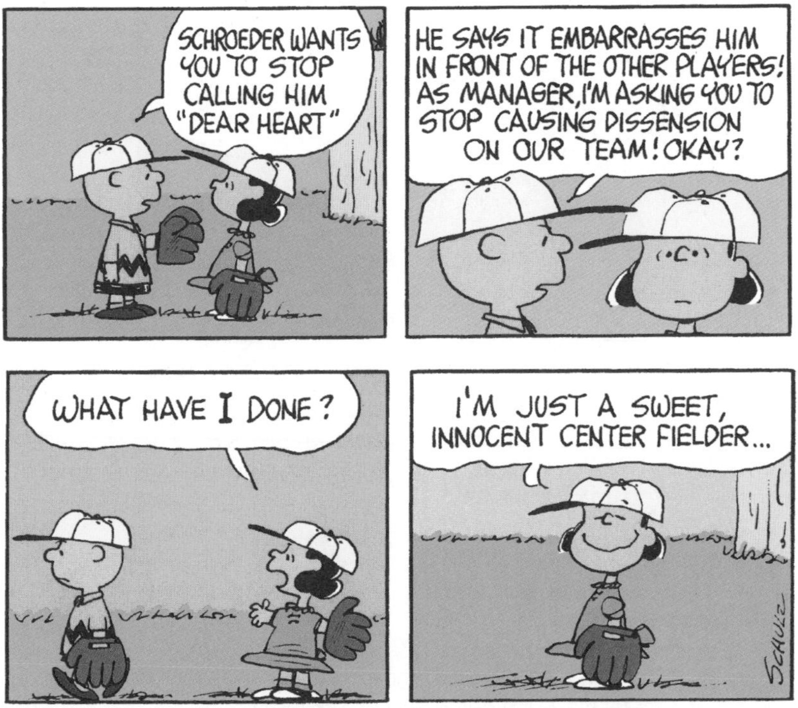
SCHROEDER WANTS YOU TO STOP CALLING HIM "DEAR HEART"
HE SAYS IT EMBARRASSES HIM IN FRONT OF THE OTHER PLAYERS! AS MANAGER, I'M ASKING YOU TO STOP CAUSING DISSENSION ON OUR TEAM! OKAY?
WHAT HAVE I DONE?
I'M JUST A SWEET, INNOCENT CENTER FIELDER...
SCHULZ

AAUGH! AAUGH!

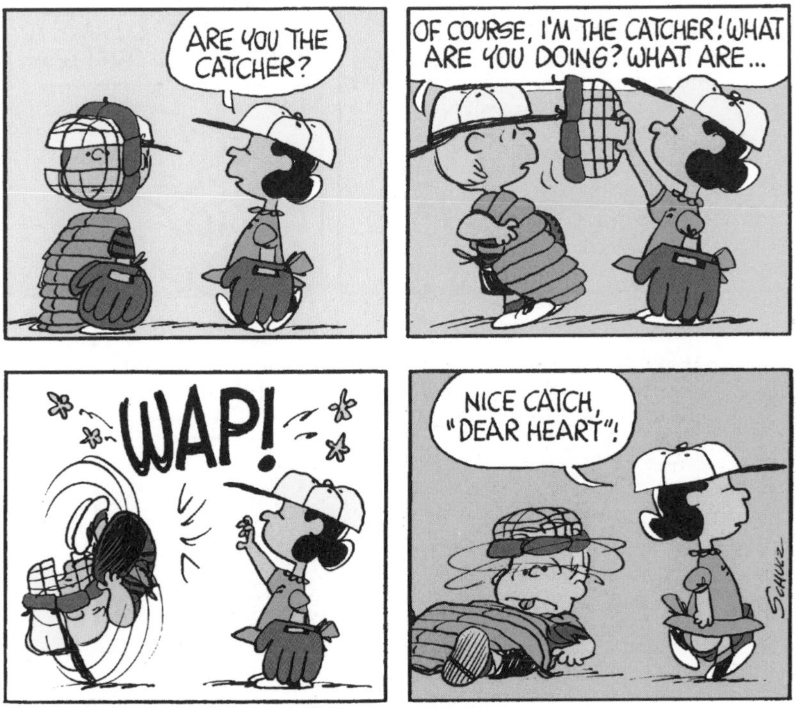
ARE YOU THE CATCHER?
OF COURSE, I'M THE CATCHER! WHAT ARE YOU DOING? WHAT ARE...
WAP!
NICE CATCH, "DEAR HEART"!
SCHULZ

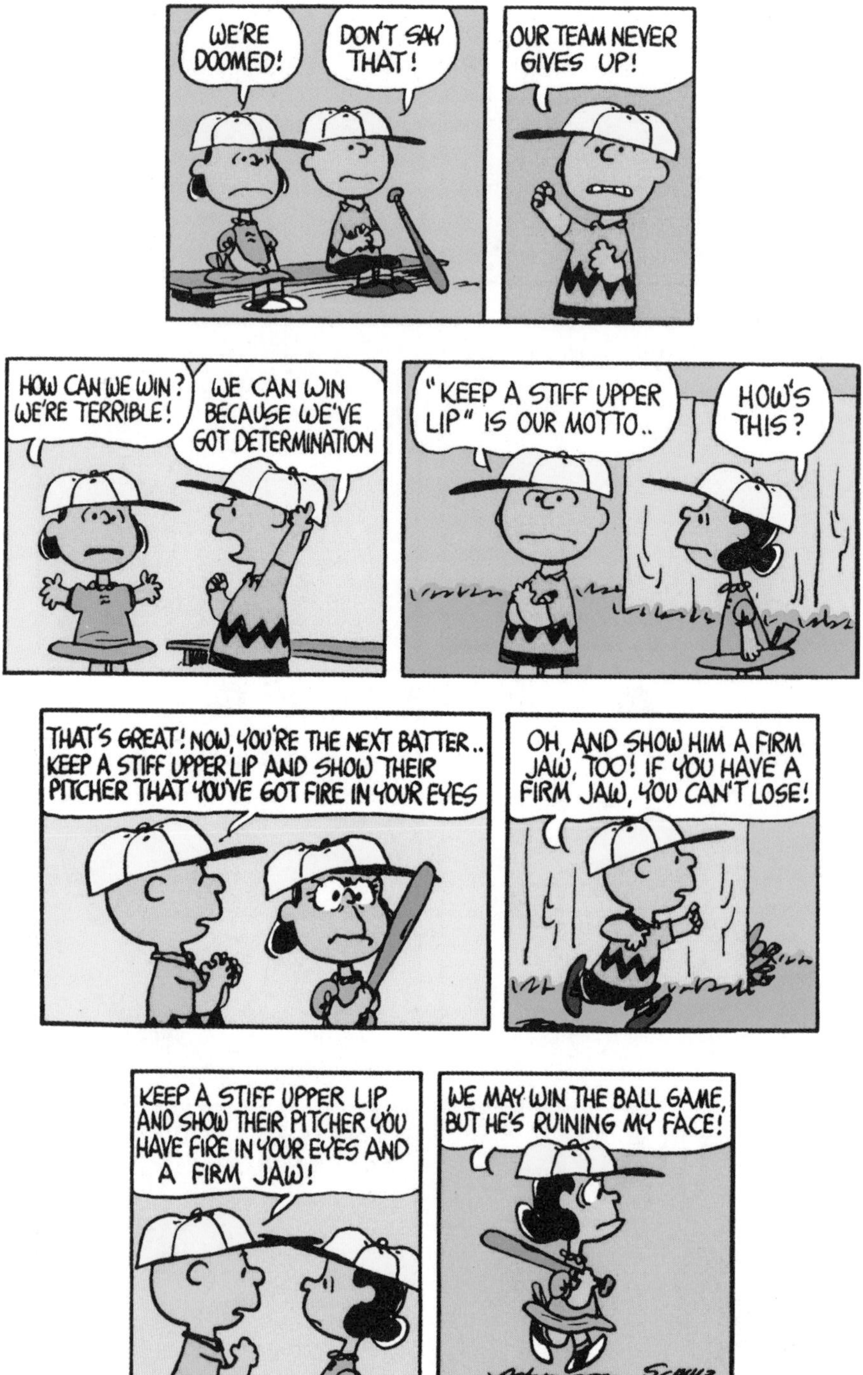
WE'RE DOOMED!
DON'T SAY THAT!
OUR TEAM NEVER GIVES UP!
HOW CAN WE WIN? WE'RE TERRIBLE!
WE CAN WIN BECAUSE WE'VE GOT DETERMINATION
"KEEP A STIFF UPPER LIP" IS OUR MOTTO..
HOW'S THIS?
THAT'S GREAT! NOW, YOU'RE THE NEXT BATTER.. KEEP A STIFF UPPER LIP AND SHOW THEIR PITCHER THAT YOU'VE GOT FIRE IN YOUR EYES
OH, AND SHOW HIM A FIRM JAW, TOO! IF YOU HAVE A FIRM JAW, YOU CAN'T LOSE!
KEEP A STIFF UPPER LIP, AND SHOW THEIR PITCHER YOU HAVE FIRE IN YOUR EYES AND A FIRM JAW!
WE MAY WIN THE BALL GAME, BUT HE'S RUINING MY FACE!
SCHULZ

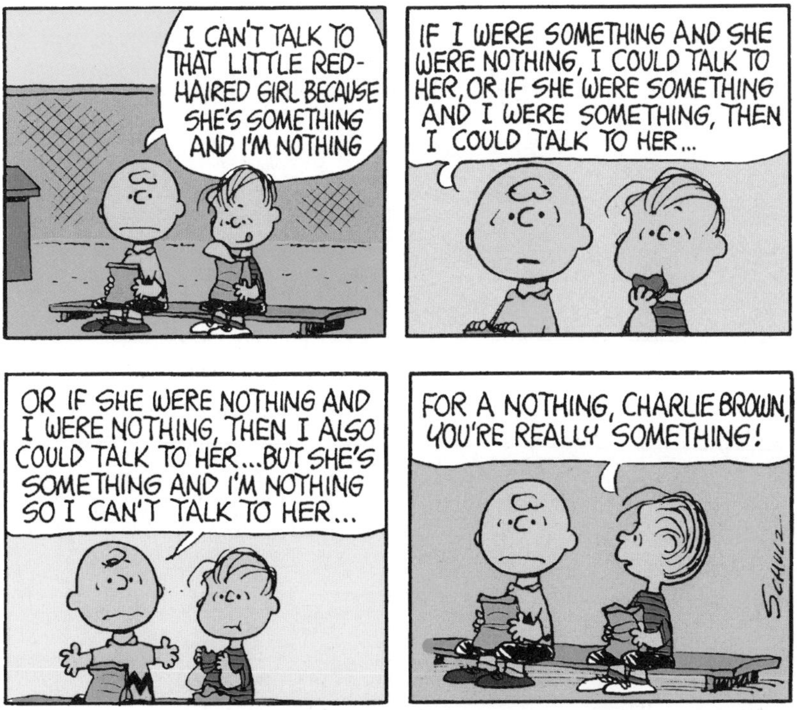
I CAN'T TALK TO THAT LITTLE RED-HAIRED GIRL BECAUSE SHE'S SOMETHING AND I'M NOTHING
IF I WERE SOMETHING AND SHE WERE NOTHING, I COULD TALK TO HER, OR IF SHE WERE SOMETHING AND I WERE SOMETHING, THEN I COULD TALK TO HER...
OR IF SHE WERE NOTHING AND I WERE NOTHING, THEN I ALSO COULD TALK TO HER...BUT SHE'S SOMETHING AND I'M NOTHING SO I CAN'T TALK TO HER...
FOR A NOTHING, CHARLIE BROWN, YOU'RE REALLY SOMETHING!
SCHULZ

AAUGH! AAUGH!

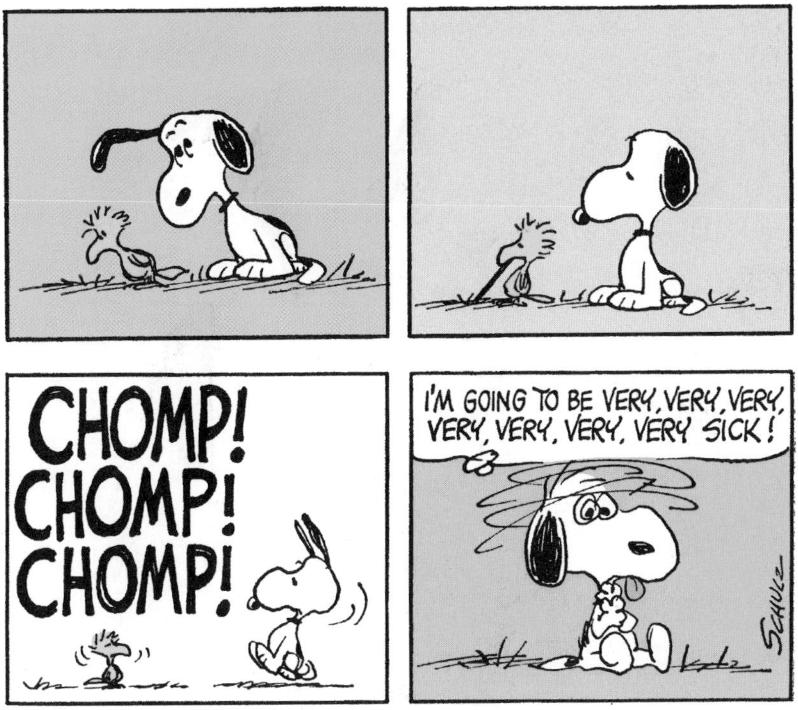
CHOMP! CHOMP! CHOMP!
I'M GOING TO BE VERY, VERY, VERY, VERY, VERY, VERY, VERY SICK!
SCHULZ

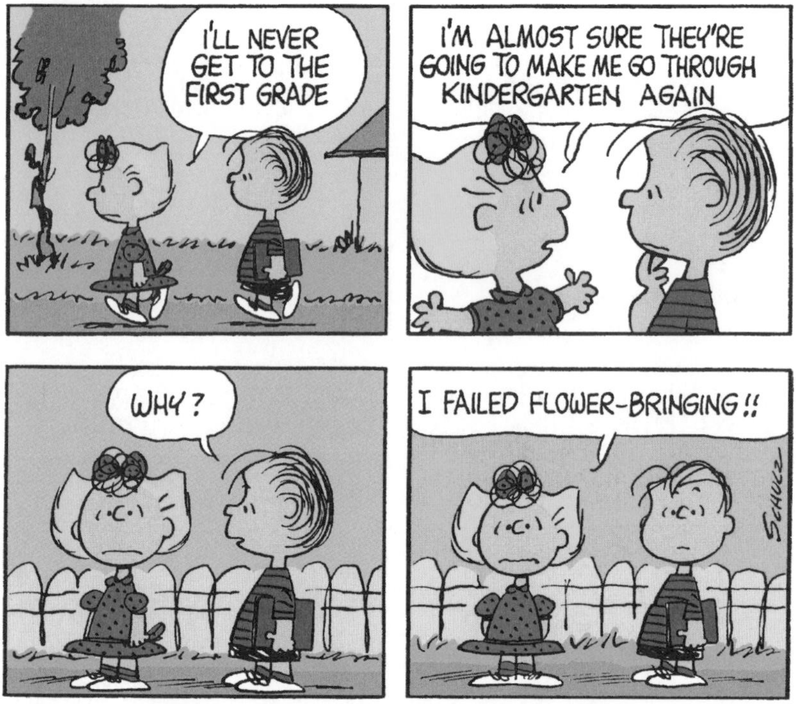
I'LL NEVER GET TO THE FIRST GRADE
I'M ALMOST SURE THEY'RE GOING TO MAKE ME GO THROUGH KINDERGARTEN AGAIN
WHY?
I FAILED FLOWER-BRINGING!!
SCHULZ

AAUGH! AAUGH!

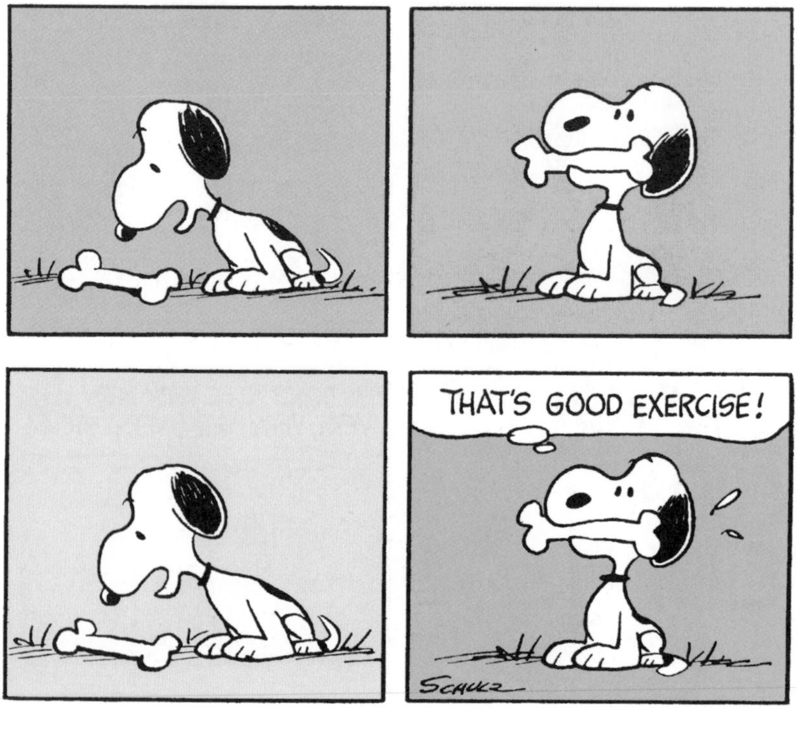
THAT'S GOOD EXERCISE!
SCHULZ

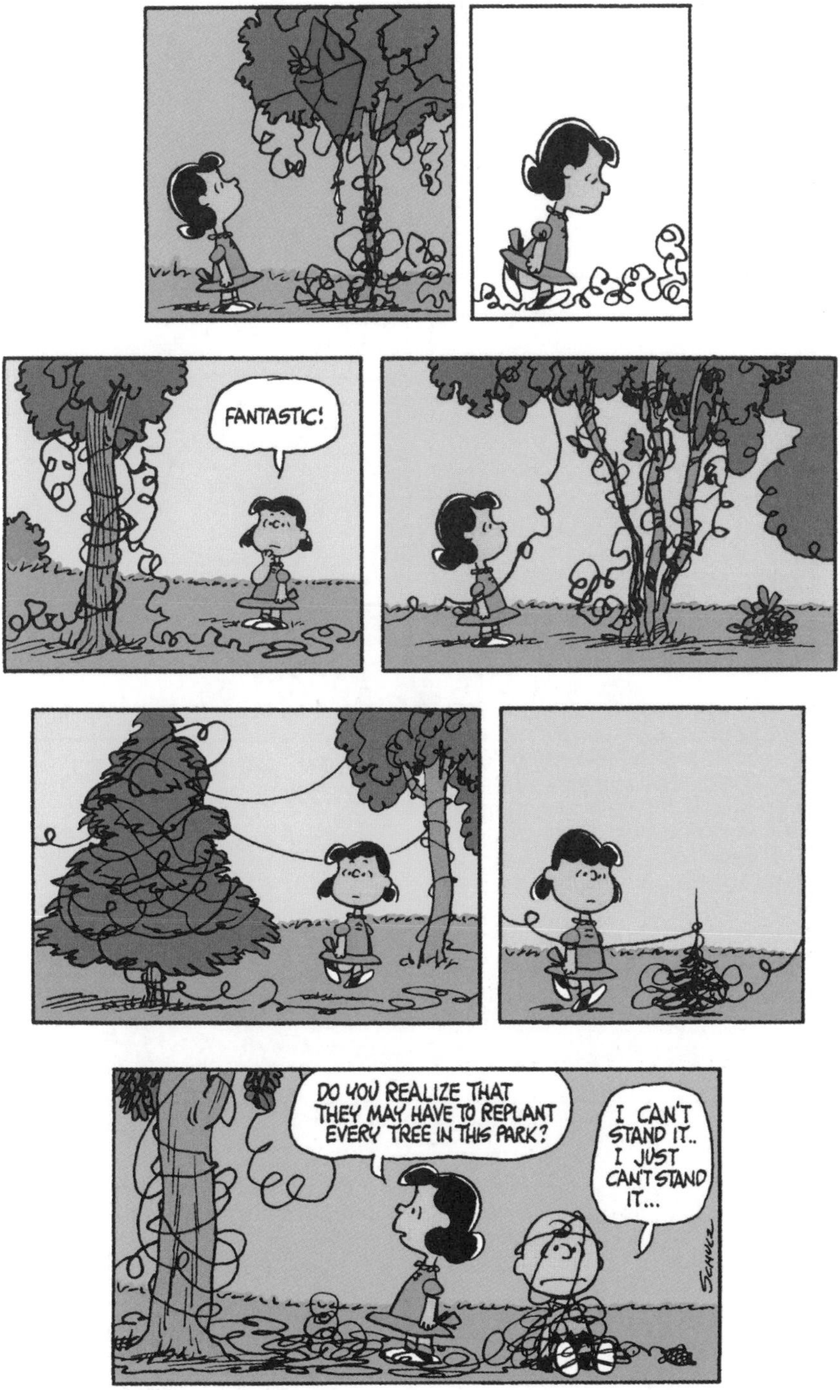
FANTASTIC!
DO YOU REALIZE THAT THEY MAY HAVE TO REPLANT EVERY TREE IN THIS PARK?
I CAN'T STAND IT.. I JUST CAN'T STAND IT...
SCHULZ

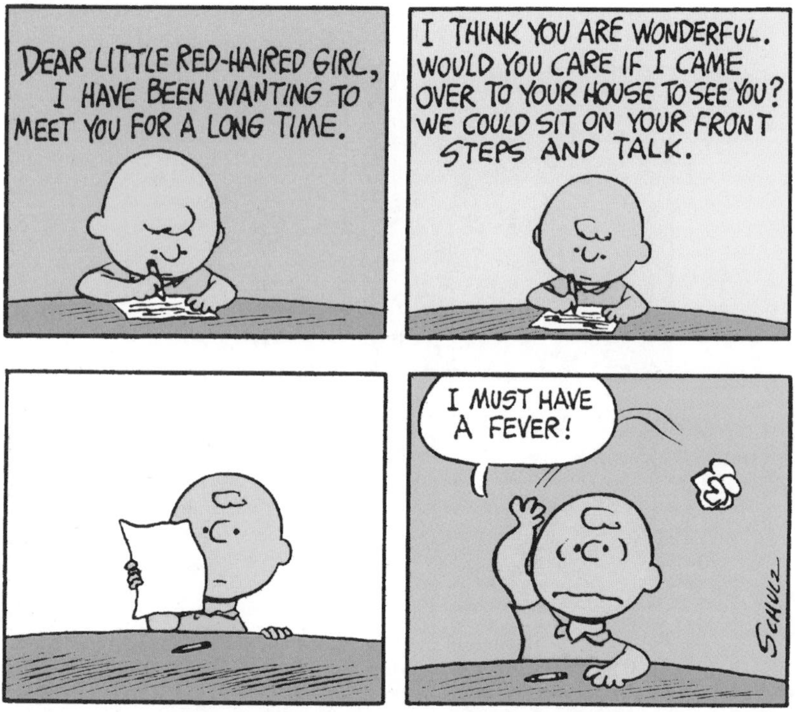
DEAR LITTLE RED-HAIRED GIRL,
I HAVE BEEN WANTING TO MEET YOU FOR A LONG TIME.
I THINK YOU ARE WONDERFUL. WOULD YOU CARE IF I CAME OVER TO YOUR HOUSE TO SEE YOU? WE COULD SIT ON YOUR FRONT STEPS AND TALK.
I MUST HAVE A FEVER!
SCHULZ

AAUGH! AAUGH!

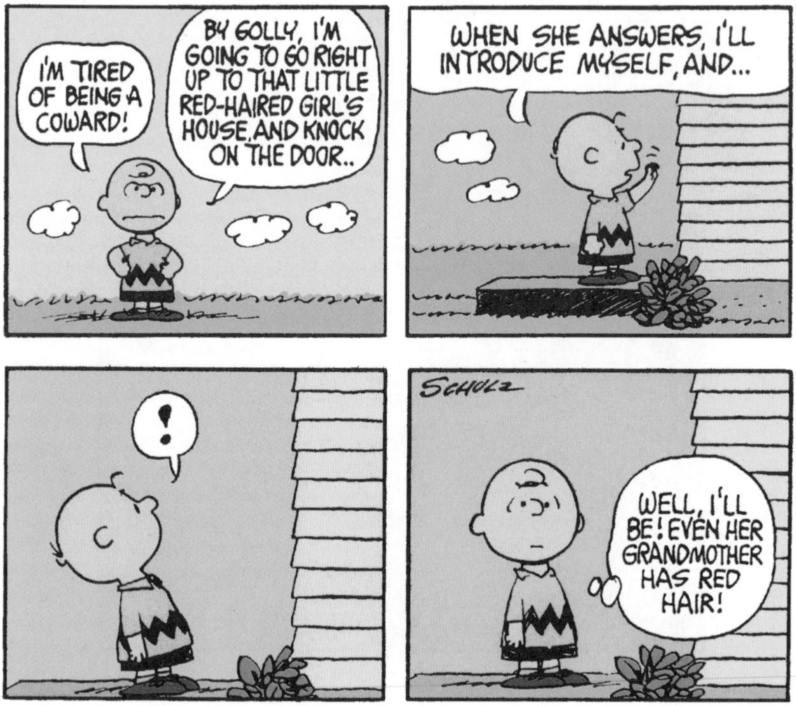
I'M TIRED OF BEING A COWARD!
BY GOLLY, I'M GOING TO GO RIGHT UP TO THAT LITTLE RED-HAIRED GIRL'S HOUSE, AND KNOCK ON THE DOOR..
WHEN SHE ANSWERS, I'LL INTRODUCE MYSELF, AND...
!
SCHULZ
WELL, I'LL BE! EVEN HER GRANDMOTHER HAS RED HAIR!

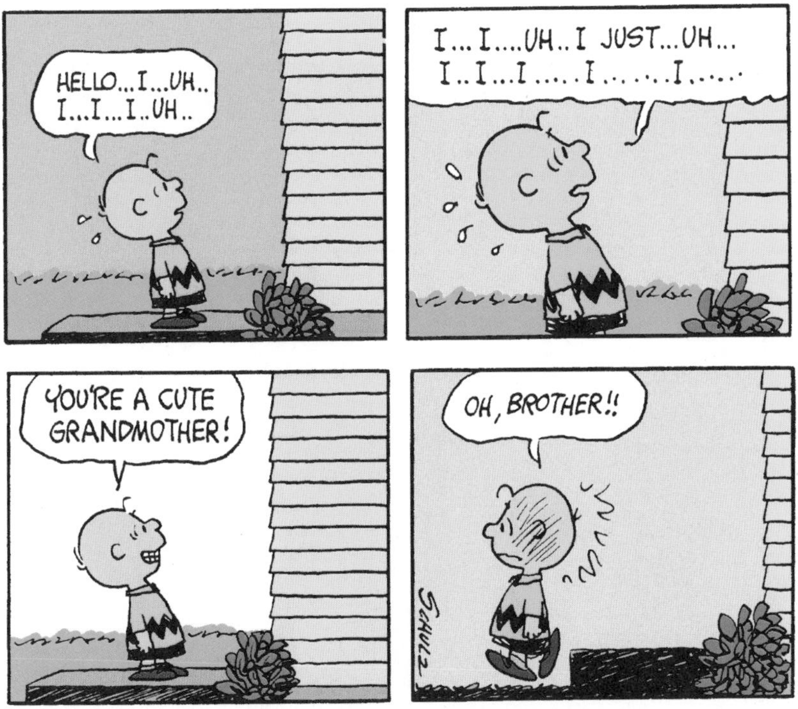
HELLO...I...UH.. I...I...I..UH..
I... I....UH.. I JUST...UH... I.. I...I..... I....... I......
YOU'RE A CUTE GRANDMOTHER!
OH, BROTHER!!
SCHULZ

AAUGH! AAUGH!

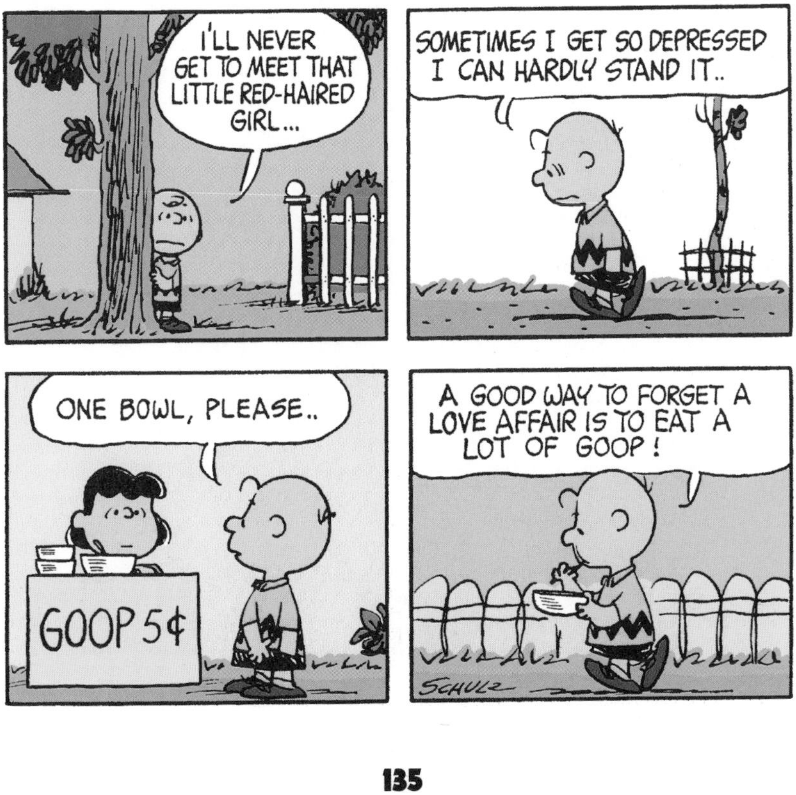
I'LL NEVER GET TO MEET THAT LITTLE RED-HAIRED GIRL...
SOMETIMES I GET SO DEPRESSED I CAN HARDLY STAND IT..
ONE BOWL, PLEASE..
GOOP 5¢
A GOOD WAY TO FORGET A LOVE AFFAIR IS TO EAT A LOT OF GOOP!
SCHULZ

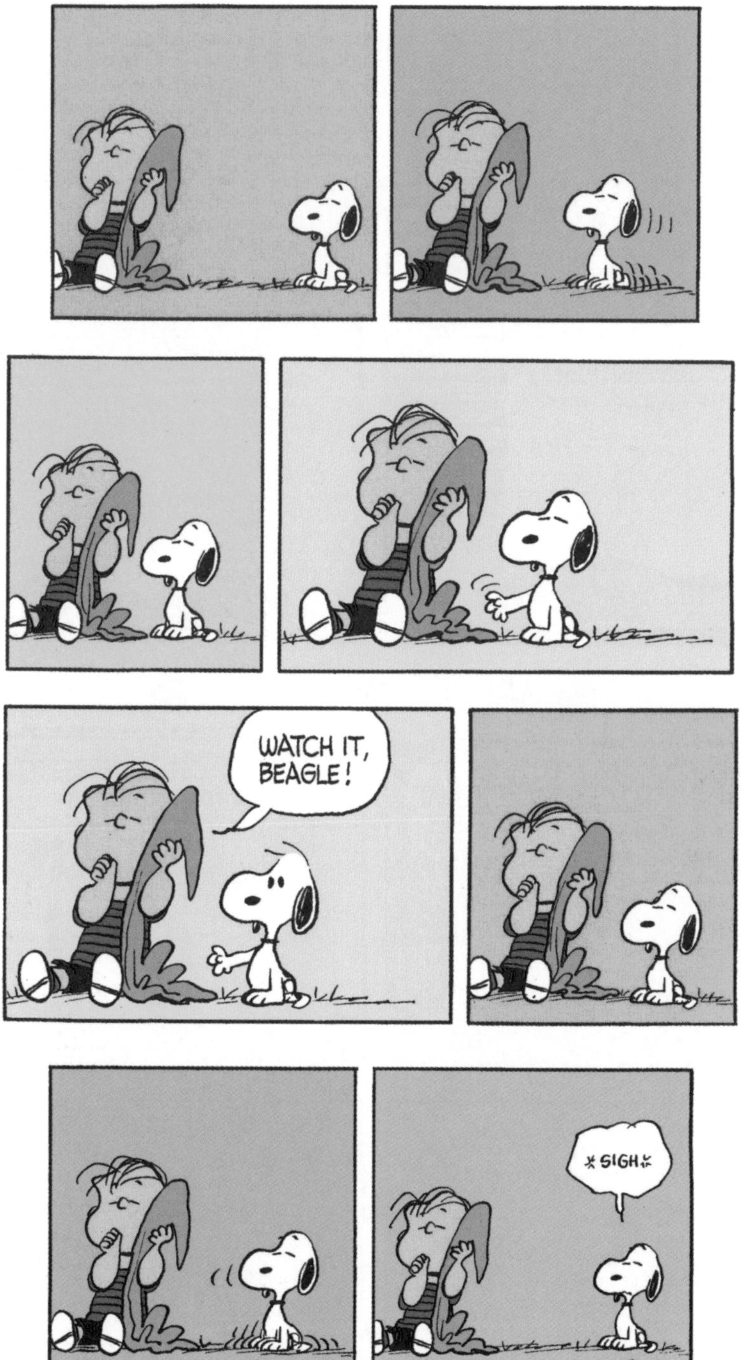
WATCH IT, BEAGLE!
SIGH
SCHULZ

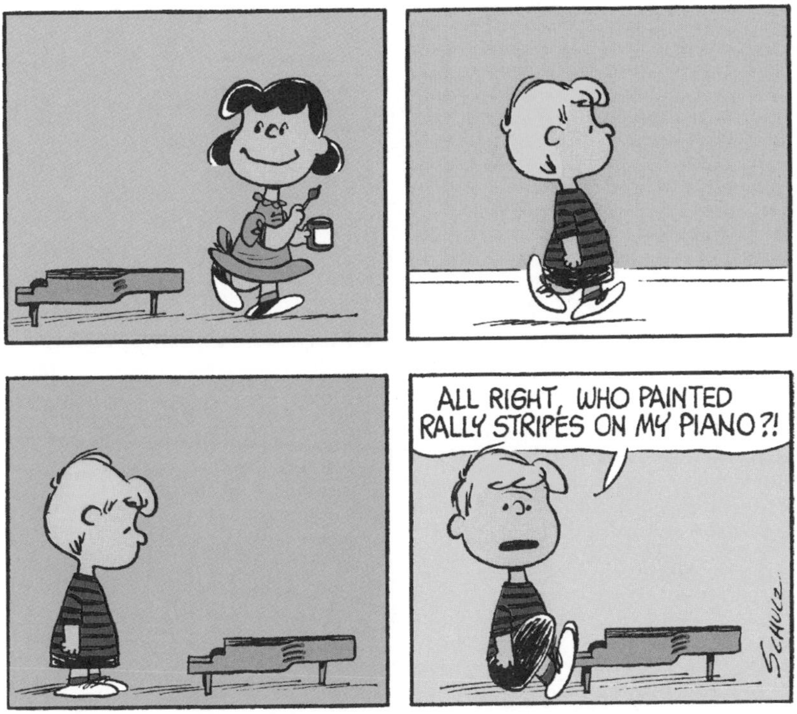
ALL RIGHT, WHO PAINTED RALLY STRIPES ON MY PIANO?!
SCHULZ

AAUGH! AAUGH!

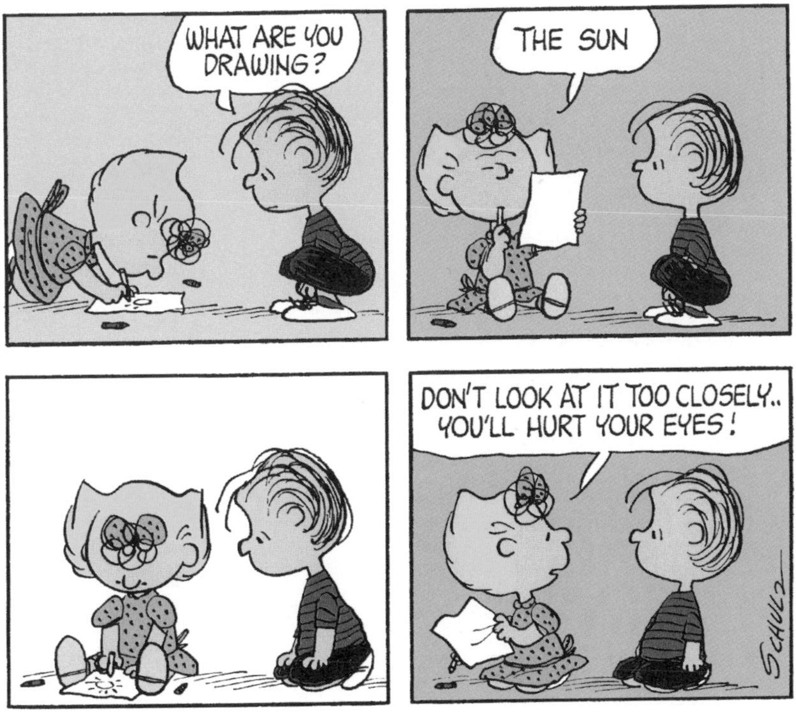
WHAT ARE YOU DRAWING?
THE SUN
DON'T LOOK AT IT TOO CLOSELY.. YOU'LL HURT YOUR EYES!
SCHULZ

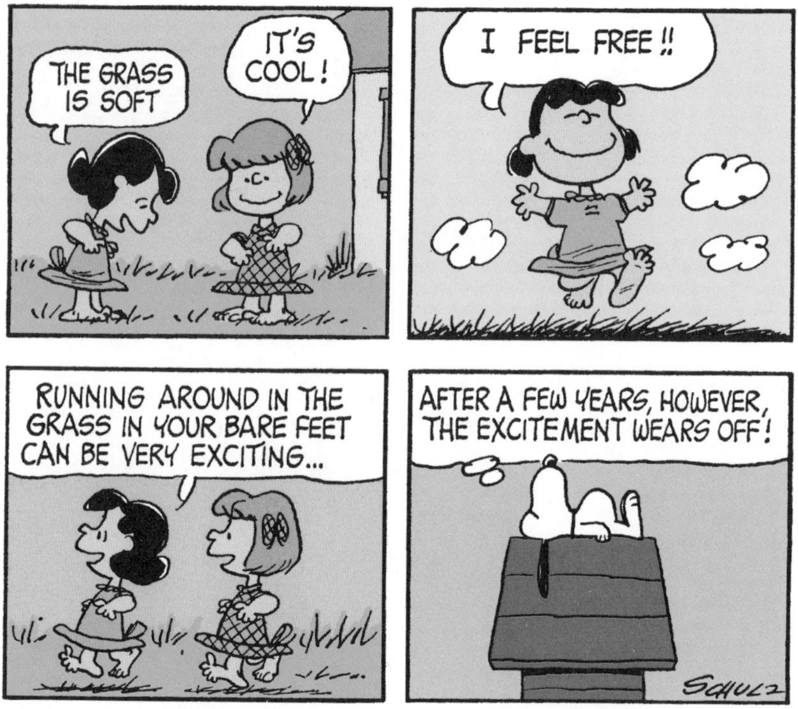
THE GRASS IS SOFT
IT'S COOL!
I FEEL FREE!!
RUNNING AROUND IN THE GRASS IN YOUR BARE FEET CAN BE VERY EXCITING...
AFTER A FEW YEARS, HOWEVER, THE EXCITEMENT WEARS OFF!
SCHULZ

AAUGH! AAUGH!

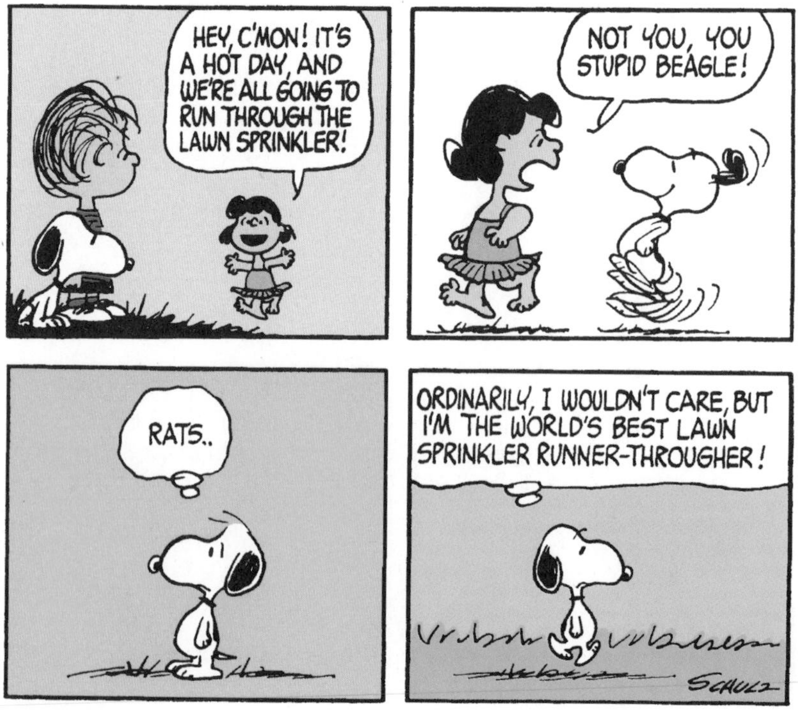
HEY, C'MON! IT'S A HOT DAY, AND WE'RE ALL GOING TO RUN THROUGH THE LAWN SPRINKLER!
NOT YOU, YOU STUPID BEAGLE!
RATS..
ORDINARILY, I WOULDN'T CARE, BUT I'M THE WORLD'S BEST LAWN SPRINKLER RUNNER-THROUGHER!
SCHULZ

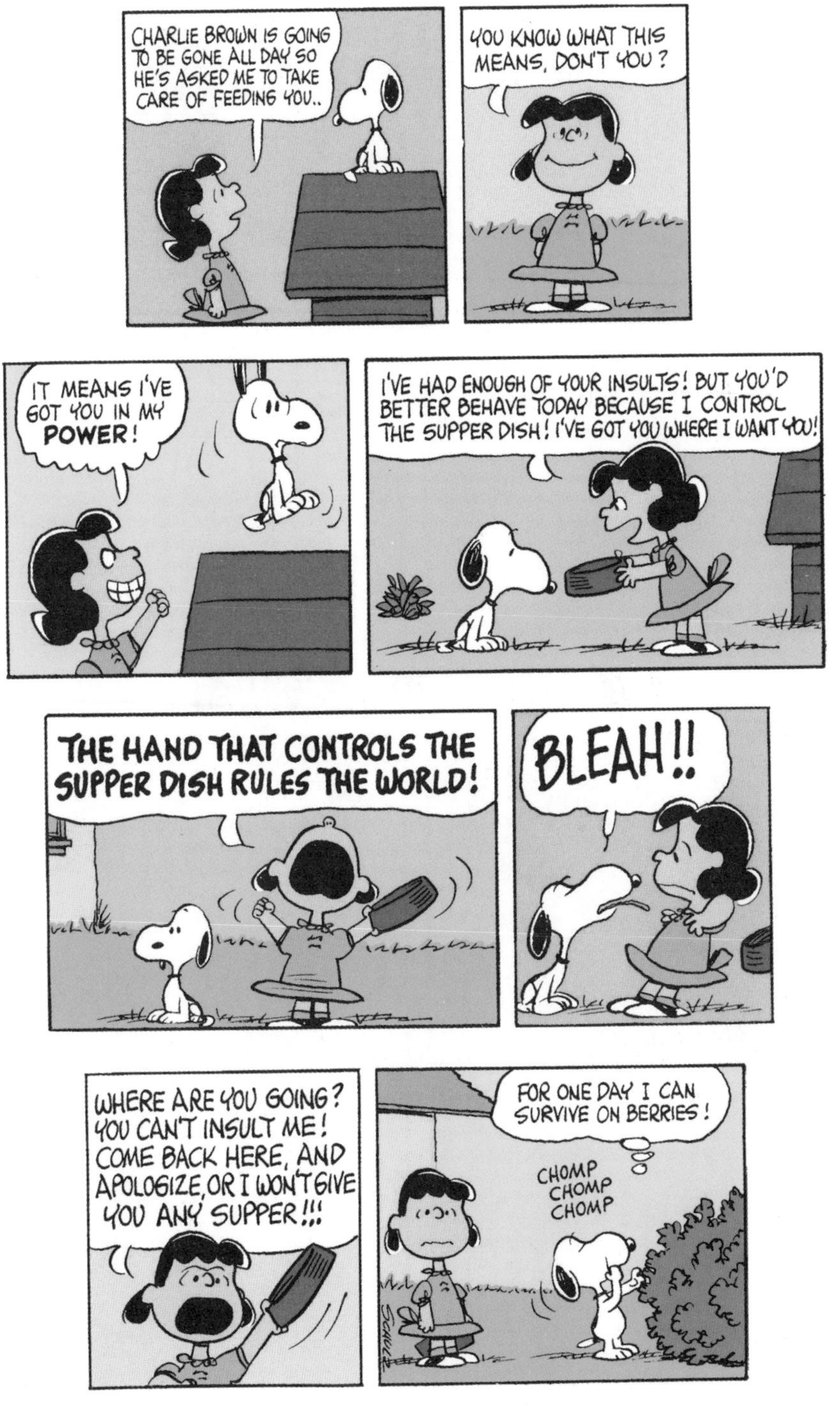
CHARLIE BROWN IS GOING TO BE GONE ALL DAY SO HE'S ASKED ME TO TAKE CARE OF FEEDING YOU..
YOU KNOW WHAT THIS MEANS, DON'T YOU?
IT MEANS I'VE GOT YOU IN MY POWER!
I'VE HAD ENOUGH OF YOUR INSULTS! BUT YOU'D BETTER BEHAVE TODAY BECAUSE I CONTROL THE SUPPER DISH! I'VE GOT YOU WHERE I WANT YOU!
THE HAND THAT CONTROLS THE SUPPER DISH RULES THE WORLD!
BLEAH!!
WHERE ARE YOU GOING? YOU CAN'T INSULT ME! COME BACK HERE, AND APOLOGIZE, OR I WON'T GIVE YOU ANY SUPPER!!!
FOR ONE DAY I CAN SURVIVE ON BERRIES!
CHOMP CHOMP CHOMP
SCHULZ

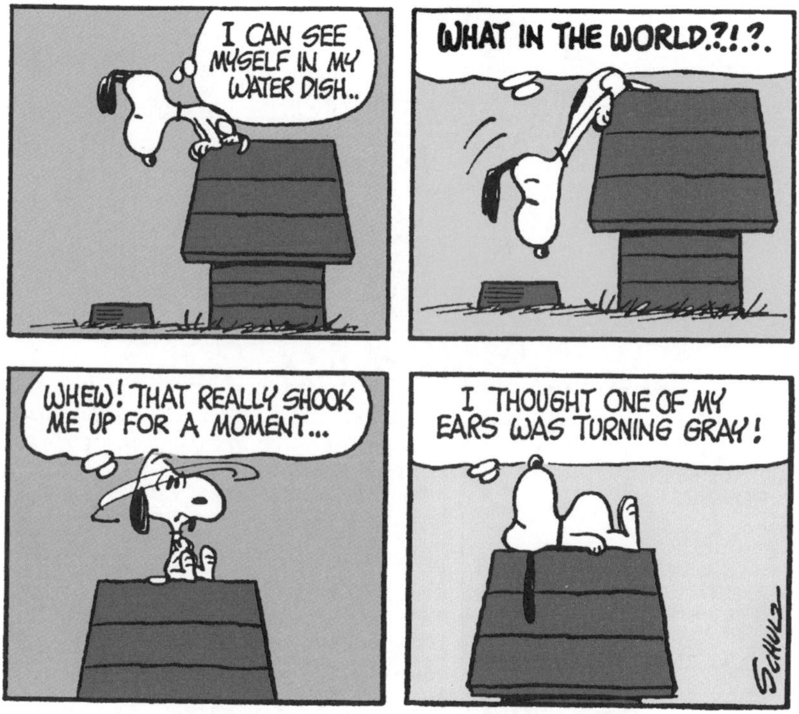
I CAN SEE MYSELF IN MY WATER DISH..
WHAT IN THE WORLD?!?!?
WHEW! THAT REALLY SHOOK ME UP FOR A MOMENT...
I THOUGHT ONE OF MY EARS WAS TURNING GRAY!
SCHULZ

AAUGH! AAUGH!

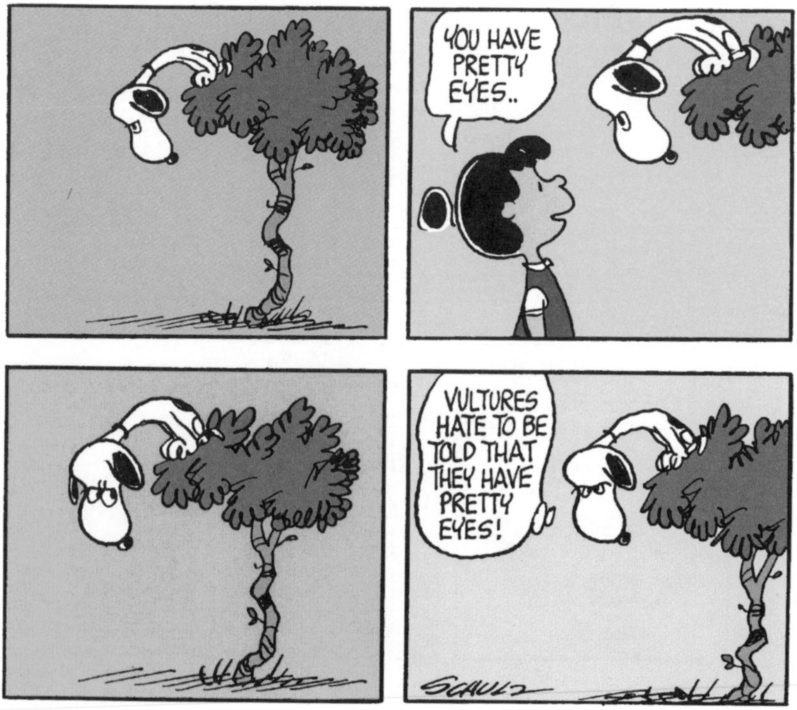
YOU HAVE PRETTY EYES..
VULTURES HATE TO BE TOLD THAT THEY HAVE PRETTY EYES!
SCHULZ

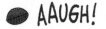

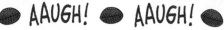

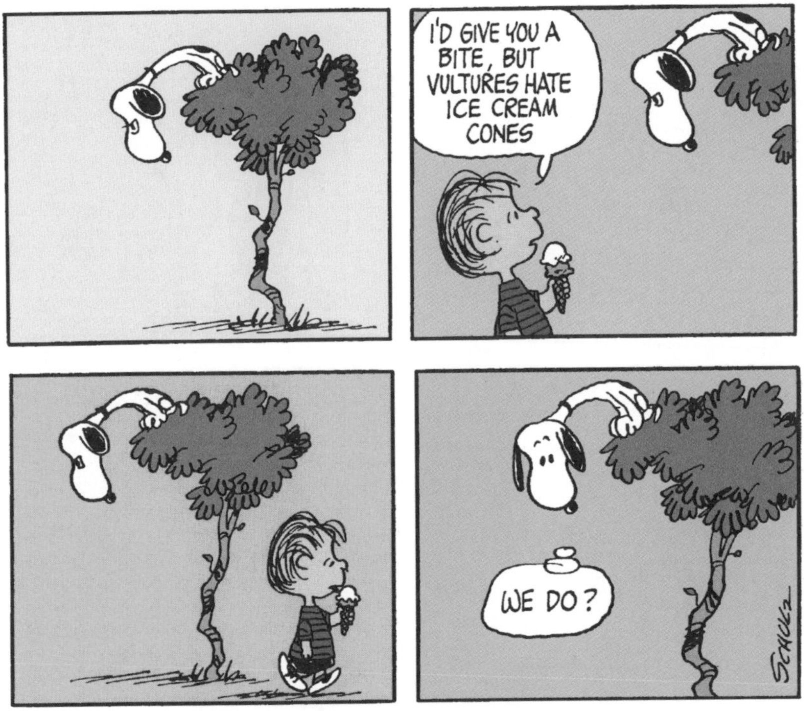
I'D GIVE YOU A BITE, BUT VULTURES HATE ICE CREAM CONES
WE DO?
SCHULZ

AAUGH! AAUGH!

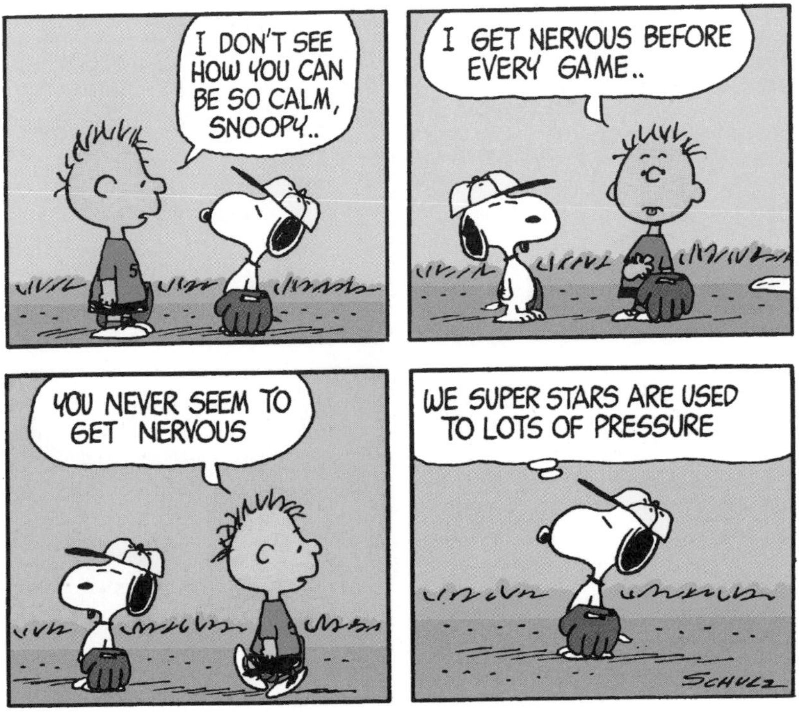
I DON'T SEE HOW YOU CAN BE SO CALM, SNOOPY..
I GET NERVOUS BEFORE EVERY GAME..
YOU NEVER SEEM TO GET NERVOUS
WE SUPER STARS ARE USED TO LOTS OF PRESSURE
SCHULZ

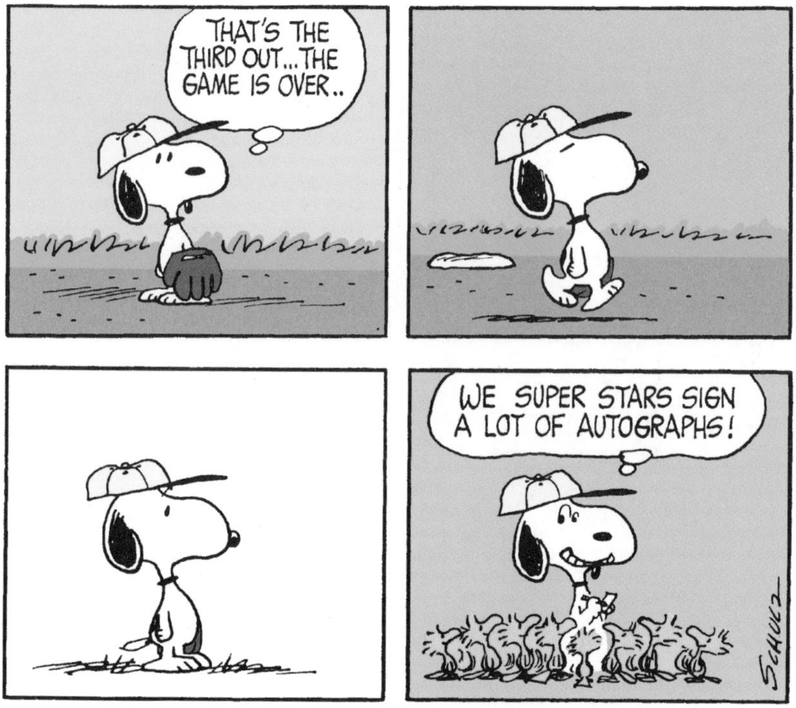
THAT'S THE THIRD OUT... THE GAME IS OVER..
WE SUPER STARS SIGN A LOT OF AUTOGRAPHS!
SCHULZ

AAUGH! AAUGH!

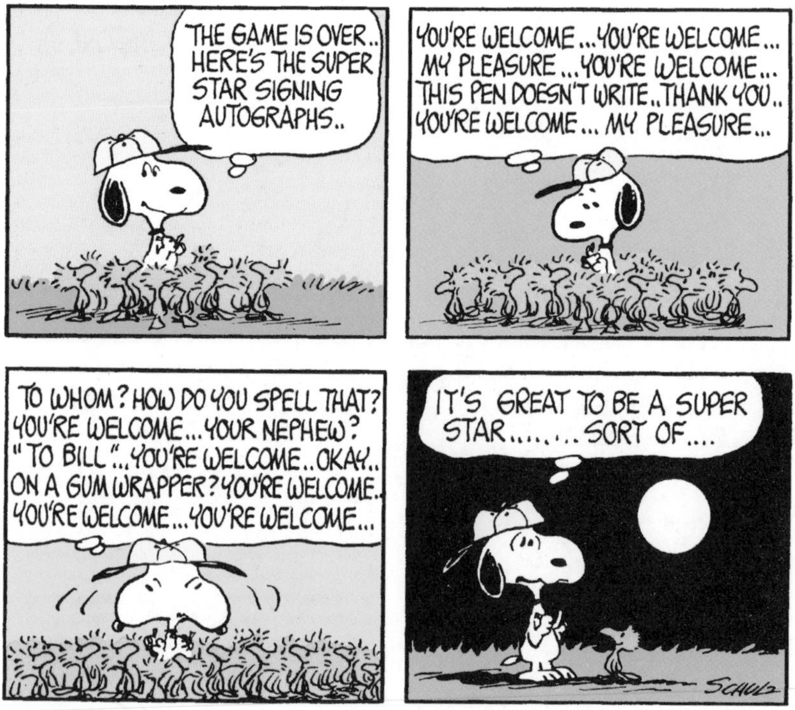
THE GAME IS OVER.. HERE'S THE SUPER STAR SIGNING AUTOGRAPHS..
YOU'RE WELCOME... YOU'RE WELCOME... MY PLEASURE... YOU'RE WELCOME... THIS PEN DOESN'T WRITE.. THANK YOU.. YOU'RE WELCOME... MY PLEASURE...
TO WHOM? HOW DO YOU SPELL THAT? YOU'RE WELCOME... YOUR NEPHEW? "TO BILL".. YOU'RE WELCOME.. OKAY.. ON A GUM WRAPPER? YOU'RE WELCOME.. YOU'RE WELCOME... YOU'RE WELCOME...
IT'S GREAT TO BE A SUPER STAR....... SORT OF....
SCHULZ

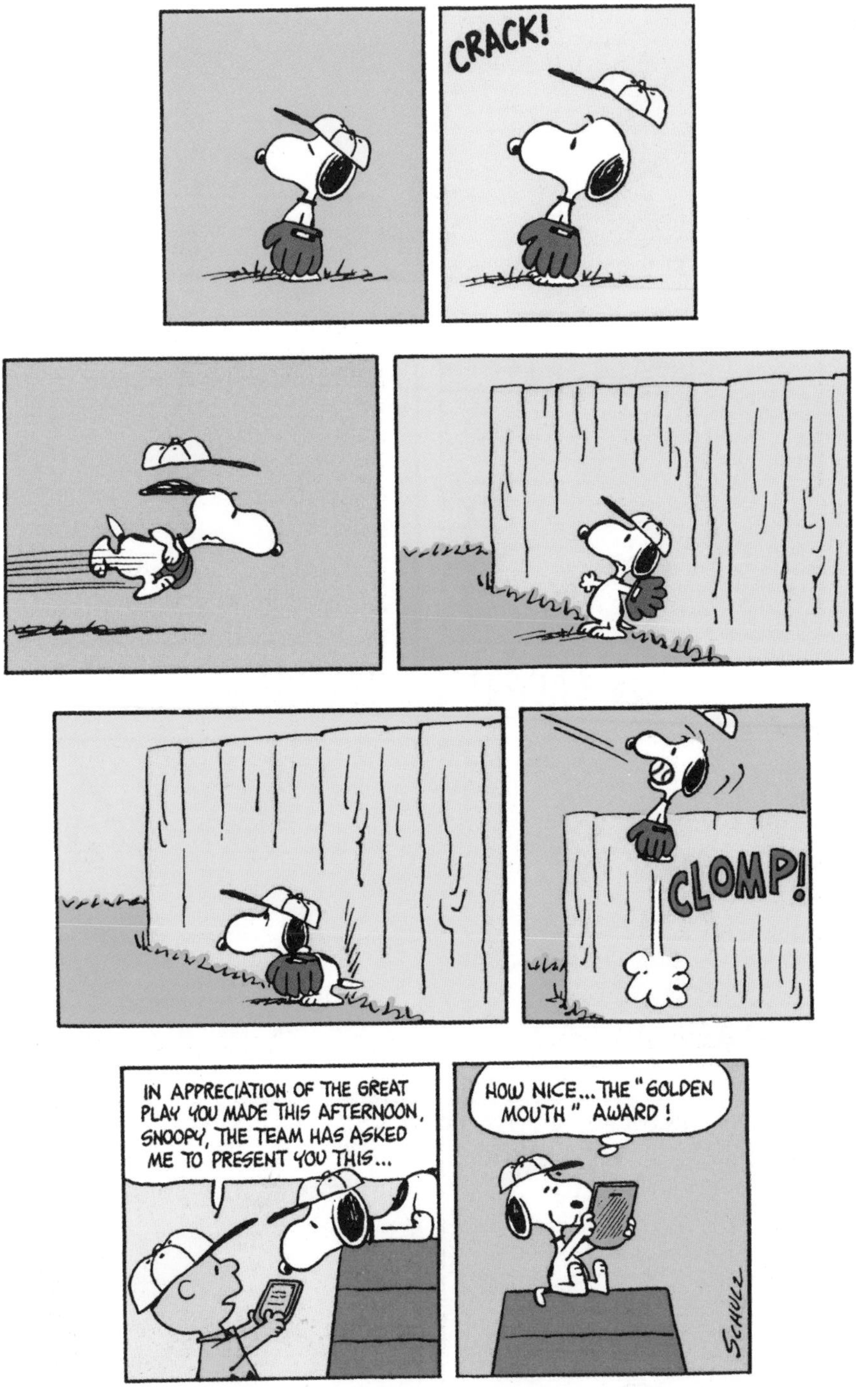
CRACK!
CLOMP!
IN APPRECIATION OF THE GREAT PLAY YOU MADE THIS AFTERNOON, SNOOPY, THE TEAM HAS ASKED ME TO PRESENT YOU THIS...
HOW NICE...THE "GOLDEN MOUTH" AWARD!
SCHULZ

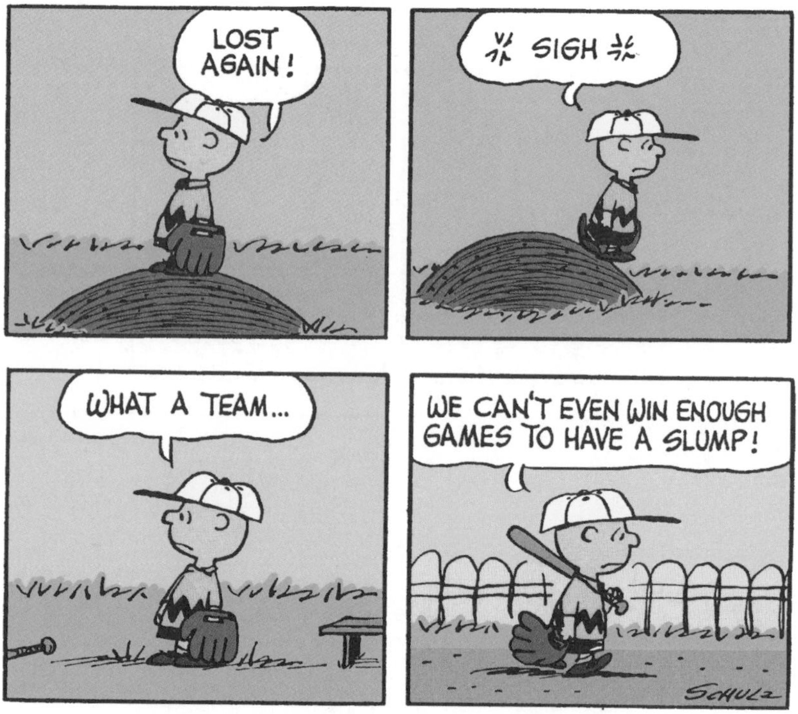
LOST AGAIN!
SIGH
WHAT A TEAM...
WE CAN'T EVEN WIN ENOUGH GAMES TO HAVE A SLUMP!
SCHULZ

AAUGH! AAUGH!

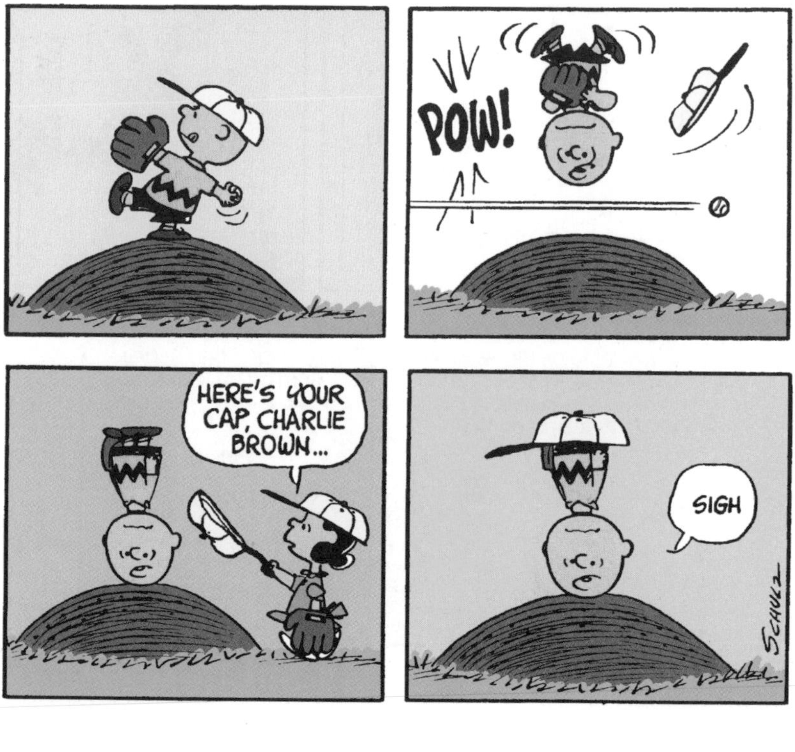
POW!
HERE'S YOUR CAP, CHARLIE BROWN...
SIGH
SCHULZ

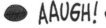

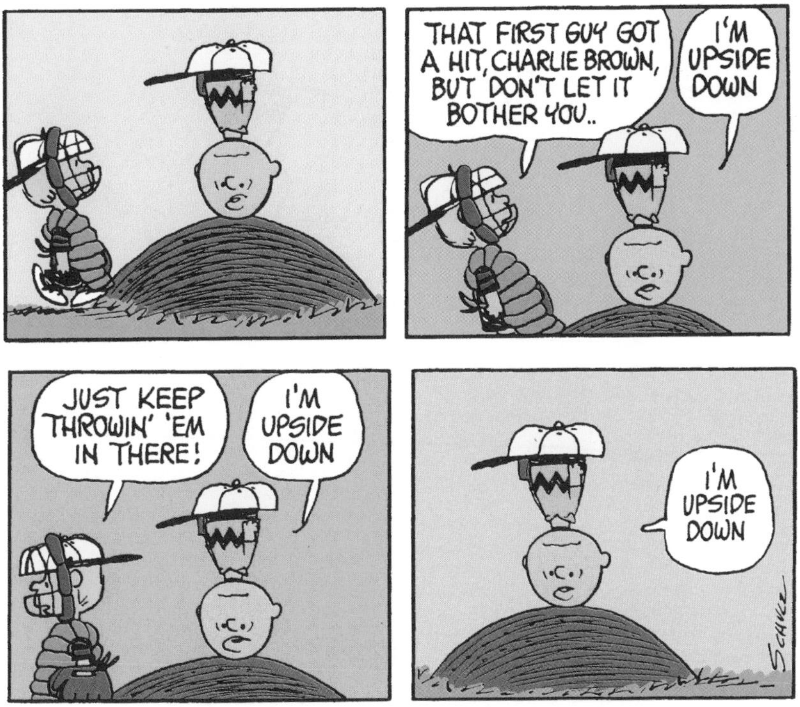
THAT FIRST GUY GOT A HIT, CHARLIE BROWN, BUT DON'T LET IT BOTHER YOU..
I'M UPSIDE DOWN
JUST KEEP THROWIN' 'EM IN THERE!
I'M UPSIDE DOWN
I'M UPSIDE DOWN

AAUGH! AAUGH!

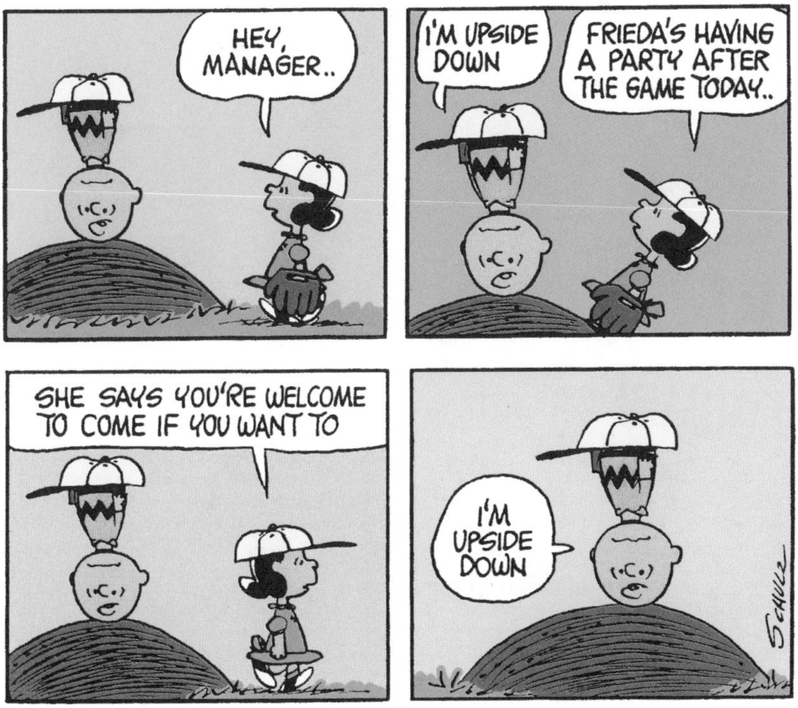
HEY, MANAGER..
I'M UPSIDE DOWN
FRIEDA'S HAVING A PARTY AFTER THE GAME TODAY..
SHE SAYS YOU'RE WELCOME TO COME IF YOU WANT TO
I'M UPSIDE DOWN

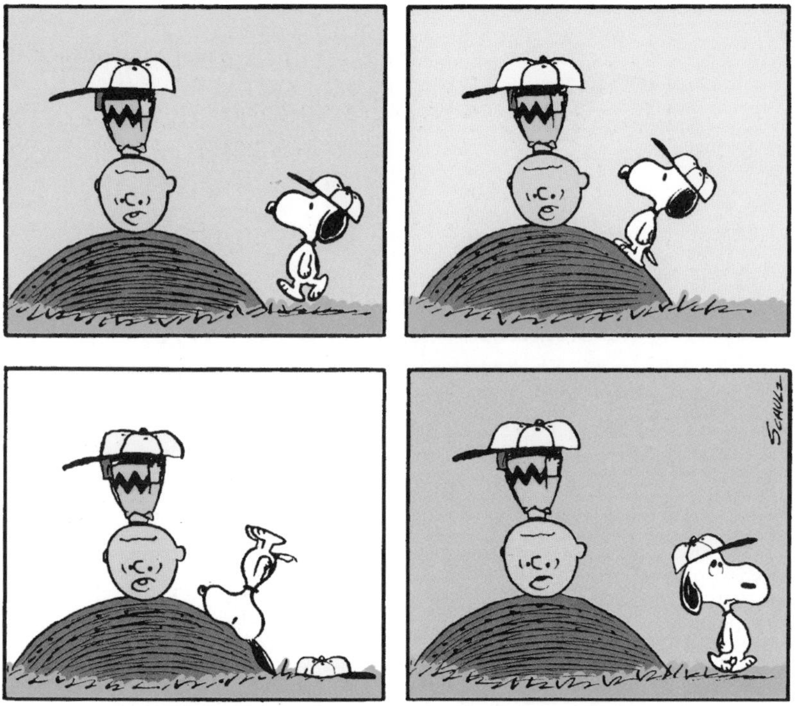
SCHULZ

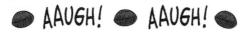

AAUGH! AAUGH!

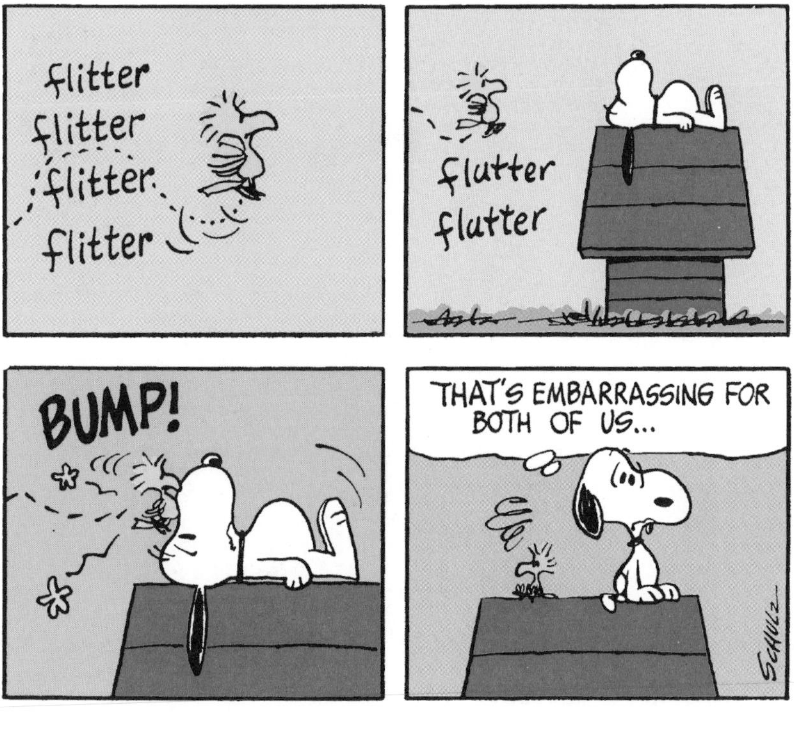
flitter
flitter
flitter
flitter
flutter
flutter
BUMP!
THAT'S EMBARRASSING FOR BOTH OF US...
SCHULZ

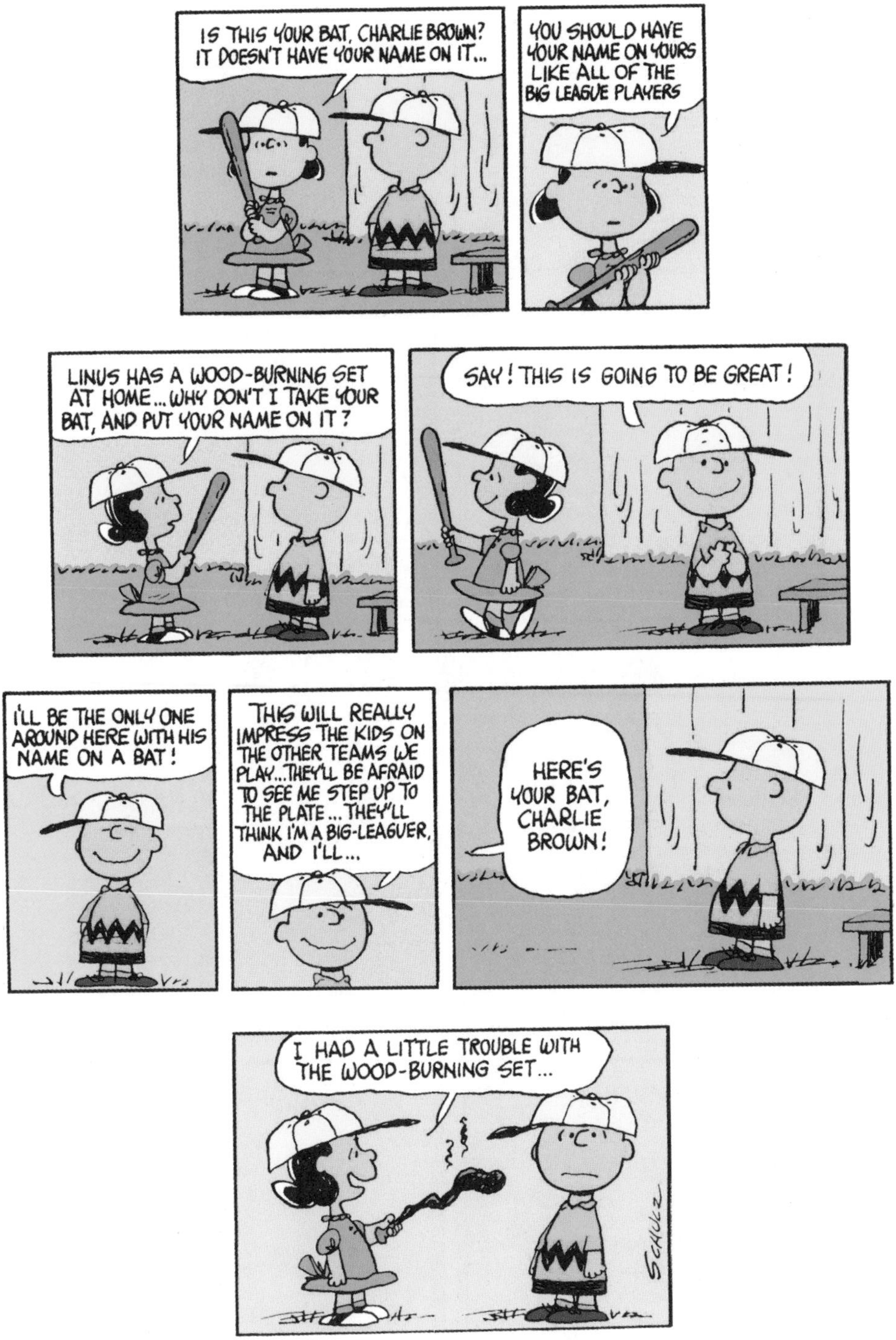
IS THIS YOUR BAT, CHARLIE BROWN? IT DOESN'T HAVE YOUR NAME ON IT...
YOU SHOULD HAVE YOUR NAME ON YOURS LIKE ALL OF THE BIG LEAGUE PLAYERS
LINUS HAS A WOOD-BURNING SET AT HOME... WHY DON'T I TAKE YOUR BAT, AND PUT YOUR NAME ON IT?
SAY! THIS IS GOING TO BE GREAT!
I'LL BE THE ONLY ONE AROUND HERE WITH HIS NAME ON A BAT!
THIS WILL REALLY IMPRESS THE KIDS ON THE OTHER TEAMS WE PLAY... THEY'LL BE AFRAID TO SEE ME STEP UP TO THE PLATE... THEY'LL THINK I'M A BIG-LEAGUER, AND I'LL...
HERE'S YOUR BAT, CHARLIE BROWN!
I HAD A LITTLE TROUBLE WITH THE WOOD-BURNING SET...
SCHULZ

YOUR BEACH BALL JUST LEFT FOR HAWAII..

AAUGH! AAUGH!

MY BEACH BALL!

YOU LET MY BEACH BALL GET AWAY! IT'S GONE! THAT BALL WILL FLOAT CLEAR TO HAWAII!

WHAT DO YOU HAVE TO SAY FOR YOURSELF?

ALOHA?

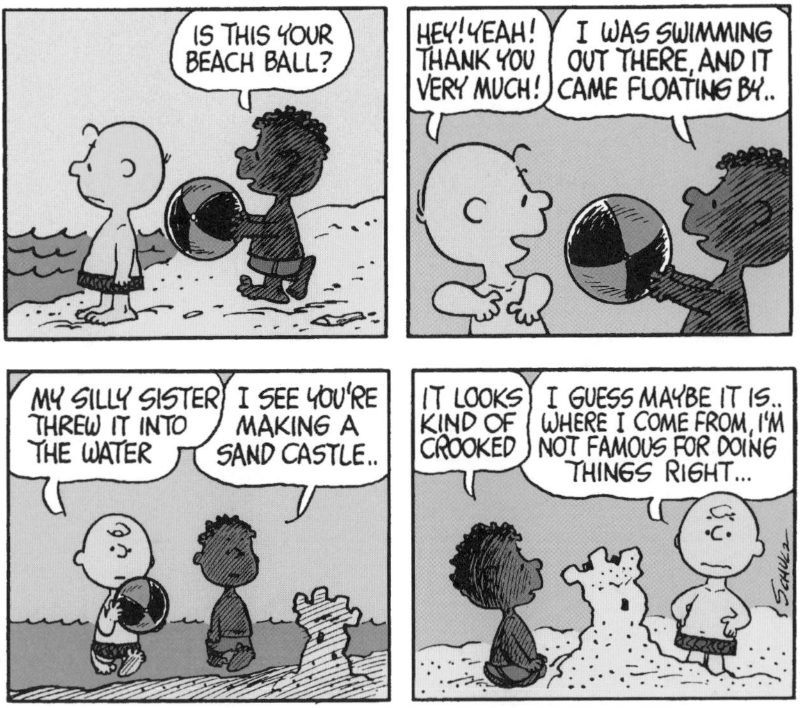
IS THIS YOUR BEACH BALL?
HEY! YEAH! THANK YOU VERY MUCH!
I WAS SWIMMING OUT THERE, AND IT CAME FLOATING BY..
MY SILLY SISTER THREW IT INTO THE WATER
I SEE YOU'RE MAKING A SAND CASTLE..
IT LOOKS KIND OF CROOKED
I GUESS MAYBE IT IS.. WHERE I COME FROM, I'M NOT FAMOUS FOR DOING THINGS RIGHT...
SCHULZ

AAUGH! AAUGH!

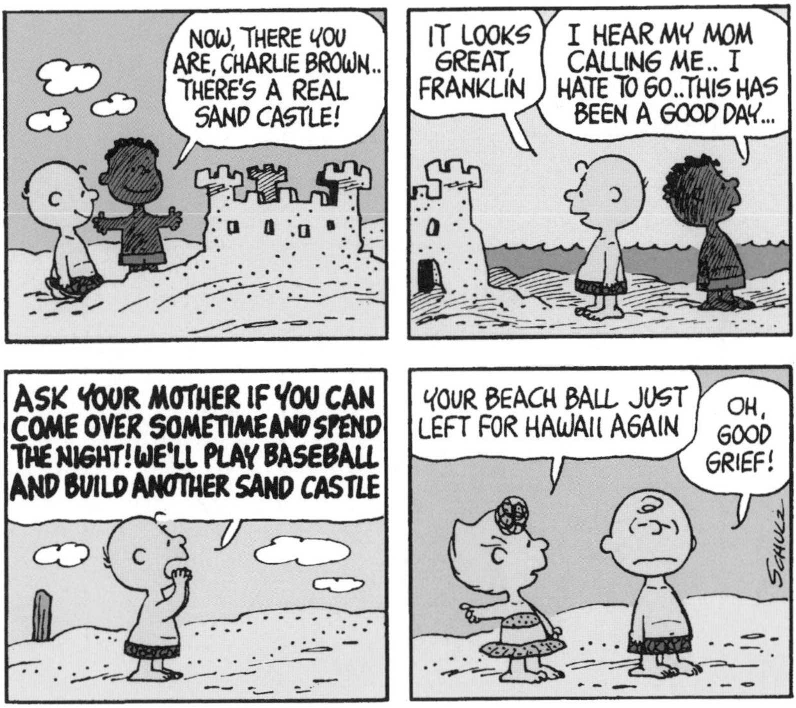
NOW, THERE YOU ARE, CHARLIE BROWN.. THERE'S A REAL SAND CASTLE!
IT LOOKS GREAT, FRANKLIN
I HEAR MY MOM CALLING ME.. I HATE TO GO..THIS HAS BEEN A GOOD DAY...
ASK YOUR MOTHER IF YOU CAN COME OVER SOMETIME AND SPEND THE NIGHT! WE'LL PLAY BASEBALL AND BUILD ANOTHER SAND CASTLE
YOUR BEACH BALL JUST LEFT FOR HAWAII AGAIN
OH, GOOD GRIEF!
SCHULZ

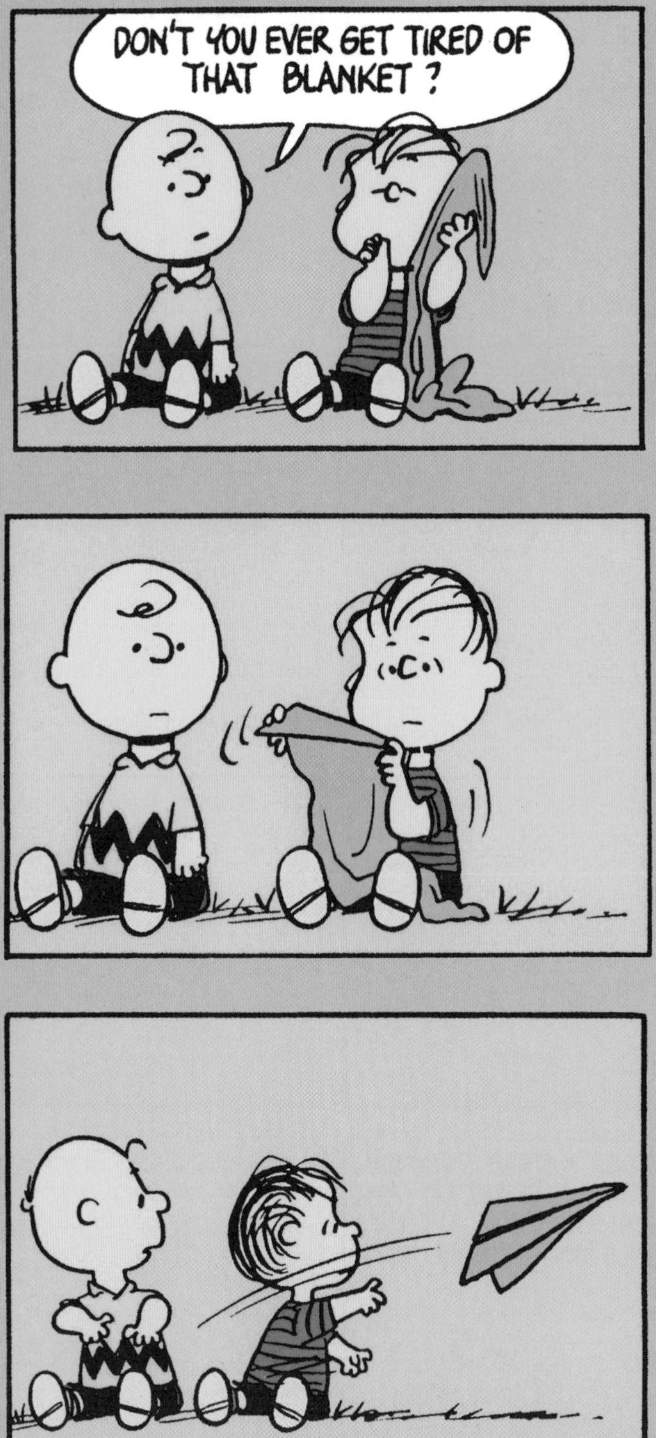
DON'T YOU EVER GET TIRED OF THAT BLANKET ?

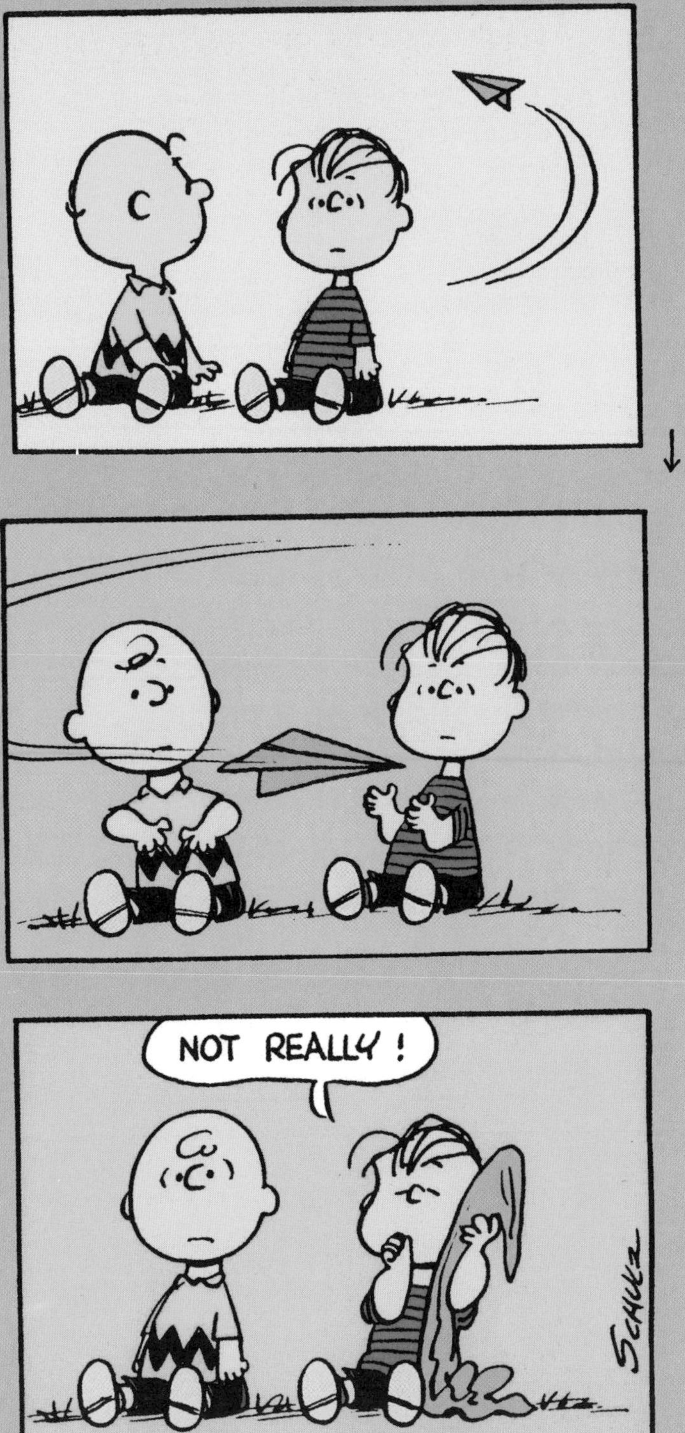
NOT REALLY !
SCHULZ

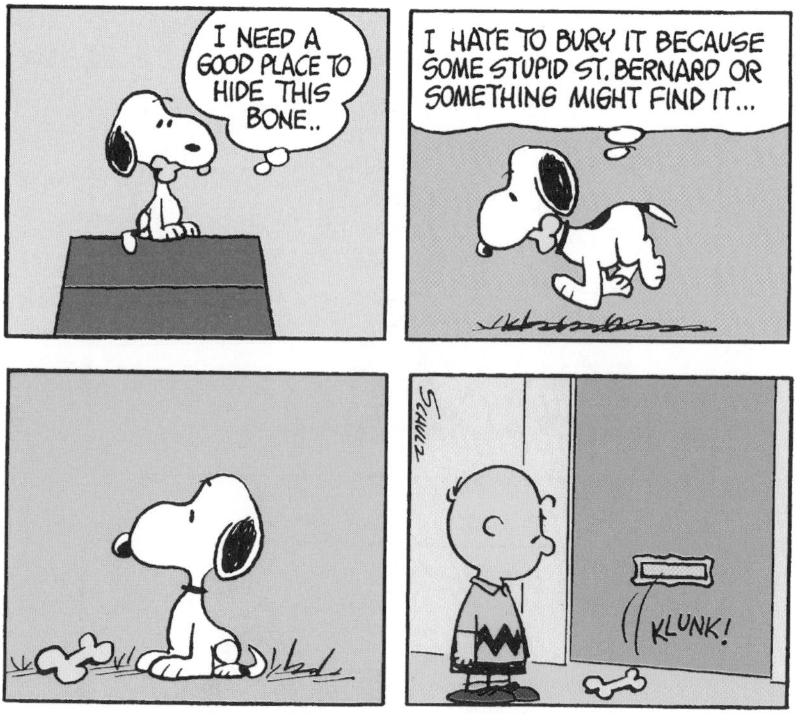
I NEED A GOOD PLACE TO HIDE THIS BONE..
I HATE TO BURY IT BECAUSE SOME STUPID ST. BERNARD OR SOMETHING MIGHT FIND IT...
KLUNK!

AAUGH! AAUGH!

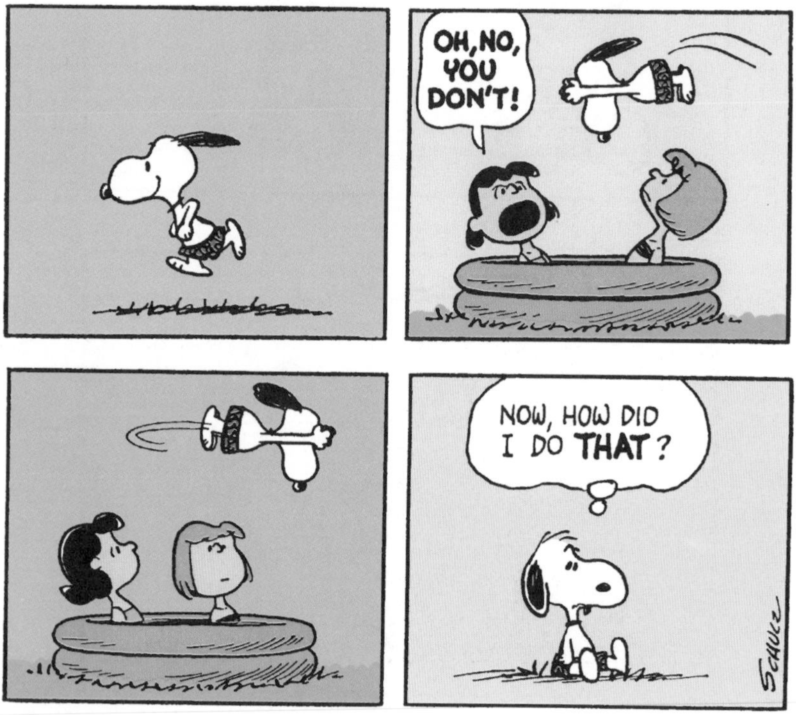
OH, NO, YOU DON'T!
NOW, HOW DID I DO **THAT**?

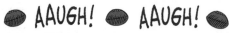

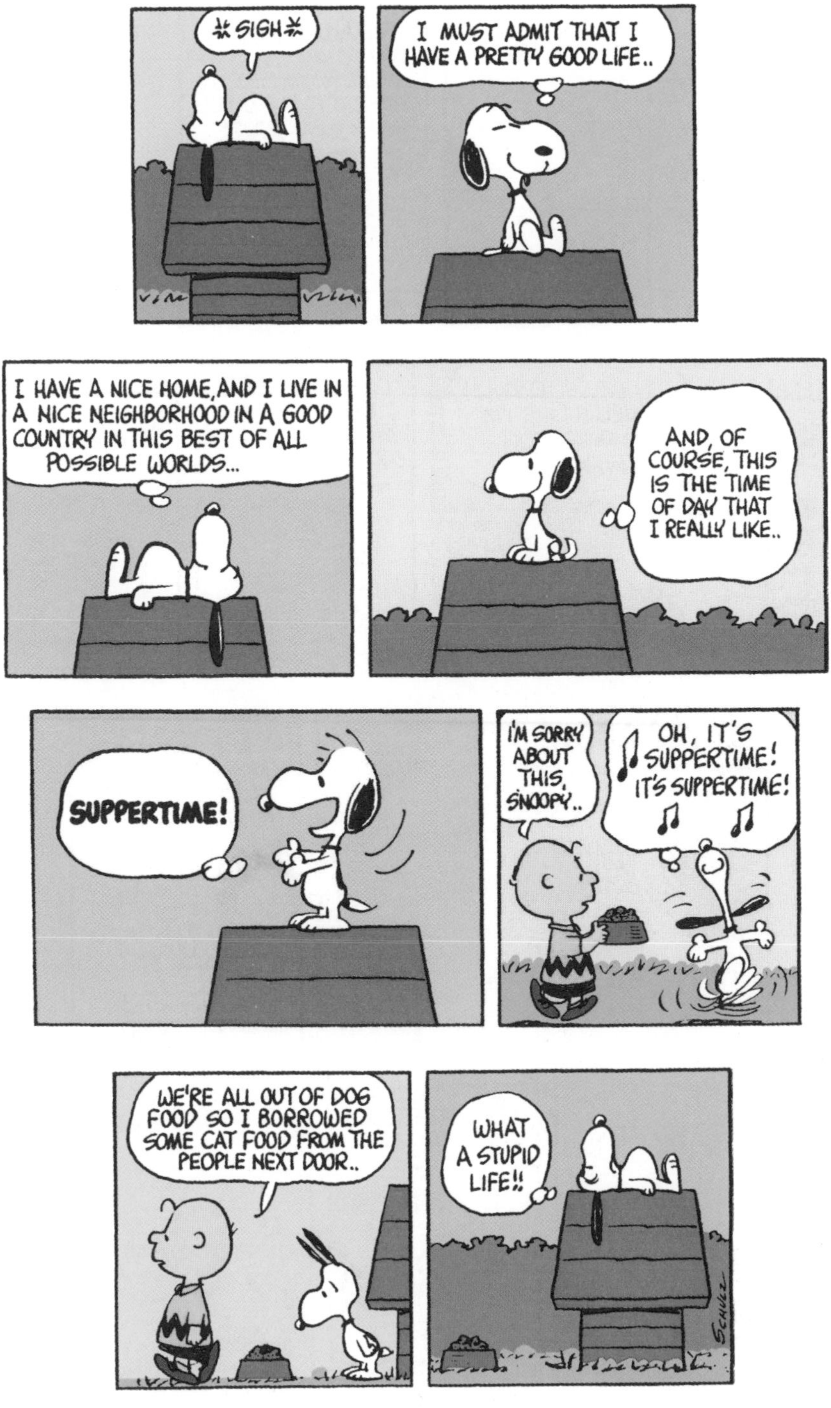
SIGH
I MUST ADMIT THAT I HAVE A PRETTY GOOD LIFE..
I HAVE A NICE HOME, AND I LIVE IN A NICE NEIGHBORHOOD IN A GOOD COUNTRY IN THIS BEST OF ALL POSSIBLE WORLDS...
AND, OF COURSE, THIS IS THE TIME OF DAY THAT I REALLY LIKE..
SUPPERTIME!
I'M SORRY ABOUT THIS, SNOOPY..
OH, IT'S SUPPERTIME! IT'S SUPPERTIME!
WE'RE ALL OUT OF DOG FOOD SO I BORROWED SOME CAT FOOD FROM THE PEOPLE NEXT DOOR..
WHAT A STUPID LIFE!!
SCHULZ

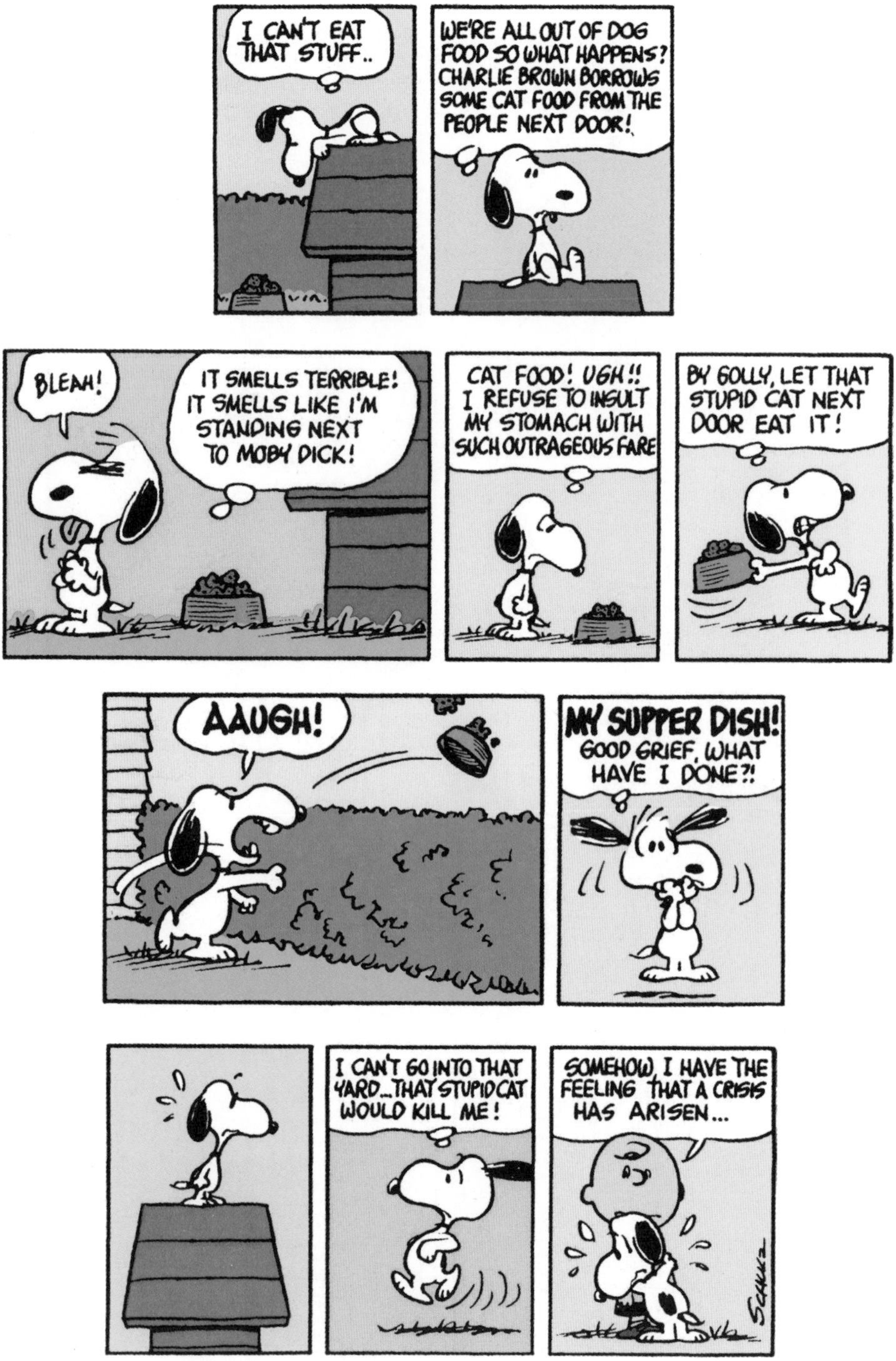
I CAN'T EAT THAT STUFF..
WE'RE ALL OUT OF DOG FOOD SO WHAT HAPPENS? CHARLIE BROWN BORROWS SOME CAT FOOD FROM THE PEOPLE NEXT DOOR!
BLEAH!
IT SMELLS TERRIBLE! IT SMELLS LIKE I'M STANDING NEXT TO MOBY DICK!
CAT FOOD! UGH!! I REFUSE TO INSULT MY STOMACH WITH SUCH OUTRAGEOUS FARE
BY GOLLY, LET THAT STUPID CAT NEXT DOOR EAT IT!
AAUGH!
MY SUPPER DISH! GOOD GRIEF, WHAT HAVE I DONE?!
I CAN'T GO INTO THAT YARD...THAT STUPID CAT WOULD KILL ME!
SOMEHOW, I HAVE THE FEELING THAT A CRISIS HAS ARISEN...
SCHULZ

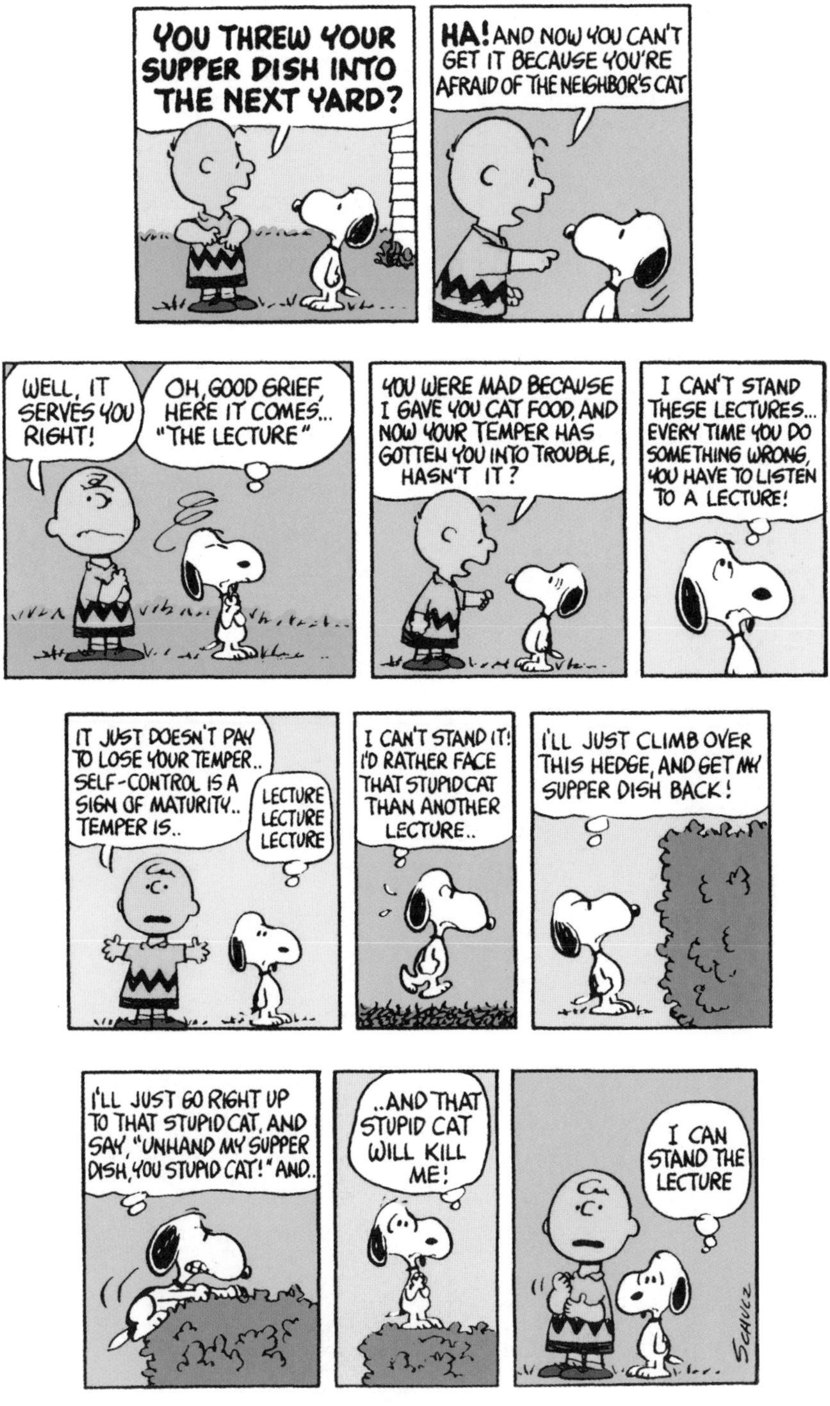
YOU THREW YOUR SUPPER DISH INTO THE NEXT YARD?
HA! AND NOW YOU CAN'T GET IT BECAUSE YOU'RE AFRAID OF THE NEIGHBOR'S CAT
WELL, IT SERVES YOU RIGHT!
OH, GOOD GRIEF, HERE IT COMES... "THE LECTURE"
YOU WERE MAD BECAUSE I GAVE YOU CAT FOOD, AND NOW YOUR TEMPER HAS GOTTEN YOU INTO TROUBLE, HASN'T IT?
I CAN'T STAND THESE LECTURES... EVERY TIME YOU DO SOMETHING WRONG, YOU HAVE TO LISTEN TO A LECTURE!
IT JUST DOESN'T PAY TO LOSE YOUR TEMPER.. SELF-CONTROL IS A SIGN OF MATURITY.. TEMPER IS..
LECTURE LECTURE LECTURE
I CAN'T STAND IT! I'D RATHER FACE THAT STUPID CAT THAN ANOTHER LECTURE..
I'LL JUST CLIMB OVER THIS HEDGE, AND GET MY SUPPER DISH BACK!
I'LL JUST GO RIGHT UP TO THAT STUPID CAT, AND SAY, "UNHAND MY SUPPER DISH, YOU STUPID CAT!" AND..
..AND THAT STUPID CAT WILL KILL ME!
I CAN STAND THE LECTURE
SCHULZ

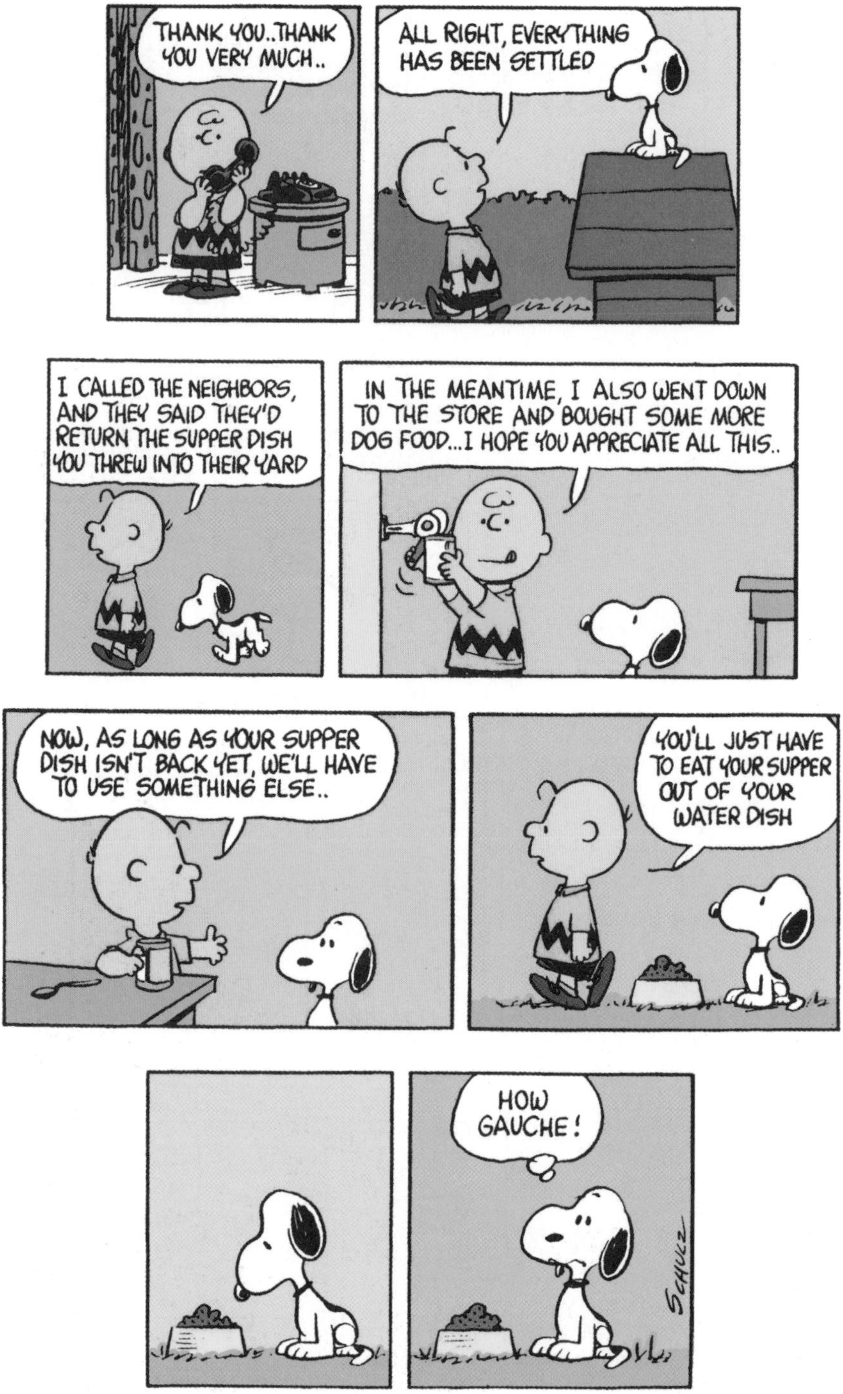
THANK YOU..THANK YOU VERY MUCH..
ALL RIGHT, EVERYTHING HAS BEEN SETTLED
I CALLED THE NEIGHBORS, AND THEY SAID THEY'D RETURN THE SUPPER DISH YOU THREW INTO THEIR YARD
IN THE MEANTIME, I ALSO WENT DOWN TO THE STORE AND BOUGHT SOME MORE DOG FOOD...I HOPE YOU APPRECIATE ALL THIS..
NOW, AS LONG AS YOUR SUPPER DISH ISN'T BACK YET, WE'LL HAVE TO USE SOMETHING ELSE..
YOU'LL JUST HAVE TO EAT YOUR SUPPER OUT OF YOUR WATER DISH
HOW GAUCHE!
SCHULZ

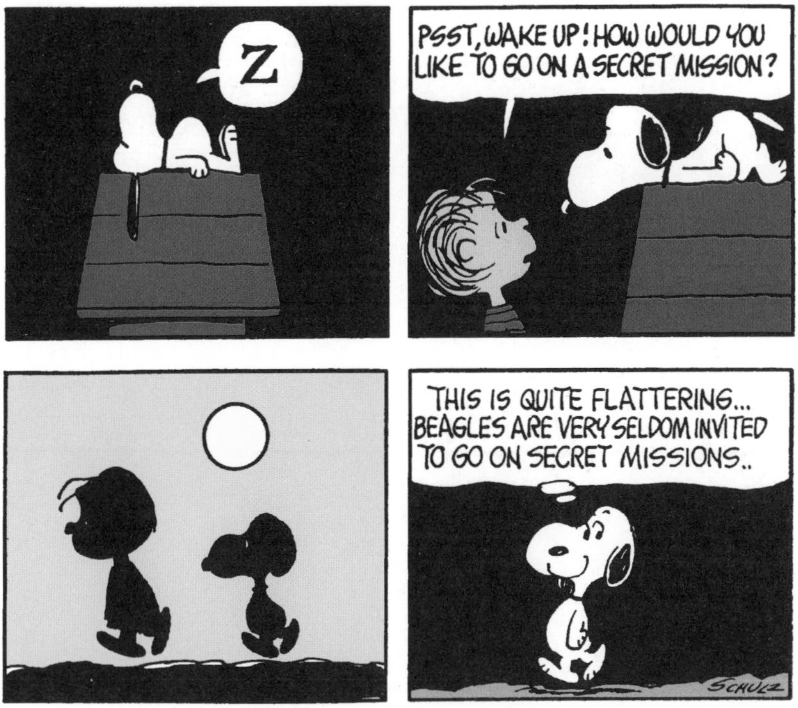
Z
PSST, WAKE UP! HOW WOULD YOU LIKE TO GO ON A SECRET MISSION?
THIS IS QUITE FLATTERING... BEAGLES ARE VERY SELDOM INVITED TO GO ON SECRET MISSIONS..
SCHULZ

AAUGH! AAUGH!

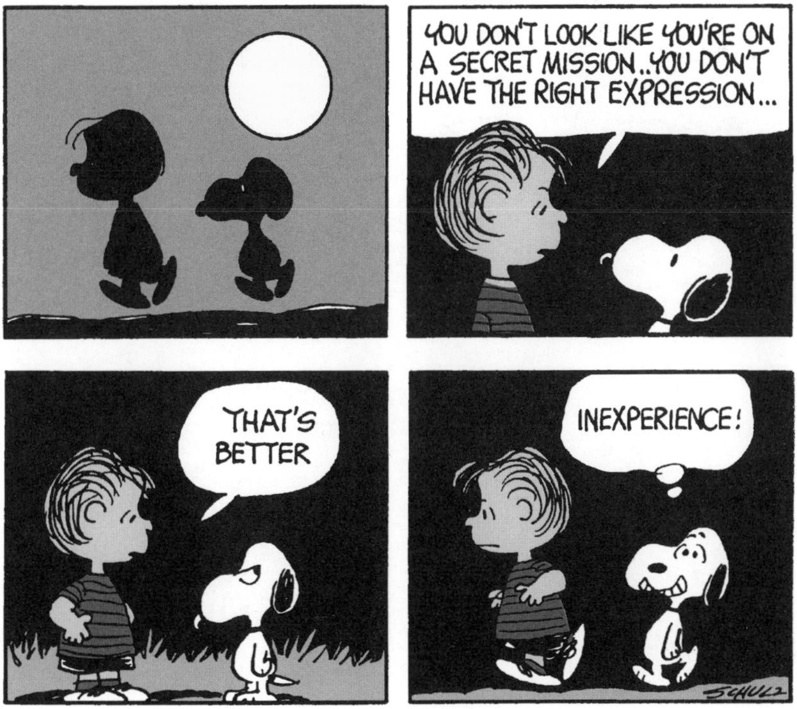
YOU DON'T LOOK LIKE YOU'RE ON A SECRET MISSION..YOU DON'T HAVE THE RIGHT EXPRESSION...
THAT'S BETTER
INEXPERIENCE!
SCHULZ

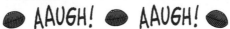

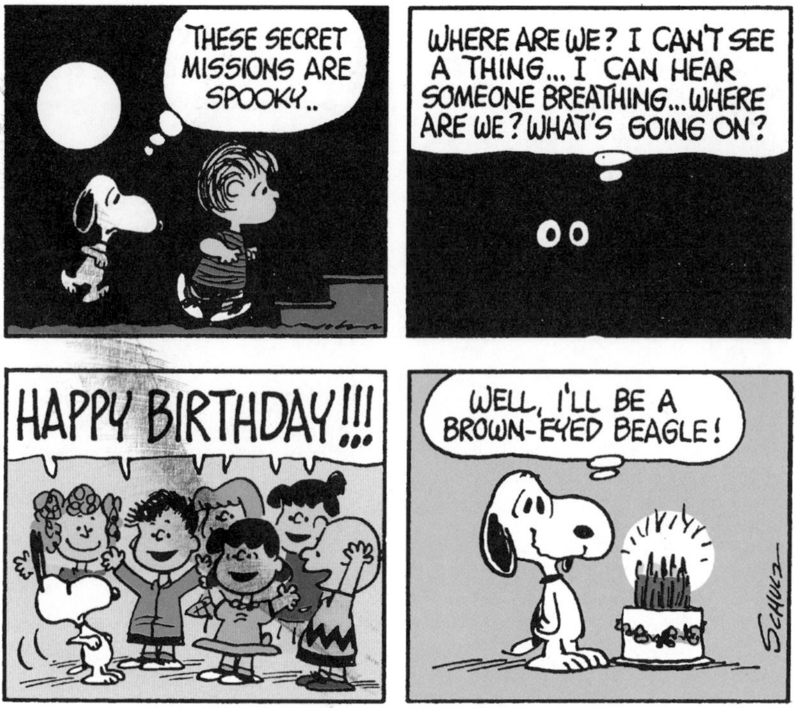
THESE SECRET MISSIONS ARE SPOOKY..
WHERE ARE WE? I CAN'T SEE A THING... I CAN HEAR SOMEONE BREATHING...WHERE ARE WE? WHAT'S GOING ON?
HAPPY BIRTHDAY!!!
WELL, I'LL BE A BROWN-EYED BEAGLE!
SCHULZ

AAUGH! AAUGH!

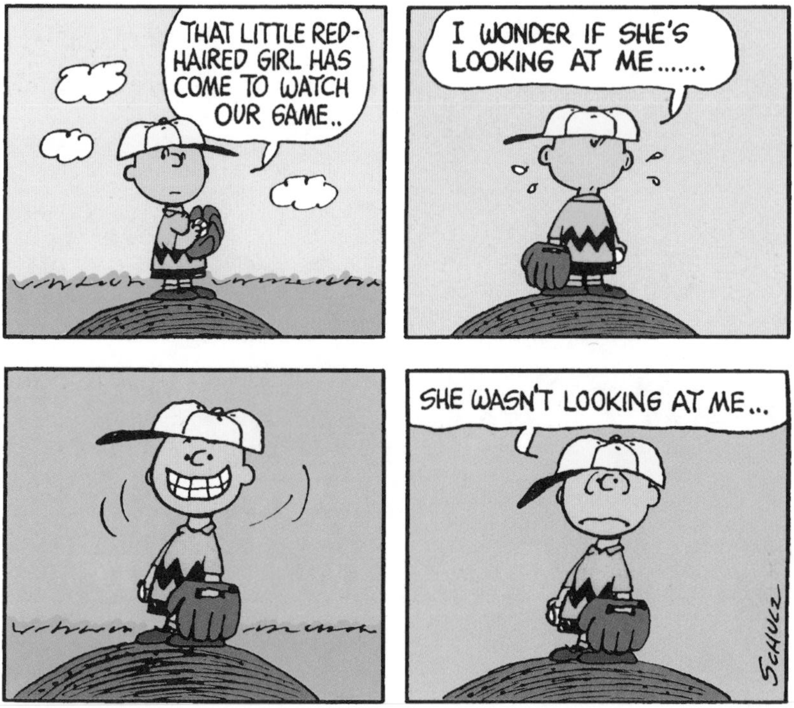
THAT LITTLE RED-HAIRED GIRL HAS COME TO WATCH OUR GAME..
I WONDER IF SHE'S LOOKING AT ME.......
SHE WASN'T LOOKING AT ME...
SCHULZ

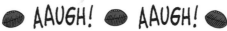

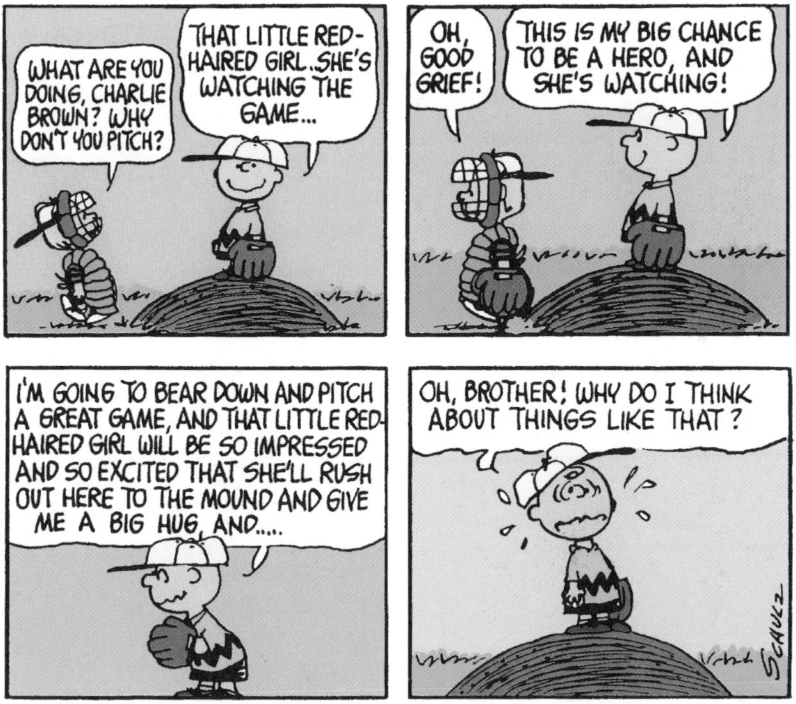
WHAT ARE YOU DOING, CHARLIE BROWN? WHY DON'T YOU PITCH?
THAT LITTLE RED-HAIRED GIRL..SHE'S WATCHING THE GAME...
OH, GOOD GRIEF!
THIS IS MY BIG CHANCE TO BE A HERO, AND SHE'S WATCHING!
I'M GOING TO BEAR DOWN AND PITCH A GREAT GAME, AND THAT LITTLE RED-HAIRED GIRL WILL BE SO IMPRESSED AND SO EXCITED THAT SHE'LL RUSH OUT HERE TO THE MOUND AND GIVE ME A BIG HUG, AND....
OH, BROTHER! WHY DO I THINK ABOUT THINGS LIKE THAT?
SCHULZ

AAUGH! AAUGH!

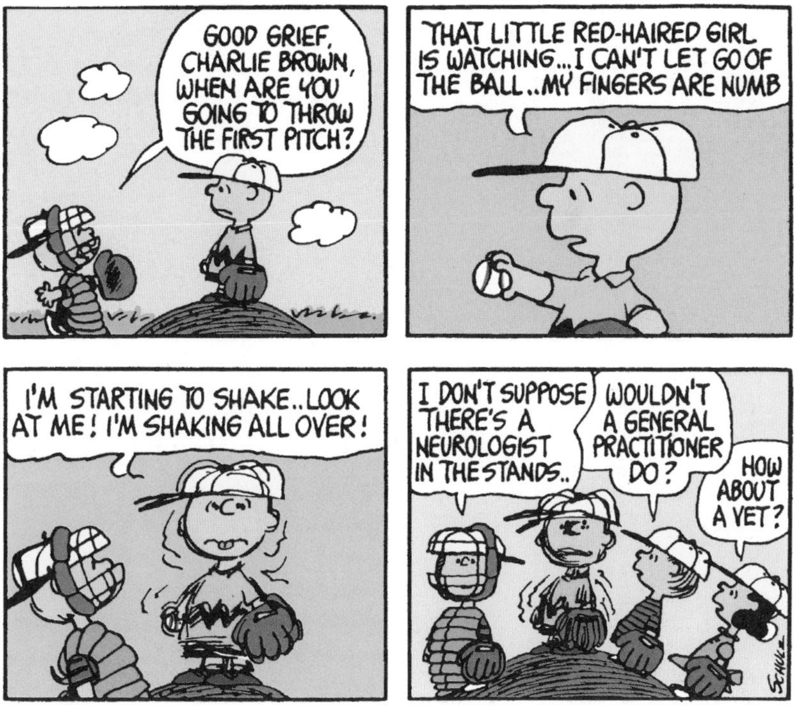
GOOD GRIEF, CHARLIE BROWN, WHEN ARE YOU GOING TO THROW THE FIRST PITCH?
THAT LITTLE RED-HAIRED GIRL IS WATCHING...I CAN'T LET GO OF THE BALL..MY FINGERS ARE NUMB
I'M STARTING TO SHAKE..LOOK AT ME! I'M SHAKING ALL OVER!
I DON'T SUPPOSE THERE'S A NEUROLOGIST IN THE STANDS..
WOULDN'T A GENERAL PRACTITIONER DO?
HOW ABOUT A VET?
SCHULZ

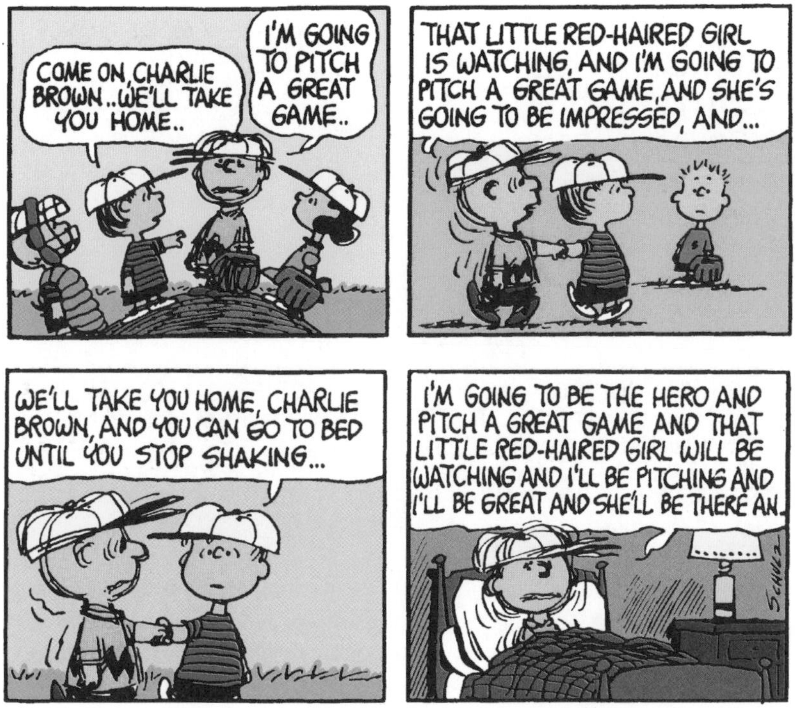
COME ON, CHARLIE BROWN..WE'LL TAKE YOU HOME..
I'M GOING TO PITCH A GREAT GAME..
THAT LITTLE RED-HAIRED GIRL IS WATCHING, AND I'M GOING TO PITCH A GREAT GAME, AND SHE'S GOING TO BE IMPRESSED, AND...
WE'LL TAKE YOU HOME, CHARLIE BROWN, AND YOU CAN GO TO BED UNTIL YOU STOP SHAKING...
I'M GOING TO BE THE HERO AND PITCH A GREAT GAME AND THAT LITTLE RED-HAIRED GIRL WILL BE WATCHING AND I'LL BE PITCHING AND I'LL BE GREAT AND SHE'LL BE THERE AN
SCHULZ

AAUGH! AAUGH!

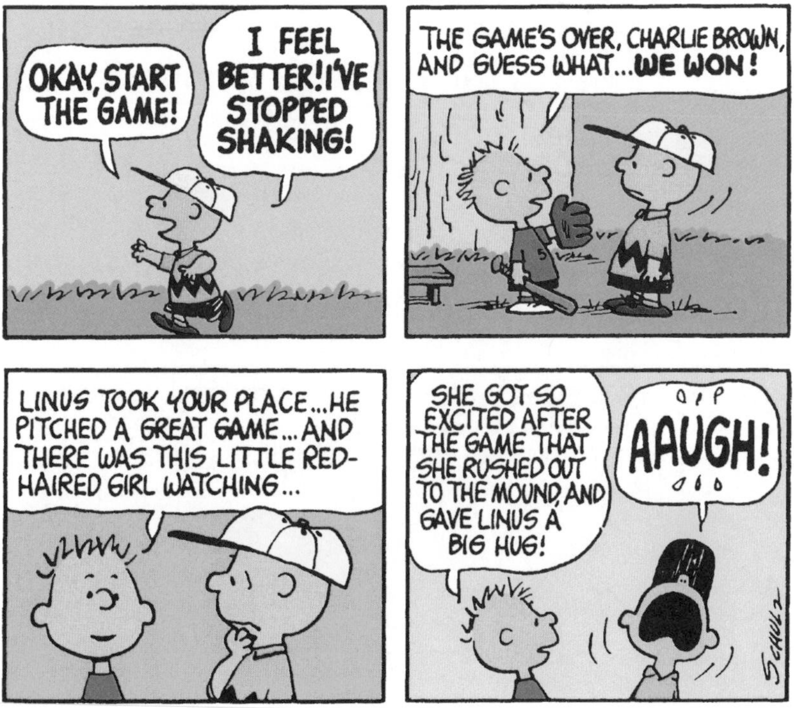
OKAY, START THE GAME!
I FEEL BETTER! I'VE STOPPED SHAKING!
THE GAME'S OVER, CHARLIE BROWN, AND GUESS WHAT...**WE WON!**
LINUS TOOK YOUR PLACE...HE PITCHED A GREAT GAME...AND THERE WAS THIS LITTLE RED-HAIRED GIRL WATCHING...
SHE GOT SO EXCITED AFTER THE GAME THAT SHE RUSHED OUT TO THE MOUND, AND GAVE LINUS A BIG HUG!
AAUGH!
SCHULZ

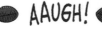

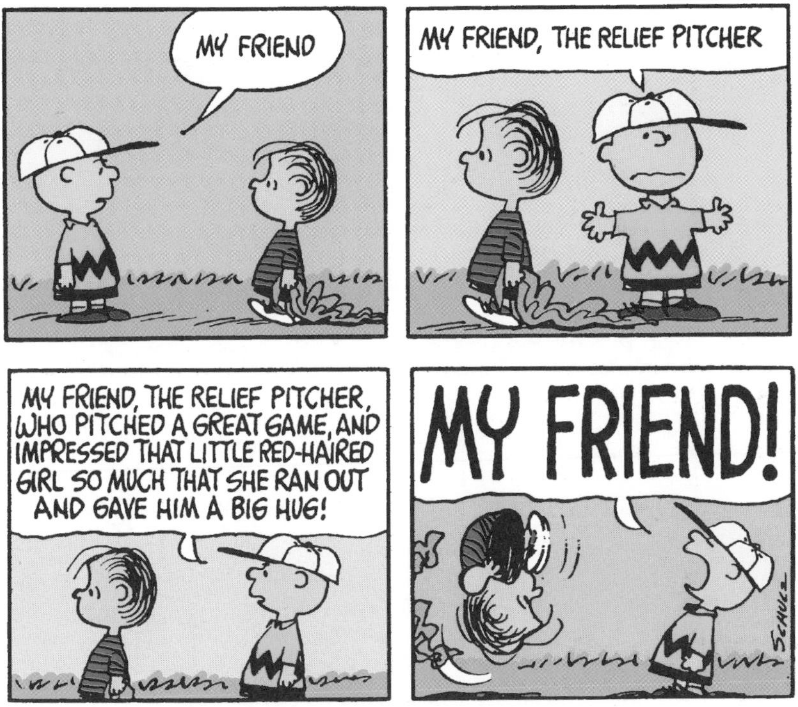
MY FRIEND
MY FRIEND, THE RELIEF PITCHER
MY FRIEND, THE RELIEF PITCHER, WHO PITCHED A GREAT GAME, AND IMPRESSED THAT LITTLE RED-HAIRED GIRL SO MUCH THAT SHE RAN OUT AND GAVE HIM A BIG HUG!
MY FRIEND!
SCHULZ

AAUGH! AAUGH!

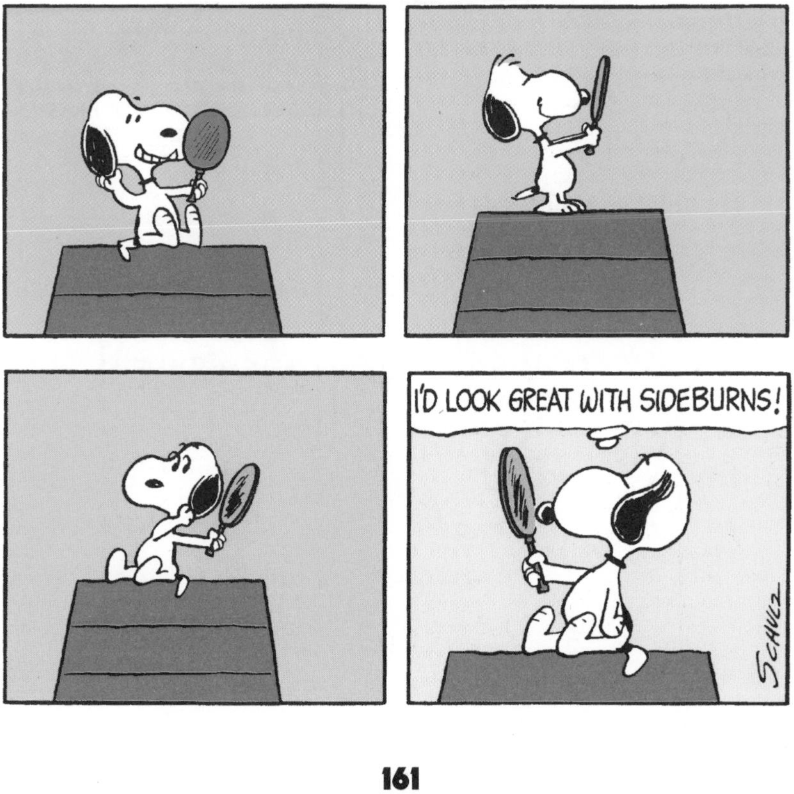
I'D LOOK GREAT WITH SIDEBURNS!
SCHULZ

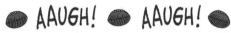

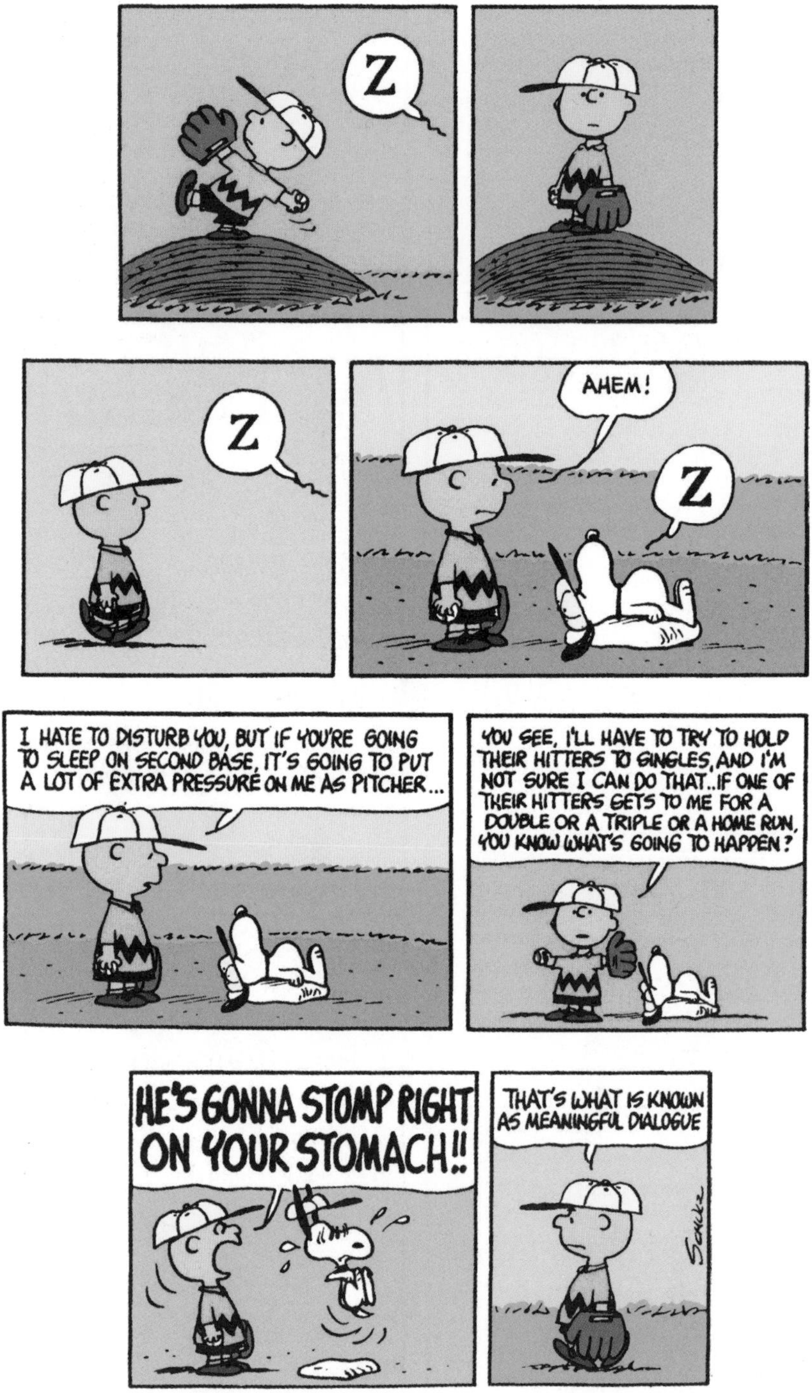
Z
Z
AHEM!
Z
I HATE TO DISTURB YOU, BUT IF YOU'RE GOING TO SLEEP ON SECOND BASE, IT'S GOING TO PUT A LOT OF EXTRA PRESSURE ON ME AS PITCHER...
YOU SEE, I'LL HAVE TO TRY TO HOLD THEIR HITTERS TO SINGLES, AND I'M NOT SURE I CAN DO THAT..IF ONE OF THEIR HITTERS GETS TO ME FOR A DOUBLE OR A TRIPLE OR A HOME RUN, YOU KNOW WHAT'S GOING TO HAPPEN?
HE'S GONNA STOMP RIGHT ON YOUR STOMACH!!
THAT'S WHAT IS KNOWN AS MEANINGFUL DIALOGUE
SCHULZ

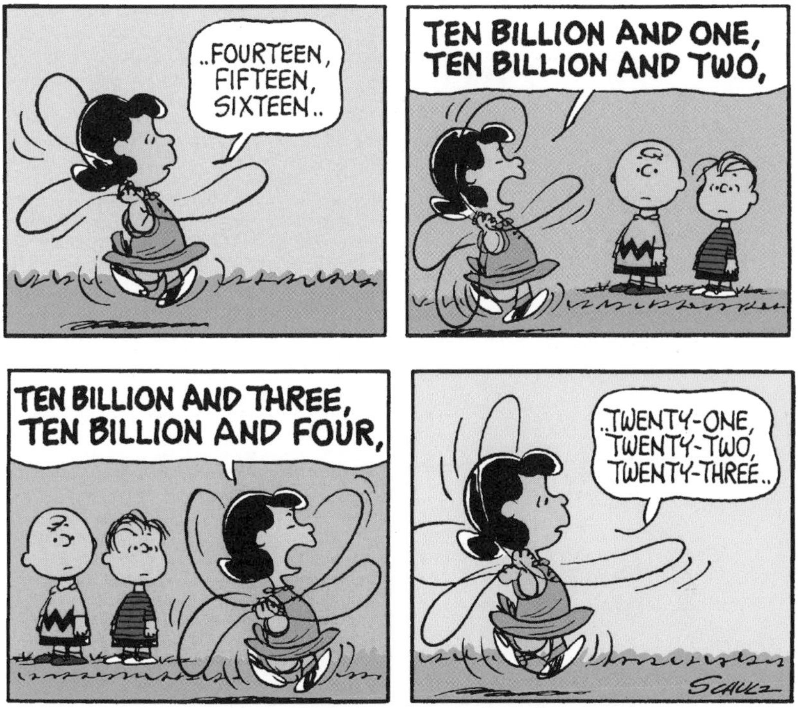
..FOURTEEN, FIFTEEN, SIXTEEN..
TEN BILLION AND ONE, TEN BILLION AND TWO,
TEN BILLION AND THREE, TEN BILLION AND FOUR,
..TWENTY-ONE, TWENTY-TWO, TWENTY-THREE..
SCHULZ

AAUGH! AAUGH!

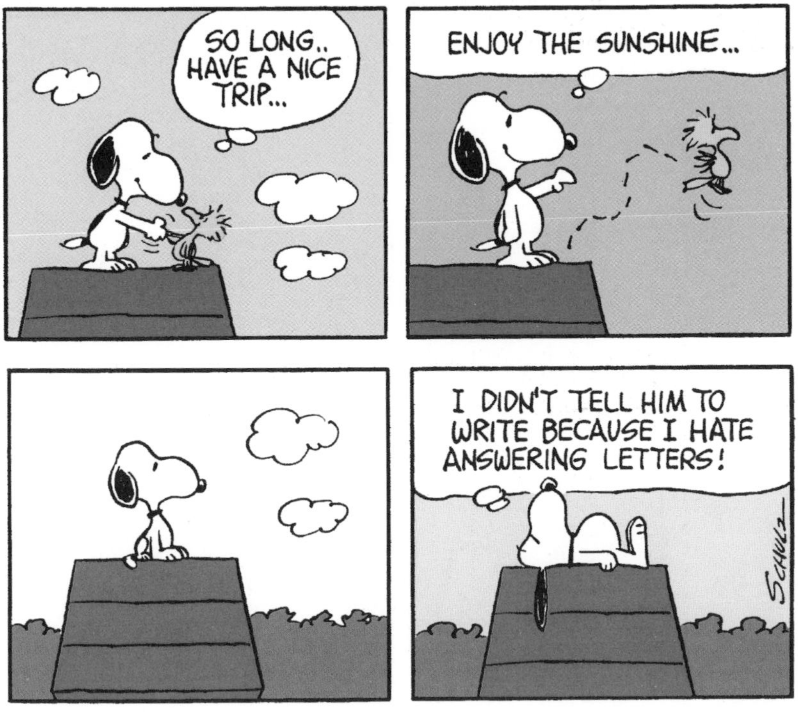
SO LONG.. HAVE A NICE TRIP...
ENJOY THE SUNSHINE...
I DIDN'T TELL HIM TO WRITE BECAUSE I HATE ANSWERING LETTERS!
SCHULZ

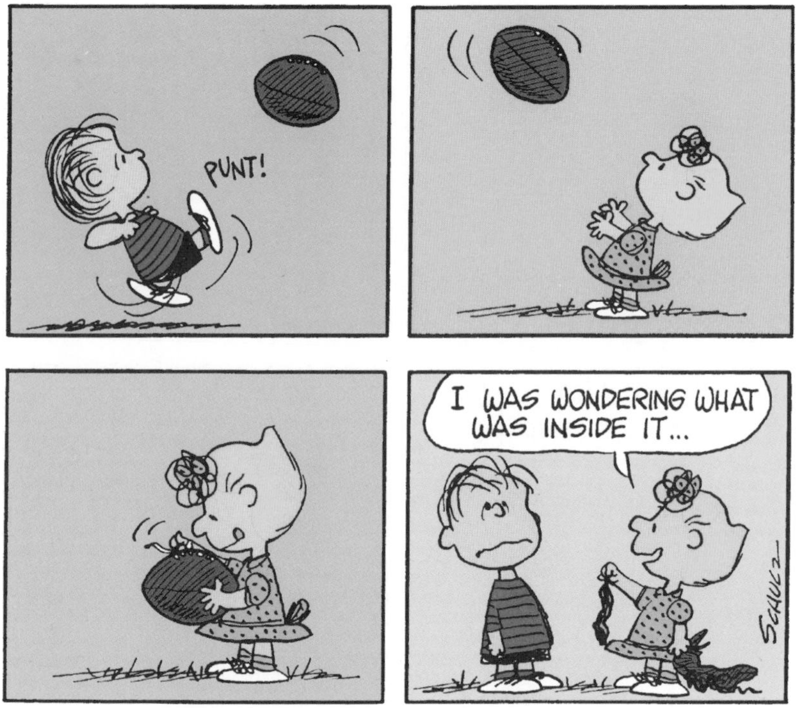
PUNT!
I WAS WONDERING WHAT WAS INSIDE IT...
SCHULZ

AAUGH! AAUGH!

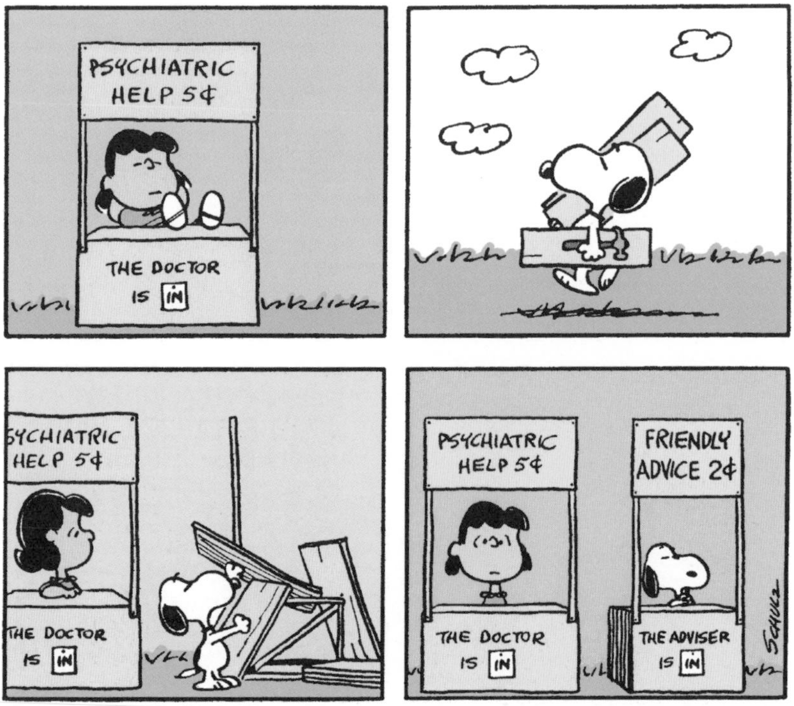
PSYCHIATRIC HELP 5¢
THE DOCTOR IS IN
SYCHIATRIC HELP 5¢
THE DOCTOR IS IN
PSYCHIATRIC HELP 5¢
THE DOCTOR IS IN
FRIENDLY ADVICE 2¢
THE ADVISER IS IN
SCHULZ

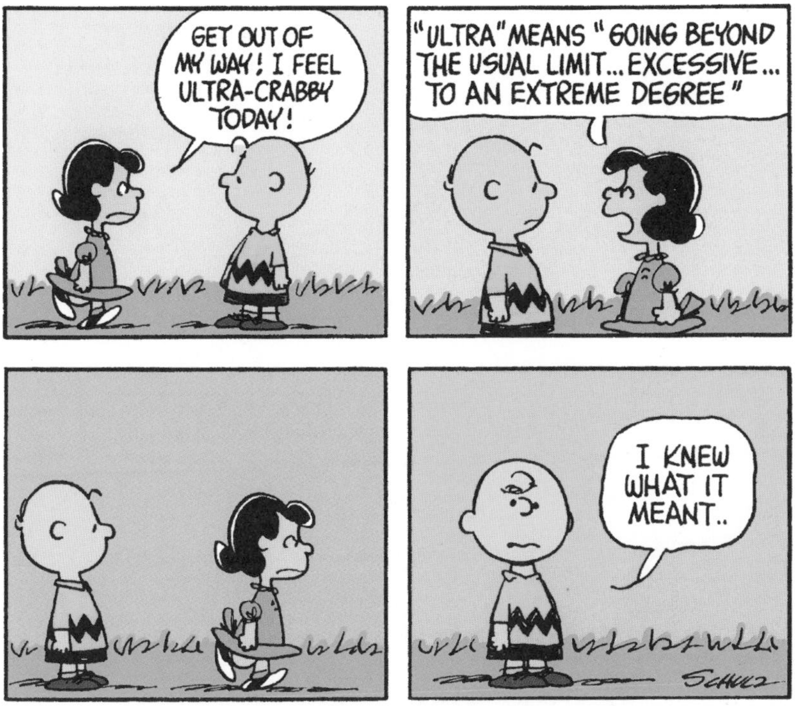
GET OUT OF MY WAY! I FEEL ULTRA-CRABBY TODAY!
"ULTRA" MEANS "GOING BEYOND THE USUAL LIMIT... EXCESSIVE... TO AN EXTREME DEGREE"
I KNEW WHAT IT MEANT..
SCHULZ

AAUGH! AAUGH!

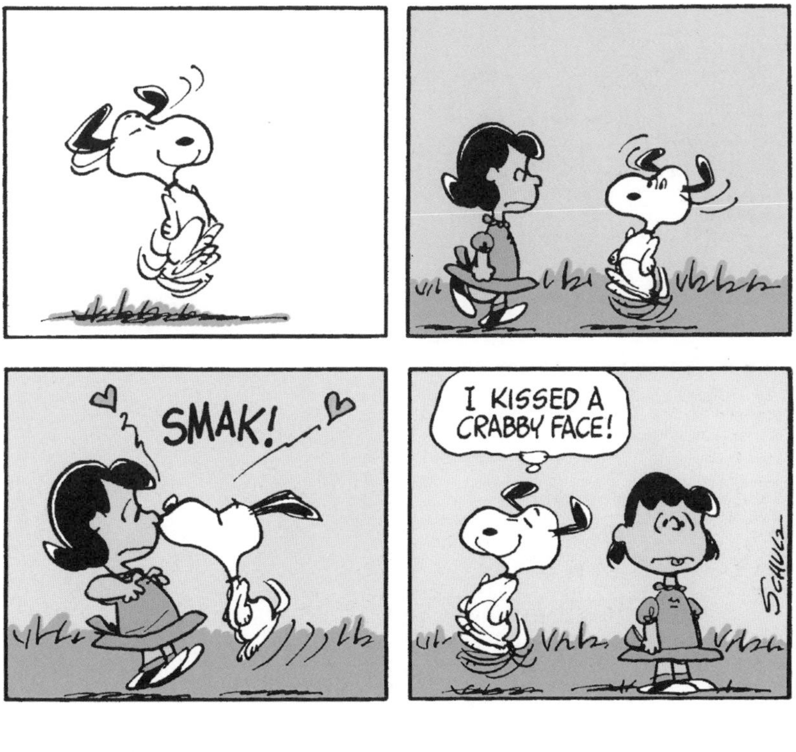
SMAK!
I KISSED A CRABBY FACE!
SCHULZ

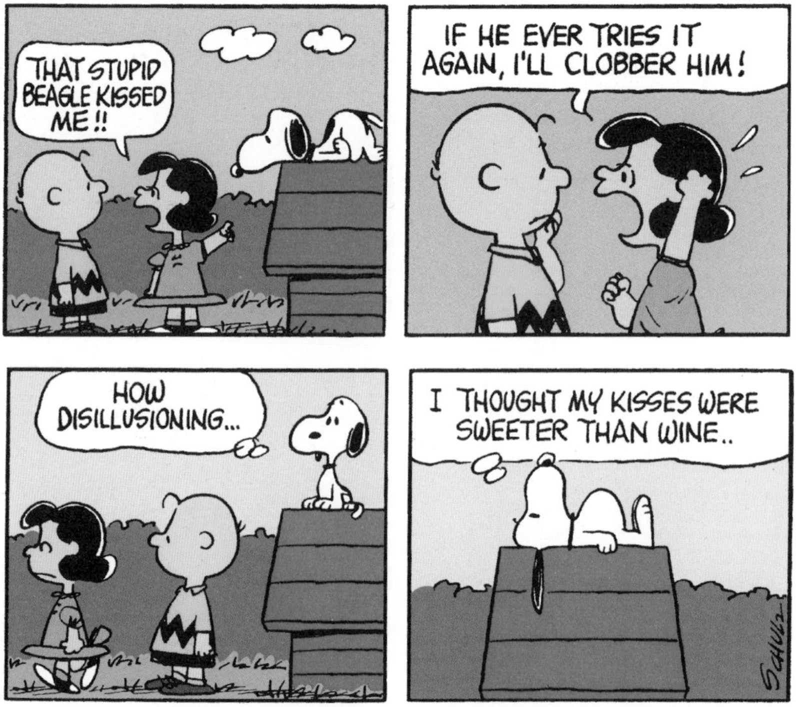
THAT STUPID BEAGLE KISSED ME!!
IF HE EVER TRIES IT AGAIN, I'LL CLOBBER HIM!
HOW DISILLUSIONING...
I THOUGHT MY KISSES WERE SWEETER THAN WINE..
SCHULZ

AAUGH! AAUGH!

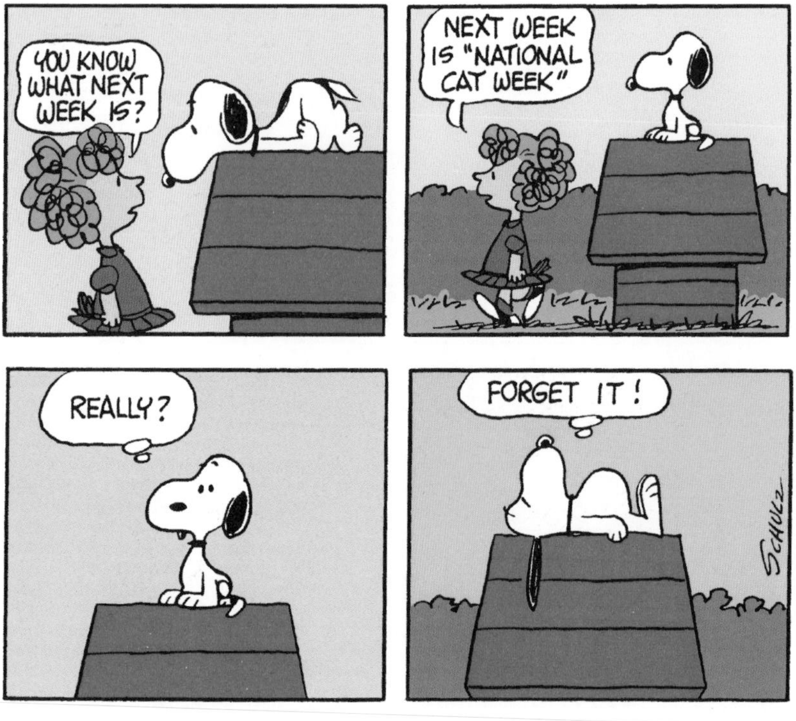
YOU KNOW WHAT NEXT WEEK IS?
NEXT WEEK IS "NATIONAL CAT WEEK"
REALLY?
FORGET IT!
SCHULZ

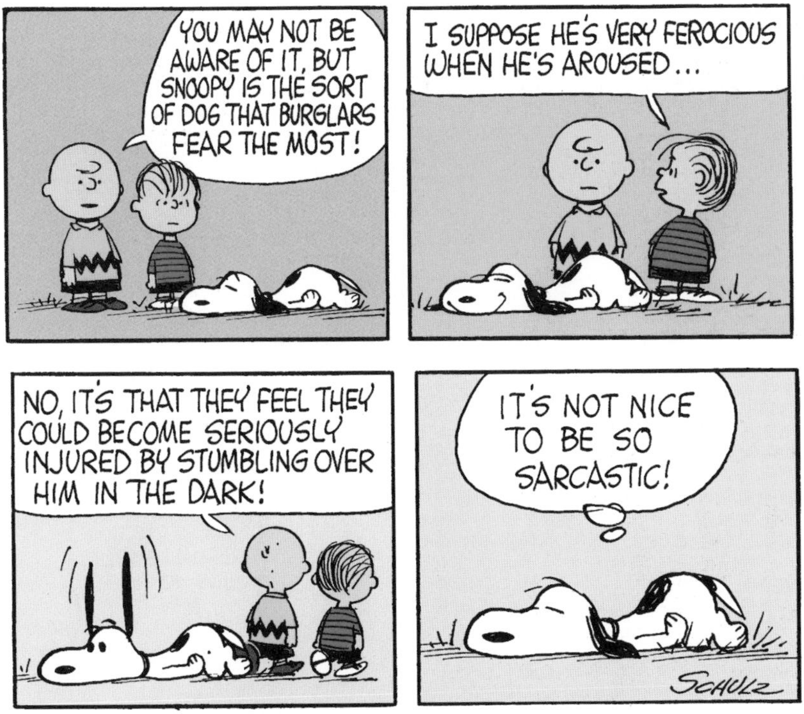
YOU MAY NOT BE AWARE OF IT, BUT SNOOPY IS THE SORT OF DOG THAT BURGLARS FEAR THE MOST!
I SUPPOSE HE'S VERY FEROCIOUS WHEN HE'S AROUSED...
NO, IT'S THAT THEY FEEL THEY COULD BECOME SERIOUSLY INJURED BY STUMBLING OVER HIM IN THE DARK!
IT'S NOT NICE TO BE SO SARCASTIC!
SCHULZ

AAUGH! AAUGH!

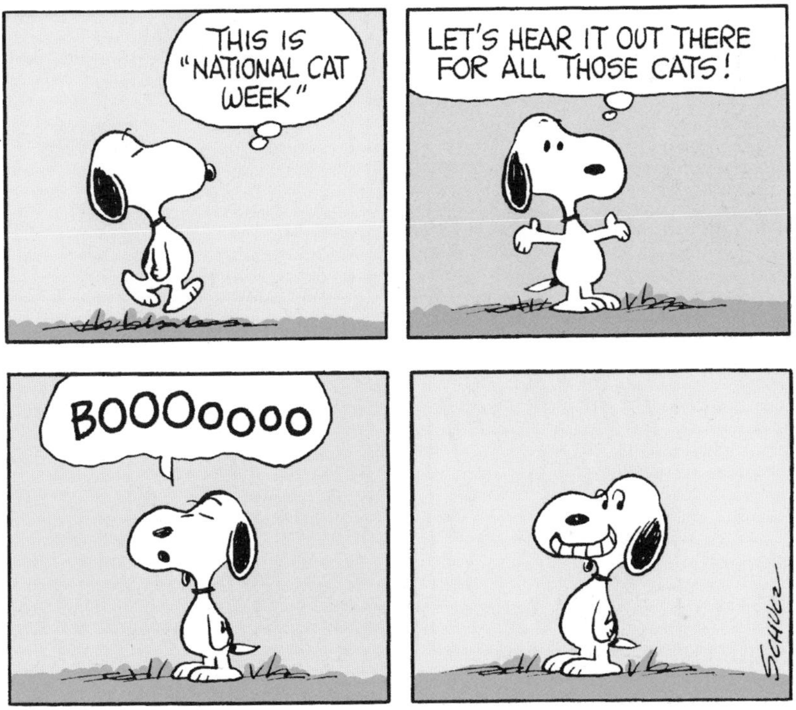
THIS IS "NATIONAL CAT WEEK"
LET'S HEAR IT OUT THERE FOR ALL THOSE CATS!
BOOOoooo
SCHULZ

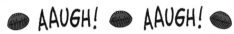

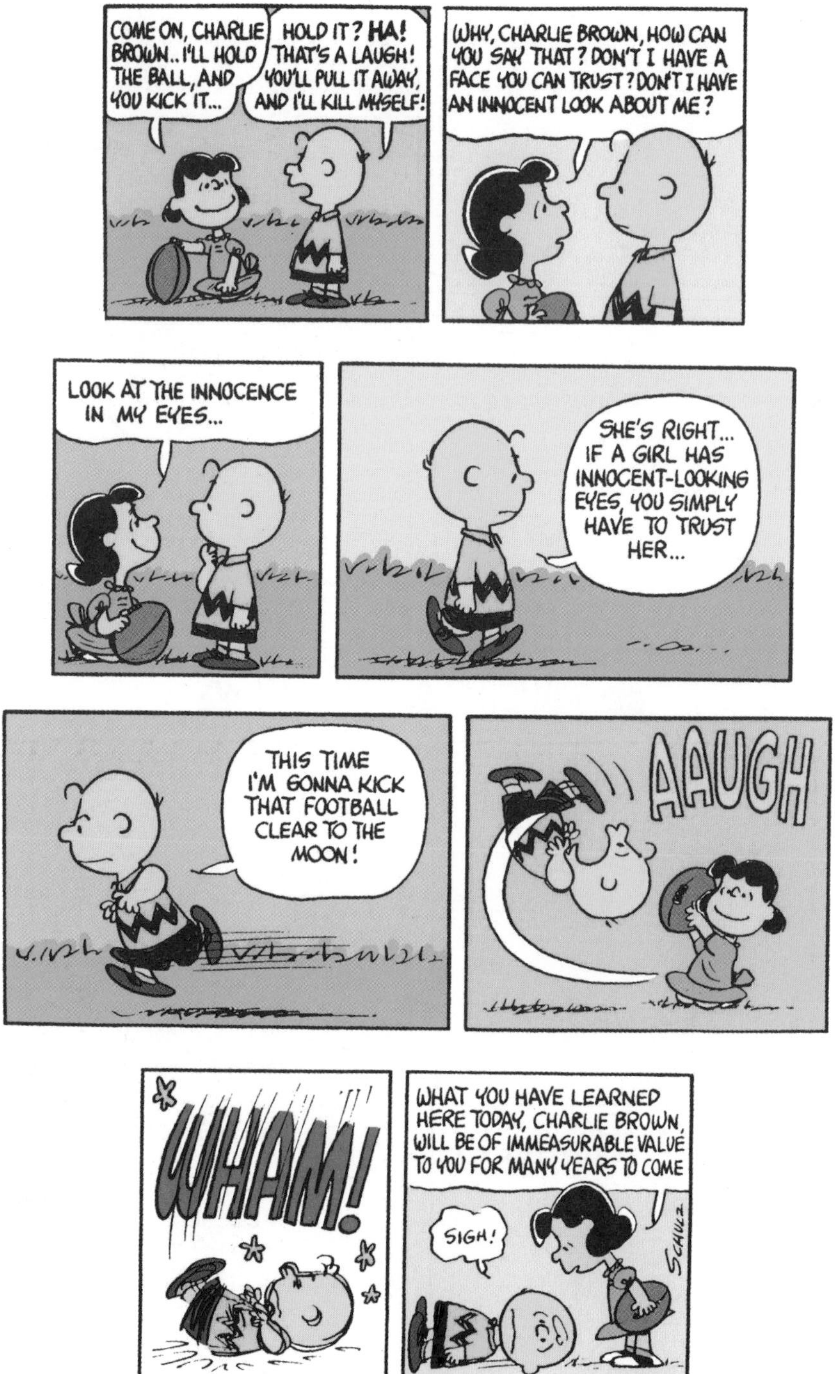
COME ON, CHARLIE BROWN.. I'LL HOLD THE BALL, AND YOU KICK IT...
HOLD IT? HA! THAT'S A LAUGH! YOU'LL PULL IT AWAY, AND I'LL KILL MYSELF!
WHY, CHARLIE BROWN, HOW CAN YOU SAY THAT? DON'T I HAVE A FACE YOU CAN TRUST? DON'T I HAVE AN INNOCENT LOOK ABOUT ME?
LOOK AT THE INNOCENCE IN MY EYES...
SHE'S RIGHT... IF A GIRL HAS INNOCENT-LOOKING EYES, YOU SIMPLY HAVE TO TRUST HER...
THIS TIME I'M GONNA KICK THAT FOOTBALL CLEAR TO THE MOON!
AAUGH
WHAM!
WHAT YOU HAVE LEARNED HERE TODAY, CHARLIE BROWN, WILL BE OF IMMEASURABLE VALUE TO YOU FOR MANY YEARS TO COME
SIGH!
SCHULZ

MORE TO EXPLORE! Featuring cool activities and fun facts!

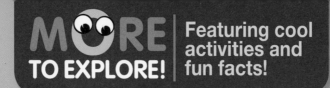

FUN ACTIVITIES FOR EVERY SEASON

No matter what season it is, the *Peanuts* gang is always up for some fun and games! Here are some fun things for you to do throughout the whole year.

SCHULZ

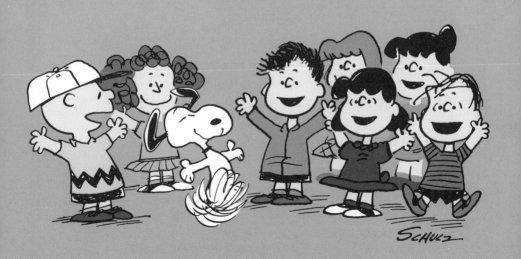

Fall

It's football season! Create your own table football for the rainy days.

How to make your own paper football (and one for a friend):

1. Take a piece of notebook paper, fold it hotdog style (lengthwise), and cut along the crease to make two strips. You will be using half; give the other half to a friend.
2. Fold your strip in half (hotdog style) again.
3. To create a triangle, take the left corner of your paper and fold it up toward the right side.
4. Fold this triangle up. Repeat until you've reached the end of the paper strip.
5. Once you've reached the end, tuck in the extra paper.

GET READY FOR A PAPER FOOTBALL GAME!

What you'll need: two plastic cups; a table; two paper footballs; a friend.

Place plastic cups on opposite ends of the table. The object of the game is to land your football into your friend's cup before he or she does. You will both be flicking your footballs across the table at the same time. Once someone makes a "touchdown" (lands his or her football into the opponent's cup), the person gets six points. The goal is to be the first person to make five touchdowns (score thirty points).

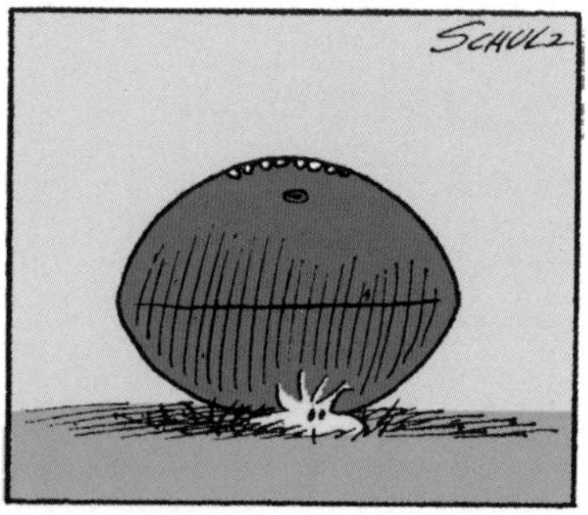
SCHULZ

Winter

SPECIAL STARGAZING

Though Lucy said there are 365 stars (one for every day), there are actually many more! Some of these stars make pictures in the sky; these pictures are known as constellations. You can see a different part of the universe during each season while the earth travels around the sun. Check out these famous constellations on a clear, dry winter's night.

Look north, and you'll catch a glimpse of **DRACO THE DRAGON** flying across the horizon.

Look east, and you'll spot **ORION** with his famous, eye-catching belt made from three very bright stars. Check out that shine!

Look west, and you'll see **PEGASUS**. The winged horse is in mid-leap!

Look south, and you'll spy **CETUS**, one of the strangest sea monsters you'll ever meet.

Look straight up, and see if you can find **PERSEUS**, the Greek hero who rescued a princess by beating Cetus in battle. Seems like those two are still clashing in our night sky.

To learn about these and many more constellations, visit: http://www.kidsastronomy.com.

Spring

GO ON A NATURE SCAVENGER HUNT

This time of year, lots of things are starting to grow. Grab a sketchbook or a camera and get ready for a nature scavenger hunt either at a nearby park or around your neighborhood. Gather a few friends and organize a competition. Whoever scores the most points wins.

ITEMS TO FIND:

Flower (2 points); Bird's nest (3 points); Weed (other than a dandelion) (5 points); Animal's footprint (5 points); Mushroom (4 points); Spider web (3 points); Garden (3 points); Pinecone (3 points); Four different types of leaves (4 points); Bug (1 point); Butterfly (3 points); Feather (2 points); Animal (other than a bird) (5 points); Bench (2 points); Spotting your state flower, bird, or animal (7 points).

HERE'S THE WORLD FAMOUS BEAGLE SCOUT LEADING HIS TROOP ON A HIKE

OUT TO THE WILD COUNTRY WHERE MAN HAS NEVER TROD!

BEYOND CIVILIZATION!

Summer

Combine your love of campfire s'mores and classic puppy chow in this winning combination.

S'MORES SNOOPY CHOW

INGREDIENTS: 6 cups Chex cereal; 3 cups Golden Grahams cereal; 2 cups marshmallows; 1 cup semi-sweet chocolate chips; ½ cup Nutella; 2 cups powdered sugar; a microwave-safe bowl; a mixing bowl; aluminum foil

This recipe makes approximately 10 cups.

INSTRUCTIONS:

1. Pour Chex, Golden Grahams, and marshmallows into a mixing bowl. Set to the side.
2. Microwave chocolate chips and Nutella for one minute. Stir, and microwave for another 20 seconds, if needed.
3. Pour the chocolate mixture onto the cereal and marshmallows in the mixing bowl.
4. Add the powdered sugar to the mix. Cover the mixing bowl with aluminum foil and shake until the cereal and marshmallows are coated.
5. Share with a friend and enjoy.

I'LL BUILD THE FIRE...YOU GET YOURSELVES SOME NICE LONG STICKS...

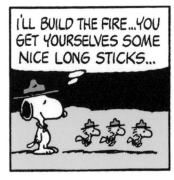

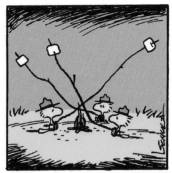

Even More to Explore!

These sources will be helpful if you wish to learn more about Charles Schulz, the Charles M. Schulz Museum and Research Center, *Peanuts*, or the art of cartooning.

WEBSITES:

www.schulzmuseum.org
- Official website of the Charles M. Schulz Museum and Research Center.

www.peanuts.com
- Thirty days' worth of *Peanuts* strips. Character profiles. Timeline about the strip. Character print-outs for coloring. Info on fellow cartoonists' tributes to Charles Schulz after he passed away.

www.fivecentsplease.org
- Recent news articles and press releases on Charles Schulz and *Peanuts*. Links to other *Peanuts*-themed websites. Info on *Peanuts* products.

www.toonopedia.com
- Info on *Peanuts* and many, many other comics—it's an "encyclopedia of 'toons."

www.gocomics.com
- Access to popular and lesser-known comic strips, as well as editorial cartoons.

www.reuben.org
- Official website of the National Cartoonists Society. Info on how to become a professional cartoonist. Info on awards given for cartooning.

www.kingfeatures.com and www.amuniversal.com
- Newspaper syndicate websites. Learn more about the distribution of comics to newspapers.

Andrews McMeel Publishing
a division of Andrews McMeel Universal
1130 Walnut Street, Kansas City, Missouri 64106

www.andrewsmcmeel.com

www.peanuts.com

16 17 18 19 20 SDB 10 9 8 7 6 5 4 3 2

ISBN: 978-1-4494-7881-0

Library of Congress Control Number: 2016932240

Made by:
Shenzhen Donnelley Printing Company Ltd.
Address and location of manufacturer:
No. 47, Wuhe Nan Road, Bantian Ind. Zone,
Shenzhen China, 518129
2nd Printing—10/17/16

ATTENTION: SCHOOLS AND BUSINESSES

Andrews McMeel books are available at quantity discounts with bulk purchase for educational, business, or sales promotional use. For information, please e-mail the Andrews McMeel Publishing Special Sales Department: specialsales@amuniversal.com.

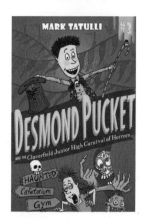